BEWITCHING DARKNESS

BEWITCHING BREWS
BOOK 2

SHERITTA BITIKOFER

Cover Design by Patrisha Badalo (Art Muse Graphic Designs)

Ebook ISBN: 978-1-946821-48-5

Print ISBN: 978-1-946821-49-2

Contents

Dedicated to all those who believe in magic, miracles, and the mystical power of a good cup of coffee.

Chapter 1

S omething soft, wet, and cold slid against Valerie's cheek. From the void of being half asleep and half awake, she heard Thor's usual high-pitched, breathy whine. Blindly, she reached out and found his massive furry paw on the edge of her bed. A few more licks to her nose and around her mouth drew her completely out of sleep and she peered through the darkness.

Her black lab's deep brown eyes greeted her with an imploring look, and though she wanted nothing more than to slip further under the warm covers, the dog would be expecting breakfast soon. With her dark hair a tangled mess around her face, she squinted at the flipping letters on her vintage alarm clock.

There was just enough dawn peeking through her black curtains to illuminate the numbers. Five forty-five.

"Shit, shit, shit!" she whispered as she frantically rolled over to get out of bed. She brought her arms close to her chest, finding her thin t-shirt hardly adequate in keeping her warm. Each day she meant to pull out her warmer sleeping clothes from the trunk in the closet, but each day she forgot.

Valerie heard the tap of dog nails on the floorboards as she tried to grab for clothes out of her closet, her eyes still not adjusted to the dim light. She managed to find a pair of dark jeans and a t-shirt she had picked up at a Five Finger Death Punch concert a few years back.

Perfect Books and Brews opened at six in the morning and though she was one of the co-owners, Krystal was getting fed up with her friend's constant tardiness. It left the task of opening up the coffee shop to her two friends while she got to snooze and that wasn't fair. She wasn't surprised she slept through all of her alarms. Again.

Struggling in and out of pants legs, Valerie found herself hopping around, trying to avoid bumping into furniture or tripping over Thor who was getting a little impatient for his breakfast. The bottom of her foot landed on something smooth and when she tried to right herself, she slipped and crashed to the floor. A few loose leaf pieces of notebook paper, the ones that belonged inside her family grimoire, were sent fluttering around half of her room.

"Val?" Shawn called from across the house. "You all right?"

Valerie groaned at the pain in her banged-up elbow and knee. She earned a couple of bruises that would show up later. "I'm fine!"

Common sense returning to her, she reached up and flicked her finger toward the ceiling light. If her magic came in handy at any time, it was in those moments when she was her laziest. It clicked and the room was finally illuminated to reveal the chaotic mess of papers atop her desk, discarded dirty clothes littered across the floor, and rock band posters tacked up on the walls.

"You tripped over something, didn't you?" he asked. Without waiting for an answer, he continued, "I told you that you need to clean that room up."

Valerie, in no mood for his shit today, grumbled out, "Go suck a –"

Just as she was about to finish, Thor vigorously licked at her mouth, urging her to get up and hurry, so he could get fed. Despite it all, Valerie smiled and pushed the lovable mutt out of her way.

Within just another minute, she was fully dressed and in the bathroom across the hall. There wasn't much time to fix her hair or her makeup. Usually she straightened her wavy, dark brown hair, so her red streaks would pop out nice and bold. Settling for a good brushing and a little hair de-frizzing charm, she went to putting on just mascara and skipped the thick black eyeliner, though it made her green eyes look a little odd without it. There was no time to complete her full, half-smoky look while she was running late.

Thor followed her every step of the way, his thick tail wagging side to side with impatience as he watched her get ready. Raised from a pup, the lab was insanely loyal, almost to a fault, and hardly ever let anyone else feed or touch him except for Valerie. Shawn was allowed his few moments, but they were few and far between. If only the dog would give a little, Valerie could have had Shawn feed him every morning.

She rushed into the kitchen and found her roommate calmly sitting at the small dining table with his tablet in one hand and a cup of coffee in the other. School was out for winter break, otherwise he would have been dressed in a pressed button-down shirt, khaki slacks, and an outrageous tie that she could tease him for. Instead, he wore a nice pair of faded jeans and a grey shirt that showed off the kind of muscles one might expect an active soccer coach to have. It was a wonder no girl had taken him up by now. If it weren't for his bright blonde hair, she might have considered him. But Valerie hated blonde hair on guys.

"Didn't you hear your alarms going off?" he questioned before taking a sip from the purple and gold LSU mug.

"No," she groaned as she grabbed Thor's bowl from the counter and the plastic cup they used to scoop out his food. "I slept through every one of those fuckers."

Shawn made a disapproving sound in his throat before swallowing. "You're going to have to watch your language. I almost cussed like that in front of my students the other day."

Valerie rolled her eyes and hurriedly dished out the dry food into the bowl. Thor was already hopping on his front paws, tongue lulling with enthusiasm.

"Sorry," she said. "Haven't had coffee yet."

By the look he gave her, she knew that he wasn't buying that excuse. It was common knowledge that she enjoyed her improvisational expletives. Shawn pointed toward the pale yellow counter where an old coffee maker sat, a half-full carafe of the brew keeping warm on the heating pad. "There's plenty if you want some before you go."

Thor already had his muzzle in the bowl before she could fully set it down on the linoleum floor.

"No. I'm running late as it is and Krystal's going to tear me a new one."

She rushed out of the kitchen, through the dining room that was only used for Shawn when he was grading papers, and into the foyer.

"Hey, just a second!" he hollered. "I think I might have found a new roommate for us."

Valerie was about to grab her dark grey wool coat and scarf from the coatrack, but dropped her hands and tilted her head back to stare at the ceiling in exasperation. "So?"

"I'm meeting up with him at Perfect Books and Brews later this morning. I want you to sit in while I interview him."

Shawn and Valerie had been in the market for a new roommate for the last two months. Their landlord was forced to raise the rent due to property taxes going up. But the task of finding a mature, responsible person who was out of their wild college phase and had a reliable source of income was proving harder than they thought.

Goldcrest Cove wasn't a big town and many of their applicants were fresh high school graduates trying to get out of their parents' house or returning college kids who didn't have a job yet. All other unmarried adults seemed to be roomed up with other friends or they were in hiding, because neither Valerie nor Shawn was hearing from them.

"I can't guarantee anything," she replied with a sigh as she took her coat off the hook and slipped her arms through. "If we get busy, I'll be behind the counter."

"Then just stop by and meet him."

So, another guy? That suited her just fine. Minimal drama, less clutter, and she'd still have plenty of cupboard space in the bathroom.

She agreed as she fastened her scarf around her neck and ducked out into the cold morning without another word. They never exchanged goodbyes or hugs or anything sentimental like that. Valerie cringed at the idea of it. She cared for Shawn, but keeping her distance was second nature to her now. Whoever this new roommate was would learn that quickly. No forced bonding or heartfelt talks. Getting too close was dangerous. Her identity as a witch forbid it.

The moment her boots hit the flagstone path leading to the driveway, Valerie nearly slipped. She let out one little curse at the thin layer of ice that had formed overnight. Checking to make sure that Shawn wasn't peeping through the window, she used her magic to instantly melt the ice and the frost on the windshield of her dark green Acura.

Such a move would have infuriated Krystal, but what the witch didn't know wouldn't hurt her. And she wouldn't know about this incident, or the ones all the way to work. Valerie figured she was doing the community a favor by thawing the roads for them – and for her.

The curbsides up and down Johnson Avenue were already packed, and from the glimpse she caught of the waiting line outside Perfect Books and Brews, Valerie knew exactly what kind of shit storm she was about to walk into.

Christmas was fast approaching, and families were already flocking to Goldcrest Cove in droves. Business was picking up for McRae's Morsels down the road, Miss Macy's Antiques, Mamma Pazzini's Italian Restaurant, and especially Amber's Bed and Breakfast. Perfect Books and Brews was not spared by this mass influx of tourists and visitors. Krystal already told them to expect hard work hours due to their growing reputation as the best – and only – coffee shop in town.

Valerie wrapped her coat around her and broke into a light jog up the street. There were at least a dozen people outside the door, but Krystal had already let several customers inside.

By the door, she recognized Devin and Aaron, two of their morning regulars and probably the town's finest police officers on the force. Devin was already taken by Krystal since this past Halloween and it was sickening the way they drooled over one another after only being together for a couple of months. It didn't help that they were true Twin Flames. They were each other's mythical soulmate that only came around once in a lifetime. Valerie was happy for her friend, but she would have rather been happy from a distance.

He, unlike Aaron, was privy to the fact that Valerie, Krystal, Alexa, and a few other women in town, were witches. It hadn't been an easy transition and he learned something new about them and their ways almost every day. In the end, it proved pretty handy to have someone on the Goldcrest Cove Police Department know their secret.

Aaron, on the other hand, still didn't have a clue about their magic.

Devin was the first to smile and rush forward to open the door for her. "Running a little late, Val?" the former Boston cop asked.

Valerie just rolled her eyes, but the moment she tried to pick up the pace, her foot slipped on a patch of snow that hadn't been cleared away. If Aaron's strong arms hadn't caught her, she would have taken a nasty spill on the pavement.

She looked up into his mocking brown eyes as the wind whipped at his curly blonde hair. Some girls might have considered him handsome, just like Shawn. Even if he didn't treat her like a joke, she couldn't bring herself to see anything good in him. She just couldn't stand him and his wisecracking. He was too cocky for his own good. His occasional snide remarks about her makeup, hair, or dress made her bristle every time.

"Watch your step, Barbie."

Once he helped her to her feet again, Valerie had to restrain herself from using her magic against him, as she had wanted to do countless times before. Too much this morning. She still hadn't had her coffee and she was growing crankier by the minute. She just set her lips in a grim line and charged inside the warm coffee shop, flipping her hair as she went. She could hear Aaron chuckle as she made her flustered exit.

Taking a few peaceful seconds, Valerie took a deep breath to let the aromatic hug of espresso beans welcome her to work. The dull roar of voices, spoons clinking against mugs, and the whirl of the grinder were as home to her as anything else she knew. The coffeeshop might not have been her idea, but it had become her baby, just as it had for Krystal and Alexa.

Once behind the counter, she slipped off her coat and scarf to hang on the wall, and then threw her bag at Krystal's feet where she stood at the register.

"You're late," her dark-haired friend said as she opened the cash register to slip in the ten she had received from Mrs. Young, who was bouncing her bundled up baby on her hip.

"I know, I know," Valerie replied as she slipped on her apron and set to helping Alexa with a big order. One of the secretaries from the town's biggest furniture store was waiting for eight drinks to go.

Even if she hadn't had her coffee yet, she could still brew up a mean espresso. Part of her and Alexa's job, along with making coffee, tea, lattes, and espressos, was keeping a keen ear out to Krystal's brief conversations with the customers while they were ordering.

Because, though they looked like any typical baristas and this coffeeshop was unassumingly stylish and homey, the three witches had a special calling. And through the low hum of voices, she picked out one customer who could use her particular expertise.

"Is your wrist feeling okay, Mrs. Robinson?" she heard Krystal ask after ringing up the customer's usual large green tea.

"It's just my arthritis," Mrs. Robinson replied. "It always gets me on these cold mornings."

Valerie didn't need to hear anymore. She grabbed a large to-go cup and poured the hot water over the hand-packed green tea bag. While the scalding hot water flowed in, steeping the dried leaves, she infused the coffee with a quick, but effective pain-relieving charm she had used for Mrs. Robinson's drinks before.

All it took was a flick of her fingers and a little sprinkling of magic. It wouldn't be instant relief, but within half an hour, Mrs. Robinson's arthritis would be subdued for a day.

Valerie lied whenever Krystal asked how many coffees and teas she had enchanted before noon, knowing the sheer total would make her friend's head spin straight off her neck. For reasons that became clearly serious in October when a charmed coffee got way out of hand, the witches tried to limit themselves to four or five charms a day and no more.

They didn't want to become a one-stop miracle shop. They helped those who were in pain, those who were down on their luck, or those who needed a little pep back in their step. All with the use of their magic.

Krystal, the eldest by four months and most fortunate of all the girls with her excellent magical parentage, had taken on the task of playing mother to both Valerie and Alexa since they were little. They were the Three Musketeers. Inseparable. When she mentioned the idea of opening a coffee shop together, Valerie was fully on-board. When they discussed the idea of breaking the cardinal rule of witchcraft and aiding non-magic folk with their daily problems, she was doubly excited. They realized long ago that if they had all these special powers, it should be used for good. And what better way than to give back to the community they loved so much?

Always ready to rebel and the one with a natural eye for style and colors, Valerie set herself to designing the place, adding the vintage, urban touches of a red brick wall and distressed hardwood floors. Alexa took care of the finances. No one would suspect that her ditzy personality, half-magical genes, and her long bleach-blonde ponytail masked a clever mind for numbers and figures. Krystal was the face of Perfect Books and Brews, the first to greet the customers and the one who gave it a homier feel with personalized mugs for regulars and a pair of listening ears to talk into when life was hard.

That suited Valerie, because most people aggravated her anyway. One who did that much too perfectly was swaggering up to the counter with his partner.

Valerie let Mrs. Robinson's tea steep while she snatched off two mugs from the shelf near the register. Aaron's, a Goldcrest Cove Police Department mug he had snitched from the station, and Devin's, a new mug Krystal bought for him. It was white except for the iconic image of a sailing ship and the words, "I'd Rather Be Fishing" glazed on the side.

She caught Krystal and Devin sharing a quick kiss over the counter.

"Do you think you could warm me up a bit?" Devin asked, flashing a flirty smile to his girlfriend.

Krystal returned the look and brushed aside her black bangs, so they wouldn't hang too low into her eye. "Not right now," she whispered.

The first of the three to discover their dark magic, Krystal was still trying to get the hang of her fire elemental abilities. If gone unchecked, she could make water boil or start a fire on the countertop. She learned early on that a passionate, emotional response was what triggered it every time, which was why Devin's presence made things interesting to say the least. It was all his fault her dark magic had developed in the first place. The entrance of a Twin Flame into a witch's life heralded all these new challenges. Another reason to steer clear of romance.

Rolling her eyes at how undeniably cute they were, she poured Officer Devin a cup of plain black coffee and handed Aaron's mug to Alexa to start his special blend. She didn't exactly trust herself with his order right now. She'd likely spike it with something sinister and she'd be found out later.

Once the timer went off for Mrs. Robinson's tea, Valerie popped a lid on the to-go cup and stepped around the counter to hand-deliver it to the older woman. That was the first time she had smiled all day and it was only for Mrs. Robinson's sake. Valerie absolutely hated her smile, especially when it was faked. Krystal told her to try and think of something funny or happy when facing the customers, but Valerie always drew a blank. There were plenty of things she enjoyed, plenty of things she could laugh at, but nothing that made her happy enough to grin from ear to ear and giggle as Alexa did at every given chance.

"Here you go, Mrs. Robinson," she said, gently handing it over to the woman who had taken a seat at one of the smaller tables near the wall of bookcases.

Mrs. Robinson smiled, her wrinkles deepening. "Thank you, Valerie."

She would have stayed and exchanged more shallow small talk, but the line still stretched clear out the door and Alexa couldn't fix all the drinks by herself. Valerie turned and hurried away, wishing she hadn't been in such a hurry to leave the house. Even just a sip of coffee would have livened her up enough to deal with the mad rush that morning.

Caleb peered through the glass pane of the window rimmed in ice crystals. Under his feet, he could hear the last of the families at the bed and breakfast leave and venture out into the snowy lane. Rose House had been the only place in town that had a vacancy. In fact, it was rather remarkable that the innkeeper, Amber McCain, had a last minute cancellation just ten minutes before he had called ahead to check.

Despite the stroke of luck at finding a room to rent when Christmas was just around the corner, Caleb was ready to find a more permanent home as soon as possible. He didn't want to stay in the same house with a witch for more than a few days. His inner wolf wouldn't allow it.

His werewolf senses told him the mistress of Rose House was a witch the moment he stepped foot on the porch. The place was smothered in the stench of magic. Undoubtedly, she knew he was a werewolf from the second she laid her appraising eyes on him. Supernatural beings had a way of finding each other, even in the most crowded cities. Mostly so they could steer clear of one another. Werewolves and witches were no exception.

With a sigh of resignation, Caleb slid his arms through his black leather jacket and shouldered his laptop bag. If he timed it just right, he could slip down the creaking stairs before Amber noticed he was gone. If his nose and ears weren't lying, she was in the kitchen washing dishes. It was nearly impossible to sneak around in the old Victorian home, but Caleb prided himself on his stealth. It came in handy, whether in human form or not.

He eased his bedroom door shut and walked down the hall without so much as a whisper of noise from the floorboards, his clothes, or even the crinkling of leather from his jacket. He made it as far as the front foyer and his wolf nearly congratulated him.

"Aren't you going to have some breakfast before you go?" Amber called out from behind the swinging door into the kitchen.

He cringed and muttered, "Fuck." His lips curled around the word with all the passion and frustration of a man who was in a hurry and in absolutely no mood to deal with the witch.

Amber wasn't unpleasant. In fact, she was too pleasant. Too willing to please, talk, and serve. It made him question her intentions. He'd had enough of those little schemes in his old pack, the one he was running from. He didn't want to deal with them here. This was supposed to be a fresh start.

Admitting defeat and coming up with no excuse for why he should leave Rose House on an empty stomach, Caleb turned and lazily strode toward the dining hall. Amber pushed her way through the galley door, her hands holding up a heaping platter of bacon and slices of seared ham. He'd been smelling it all morning from his room and he'd be lying if he said his mouth wasn't watering. But his hunger was rivaled by the tingling, needling sensation of her magical essence when she stepped into the room.

"I made up an extra helping just for you," she said as she tossed her dark purple hair over her shoulder before setting the plate down at one of the empty places at the table. The rest of the dishes had been cleared away, leaving only the pine sprig and fake ice crystal centerpiece in the center of a pristine white table cloth. "I've never had a werewolf stay here before, but I imagine you have a hearty appetite, right?"

Caleb slid a glance her way. "I'm in a bit of a hurry."

"Oh? Where are you off to?" Amber asked with a big grin. "I don't think there are any other werewolves in town." She propped her hands on her hips. That's when he noticed her black apron was stained with oil and flour from prepping breakfast for a full house earlier that morning. If she had gone through the trouble of fixing him a special meal, then the least he could do was eat half.

Begrudgingly, he sat himself down and she went to the sideboard against the wall to pour him a bit of leftover orange juice from a pitcher.

"I'm meeting a man in town about a house to rent."

At this, she became even more animated – if that was even possible. "Really? Are you going to rent a room with Shawn and Valerie?"

He chewed a little slower and swallowed, trying not to be surprised by how much she already knew. It was a small town, and perhaps that was a good thing. In bigger cities, a man like him could get lost, but it wouldn't be conducive to his reclusive nature. Then again, if he spent too much time in the public eye in Goldcrest Cove, everyone would begin to speculate about him. Just one slipup and he'd have to move. Again.

Making the decision to leave his pack in Bridgewater wasn't easy, but picking a new home in Massachusetts proved rather simple. All he needed was a map, a dart, and a random bit of skill. The needle landed right on Goldcrest Cove, a place he had never heard of. It was a chance for a new life, a solitary life. The one he wanted. But late at night, he still wondered at what cost.

"I talked to Shawn over the phone last night," Caleb replied as he took a draught from the glass after Amber had set it in front of him. There was no use denying his plans if the witch already knew. From what he understood, they could sniff out a lie as easily as he could.

"They're good friends of mine. Good people." She pulled up a chair next to him and he had to resist the urge to lean away. "Where are you meeting him?"

Caleb looked sideways at her wondering if now would be an appropriate time to tell her how nosy she was. If all went well, he'd be out of Rose House by the end of the day and he could insult her all he wanted. But, he refrained. His mother taught him better than to disrespect a lady to her face.

"One of the coffee shops on Johnson Avenue," he replied, tucking some of the ham against his cheek, so he could talk clearly.

Amber beamed. "You mean the *only* coffee shop. Perfect Books and Brews. Great place and great coffee. You should have Krystal make you a cup. It's amazing stuff. Actually, the coffee I have here is the same as over there. I made a deal with them, so I could buy discounted grounds from them and then serve it to my guests and –"

Right about there is when he stopped listening and continued to eat. He let her talk, nodding politely to make her believe that he was actually interested in what she had to say. All the while, he thought about the route he would have to take down the residential roads to get to Johnson Avenue. He had only been in Goldcrest Cove for a couple of days and already he could tell that he liked the looks of the town. Plenty of old houses. It'd be even more beautiful in the spring and fall seasons.

He looked at the grandfather clock on the other side of the dining room. He had just fifteen minutes before he had to meet with Shawn.

Scarfing down a few more strips of bacon from the platter, he stood from the table. "Thanks for the meal," he said, then wiped his mouth on his sleeve and made for the front door.

"Do you want me to save any of it for when you come back?"

He wanted to say that he wasn't likely to come back except to get his things, but shook off the impulse. "No, thanks. Feed it to the cats."

Wherever they were.

Amber bragged that she took care of at least twenty cats that hung around inside and outside the bed and breakfast. Since he'd arrived, he hadn't seen a single one. Perhaps that was for the best. He'd been on the bad end of plenty of feisty cats that considered him a threat. He could heal from their scratches and bites, but it was still a terrible inconvenience. His whole life might as well have been inconvenient.

He marched out the door before Amber could ask any more questions or ensnare him in another one-sided conversation.

The trailer rental sat on the newly paved driveway, loaded down with all his worldly possessions that amounted to a few dozen boxes of books, a metal bed frame, and a queen-sized mattress. Beside it was his faithful pickup truck that he'd had for almost fifty years. It had been with him through three pack changes and had gotten him this far, but he wondered how it would react to the cold winters that Massachusetts could dish out. He'd have to invest in snow tires or chains at some point.

Once the engine was cranked up and warm enough, he rolled down the quaint, narrow streets of Goldcrest Cove until he arrived at Johnson Avenue. He spotted the gold and purple sign for Perfect Books and Brews, but there wasn't a single place to park on either side of the street. He managed to find a spot about three blocks down and then braved the cold to walk the rest of the way. The ice might have deterred others, but his uncanny balance, along with traction boots, made for an easy trek.

He passed by small shops, a restaurant or two, and gave friendly nods to other pedestrians who slid him cautious looks. He wasn't nearly as bundled up as they were in their scarves, gloves, hats, and at least three layers, while he wore only a simple t-shirt underneath his leather jacket. They must have thought him insane. He didn't even wear a stocking cap to cover his short dark hair. Though he was a born and raised southern boy, the cold hardly fazed him.

Still a block away, he breathed in the smell of the coffee beans, toffee syrup, dark chocolate powders, and caramel drizzle. It had been ages since he'd had a good cup of coffee and though his werewolf stomach couldn't handle that much caffeine anymore, he still enjoyed the smell of the brew.

The lobby was packed with customers. Families, couples, and students taking advantage of their winter break filled the tables across the expansive dining area. It was a good thing he hadn't relied on this place for breakfast, because there wasn't a single egg sandwich or pastry in sight. However, there was a drink in every hand and a smile on everyone's face. Caleb even caught himself smiling when he looked up and saw the rows upon rows of books against the far brick wall. But it was a fleeting grin, because within seconds of him stepping through the door, another sensation hit him like a slap in the face.

Witches. Magic. It was everywhere.

He let out an audible groan when he realized where it was coming from. The three girls behind the counter were the source. No wonder Amber liked this place.

Caleb had never been in a town with this many witches before and as he staggered up to wait in line, he wondered how many more there might be. He readjusted the strap on his laptop bag and reached into his back pocket to pull out his wallet in preparation for his purchase, all the while thinking what a load of bullshit it was to be living in a town so infested with magic. Just when he thought the dart had taken him someplace worthwhile, he regretted not giving it another toss.

At first, he had no intention of making nice with the witches. The one at the register, her black hair pulled back and brown eyes serene, seemed nice and would probably be as polite as a witch could to a werewolf. The other two who were hard at work making the drinks, he wasn't so sure. The blonde flitted from espresso machine to counter with a light skip in her step that reminded him of a gleeful child.

The third, who faced away from him for the majority of the time while he stood in line, seemed different than the others. There was a tenseness across her shoulders, a stiff and aggravated attitude in her movements. With each turn of her head, he thought he caught something peculiar about her. It took a few moments for him to realize that what he saw in the sparse lighting of the coffee shop were burgundy streaks woven through her dark brown, wavy hair. He watched her more closely than the others, waiting for her to turn around, so he could get a better look. Though, he wasn't sure why he should have taken any special interest in her. She was just a witch.

When she did turn around, his lips parted just enough for a hissing utterance of, "Shit" to slide out. She was stunning, more so than the other two witches who were fairly pretty all by themselves. But this girl, wearing a Five Finger Death Punch touring shirt stole the breath from his very lungs.

His talents as a wordsmith were useless as he went through the various phrases and comparisons to accurately describe her. Stunning didn't cut it. It was in the way her dark emerald eyes offset her skin tinted by a tan she must have acquired over the summer. It was in the way her lips formed a tight, suppressed scowl and how her thin black brows slanted in a look of concentration. It was the way her jeans hugged her firm curves. It was how the shirt wasn't quite long enough to hide the stretch of skin on the small of her back when she reached up for something from an upper cabinet or bent down low to grab a sleeve of to-go cups from under her station. She didn't have to be wearing anything provocative to make him keenly aware of how his body responded to her.

Caleb stared as she deftly handled the machines, pouring drink after drink and dropping tea bags as the orders continued to fly at her. Hardworking, determined, and completely oblivious to how captivating she was. He had to know her name. Even his wolf was straining for him to get closer. If the animal spirit within him was physical at all, it would have been pulling against his leash for a chance just to sit next to the barista. His wolf hardly ever wanted something so badly.

As soon as the thought entered his mind, he squirmed uncomfortably at the mixed feelings that now burned in his chest. She was a witch, something that he couldn't ignore. Caleb let out a tired sigh and passed a hand over his eyes.

One thing all of his former alphas had made perfectly clear to him. Witches, and other magical beings like them, didn't take kindly to werewolves. There were centuries worth of hostilities between their kinds that would never die. They usually didn't inhabit the same territories and avoided one another like the plague. He would be shattering that taboo by staying in the same town where four witches lived and worked.

Amber was nice enough, and none of these girls seemed to be immediately bothered by his presence, but who was to say this wouldn't blow up in his face later down the road? He wasn't in a pack anymore and they could easily run him off. Then again, maybe his new solitary living would make him less of a threat. It all hinged upon how these girls saw him, what they thought of his kind, and if they already had a severe prejudice. If they did, it was game-over before he could even pass the first level.

Caleb was just two customers away from standing in front of the cashier and he risked another glance toward the witch that caught his eye. His heart nearly stopped beating when their eyes locked. It may have only been four or five seconds, but it might as well have been a lifetime.

They gazed at one another, both startled expressions mixed with a spark of interest and confusion. She must have known what he was. There was no way she couldn't sense it with her magic. He had come into contact with plenty of other supernatural beings, but never had he felt so naked and vulnerable than under her stare. He wanted to give her an apology just for being there, but he shouldn't have been sorry for what he was. There was nothing to be ashamed of. So why did he care about what she thought of him? Why should he care if he frightened her?

The line moved and he took a dragging step forward, breaking the enchantment. The witch looked away and continued working, but there was a noticeable difference in her now. Her hands weren't as precise, and he saw the way her fingers trembled a bit as she pressed buttons and pulled levers on the espresso machines.

He took another step and found himself facing the cashier. The smile she afforded to each of the customers completely dropped as soon as she saw him.

He held up his hands in surrender, his wallet still gripped in one of them as an offering. He could already predict what would come out of her mouth by the flinty look of her glare. No, she wasn't going to be as amiable as Amber. He checked the nametag pinned to her apron.

"I come in peace," he said to Krystal, letting his voice drop low. The witch he fancied shuddered and slowed in her movements even further.

Krystal lifted her chin, dark eyes assessing him. "You better," she replied softly, her feminine voice hardened. "This is a good town with good people and we don't need any trouble here."

Caleb couldn't keep his brows from furrowing. "Trouble?" he repeated, lowering his hands to the edge of the counter. "What kind of trouble could I possibly cause?"

He didn't have to look to know that the other pairs of witch eyes locked on him in that moment. They were all aware of what his kind could do, if they really wanted to.

Krystal did a good job of remaining calm if she thought she was speaking with a vicious, savage beast. "I've been told about the kind of stuff werewolves pull. Just know that we have connections with the police department and I can tell them to keep a close eye on you."

Caleb let out a huff of a laugh. "Seriously? You think I'm going to do some crazy shit like rob a house or something?"

"We've already had one murderer caught in this town this year. Don't make it two."

At this, his eyes went wide. "Murder?" he drawled out in disgust. "You don't even know me, and you think I'm going to go out and kill someone?" Krystal opened her mouth, but he held up his hand to keep her from answering his rhetorical question. "You know what, forget it. Can I just get a hot Earl Gray tea with a tablespoon of honey, please?"

What fucking right did she have to accuse him of going off and murdering someone in this town? Werewolves hunted deer in the forests, they bought meat from the supermarket, or they starved. Those were the only options, but evidently these witches had heard otherwise. Maybe word about what happened with his pack in Bainbridge had leaked this far north, though he couldn't imagine how.

Any other sensible werewolf would have turned around, walked out of that coffee shop and found another town to take refuge in. But something told Caleb to hang on. Give it some time. Maybe, he could prove these witches wrong. He wasn't sure if it was his pride, his usual untimely optimism toward stupid decisions, or the way those captivating green eyes had looked at him a moment ago.

Willing to let the matter drop for now, Krystal turned to her register screen. "What size?"

"Large," he snapped.

Normally, he only ordered a medium, but after this encounter, he needed something to calm his nerves.

The transaction was complete and before Caleb stepped away from the counter, he glanced back one more time to the green-eyed witch. She was watching him too, her hands stilled over the espresso machine. He just gave a nod and weak, unconvincing smile to show her that all was well, and then turned away. Damn him and his fickle heart. He wanted to hate the witch, Krystal, for insulting him so biasedly, while he wanted to get the number for the girl he had nearly terrified just by walking into the shop.

Then again, was that even fear? He was usually pretty adept at picking up that acrid, peppery scent of fear from the humans around him. Even the strong magical energy that infused the air couldn't block out something his wolf – to his chagrin – sometimes reveled in. But there was no fear. Not with any of the witches. Not even the one with the green eyes.

Chapter 2

Valerie's body hummed from her scalp to her toes, thrumming with an energy she had never felt before. She couldn't understand it. She felt fine just before that guy – that werewolf – walked into the shop. Her hands were steady, her heartrate might have been a little high but that was typical while she worked.

But when she laid sights on those green eyes, eyes the color of spring leaves in the sunshine, it was like the brakes had been pulled and alarms sounded through her bones. Nothing wanted to work right after that brief, heart-stopping moment.

She couldn't grip the handle on the espresso machine. Her palms were sweating, her knees weak. The temperature in the room skyrocketed and focusing on the task at hand seemed nearly impossible. All her attention riveted upon the man.

Where he was, what he was doing, what he was saying. She wasn't usually this hyper-aware about anyone or anything. What the hell was wrong with her?

It was just a guy. Dozens like him came through every day like clockwork. Even ones as smoking hot as he was. But this was different. He was a werewolf, a man who could shift into a beast at will. Of course, just like witches, werewolves weren't what Hollywood and mythology made them out to be. They were still dangerous, that much she understood. Something to be avoided. They didn't travel in the same circles for a reason. While witches were sworn to do no harm, werewolves could do nothing but harm. At least, that's what she understood.

The rivalry between their races had been around since humans first became superstitious. Witches were blamed for the creation of werewolves – whether that was true or not, Valerie couldn't say. And werewolves were burned at the stake for being accused of witchcraft. The packs retaliated against the covens and nothing had been peaceful between their kinds since. Even in the twenty-first century, incidents still popped up here and there.

Of course, none of that had to do with her. She had no beef with the shifters and they shouldn't have a reason to think ill of her either. From the sounds of it, the werewolf who just came to Goldcrest Cove knew how to mind his own business too. That, in itself, could be a relief.

Valerie wanted nothing more than for the man to go away and to stop looking at her from across the coffeeshop. Every chance, she glanced toward his little table near the wall of bookcases, just to make sure he was still there, typing away on his laptop. And it seemed each time she caught herself staring, he'd happen to glance up and meet her eyes so directly that her breath would hitch for a second before she turned away.

God fucking damnit, she swore to herself. *Stop looking at him!*

But only a minute or so would pass before she caught herself taking another peek. The scruff on his face, his strong features, the way his muscled body filled out his shirt, and how his gaze seemed to penetrate to her very soul. All of it was too much. Too good. Too addictive.

Once the rush of the morning died down, Valerie brewed her usual café mocha with chocolate powder and whip cream, then ducked into a corner of the work station where she wouldn't be tempted by the werewolf again. From here, she could neither see him nor be seen by him.

He had been in the store for all of half an hour, but she could pull up his face in her mind so clearly, so vividly, that her core warmed at the remembrance of him. The sound of his deep, bass-like voice played on loop in her ears. She picked up on the slight southern drawl in his words and that didn't help her at all. That little smile and nod in her direction after he took his tea set her nerves on fire. Why did he do that? Why keep looking at her? Why stay in a coffeeshop with three witches when he knew damned well that he wasn't welcome by at least one of the owners?

"Isn't he a cute little puppy?" Alexa crooned as she joined Valerie. Her purple fairy mug was filled with a fresh refill of her caramel macchiato, but the witch didn't need any more caffeine. She hardly needed any to begin with.

Krystal turned and folded her arms before leaning against the counter. "That's no puppy, that's a werewolf." A blind man would have known that she wasn't comfortable at all with the idea of a man like him in Goldcrest Cove, much less in their coffeeshop.

"Right, puppies are supposed to have brown eyes. He has blue eyes." The way Alexa joked, Valerie might have thought the half-witch didn't even known what a werewolf was. At least they were of similar opinions about the creatures.

Thankfully, something of her humor was affecting Krystal and she cracked a tiny, sadistic smile. "Maybe he can shift into a Siberian Husky instead."

Alexa wagged her brows. "More like Siberian Hunky."

Valerie spoke up for the first time since the werewolf came in, unable to keep quiet in the face of such an inaccurate statement. "He has green eyes, not blue. And huskies don't have green eyes"

She dearly hoped that neither of her friends would realize she had been looking close enough at the man to know his eye color.

"What dog has green eyes?" Krystal asked, perhaps trying to change the subject.

No such luck with Alexa's hyper brain. "Does it matter? He's still adorable." Her eyes took on a mischievous glimmer. "I wonder how he would look with a collar and leash"

Krystal, however, would not go so far. "We might need to put one on him if he doesn't behave."

The blonde giggled. "Spank him with a rolled up newspaper too?"

"He'll learn pretty quick who's the master in this town." Krystal's lips quirked up in a devious way that made Valerie wonder if they had both lost their minds.

Alexa suggestively wiggled her hips. "He's one dog I wouldn't mind getting on the furniture with, though."

"Do you think they have sex like dogs too?"

Valerie pressed her fingers between her eyes and groaned as a wave of heat crept up her neck. One friend wanted to jump the werewolf's bones and the other was bent on ridiculing him. It painted contrasting pictures in her mind's eye that might never be erased.

"You do realize I can hear everything you're saying?"

Valerie jumped and spilled some of her coffee over her apron at the sound of the werewolf's voice coming from the front counter. All three witches turned to see him there with his empty to-go cup. The frustrated set of his brows told her that he was just as amused about the banter as she was.

The elder of the witches hardened while a deep red colored Alexa's cheeks.

"This is our shop and we can talk about whatever we want," Krystal snapped at him, minding to keep her voice down, so no other customer would hear her rude remark.

"Can I just get another tea?" he asked, offering out the cup. Valerie could see the way his eyes struggled to stay focused on Krystal, wanting to flit to the other witches huddled in the corner.

"You'll have to pay for it."

The werewolf glanced to the chalkboard sign hanging above the cash register. "It says refills are free."

"Not for you, they aren't."

Valerie nettled. Why was her friend acting so cold? Yes, he was a werewolf, but was all of that necessary? He hadn't done anything to deserve it.

The werewolf huffed. "Wonderful customer service."

"Just making sure you know where you stand with us."

A sparkle of gold flashed in the man's eyes and electricity shot through Valerie's chest and straight down her legs. "Oh, I know where I stand. You've all made it perfectly clear."

For a second, Valerie was ashamed. Mostly for how her friends were treating him, but also for how she wasn't doing anything to stop it.

She could tell that Krystal was gearing herself up for a little supernatural lecture, but Valerie couldn't take it anymore. He was making her come undone and the longer they argued, the longer he would be there, driving her crazy.

Valerie set down her mug and stormed up to him. "Quit being a bitch and give the guy a fucking refill," she growled, snatching the cup from the werewolf's hand.

Krystal and Alexa were struck speechless. It wasn't often that Valerie would snap at her friends like that. At Aaron or anyone else who pissed her off, yes, but not them.

The man, however, was still lucid. "One tablespoon – "

"Of honey," Valerie finished without looking over her shoulder. "I know." Of course she knew. She wasn't sure she'd easily forget it. Hot Earl Grey tea.

The entire time she prepared it, she could feel his stare hot on her back, even while Krystal interrogated him.

"How long will you be in Goldcrest Cove?" she asked.

"It's none of your business."

"It is my business. How long are you staying?"

"I don't know. As long as I want, really."

Valerie cringed as she stirred in the honey with the hot water.

"Why are you here?"

"Again, that's my business."

Valerie dropped the teabag into the water and put on a fresh cap before hurrying back to the counter.

"How many more are with you?" Krystal asked.

"It's just me."

"Are more following you?"

She couldn't stand much more of this and slammed down his drink. "I'm taking the coffee to Amber's," she declared, heedless to the fact that she was interrupting. "I'll be back in a little bit."

Valerie wouldn't look at the werewolf as she bent down to retrieve the delivery box from under the counter. Amber had told them that she was getting low on coffee for her bed and breakfast. Usually, the innkeeper came in to get the supplies herself, but said that she'd have her hands full that morning. That was a week ago. With her scrying abilities, Amber could predict just about everything. Maybe she knew that Valerie would need this excuse to leave the coffeeshop.

"Thank you, ma'am," the werewolf said as she rounded the counter.

She wouldn't acknowledge him. Nor would she reply to her friends who were insisting that she stay and wait until later that afternoon to make the delivery. Hopefully they wouldn't think anything of this speedy flight. Maybe if she put some distance between herself and the werewolf, she wouldn't feel on the brink of a total meltdown.

What scared her the most was that the feeling wasn't altogether unpleasant. She felt light, airy, like the air around her had been infused with some sort of new and powerful energy that livened her instead of dragging her down. But it was that liveliness, that total sensation of ecstatic that frightened her the most. She didn't want to feel that giddy, that high.

Uncaring of who saw her, Valerie flicked her fingers at the icy sidewalk the moment she stepped out of the coffeeshop. That was before she realized that Shawn was about a block away from the coffeeshop and headed right for her.

"Where are you going?" he asked as a cold wind tossed the ends of his scarf. It reminded her that she wasn't wearing a jacket. Funny enough, she didn't feel the winter chill at all.

"I'm taking this to Amber."

It was then she remembered that they were going to meet with the new room-mate. Shawn was about to start in on a tirade about that and she cut him off.

"I know, I know! Just make sure he's not an asshole. Otherwise, I really don't care right now."

"You're not even curious?"

Valerie couldn't think, couldn't reason. She just needed to get away from the shop, away from that werewolf. "No. I'm not. Just go without me. It'll be fine."

She heard nothing else from him and hurried to her car, unsettled that no matter how fast she walked or how far she drove away from Johnson Avenue, the feeling persisted. What the hell was that werewolf doing to her?

Caleb couldn't catch his breath, couldn't stop grinding his teeth, couldn't reign in his wolf that pled for him to run after the girl. She had a funny way of showing the difference between her and her witch friends. She was still cold, but she stood up for him. At least, that's how he wanted to perceive it. It was just a cup of tea, but it was the best handout he'd received since he came in that morning.

He sipped on his drink and tried to focus on the half-page worth of the next chapter in his novel, but his mind was on anything else. The girl's eyes stared back at him through the white space below his words. Her voice sounded louder than any of the noise around him. His fingers wouldn't type out what he needed to say. All he could do was replay the scene in his mind, relive the moment their fingers brushed when she took his cup, and hold onto her scent that was already fading from his senses.

"Hey. Are you Caleb?"

He stiffened and looked up to the man standing next to his table. In his hand was a white mug with the words "#1 Teacher" printed across it. He had seen several customers receive a special mug when they ordered their drinks. It must have been a "regular" sort of thing. He knew he wouldn't have his own, even if he came here every day for years. Those witches would make sure of it.

"Yeah. Shawn?"

The tall man smiled and nodded. They shook hands and exchanged greetings as Caleb closed his laptop and set it aside. Shawn sat down across from him.

"I hope you haven't been waiting long," he said.

Caleb shook his head, hoping it would rid him of the girl's memory for just a moment, so he could focus on this interview. "Not at all. I had some work to do anyway, so I came in early."

Shawn gestured his brimming coffee mug toward the laptop. "And what exactly do you do?"

"I'm an author," he replied. "A successful one. I have a few bestsellers."

At least, that's what he was endeavoring to do in this century. If he were to give an unapologetic resume, the man's head would spin.

Blonde eyebrows arched in surprise. "Really? I've never heard of you."

"I write under a penname. I prefer it that way. Maybe you've heard of C. L Winscott."

Recognition dawned in his eyes. "I have. A coworker of mine loves your books. It's mystery stuff, right? I don't read too much fiction. I'm a history teacher at the high school. Soccer coach too."

Small talk. Caleb endured it for the sake of a place to live, but he sincerely hoped it wouldn't be a normal thing.

"Have you been doing that for long?"

Shawn shrugged. "Just for six or so years."

Caleb showed his appreciation and took a draught of his tea.

"So, how stable is your job?" Shawn questioned with a note of skepticism. "I mean, you're a writer, and obviously a good one, but we're looking for someone who can still pull their own weight. Financially, that is."

He suppressed a chuckle, knowing this had to be typical. Caleb rarely had to worry about finding a place of his own. He had his pack, no matter where he lived. His alpha pulled strings to get him the best landlords. He was given an address and a move-in date, and that was it. If he couldn't afford his rent one month, someone covered the difference. Now, he was on his own. He'd be doing this all alone, without a safety net. That's what he wanted. Wasn't it?

"I have a steady flow of income. No need to worry about that." There was no point in telling him about the stocks and investments that filled in the gaps every so often. He had enough savings built up from over the years that he could have paid the rent in its entirety. Maybe even buy the damn house, but he wouldn't boast.

Shawn nodded and sipped his coffee. "What made you decide on Goldcrest Cove?"

Caleb went into explaining about the map, the dart, and the fact that he wanted a fresh start.

"I bet this will be good for your muse, or your creative flow, or whatever it is you artist types need."

"I think it'll be a good change." Caleb cut his eyes toward the counter and saw the dark-haired witch, Krystal, peering at him with as much tenderness as a cobra.

"I'll be honest," Shawn continued with a laugh. "You don't look like a writer at all."

No, he wouldn't. His physique alone would never pin him for a man who spent much of his time hunched over a computer. He might have been a half-recluse, but being a werewolf kept him in shape. "You can't always judge a book by its cover."

Shawn pointed a finger at him. "Touché."

"You mentioned there would be a third housemate?"

"Yeah. That's Valerie."

Caleb noticed the slight flicker of hesitation. "Your girlfriend?"

That earned him a laugh. "God, no! She's just a friend. She's got her own way of doing things, but as long as you stay out of her way, she gets along with most people."

"I can respect that," Caleb replied, only slightly curious as to what he was getting himself into. "Everyone has their own bedroom?"

He nodded. "I cleaned out my office. It's about the same size as the other rooms."

"I'm sorry if I'm putting you out."

Shawn set his mug on the table. "Not you. Our landlord raising our rent last month put us in a bit of a bind. I didn't have much in the office anyway. I grade my papers in our dining room. There's the kitchen, a fenced-in yard, living room of course, and one bathroom."

Caleb cocked an eyebrow. "One bathroom?"

His interviewer winced. "It's an older house. The bathroom's in the hall and we share it. Valerie's not a girly type, so she doesn't hog the hot water or anything. And she's quick in the morning. Fifteen minutes tops."

Caleb wondered how he'd deal with being roommates with a female. He had never had to live with one he wasn't related to. "As long as we can all respect our own spaces, I think it'll be fine."

By the way Shawn's shoulders steadily relaxed through their interview, he guessed this was going well. His posture was loose, more open, slumped in the chair with his legs casually crossed. Everything told Caleb that he was putting on a good show.

They discussed the specifics of the rent, utilities, and general house rules. They took turns with the chores and chipped in for the groceries each week. It would be incredibly different than living alone, or even living in a pack. But he'd have to make it work.

"I think I can agree to all of those terms."

Shawn grinned and offered out his hand. "Then I think we've got our new tenant."

They shook on it, but the meeting wasn't over.

"Now, I have to warn you that I'll be leaving for about a week or two," Shawn continued. "I've got family I'm planning to visit up in New York for the holidays. It'll be just you and Valerie in the house."

Caleb felt a cold streak race down his spine, but he nodded. "Stay out of her way and no trouble, right?"

"Yep. Pretty much. You'll meet her tonight after she gets off work. I wanted her to meet you now, but she had something she needed to do."

Shawn then went into a discourse on Goldcrest Cove. Where to shop, who to make friends with, the best places to eat, and everything in between. It was a lot to take in, but there was one thing on Caleb's mind.

He leaned forward on his elbows and the table tilted slightly under his weight. "Are there any other places in town with free Wi-Fi?"

Shawn downed the last of his cup. "Nope. Perfect Books and Brews is pretty much the place. We have internet at the house, though. If you don't feel like coming here, you can always stay at home."

That tore him. While he might have the house to himself during the day, Caleb knew he'd want to get out every once and a while to write. He needed to watch people, listen to conversations, get a grip on the human condition enough to flesh out his characters the way he needed to. Wherever he lived, there was always a coffeeshop or two he could visit for such research.

If Perfect Books and Brews was his only option, he needed to find some place else. As much as he wanted to see that girl every day, her friends would make sure that his time there was a living hell.

And just like that, his mind drifted back to the barista. She said she was going to Amber's. Was it the same Amber who owned Rose House? If it was, maybe they would run into one another when he went to get his stuff. She'd walk the same floors that he did. She'd see his trailer, loaded down with his possessions.

"You all right?"

Caleb looked up and realized he must have zoned out for a minute. "Yeah, I'm good. I can bring my stuff by this afternoon if that'll work for you."

"Are you still on the clock?" Amber asked as she took a seat across from Valerie in the parlor.

With her hands firmly clasped around the blue mug, she nodded. "Yep. Just... taking a little breather. It was a busy morning."

Amber slowly nodded, and Valerie knew she had been caught in the lie. "Uh huh..."

They had the old house to themselves. Soft classical music played from the radio in the dining room and Valerie could smell muffins baking in the oven. She must have had a new guest arriving later that afternoon. Amber only spiffed up the place when she knew she was receiving another patron. Otherwise, pop music would be playing on the radio and some sort of hard liquor would have been offered with her coffee.

All of it should have been relaxing, but Valerie's nerves were still rattled by the werewolf. Distance hadn't helped the tremor in her hands, but the charm she put over her coffee would take affect soon enough. Just another ten or fifteen minutes and she might be safe to drive back to the coffeeshop. Goddess willing, the werewolf would be gone by then.

"So, did you meet him?"

Cold gushed through her veins and Valerie wondered if she'd have to double the charm. "Him?"

Amber grinned like a Cheshire cat. "The werewolf." The hostess leaned against the arm of the sofa and crossed her legs. "He said he was going to Perfect Books and Brews this morning."

Valerie took a hasty sip of her coffee, hating the utter lack of chocolate in the blend. She would have rather had her mocha. "Yeah, I saw him. How did you know about him?"

"That's his stuff out in the driveway." She jerked her head toward the wide window that overlooked the frost-tinged lawn. "He's been here a couple of days."

"You knew there was a werewolf in town and you didn't tell anyone?" Valerie fought the deep-seated urge to feel betrayed. Amber was under no obligation to tell anyone anything, but since she was the only witch in town who could scry, she should have warned someone. Especially her fellow witches. At least she didn't seem so averse to the man as Krystal had been.

"Oh, honey, I've known for a few weeks he was coming. I made sure there was a room open for him."

That's why she looked so clever about the whole thing.

"Do you know what he wants?" Valerie asked, trying to keep the panic from her tone.

She shrugged her shoulders. "I figured it'd be obvious. Just a place to stay."

Valerie closed her eyes against the answer. It was just as she feared. The werewolf was going to make a home in Goldcrest Cove. "Krystal gave him the third-degree at the coffeeshop. He said he was alone."

"He is alone," Amber confirmed.

"But that doesn't make him any less dangerous, right?"

Amber gave her a look as if she had just said something rude. "Dangerous? I mean, Caleb's a little rough around the edges, but aren't we all?"

Caleb. Valerie let the name roll around in her head. She let it connect with the memory of his eyes, his voice, his essence. He certainly looked and acted like a Caleb. She found herself drifting when something of the charm finally grounded her in the present.

"So, you don't think he's a threat?"

Amber blew air between her lips. "Fuck, no."

"Even though he's a werewolf?"

"You say that like he's some felon or a terrorist."

Valerie shifted on the thin cushion of the Victorian settee. "I admit I don't know a lot about them, but I haven't exactly heard any good stories either."

The innkeeper's face wrinkled. "Neither have I, but I can pick up on intent. This dude isn't going to hurt anyone."

"Krystal doesn't seem to think so." Valerie took another sip of her coffee, feeling her face grow hot from its magical remedy. Calm and courage. That's all she needed.

"Krystal and Sierra hear things from their parents and all their parents know is the council and all the shit that they have to deal with. I reserve judgement until I've experienced it firsthand."

Amber had a point and Valerie could share in the sentiment. Gordon and Catherine Hayden were part of the council put in place to police all magical disturbances in the country. They were the ones who disciplined rogue witches and dealt with other supernatural upheavals. They would know what kind of trouble a werewolf could cause.

But none of that had to do with Caleb. He hadn't done anything wrong yet. Maybe part of her wanted there to be something wrong with him. She wanted him to be a criminal, to be a dangerous citizen. Then, she would have a reason not to like him. She'd have a solid excuse not to get close and to avoid him, instead of this nameless discomfort that made her so undone.

"I'll tell you what, though," Amber continued with refreshed enthusiasm. "He's hot as hell." She fanned herself and swept back her purple hair. "Damn, that man is fine."

Valerie cracked a tiny smile, but she didn't openly agree. She never would, if she could help it.

Chapter 3

By the grace of the Goddess, Caleb was not at the coffeeshop when Valerie came back from the delivery. It was his absence that gave Krystal and Alexa the impression that they could talk about werewolves to their hearts' content. She shut them up real quick before they could start gabbing about the man who had lit something inside of her that needed to be doused.

She couldn't explain it. Neither did she want to. The werewolf was gone, and if he had any sense, he wouldn't come back to the coffeeshop. If Caleb intended to live in Goldcrest Cove, there might be other run-ins with him, but she would cross that bridge when she came to it. For now, Valerie shushed the other two witches and poured herself into her work. She even elected to stay late, just to distract herself for a little longer. If she stayed busy, she wouldn't think about him.

The charm was just wearing off when she pulled into the driveway. Night had come and with it a clear sky, lit by a billion brilliant stars that gave her some ease. The moon, a bright beacon outshining everything else, wasn't quite full, but cast a bluish, silver glow over the patches of snow across the lawn.

Her tired muscles, aching head, and growling stomach kept her from enjoying the wintery scene as much as she wanted to. Nature and all its natural beauty were the only pleasures she could afford nowadays. Everything else was hustle and work. Taking just a few minutes to breathe in the crisp, clean air seemed so vital nowadays.

Though, right now, all she wanted was a hot meal, steaming bath, and a bed. And maybe a few cold kisses from Thor.

Warm air hit her when she tried to open the door. It hit something and wouldn't swing all the way. She peeked around and saw the stack of cardboard boxes in the hall.

"That you, Val?" Shawn called from the living room.

Valerie squeezed her way through the door and shut it behind her. "Yeah. I worked late."

The mess just by the door flowed into the dining room, where more boxes of various sizes were scattered. Labels written in black marker were scrawled across the sides, still taped shut. She didn't need to ask if the interview went well. Looks like they found their new tenant. That must have been his truck parked on the curb.

She dropped her bag by the pile of shoes in the foyer and slipped off her own while shrugging her jacket from her shoulders.

It was then that she realized something else. Thor was usually the first one to greet her at the door. She neither heard his claws tapping against the hardwood floors, nor his muffled barking from the backyard.

"Where's Thor?" she asked as she strode into the living room, glancing around for her lab.

Shawn sat on the sofa, his elbows upon his knees and game controller between his hands. His eyes were focused upon the combat scene on the television, the sound turned down so low that she could only hear the sharp grunts of the characters in the melee.

"He was in the way when we were bringing in the boxes. He's in your room. Don't worry, I put some food and water in there for him."

Valerie rolled her eyes and headed toward the kitchen. "You could have let him out in the backyard."

"He wouldn't get out of the hallway. Just kept barking his damned head off."

Just as she was wondering if Thor's aggression had anything to do with the new guy, she rounded the corner and looked up. There, standing in the middle of her kitchen with a knife in his hand, was the werewolf. *Caleb.*

Too startled to think straight, Valerie let out a shriek. She threw up her hands, and a whirlwind crashed through the room. The knife was knocked from Caleb's hand and he was lifted clean off his feet. The backdoor flew open and the werewolf was forced out by her magic. The door closed and the locking mechanisms clicked securely into place.

It all happened in less than three seconds and Valerie never had to move. Her heart pounded out of her chest and her body shook. Adrenaline and fear spiked through her nerves. Her lungs refused to work and she couldn't draw a solid breath. She just stood there, trembling and gasping for air.

She had never used her magic so violently in the house, nor so close to Shawn. Dangerous didn't begin to describe what she just did out of pure impulse.

"Valerie?" The game was paused and Shawn was behind her in an instant.

As if the fear of showing her shock overrode her fear of Caleb, Valerie sobered and crossed her arms over her chest. "Who the hell was that?" she demanded.

Shawn looked from her to the back door, colored in utter bewilderment. "That was Caleb. Our new roommate... Did you shove him out?"

Caleb was on the other side of the door, watching them through the window with the light from the kitchen illuminating his disgruntled look. Shawn hurried forward and proceeded to unlatch the various locks barring him from reentering.

Valerie's mind snagged on that simple answer. *Our new roommate.* There wasn't a strong enough word in the English language to accurately voice her feelings on that account.

"I... I thought he was a burglar or something. He had a knife!" She gestured toward the floor where the knife had fallen, and it was then she saw the truth to the matter. A cutting board was on the counter, a slab of flank steak still in the wrapper sitting beside it. The oven was on, and a pot of chopped potatoes was boiling on the stove.

Caleb, the werewolf, was cooking dinner.

Shawn opened the door to let the man in, and Valerie wouldn't dare to meet his stare. Not out of embarrassment, but because she was too furious to think straight.

"This is one hell of a way to greet your new roommate," Shawn scolded.

"It's all right," Caleb replied, his deep, southern drawl electrifying the air around her. "I would be startled too, if I saw a stranger in my kitchen."

"Valerie, this is Caleb. Caleb, Valerie."

Their first real introduction was made hastily, thanks to the already hostile tension between them. She could feel his gaze on her, burning, begging her to look up. She swallowed hard and did the one thing she wished she would never have to do again.

He was just as hot as she remembered. Now, with his jacket off, he displayed all of his masculinity that frightened and excited her at the same time. But she couldn't show her weakness. She understood canine mentality. She knew everything about territories, dominance, and the need to establish rank quickly. Wolves might have been a totally different thing than dogs, but it was close enough.

Valerie lifted her chin and gave as stern a look as she expected to receive from a beast. His eyes, however, stayed calm, touched with a bit of intensity that she recognized from earlier that day. As if he were trying to peer into her very soul. He'd find little worth exploiting.

Time seemed to stand still with all three of them in the kitchen, waiting for the muted battle of wills to be won or lost already.

"Is there going to be a problem?" Shawn finally asked, attempting to fracture the tension just a little.

Caleb was the first to break eye contact and turned to Shawn. "I don't have a problem." Then he turned back to Valerie. "Do you?"

That had to be the most loaded question ever to be formed by human lips. Was she okay with having a werewolf for a roommate? Was she okay with keeping another secret from Shawn? Could she promise to behave? All of it was a resounding, "no", but logic took over.

They needed the help with the rent, at least for now. If Caleb moved out, they'd have to start their tiring search all over again and neither she, nor Shawn, had the patience for that. As long as Caleb could play nice, then she would have to as well. Besides, it would give her time to see if any of the stories about werewolves were true.

"Nope. No problem."

Shawn nodded and slapped Caleb on the back. "Great then. You two take some time and get acquainted, since you didn't earlier at the coffeeshop."

He gave a cautionary look to Valerie as he passed, silently ordering her not to screw this up. In any other situation, she would stick her tongue out at him or make some smartass comment, but her chest was still tight from the shock of it all.

They stood alone in the kitchen, the simmering of the water on the stove and Shawn's videogame sounding louder in her ears than before.

"I have no intention of causing trouble for you," Caleb began. "If I had known – "

"What? You would have told him, 'Sorry, I can't live with you, because you also live with a witch?'" Valerie kept her voice to a low whisper, fully aware that he could hear her while Shawn wouldn't.

A muscle jumped in Caleb's jaw, but he said nothing. Unable to stop herself, Valerie marched forward and jabbed a finger at his chest.

"I swear by the Goddess Trinity that if you do anything to hurt me, Shawn, or any of my friends, I'll make sure you won't be able to eat solid meat or shift into your little puppy form for a fucking year. And you know I can do it."

Up this close, his height and stature were fully realized. He was so much taller and bulkier than she was. He could snap her like a dead twig and she had the balls to bow up to him like this. The scene might have looked comical from outside eyes. Once more, the thought of his massive, chiseled body so near to hers, made heat flash across her skin. It'd be impossible to intimidate him, but her magic could easily throw him across the street if needed.

From afar, his werewolf spirit was tangible, but not overpowering. This close, it engulfed her, along with the aroma of the earth. Pine, oaks, and a tinge of wild echoed through her soul. Whether it was his aftershave, his cologne, or maybe it was his normal, unaltered scent, she didn't know. All she knew was that the combination of it thrilled her like nothing else she had ever experienced.

Valerie tried to tell herself that she was safe, that this man couldn't and wouldn't lay a single claw on her. Then why did she still feel as if she were just cast into a whirlpool of emotions she couldn't describe?

"I know you can," he replied, his voice dropping, if that was even possible. "But you won't."

Valerie's nose wrinkled in disdain. "Don't tell me what I will or won't do. You don't know a goddamn thing about me."

One corner of his lip tilted up in a mocking smirk. "I say you won't, because I won't give you a reason to."

She felt as if a bucket of cold water had just been tossed in the direction of her blind hatred for the guy. It threatened to pacify her, to calm her riled nerves. She didn't want to be calm. She wanted – needed – to stay mad. As long as she could hate him, she couldn't feel anything else. He was just being too damn agreeable.

"Would you like any dinner? I'm making – "

"No."

Valerie whisked around and charged out of the kitchen, yielding the field to the werewolf and unsure who just came out as top dog. She wouldn't look to Shawn or even snatch up her bag before sulking away to her bedroom.

The moment she opened the door, Thor came tearing out, ramming into her leg and bolting for the kitchen.

"Thor, no!" she shouted, more afraid for her dog than for what might happen to Caleb. The lab began barking and growling so viciously that Valerie was sure blood would be spilled.

"You see!" Shawn cried. "That's what he was doing all afternoon."

Thor wouldn't trespass into the kitchen, but stood there, ears perked and tail erect as he continued to go ballistic on Caleb. The werewolf, astonishingly, didn't seem that concerned at all and was too busy rinsing off the knife to care about the dog.

Valerie hooked her thumb around Thor's blue collar and tried to pull him away, but it was no use. Thor's territory was being violated and the lab couldn't tell the difference between a rival dog and a man. Caleb was more of an invader to him than anyone else.

After a bout of shouting and tugging, she finally gave in and used her magic. Just a quick tempering charm to make the dog more manageable.

"Can you just turn off whatever it is that makes him nuts like that?" Valerie beseeched the werewolf, who would always be the offending party in her mind, no matter the situation. He had to be, for the sake of her own sanity.

Caleb chuckled and it nearly broke her.

"You think I can just turn off who I am? You clearly don't know a goddamn thing about me either."

Valerie narrowed her eyes upon his back. If looks could kill, he would be six feet under already.

Thor let out a whine and let himself be taken outside for a potty break, then back inside to her room. With her door closed, shutting out the smell of the cooking dinner, Valerie tried not to let herself get worked up about the whole thing. Her life had just taken a crazy, unpredictable turn and she didn't know how to handle it.

Caleb made her feel so much that it was nothing more than a big mass of energy in her stomach that wouldn't go away. It constricted her lungs, and wouldn't let her heartrate slow for one second. Her limbs were tingling, her thoughts racing. It was like what she experienced in the coffeeshop, but so much more acute, stronger, unavoidable.

She didn't want to feel like this, but she knew that she couldn't dope herself up on charms every day just to feel normal again. Part of her, the part that didn't want to hate Caleb, told her to just let it all go. To release these energies that were slowly eating away at her insides.

But letting go had never been easy for her, and it never would be.

Wildflowers. That's what she smelled like. That fact wasn't cemented until he came onto the property and stepped into the foyer. Her scent and her magic infected everything in the house and it didn't take him long to put the pieces together. His new roommate was the witch from the coffeeshop. The same witch that had caught his eye and occupied his every waking thought.

He was granted a few hours to collect whatever reason was left in him and plan what he would say and do when she walked in the door. Even if he had several days, he might not have been prepared for her reaction. It was the first time he had ever came in direct contact with magic, and he hoped it would be the last. As he told Valerie, he would never intentionally make her fulfill that threat.

He also hadn't expected to see that fire behind her eyes, nor hear the biting tone of her words that made him reassess everything he had thought of her. Next to Amber, he thought Valerie would prove to be an ally. Her warning, the way she glared at him from across the kitchen, all of it suggested that he had been wrong.

Yet, there was something else beneath all the hostility. Behind the walls she threw up, he sensed something else. It was a glimmer, a dim spark of an emotion that she covered well. He saw it, and he'd hold onto it as the only bit of proof that she wasn't as cold and prejudice as her friends.

It was happiness. For just a second, Valerie was happy. Of course, on the outside she didn't give any hint of it. There was no smile, no brightening of the expression or exclamation of joy. It was the moment she laid eyes on him, just before she threw her hands up and whisked him out of the house with her magic. For that millisecond in time, she was happy to see him. Not frightened, not angry. Did she even realize what it was?

Caleb wanted to know why it was there, why he could manifest something so simple and yet fundamental in another being. For as long as he could remember, he had never seen that kind of true happiness in another's face when they looked at him.

All the while he and Shawn played co-op in his science fiction shooter game, Caleb kept one ear out for Valerie, absently listening to the conversation within her bedroom. From what he gathered, she must have been in a three-way call with the other witches, appraising them of her situation.

"I will seriously send Devin down there to keep an eye on the house," said Krystal. "I'm not afraid to call him up right now. Just say the word."

As much as he resented her prejudice, Caleb could admire her spirit. Krystal was a born alpha, a defender and protector. That much he could understand. The rest was unnecessary.

"Aren't you scared at all? I mean, he's right down the hall from you."

Caleb shook his head at the petite blonde who made such bold statements in the coffeeshop. By the fear that wafted off of her when he came up for his refill, he knew she was just blowing smoke. Same as now.

"He can't do shit to me," Valerie replied confidently. "He knows who has more power here and he's definitely not it."

He shrugged his brows as he smashed his thumb into the controller buttons during the combat sequence. Shawn's excited shouts were almost drowning out the rest of the girl-talk down the hall. Power and competition were not his thing. If Valerie wanted to be in control, she'd have it. All Caleb wanted was peace. That's why he was here.

"What's he doing now?"

There was a pause and Shawn answered for her as he screamed at the avatars in the game.

"With Shawn playing Call of Duty."

"What does Shawn think of him?"

"How should I know? I've barely spent any time outside my bedroom since I got home."

"Good call. The less contact the better."

He frowned. Caleb didn't need her friends trying to tell her what to do or how to think. It wouldn't help him in the least and it would only thicken the walls between them.

"Has he done anything yet?" Krystal asked, probably hinting to a deeper question. Had he done anything "werewolf" yet?

"He was cooking dinner and now he's playing a game. Pretty normal to me."

There. Caleb would hold onto that. Another time she came to his defense.

"Cooked dinner?" the blonde asked. "Like, skinned a deer and roasted it over a spit or…"

Valerie's tone became flavored with impatience. "No, it was out of a package. You think that sort of thing would just fly under the radar with Shawn home?"

"I guess not… So, he's just out there in the living room?"

"Listen," Valerie snapped. "I just wanted to tell you two that he's living with me. Not to give a play-by-play of everything he does."

"But, like, does he have his stuff in the bathroom already? Does he use dog shampoo or regular guy shampoo?"

Caleb had to shake his head. Never mind about prejudices. These girls were downright ignorant. He could almost forgive them for knowing absolutely nothing.

There came a subtle shift in the air inside the house, as if everything became slow and sluggish. The lights even seemed to dim, but he might have been the only one to notice. His wolf stiffened at the change, but he reasoned the power lines must have been affected by the cold somehow.

"Please, I don't want to think about this asshole anymore," Valerie pleaded. "And my phone's almost dead. I'll talk to you tomorrow, okay?"

At this, she unceremoniously hung up with her friends. The thickness in the atmosphere persisted and his wolf chafed at its potency. It wasn't a coming storm. He knew what those felt like. His joints would ache and his wolf would press him to take a run through the woods during those evening thunderstorms. This was different. More suffocating and draining.

Beside him, Shawn suddenly yawned. He checked the time.

"When does your flight leave tomorrow?" Caleb asked.

"Ten in the morning. You're still good to drive me there?"

"Sure. But you look beat."

Shawn paused the game, the opaque menu blurring the wide television screen. "Yeah, I don't know what it is, but I just got super tired all of the sudden." He stretched his arms and set the controller on the table. "That's weird, because I hardly ever get tired playing this."

Caleb leaned back against the couch cushion and set his own controller in his lap. "You should turn in then."

Right as he said that, Valerie's door opened. The darkened hallway became illuminated by the light that poured from her bedroom. A moment later, she appeared at the corner, wearing a pair of flannel pajama pants and oversized Metallica shirt. It obscured her figure, but somehow, she looked even sexier dressed down than in jeans. His wolf agreed, and the nasty scowl on her face only added to the appeal somehow.

"Did you take my charger?" she demanded of Shawn.

The only human in the house looked up and his brows furrowed. "No. I don't touch your stuff."

"Well, it's missing and my phone's dead."

That was quick. Just a moment ago, she said it was dying.

"Are you sure you didn't use it somewhere else and forget?"

Valerie propped a hand on her hip. "I looked everywhere in my room and I couldn't find it."

"What kind of phone do you have?" Caleb asked, stunning them both into silence. They couldn't have forgotten that he was there.

It took her a minute to gather her wits long enough to reply. "Android."

He nodded. "I just switched to an iPhone from an Android. Do you want my old charger?"

Her lips parted, but no words came out. It was as if this were the first time anyone had shown her a bit of kindness or unselfish compassion.

"This is where you say, 'Thank you, Caleb. That's very nice of you.'" Shawn's teasing went over just about as well as Caleb expected.

She shot him a fiery glare. "I'm not one of your kids and this isn't a classroom."

Caleb stood up and placed his controller in his seat before locating the box with all of his office supplies. He found the charger coiled up on top and brought it back to her. "You can have it."

Valerie's gaze shifted from him to the charger and back again, hesitant and completely untrusting of him. But he wouldn't give away the wounds she inflicted. Like a skittish deer, she edged closer to him and then snatched the charger from his hand before retreating back down the hall.

Caleb continued to watch her until she was safely sequestered in her room again. He heard the lock on the knob turn and his back muscles stiffened at the insult.

"I don't know what's gotten into her. She's normally not such a nutcase, I promise."

Shawn's apology wasn't necessary, but it both hurt and intrigued him at the same time. She acted this way, because he was a werewolf. Not just a stranger or an intimidating male. She knew the truth about him, and it tainted whatever friendship they could have.

It only challenged him more to find out what made her so hesitant to accept his olive branch. He wanted to understand her, to find out what it would take to make her at ease again. He had to come up with some way to break those defenses and prove that he wasn't the monster the fairytales made him out to be. He was more than that.

Chapter 4

Valerie had no dreams that night. None that she could remember. No visions of rolling fog or car crashes. No sensation of falling and watching the ground rush up to meet her. No hellish screams or howling winds. Absolutely nothing. That was a first.

Sleep, as necessary as it was, eluded her more often than she liked to admit. Granted, the nightmares had become something of routine. It was a game of roulette. Which horror would startle her awake after she spent hours trying to fall asleep? How many times would she feel Thor's nudging muzzle against her shoulder to help sooth her out of her terrors?

But that night, the one night she thought she'd get absolutely no sleep whatsoever with a werewolf in the house, she woke up earlier than she had in years and actually had time to fix her own coffee.

She beat both of the boys out of bed, and caught herself listening to them, trying to determine which one was Shawn and which was Caleb. His door opened and she heard him make his way to the bathroom, but that was it. The sound of the shower running told her enough and she squeezed her mug handle a little tighter.

The werewolf was naked in her house. Completely naked. Though she absent-mindedly scrolled through her social media, her thoughts wandered to things she never wanted to consider. What did he look like without his shirt? Without his pants? All that hot water rolling down the smooth, sculpted muscles of his arms and chest... down his abs... his legs.

Her phone beeped, snapping her out of this destructive chain of thoughts. The screen had dimmed and the warning light on her battery was glaring a nasty red. She left the phone to charge all night and it was fine just a few minutes ago. How could it be dying already? It must have been something with her battery.

When Shawn shuffled into the kitchen, squinting against the bright light, he seemed genuinely surprised to see her sitting at the table.

"You feeling okay?" he asked groggily as he scratched at his flat stomach.

Valerie knew the answer she was supposed to give. She was supposed to say that she was fine, but maybe it was the good night's rest that made her more honest than usual. "No," she replied flatly and set down her phone. "You're going away for almost two weeks and leaving me here with that guy."

Shawn smirked. "His name is Caleb and he's not that bad." He made his way toward the coffeemaker and poured himself a cup. "I told him to give you a wide berth."

She resisted the impulse to huff and tell him exactly how wide of a berth she needed. How could she last two weeks without Shawn as a mediator? Maybe she could stay with Krystal for a while. Alexa's little apartment over the antique store was too small, even for her. And Miss Macy would never allow her to bring Thor there. Then again, Thor would try to eat Artemis, Krystal's overweight Siamese cat.

Sipping her coffee, she listened again to the sporadic patter of water hitting the floor of the bathtub. How long did he really need to be in there? Or was he the sort of guy that needed to do other things in the shower besides bathe himself?

Once more, Valerie's mind slipped into the gutter and she felt like she'd explode at the imagery.

"Did you make the coffee?" Shawn asked after making a deep-throated noise of disgust.

Valerie turned and hoped that her roommate wouldn't notice her cheeks had grown hot. "Yeah. Why?"

Shawn's face wrinkled and he poured out the contents of his mug into the sink. "It tastes like shit. I guess it's been sitting too long."

Glancing to her own mug, she took another sip. "Mine's fine." She then offered it out to him. After living together for a few years, germs were the least of her concerns. They had seen each other in their underwear on a few occasions and neither were squeamish about that sort of thing anyway.

Shawn took the mug from her and finished it off while she sat with her arms folded.

"I might have to go to the phone store after work. My battery won't stay charged."

"That's weird," he replied as he proceeded to fix himself breakfast. Same thing every morning. Scrambled eggs and toast. "Do you think it's just getting old?"

Valerie frowned at her phone. "I just got it a year ago. It shouldn't be having issues."

At her feet, Thor lifted his head and growled toward the entryway to the living room. It didn't take a rocket scientist to figure out that Thor didn't like Caleb one bit. Even if the man was across the house and well out of sight, the lab knew what was up. She could only hope that he'd calm down one day, so she could stop charming him to keep him submissive.

"Do you think Krystal will let me bring Thor to the coffeeshop?" Valerie asked, once more listening for the water while Shawn cracked an egg over the heated skillet.

"Why don't you just keep him in your room?"

Valerie thought of her family grimoire and all the loose-leaf sheets that Thor could easily tear into. He was – normally – well behaved, but the environment had changed. With Caleb present, it'd throw off everything. Aggression and destructive behaviors might make an untimely appearance.

"I don't want him taking a dump in my closet or something. I can't keep him cooped up all day."

Shawn shrugged his broad shoulders. "Let Caleb take care of him, then. Give them time to get to know one another."

That would go over about as well as an addict's first week of cold-turkey rehab. "I don't want Thor to hurt him."

And there it was. A condemning admittance. She wanted to snatch the words from the air and stuff them in the toaster along with the slices of bread Shawn just crammed in. Anything to hide them, to make them disappear.

The history teacher glanced back to her, utterly amused. "Oh? Is that a sign that you actually care? And here I thought you hated the guy."

"I do!" Valerie insisted, overcompensating for her slipup. "I don't feel comfortable around him. He looks like a felon or something. And if Thor doesn't like him, that's a sign. You should have never let him move in."

Shawn turned and leaned against the counter, amusement morphing into disbelief. "Val, you don't even know him. I've never known you to be so... judgmental. What the hell is up with you?"

She slunk lower in her chair like she was one of his students and he had just called her out for something. This had nothing to do with stereotypes. She never bought into them. Mostly because she knew what it felt like to be judged. She thought of Aaron and his smartass remarks about her makeup and clothes. She thought about all the kids in high school that called her a freak, because she liked to listen to heavy metal. Bullying and labeling was something she was determined to never do.

She had no reason to hate him as much as she did. So far, he had been nothing but polite and courteous. He gave her that charger, after all. And he could have made his own threats the night before, but he didn't lift a finger to put her in her place. Caleb was the first werewolf she had ever met, and he was making a good impression. A damn good impression. That was why it was so hard to truly dislike him.

Refusing to give into the reprimand, Valerie stood and made her way back to the hall, her phone in one hand and Thor trailing close on her heels. She had some time to try and charge up her battery before going to work.

So lost in her introspection, she didn't notice that the shower water had stopped until it was too late. She passed by the bathroom door, and was determined not to look in that general direction.

Caleb forced her to.

The door swung open, steam and light streaming into the hall. Valerie lifted her gaze, and froze. Her legs wouldn't respond, her heart ceased beating, everything just came jerking to a complete stop when she saw him. Standing in a towel, droplets speckled across his tanned skin and dripping from his chin, he met her stare.

Valerie thought she would die. Right there, without cause or reason. Her whole body imploded with a radiating heat that had to have turned her face an unattractive shade of red. The way the light seemed to curve around his form, how he stood in place just as fixated as she was, the power behind his eyes, all of it made the floor tilt out from beneath her feet.

One hand held the towel fast around his hips while the other still gripped the door. "Did you need to use the bathroom?" he asked. "I think I left you some hot water."

Valerie's throat worked to produce the words, but they wouldn't come right away. "I... No... I mean, not right now."

Getting a hold of herself, she hurried away toward her room. Thor was slow to follow, and probably gave Caleb the dog equivalent of the stink-eye before darting into the bedroom with her.

Once the door was closed and Valerie was safe from the werewolf, she let her legs collapse from underneath her. She slid to the floor and sat there, dumbstruck and on the verge of her first panic attack in years.

He was, for lack of a less cheesy term, absolutely magnificent. Her imagination couldn't do him justice, even if she had the dirtiest mind in all of Massachusetts. How could someone be so hot, so gorgeous, and be real? Was this a werewolf thing? Or a Caleb thing?

Her whole body ached. Ached for air, for his touch, for all the things that terrified her and yet thrilled her at the same time. Valerie pressed her hand against her fevered brow. This was insane. This feeling of total unhinged bliss. Caleb was a werewolf and she had the hots for him.

Valerie shook her head. She couldn't lose her mind over a boy. That wasn't her. Wasn't her style. She never really dated and never really wanted to. But this guy made her want to do that and so much more. How could she survive this?

Caleb turned her on. The thought still made his lips curl into a soft, betraying smile. It wasn't planned. He knew that she would pass by the bathroom, but he hadn't expected her to stop and stare the way she did. When the scent of her arousal passed under his nose, Caleb grasped the truth of everything.

Scents didn't lie. Heartbeats, sweat, the racing of blood in her veins, the subtle change in her hormones, all of it gave her away in just the span of a few seconds. She wanted him, but she didn't want to want him.

Still, he couldn't understand why he would smile at that. She was a witch. But Valerie was different somehow. Just how, he couldn't tell.

He thought about it all the way to the airport in Boston to drop off Shawn for his flight. While her emotions were clear enough, her thoughts and motives weren't. Why resist the pull? Why put on an act to make them all believe that she hated him when she might have been inclined to care?

His brain, so wired to untangle the jumbled mess of a mystery, came up with plenty of reasons. She didn't want to be the only witch in town that didn't hate him. She feared what her friends would think. She was secretly afraid of him. Perhaps she had been hurt in the past and her heart was unwilling to let him in.

The most disturbing of the explanations, was that she was already in a relationship and didn't want to be unfaithful. But in all the clipped conversations about Valerie, there was no mention of a boyfriend. Unless she kept that a secret as well. Her need for privacy was made all too apparent by everyone, including her. It wouldn't have surprised him if she were harboring more than just her feelings for him.

They pulled into the drop-off zone at the airport and Shawn hopped out of Caleb's truck.

"I'm coming back on the twenty-seventh. I'll give you a call before my final layover."

Caleb gave him the thumbs-up as another Garth Brooks song began to play over the crackling radio. "Have a great time with your family."

Shawn thanked him, and just before he closed the door, another thought occurred to him and he reopened it. "Are you sure you're going to get along with Valerie all right? I know you told me this morning you've got it handled, but…" He shrugged, as if that should have been sign enough. It was. Valerie was the wild card in the whole scheme. If she wasn't game for playing nice, they wouldn't. If anyone was alpha in that house, it was her.

"We'll be just fine." He smiled for emphasis, but in truth, Caleb wasn't one-hundred-percent sure of himself.

"Good," Shawn said with a nod. "Because if you hurt her, I just might have to kill you."

Caleb deduced long ago that Shawn was no threat. The man had muscles, but he was no match for a werewolf or a witch. He couldn't fully comprehend his long list of disadvantages.

"I think she'd kill me first."

They had a good-natured laugh about that and Shawn finally shut the door. He pulled his duffle bag from the bed of his truck and hurried toward the check-in terminal with the rest of the passengers. Families and couples all flocked to the revolving doors, off to see their relatives for the holidays. Caleb could hear their excited plans over the rumble of his truck engine.

Everyone was going somewhere, but not him. Even when he had a pack, he didn't do much with them. There were parties, gatherings, hunting excursions, but nothing he was interested in. He had been that way for a couple hundred years and he didn't see himself changing anytime soon. That was just the way things were and he never sought to do anything different.

Now, seeing life move on without him, and knowing that there would be no more invites, no more unexpected guests, and no more nights out at the bar with the guys, Caleb and his wolf grieved. But he couldn't begin to understand why.

A security officer caught his eye and gave a gesture that told him he needed to move. With a sigh, he put the truck in drive and pulled into traffic. He'd have a few more hours to rid himself of this unpleasant feeling before he arrived back in Goldcrest Cove.

Valerie couldn't get out of town fast enough. The moment they locked the doors that Sunday afternoon, she booked it out of there and went straight for the dog shelter. She normally walked the dogs on Monday and Thursdays, the only days of the week she was given the afternoon off, leaving Sundays for playing videogames with Shawn.

But since he was gone, and home had become something of a battle zone, Valerie wanted to be anywhere but in Goldcrest Cove. A brisk walk with the shelter dogs always helped to clear her head and give her heart a little breathing room. Along with brewing a mean espresso, taking care of animals was something she could do right. Something she could get excited about that didn't turn sour in the end.

She parked her Acura next to the lone office building. Even before she climbed out of the car, she could hear the dogs barking in their open kennels down the dirt lane. The shelter, situated in the middle of an expansive piece of private property, became the temporary home for all the mistreated and forgotten animals from all over the county. Sheep, horses, goats, even parrots, were surrendered here in hopes that they would find their forever home.

Staffed almost exclusively with volunteers, people like Valerie kept the place running like a well-oiled machine. Animals were adopted out every day of the week, and it was a good day when they sent out more dogs than they received. As of right now, the kennels were all full.

She walked up the ramp to the front door, careful to avoid the icy patches that hadn't been swept aside. The inside of the office was warm and smelled of cinnamon, but the receptionist, Becky, was nowhere in sight. Long John, the office's favorite parrot, was perched upon his stand and squawked at the visitor. Valerie grinned and snatched up a nut from one of the bowls on the front desk.

"Intruder alert! Intruder alert!" the parrot screeched. Whoever had owned the parrot before the shelter took him in had trained him well. He knew plenty of words, including some that weren't so appropriate for their younger visitors.

"Aw, come on. Don't be that way," she pouted playfully.

Just as she came up to feed the talkative bird, Becky came hurrying into the main room with a stack of folders in her arms. "Oh! I didn't know you were volunteering today."

Long John daintily pinched the nut in his beak and took it from Valerie. The bird was satisfied and stopped in his obnoxious impression of a burglar alarm.

"Yeah, I found some free time. Do you have a full walking team today or can I help?"

Becky set the folders down on the desk and let out a breath. "Of course you can help! The dogs all love you. Especially Brody."

Taking the misfits and county shelter rejects meant taking on some of the harder cases that most adoption places, and even foster homes, didn't want to mess with. Brody, a rough-looking pit bull with a gnarled ear was the perfect example. Sweet as pie, but judged mercilessly. Some of the volunteers wouldn't even bother trying to put him in a harness. Sometimes, she thought she understood dogs better than any other human being on earth.

Tapping Long John on the head, she went back to the desk and signed her name on the volunteer clipboard. "In that case, I'll get started."

She bid her goodbye to Becky and went straight for the kennels. For the first time in two days, she felt as if all her problems were lightyears away. A weight was lifted, and she was able to forget about her work and Caleb for just a little while.

Taking a leash from the hook on the supply shed wall, she went straight for Brody's kennel. The smoky grey pit bull saw her coming and let out a tremendous bark of greeting. His face split in one of those adorable pitty grins and the massive dog began to prance and jump on his feet, just like Thor did when he was excited.

She slid her way into Brody's fenced run and was met by a slop of happy dog kisses. This was simple. This had nothing to do with magic or werewolves or nightmares. Here, she didn't have to remember anything. Not her family, her childhood, or her own failures. It was just her and the dogs. This was easy and painless.

Valerie needed more of that. Magic and charms could only do so much to heal the past.

Could Caleb have been more of a damned idiot? The moment he stepped up to the front door, he realized it. No key. He searched under the mat for a spare, but no such luck. In the rush to get ready, amidst the critical obsessing over Valerie's behavior, his key was left on the kitchen counter. He should have put it on his keyring the moment Shawn handed it to him.

Even the backdoor was locked tight, and unless he wanted to pay for damages to any of the doors and windows, he needed to figure out another way in. That's why he came to Perfect Books and Brews.

The utter lack of noise or potent aroma of ground coffee beans had him cringing and cussing before he even reached the shop. Just as he suspected, the place was dark and empty. The closed sign on the door was flipped, and not a single witch or customer in sight.

He tested the door, just to be sure, and let out a frustrated growl.

He needed Valerie. She was the only one in town that would have a key, unless he wanted to call a locksmith. Even then, he'd have to explain his need to get into the house. His name wasn't legally on the lease yet, and the landlord knew little about him. He didn't have the witch's number, and it was likely that Shawn would already be catching up with his family and out of pocket.

Caleb glanced up and down Johnson Avenue, but he couldn't find Valerie's green car anywhere along the curb. It was only a little after noon. If she wasn't home, where could she possibly be?

The errant image of Valerie with her witch friends dancing around a burning altar came to mind and he berated himself. Even if it was the truth, he shouldn't have assumed it.

"Hey!"

Caleb turned and saw a cop striding toward him down the sidewalk. Talk, dark haired, and flashing blue eyes that fixed on him with that familiar alpha authority. Not wanting to make a scene, even if his wolf protested, Caleb waited to be interrogated.

"The coffeeshop's closed," he said firmly. "They'll be open in the morning."

The way the cop's hands settled on his hips, it pulled back his jacket just enough that Caleb spotted the holstered gun. He knew, mostly from research, that a cop wouldn't pull on a civilian unless he felt the need. A werewolf, likewise, wouldn't make a threat without due cause, or without intention to back it up.

Then again, this could be an opportunity. Krystal said they had connections with the police. If he could play ball with the cop and prove that he wasn't the villain in this story, maybe he'd put a good word in for him with the witches who were so close-minded to his true character.

"I was looking for one of the girls who works here." He offered out his hand. "I'm Caleb Lancaster."

The cop shook his hand, mostly out of politeness. There was still an edge about him that Caleb hoped to dull within a few minutes. "Yeah, I've heard about you. New guy in town."

So, he was right. No doubt Krystal told him everything.

"Yep. Just came in last week. I'm staying with Shawn and Valerie."

This, however, was news. The cop seemed thoroughly surprised. "So, you're looking for Valerie?"

Caleb faked embarrassment. "Yeah. I locked myself out of the house. I was hoping I could borrow her key. Shawn's out of town. I just got back from dropping him off at the airport."

The officer nodded. "I see. Well, I guess you're pretty stuck until Valerie gets home, then."

He narrowed his eyes. No offer to help, not even to get Valerie's phone number for him, though he was obviously connected with the witches somehow. Dulling that edge might prove a little more difficult than he thought.

"I'm sorry, what did you say your name was?" Caleb asked.

"Devin Daniels. Krystal Hayden's my girlfriend."

Admitting that bit of personal information was promising. Caleb gave him a smile, but he knew it was strained. "I met Krystal yesterday." Normally, he would add on some compliment to Krystal's friendliness, but he would never tell a lie he couldn't tell easily.

"She told me... So, you're a..."

It was odd, knowing that a human was fully aware of what he was. Few outside of his pack ever knew, and it was an accident if they found out at all.

"I am. And I'm sure she's told you a lot more about... my kind, but please hear me out." The cop crossed his arms as Caleb ventured to form the right words. Respect earns respect. If he was open, the cop would be more willing to believe him. "I have no intention of causing you or your friends any trouble. I'm... I'm getting away from a bad situation and all I want is to live in peace. I'm a lone wolf now, if you want to be whimsical about it." Caleb's stab at humor missed its mark, but he continued. "I don't know why Krystal and the others would think ill of me, but I'd appreciate it if someone would try to reserve their judgement until they got to know me. I'm not an alpha. I'm not aggressive. I've never killed anyone."

It was then he noticed something. Devin was checking his story. Not literally, but in his eyes. Caleb was being studied. Body language, gestures, pupil dilation, the whole nine yards. Devin was checking for a lie. He'd find none. It was all true, as upsetting as it would be for the witches to be proved wrong.

"And you'll do... your... your business outside of town?"

Caleb's lips quirked in a displeased way. To call shifting his "business" made it sound underhanded somehow. "Yes, my business will be conducted far away from the human population as long as I can help it."

That seemed to satisfy him. "It'd be a good idea if you made sure of it."

Was that a threat? It was laughable to think that Devin's bullets would stand a chance against him.

"I'll do my best."

"Good. Now, I'm going to have to ask you to leave. There are plenty of other places in town you can wait at until Valerie gets home. I think she volunteers at a dog shelter when she's off in the evenings."

While Caleb could have been offended about the order to move on, he accepted this little insight into Valerie. A dog shelter? So, she had a soft spot for animals. That was in his favor.

One thing that wasn't in his favor was that his laptop was still in the house. He had no means of keeping busy while she finished up her volunteering at the shelter. He waved off Devin and marched toward his truck. There had to be something he could do in this small town.

And the moment he turned the key in his ignition, it came. That itching wild beneath his skin, directly from his wolf. That desire to escape. That need to feel the dirt beneath his paws and the wind in his fur.

His lips curved into a grin. "Really?" he asked his wolf aloud. "It's freezing out there."

Still, his wolf demanded it. His pelt would keep him safe from the winter cold. Besides, he needed to scout for the best shifting places. Those spots that would be far from the inhabitants of Goldcrest Cove. Even if the cop rubbed him the wrong way, he'd keep his promise to stay clear of the humans. He just needed to find a good place to do it. This might be his chance.

Chapter 5

Valerie gripped the steering wheel until the leather crinkled in her palms. The cemetery welcome sign was lit by the solar yard lights around the perimeter of the fence. Patches of snow covered the brick barrier between the graves and the parking lot. In the waning evening light, she could just see the outline of the headstones in the darkness.

Way in the far back corner, out of reach from her headlights, was her family plot. The one they had maintained for generations. Her grandparents were there, great-grandparents, and even further back. This cemetery was so old it contained the remains of some of the founding members of Goldcrest Cove.

Somewhere amongst them, was her aunt and her parents. Shiny new marble slabs marked their places. She hadn't visited them since her Aunt Maggie was laid to rest. That was three years ago. Why did her spirit draw her here now?

Maybe it was that need to ground herself again. She had spent so much time with the dogs at the shelter, talking and laughing with the other volunteers until she was the last one on site. She had been happy. Now, she was returning to town. Returning to real life.

If she thought she could quit the coffeeshop and work in the shelter, she would. But she was too loyal for that. Too damn loyal and too trapped in the way things had always been. She always had Krystal and Alexa. When everyone else left, they remained. Maybe that's why she was back here. To remind herself of what she lost and that she could never leave that comfort zone. She had always been a glutton for punishment.

Valerie shut off her engine and angled out of the car. The crisp night air swirled around her, the breeze tossing the wavy curls of her hair around her shoulders. Nothing but the sound of her footfalls on the ground, a strangle, rhythmic crunching of snow and dead grass as she made her way through the gate.

The cemetery was so distant from town, so isolated from the rest of the world. This was a place of death, of mourning, of grieving. It had no place in the daily lives of those still breathing. Nothing about this place should have been comforting. And yet, Valerie felt her spirit stir, as if she needed to be here too.

Sensation left her. Everything dulled as she ventured deeper under the spindly shade of the leafless, twisted oaks. The moon was just ready to make its appearance, to chase away the gray twilight and drape it with silver. In just a little while, this place would be beautifully painted with moonlight.

She found the Lloyd family plot. Forethought and reverence for the founding members allowed them several more spots. Many descendants had moved away or chosen to be buried elsewhere. Valerie was the final one. The last Lloyd witch in Goldcrest Cove. Her spot was right next to her mother and it was there that she sat, temporarily occupying the space she was destined for.

Valerie's butt began to numb on the frozen ground as she looked down the row of graves to the perimeter fence. The grid-like pattern of ancestors and relatives that she had never met spread out in front of her like a morbid family reunion.

She said nothing. She knew there was no point. Their souls had rejoined the ether or moved on to reincarnate. They weren't here to help her pick up the pieces or give her safe advice that would help her along in life. That's why she never came back. What was the use?

Yet, as she read their names and the dates separated by a dash, she heard that soft reminder.

Don't screw it up. Don't waste what you have.

Already, Valerie felt as if she were failing them somehow. She wasn't some great, accomplished witch with lots of friends and a future. She was just... her. But she was trying. She really was trying.

A silent tear stung at her eyes and she sniffled it back just before she heard a noise from the forest. It didn't come just once, but several times. The cadence of footsteps in the snow. Valerie looked, but couldn't see anyone coming.

That classic, cheesy horror movie scene came to mind. This was how the pretty girls died. They'd call out into the void, ask who was there, and then go investigate. Valerie wasn't stupid like that. Besides, she had her magic. Nobody was going to catch her off guard.

She watched the tree line through the chain-link fence that comprised the rear boundary of the cemetery. The shadows didn't move, though the footsteps came closer and closer. Despite the knowledge that she'd be perfectly safe, her heart began to pound. Heat rose up her neck and she could feel her blood race with that familiar speed of fear and uncertainty.

Then, she saw it. Two glinting eyes refracted what little light could reach them. As her own vision adjusted, she saw the outline of the ears, the muzzle, and the front legs. It was a dog. A huge one by the looks of it.

It stopped and she somehow intuitively knew that it had seen her. Its head lowered and time seemed to freeze. Something in the air felt familiar. Like she had experienced this total stagger of existence before and recently. Very recently.

That's when she understood. This wasn't some stray dog. Any dog, no matter how feral, would be curious enough to approach her. This one didn't. As she stared, unblinking into the murky black, she knew what this was. It was a wolf, and that meant it wasn't just any wolf. There hadn't been real wolves in Massachusetts in ages.

This was a werewolf. And that could only mean this was Caleb.

She hadn't quite imagined werewolves to take the shape of a true wolf. She thought of the beasts from the Hollywood movies that looked like some hulking beast without reason or humanity. But the way that Caleb looked at her now, it all made sense. The stare of the wolf was the same as the man. Penetrating, examining, alluring. Every bit of understanding was there. Caleb saw her and knew her.

And he did nothing. He didn't trot up to the fence to meet her, didn't turn and run. He just stood there in the dark, watching her with those golden eyes.

For what seemed like an eternity, she didn't move either. It seemed like everything in the universe ceased to be except in this one ethereal moment of connection. This surpassed anything she had experienced in nature. Not even the moon could beat this warmth and tingling that spread through her.

In one moment, it all clicked. Caleb might have been more tied to the spiritual than any of them in Goldcrest Cove. He was man and he was animal. He belonged in the woods and on the streets. He was the perfect blend of the natural and unnatural. The ultimate in connection with the old Gods. Maybe it was because of his superior connection that she was so drawn to him. She would have taken that explanation over any kind of gushy excuse someone like Alexa could come up with.

Whatever it was, whatever her spirit was trying to tell her, Valerie realized one crucial thing. With Caleb, she felt good. It took her spiraling to this low, submerged in so much death and tragedy, for her to understand that was what she felt. In the wake of his presence, she couldn't force herself to be sad over all her losses. In that revelation, the cold talons of guilt latched into her stomach. What right did she have to be even fractionally happy sitting next to her mother's grave?

Caleb was the first to move and break the spell of fixation. One of his ears rotated, as if he heard something else that her human senses wouldn't pick up.

There was her chance. Valerie slowly rose to her feet, never breaking eye contact until absolutely necessary.

She turned down the worn path amongst the headstones, giving her back to the wolf. All the way to the car, she tried to catch her breath. She couldn't stop thinking about those eyes, and with distance, the feeling in her chest faded. It was a good thing too. Coming home to Caleb wouldn't be easy after this. But she had to be strong in the face of the one who had just shaken her foundations. No one was allowed to do that. Not even a werewolf.

Then, she stopped. The wind picked up and a voice carried upon it. A voice of the past that she was sure existed only in her head.

Don't waste this.

Again, came that goading. It must have meant something. Maybe none of this was coincidence. The graveyard, Caleb, this burning in her blood. Maybe it was all linked somehow. Maybe this was all some orchestration to help her pierce the veil and find something she didn't think she deserved. Peace.

She looked back, but the wolf was gone.

Valerie's eyes scanned the tree line and the graveyard for any sign of Caleb, but he had vanished. He couldn't run forever. They'd meet later that night, or maybe in the morning. Only then would she have her chance. The chance she shouldn't waste.

What were the odds that Valerie would be in that cemetery at the exact moment he was? He hadn't planned it that way, but he was almost thankful for his wolf's suggestion. He got to see her in a different light. Vulnerable. Hurting. She looked at him, not in anger, but with a slight sparkle of admiration. For a moment, Caleb wondered if this wasn't going to turn out so bad after all.

All the way back to Goldcrest Cove, he rehearsed how he would apologize to her. Mostly for intruding on her quiet time, visiting whoever she had once known that now resided in the cemetery. If he thought she'd leave, he would have been the first to turn away. This was her town, and it wasn't his intention to leave his mark everywhere.

The lights were on, despite the late hour. It was nearly midnight now. If Caleb had his way, he might have stayed out until dawn, but the promise of seeing Valerie wouldn't keep him away for long.

He climbed out of his truck and could hear the heavy metal music playing from inside the house.

Thor met him as soon as he shut the door and locked it. The lab detested him, but it was expected. Most dogs did. They sensed the predator in him and it was only natural for them to respond to it. He stood in the foyer amongst his boxes, thumbs slung in his pockets as he waited for Valerie to rescue him. All the while, Thor barked and growled as if he were the epitome of evil in the canine world. None of this fazed him anymore.

He heard her bare feet hurry down the hall and she soon appeared, hair wet and dressed down in her pajamas. The same pair she wore the night before that drove him wild. She bent down to grab Thor and the collar of her billowy shirt dipped with her. He caught a peak of her breasts and immediately dropped his eyes out of respect.

While she wrangled her lab out of the foyer, Caleb tried to remember the words he had planned to say. Now, all he could think about was the smell of her bodywash that added so much to her natural, feminine scent. This was easier when he was alone and away from her influences.

"Is this going to be a constant thing?" she asked, drawing him out of his thoughts. "Because I'm not getting rid of Thor just because of you."

Caleb slowly ambled into the living room as Valerie shut Thor in her bedroom.

"I would never expect you to do that." Taking a breath, he gathered his wits again and went into his speech. "I know this isn't an ideal situation. I know you're not happy with it either. You've made that perfectly clear, but you have to know my intentions are..."

His voice absently trailed off when she came to stand a few yards away, the sofa separating them. She crossed her arms and the fabric of her shirt tightened across her chest, that same chest he had glimpsed a moment before. He lost his thoughts again, but only for a second.

"My intentions are purely peaceful. I'm sure that's hard for any of you witches to believe, but it's true. I'd be a fool to expect anything close to friendship, but all I ask is that we at least be cordial with one another."

Valerie huffed and lips that were always marred by a scowl turned up into a simper. "Cordial? Are we in the eighteenth century?"

Caleb opened his mouth to respond, but then it occurred to him that he had slipped into his old vernacular. Was he that nervous? "You know what I mean," he said, choosing his words more plainly. "We should get along. All of us. Can we at least agree on that?"

Green eyes looked him up and down, and he spotted the tiniest bit of her pink tongue dart out to lick her lips in that thoughtful way. Damn, if there was anything more erotic than that. His own request reminded him that, just as he said, there was little hope for anything beyond politeness. He'd take whatever bones she'd throw his way, though.

Finally, she nodded. "Yeah. I can try... I can't say the same for Krystal. You'll have to earn her trust."

Caleb almost rolled his eyes. "I have a feeling I won't get far with her."

"It'll be tough. Her parents are on the witches' council, so she's heard some pretty fucked up stories about werewolves."

He couldn't recall a time that he'd had such an honest conversation with someone outside of his pack. Then again, Valerie could very well be part of his pack now. In an odd, dysfunctional sort of way. Same for Shawn.

"And I'm sure if I tell her that they don't represent the whole of my race, she won't believe me."

Valerie shrugged and pulled a face. "Probably not. You have a lot of making up to do. Centuries worth."

"That hardly seems fair," he remarked as he drew in a deep breath, thinking of all the ways he had to atone for the sins that were not his own.

"I'm sure we have some making up to do, too," Valerie said, her voice dropping from snarky to somber. "I bet the werewolves tell plenty of stories about us. There's a long history there, you know."

Caleb minutely nodded. "They do. Our kind have been jilted by your people just as cruelly."

That, somehow, merited him a smile. "There you go with that talk again... How old are you anyway?"

At least she knew how exactly to ask that. And she knew well enough that werewolves rarely ever looked their age.

"I was born in 1842."

That wasn't what she was expecting. Her eyes went wide. "You're one hundred and sixty-seven years old?"

Caleb smiled, partially proud that he could astonish her so well. "I will be on December thirtieth."

"Still! That's... wow..." Valerie seemed genuinely floored by the notion that he could stand in front of her, as ancient as he was, and look only slightly older than her. If only he could reciprocate that same awe, then perhaps those numbers wouldn't carry such a heavy weight for him. "You and Shawn should get along fine. He loves history."

Caleb cast his gaze to the back of the sofa. "You won't hear me talk much about it. Living that long isn't something I'd brag about."

Valerie's slight enthusiasm dimmed. "Immortality that bad, huh?"

A bit of his wolfish temper had to be forced back down. She didn't understand what it was like to lose so much. A pack was the only constant a werewolf could have. And even then, there was loss and hardships that she, as a witch, couldn't possibly understand.

"As I said, don't expect me to talk about it." He gave her a tight-lipped smile and hoped this was a step in the right direction. Being open was the way to make friends, wasn't it?

"Fair enough. I won't ask."

A pause stretched between them with only the music coming from her bedroom and Thor's nervous pacing to break the silence. After a moment of looking at everything else except one another, Caleb spoke. "I apologize for... bothering you earlier this evening."

Valerie's scent changed. It was just enough for him to notice, but he couldn't distinguish what it was. "You didn't bother me."

"Your heart was racing when you saw me."

Valerie turned pale. "You could hear that?"

Caleb suddenly felt something akin to bashful for admitting so much, even if it was the truth. "There's a lot of things I hear, but plenty of things I don't... Like intentions."

She seemed to catch his meaning, though not completely. "I was... I was just paying respects. I was pretty much done by the time you showed up."

"That's good... That you were done. Not that you had to pay respects."

Her expression hardened. "You'll find out that's something I'm not willing to talk about either."

The tightness in her tone caught his attention and Caleb met her stare with all the severity that the topic warranted. "Fair enough. Then I won't ask."

They finally found some mutual ground, though it was buried under layers of grief and secrets. The ground rules had been laid and they both knew exactly where not to step. This was good, he told himself.

Valerie thumbed toward the hall that led to her bedroom. "I'm going to turn in. I have work in the morning. You may hear my alarm go off... I guess you'll hear a lot, but I thought I'd warn you."

Caleb allowed himself a smile. "I've trained myself to sleep through most anything. It won't bother me."

With a nod, she turned and began to walk away. His gaze drifted down to her ass and watched the way it swung with each step. The moment she spun back around, his eyes were on hers. "And, by the way, Thor loves treats. You might not be able to turn off your..." She made some gesture toward him, "whatever it is that makes you what you are, but you can try and win him over with treats. It worked for Shawn."

If his nose was right, he knew exactly where these treats were. Sharing this trick was also a good sign. Valerie didn't want him to be at odds with her dog any more than he did. He nodded his appreciation and she disappeared into the hall.

He waited until her door was shut to let out the breath he had been holding. Damn. She really got to him. Smitten was too light of a term, infatuated was far closer to what he felt. Friendliness wasn't going to last for long, but Caleb had to bide his time. Krystal and Thor's trust weren't the only things he'd have to earn.

Valerie's approval mattered to him far more than anything else, and he couldn't understand just why. Yes, she was hot and fiery in her own way, yet there was a pull for him to pry deeper, to pull back the clamped edges of her shell and see what it was inside that drove him and his wolf mad with desire.

One day at a time. That's how he'd get through this. One day at a time.

Chapter 6

Valerie's smile didn't have to be faked that morning. She usually resented being put on cashier duty during the Monday rush, but everyone agreed that Krystal was faster at mixing the special brews. That, and she wanted to take the chance to instruct Alexa on the finer points of charming the coffee, though all three knew that she was hesitant beyond words. After the fiasco around Samhain, Valerie hadn't seen her even attempt a charm or spell.

The line of customers stretched down the frozen sidewalk, but they at least had the sense to keep the door closed after the line was finished moving. Chitchat wasn't as much of a priority as it could have been, but Valerie dropped the necessary hints every now and again. Mr. Kendrick's back was hurting. Mrs. Rodman didn't sleep well. The Gilbert couple were worried about their daughter being able to get off work for the holidays. Which ones were charmed by Krystal, Valerie didn't know exactly. It didn't matter. She was on Cloud Nine anyway.

For the first time in a long time, Valerie allowed herself to be happy. She hadn't fully convinced herself that this whole thing with Caleb wouldn't end in flames like everything else did, but maybe something good could come of it. As long as she was careful. If she played it right, they wouldn't get too close and it wouldn't get to the point of ruin.

Last night, the line in the sand had been drawn. They knew each other's buttons, and though her curiosity burned to know all the details of his past, she'd keep her lips sealed on the subject. He didn't want to talk about his childhood and she didn't want to talk about all the graves outside of town. That was their arrangement. Everything else would be worked out as they came to it.

The fact that he was a werewolf eluded her sometimes when she thought of him. Only the remembrance of the wolf in the snow could set her back on stable ground. The rest of the time, she was all smiles and reveled in the little things about him that she was allowing herself to enjoy.

Like how he cooked. That morning, he was in the process of whipping up gourmet omelets. She had never seen anyone make one before except on television. The way his shoulders flexed as he chopped up the veggies and reached for the spices in the cabinet was entertainment enough. If he could hear her heart beating, she wondered if he could feel her staring. Because she was doing plenty of that while she sipped her coffee at the table in the kitchen.

If any of the girls found out she was getting the hots for the werewolf, she didn't want to think of how they would react. None of them would understand. Hell, she didn't even understand it completely. Her friends, her dog, the rest of the witch community, all of them were an excuse to turn back from these feelings. But now that she had dipped her toes in them and waded into the shallows, Valerie had to hold herself back from taking the final dive.

The rush died down and she could see the end of the line. And still, this high on Caleb hadn't weakened.

Alexa came up beside her to deliver a big to-go order to a customer near the counter. "Did you sleep good last night or something?"

Valerie counted out some change and grinned. "Or something."

"You weren't even snippy with Aaron when he came in earlier with Devin."

She shrugged. "He's not worth it." Giving the customer the change, she happened to glance out the storefront window. Walking past with his collar turned up was Caleb. He glanced her way and it took some effort not to look ridiculous at the sight of him.

A soft smile graced his lips and it was then she saw the laptop bag strapped across his shoulder. His eyes shifted toward the front door and she knew he was coming in. Instantly, anxiety chased away all those lovely thoughts and she worried about pointless things. Did her hair look all right? It wasn't too warm in the coffeeshop, but did any of her makeup smear during the rush? Would she make his tea or let one of the girls do it?

The crazy-train of silly girlish thoughts was derailed when Krystal came up and flicked her fingers toward the door. Valerie watched as Caleb reached for the handle, but drew back his hand as if he had touched something hot. His lips formed a curse as he stepped back and looked to the witches inside.

"Did you really just fucking do that?" Valerie asked her friend in disbelief. Krystal hadn't openly used that kind of magic in months.

Krystal glared at the werewolf. "He's not welcome here and he knows that."

A couple came up to the coffeeshop door and they were permitted to enter without trouble. When Caleb tried to follow in behind them without touching the door, it was as if he had hit a wall and stumbled backward onto the sidewalk. He nearly slipped on some ice.

Alexa giggled, but Valerie found none of it amusing.

"What has he done to you?" she snapped, all happy flutters in her stomach gone in the face of her friend's total bitchiness. "He's only been in town for a few days, he's done nothing wrong, and you're treating him like a damn felon."

Without asking permission, she snapped her fingers toward the door and broke the seal Krystal had set in place. With hesitance, Caleb gave it one more try, his fingers just tapping on the handle before taking a firm hold of it.

Krystal's jaw went slack. "I'm trying to protect this community and our customers."

Valerie had never been this upset with her before. They had been friends since they were kids and been through a lot of shit, but right now, Krystal was earning a place on Valerie's rather long, extensive list of people she detested. There had never been a moment before now when she thought the witch deserved a spot on that list.

"Why not practice that old adage of 'innocent until proven guilty'?"

"There's such a thing as taking preventative measures too."

Valerie pointed to Caleb and put every effort into not yelling. "What is he going to do? Rip out someone's throat and steal their coffee?"

She knew that Caleb could hear every bit of this argument, even if it had been taken toward the back of the brewing station. Alexa stepped up to take care of the new orders that were piling up against them.

"I don't want to take any chances with this guy," Krystal argued. "Ever hear of the term, 'A wolf in sheep's wool'? He'll act all nice and polite until it no longer serves him. That's how they operate."

Valerie put her hand on her hip. "And I assume your parents told you that?"

"They did." Her friend's lips twisted in a nasty way. "I never remember you distrusting their word before now."

In truth, she hadn't. She had no reason to. Gordon and Catherine had earned everyone's respect. They were knowledgeable and more than loyal to the people of Goldcrest Cove. They did much more for Valerie than she could ever repay, and guilt sucker-punched her at the remembrance of it. She owed them so much, but she couldn't be on their side about this. It just didn't feel right.

"We don't have time for this petty shit, Krystal." Valerie's nostrils flared. "Quit acting like you run this town and get your priorities straight."

She turned away and set herself upon the drink orders. All the while, she could feel that indignation inside of her build and build. There weren't words strong enough to get across her meaning. Krystal had never been this prejudice. Not toward other magical beings, nor toward humans. Whatever it was she thought she knew about werewolves, whatever it was her parents had told her, Valerie was sick of it turning her friend into a bigot.

Thankfully, this little verbal sparring didn't keep them from working together. Krystal was pissed about being put in her place, but they still performed like a great well-oiled machine in conquering all the backorders.

A white tea, a couple of espressos, her signature mocha, and finally she came to Caleb's drink. Hot Earl Grey with honey. She didn't have to hear the order passed along by the nervous Alexa at the register. The minute his card was charged, she was bringing it to him. She didn't trust anyone else to do it. Not anymore.

Caleb gave her a nod of appreciation, the same he had given her the first day they met.

"Thank you for that," he said, just loud enough for her ears only. "I was worried she wouldn't let me in."

Valerie, though wholly determined to make up for her friends' intolerance, wouldn't give him too much hope. Not yet. "I don't recommend you stay long, though. In case I get overruled."

Caleb patted his laptop bag. "Just wanted to get some fresh air and write. That's all. I'll behave."

Despite herself, she smiled. "I know you will. That's why I'm not worried like they are."

A sparkle of some unnamed emotion shone in his eyes and Valerie became transfixed. "That means a lot. I'll just punch out a chapter or two and be on my way." In a bold move that Valerie admired, he tilted his to-go mug toward the other two witches. "Thank you, ladies for being so hospitable."

A bit of red showed on Alexa's cheeks, but the crimson in Krystal's face was brought on by another sentiment entirely. Valerie watched him walk away and suppressed a giggle. It was the sort of thing she would have done in the face of people who didn't like her style either. One more thing they had in common.

Before she could let her mind run rampant on that idea, one of their recent customers approached. She recognized him as a newly graduated college kid who had come back to find a job in Goldcrest Cove. They didn't charm his white tea, but he could have probably used a bit of luck with his weak resume.

"Hey, I'm sorry, but I ordered a white tea and you gave me black tea."

Valerie knew for a fact that she didn't give him black tea, but she took the cup anyway. "Oh, I'm so sorry. Let me get you a fresh cup."

She turned and poured out the perfectly fine brew into the sink before starting in on a new order. It was hard to get the teas mixed around. They steeped everything from scratch, storing the tealeaves in separate jars. Their differences were plain to see, even if the containers weren't labeled.

Still, while the water was boiling, she made sure that she scooped into the right jar this time. The creamy, off-white tealeaves were in her dispenser when she saw it. They changed. Right in front of her eyes, the stringy bits of tealeaves began to darken and shrivel to emulate black tealeaves.

Valerie stared at the leaves in the scoop for a minute, too stunned to act. She took a breath and ignored the way her heart thudded inside her chest. It had to be magic. White tealeaves wouldn't wilt and age that quickly.

Slowly, she dumped out the leaves and scooped out a new serving. Once again, the leaves turned black before she could even put them in the infuser. Angling the scoop in a different light, just to make sure it wasn't her eyes playing a trick on her, she saw they were the same in every sense. They even smelled like black tealeaves now.

Valerie set down the scoop to test if the leaves would revive, but they didn't. Whatever had happened, it was irreversible.

"Krystal? Can you make this guy's white tea for me?"

The older witch glanced her way. "Why? You're right there. Can't you make it?"

Valerie looked from the jar of tealeaves to the steaming water. "I... Can you just do it? I'll take over that cappuccino."

Krystal let out a sigh and with quick hands, did just as she was asked. Valerie watched her carefully, but the leaves didn't change like they had a moment ago. The customer was given the tea with Krystal's personal apologies. When he sipped it, he nodded in approval and walked away.

What had just happened? Valerie wasn't consciously putting off magic. None that she knew of. She wasn't even trying to charm that guy's tea. It didn't make sense.

When they had the chance and Krystal went to the back office, Valerie tested the tea one more time. Now, they didn't age. But that was at least fifteen minutes after the first incident. What was different? Had she really made them age or was it something else? Valerie was glad that she had the evening off. Maybe all this stuff with Caleb was getting to her. She needed a chance to relax again. A few walks with the shelter dogs would do her good. A chance to get away again and clear her head.

Caleb wasn't sure how long he had been sitting cross-legged at the mouth of the hallway. But it was long enough that the dog biscuit in his hand was looking like a viable snack. He was hungry and he had to take a piss eventually. But this damn dog wasn't moving.

If a dog could make an expression, this one would have killed him. Immortality or not. Thor was not giving an inch and wouldn't let him anywhere near the bedrooms or the only bathroom in the house. Each time he tried to offer out the treat, he wouldn't even look at it. The lab simply kept staring at Caleb, lips twitching into a muted growl each time the human made a move he didn't like.

"Come on, bud," Caleb groaned. "We're on the same team."

Caleb's wolf was no help. He wasn't doing anything to provoke the dog, but he wasn't doing much to help. Just existing within Caleb's soul was enough to aggravate the situation.

He held out the treat, which Valerie claimed was his favorite, and once more tried to lower his dominance. He might not have been able to turn it off completely, but Caleb could at least control how potent it was.

Every werewolf carried an inner power, a dominance that helped to rank them within a pack. It went beyond charisma and strength. He had met some dudes bigger than him who had little dominance at all, and werewolf women who possessed the most dominance out of everyone in the room. Caleb, thankfully, was gifted with just enough dominance that he wasn't a pushover, but not enough that he would have to compete for his place in a pack.

Right now, that dominance was the right amount to set Thor on edge.

One of Thor's floppy ears perked at the sound of a car pulling into the drive. Caleb might not have known what time it was, but he knew it was too early for Valerie to be home. They left the coffeeshop around the same time. Her shift finished at about four in the afternoon, but he was unwilling to stick around without her. She had staked herself as his defender in front of her friends. Yes, he decided to hide behind a witch. If his former alpha found out, Caleb would never live it down.

For a moment, neither werewolf nor dog moved from their spot. Not until Valerie's key was in the door. Thor whizzed past him in a flurry of black and went straight for the foyer. Caleb dropped the dog biscuit and stood, listening to Valerie's cheerful greeting and the hard thudding of Thor's wagging tail against everything from her legs to the wall and the sideboard. If his own tail had been out, it would have been wagging just as spiritedly.

Caleb made the mistake of intruding on the pair when he stepped just within view of the door with his hands buried in his pockets. Thor immediately turned and gave a reprimanding bark that didn't scare anyone.

"For the love of the Goddess, calm down!" Valerie begged.

"I've been trying all evening to get him to take a treat from me, but he wouldn't budge."

Valerie looked up and it was then he saw the weariness in her. His wolf went into action, covertly testing the air and the hormones that just entered the house. Something was wrong.

"You okay?" he asked as she managed to sooth Thor by massaging his ears.

For a second, she seemed befuddled, lost for the words to give him a decent response. "Yeah... I... Okay, maybe not." Valerie stood upright, her thick gray coat draping her frame. "I volunteer at an animal shelter in the afternoons and there's this dog I always walk. He's super sweet, but he's a pit bull, so hardly anyone is willing to work with him. But we've really bonded, you know? And when I went there today, he was at the vet's. He's sick and won't eat and they don't know why, but he's really dehydrated and just doesn't want to move and..."

Her throat worked and if Thor wasn't standing between them, he would gone to her. Wolves and dogs might have been on opposite sides of the evolutionary scale, but some things they still shared. Their intuition to comfort the broken and be there for loved ones was still strong. Caleb wanted to reach out and wrap his arms around Valerie until the pain of this news dissolved into himself.

It would be platonic, a pure instinctive move to heal the hurt. But he had to stay rooted where he was. They weren't to that place yet. He gritted his teeth at the unfairness of it and could do little more than convey his sympathies. Whatever damn little that could do.

"They don't know why?" Caleb asked.

Valerie blinked and began to shrug off her winter layers. Beneath her coat, she wore a button-down black shirt with dark purple stitching that accentuated her shape just enough that the hug he desired might not have been too platonic after all.

"They really don't know. His white blood cell count is high, which is good. Whatever he's got, he's fighting... They've got him on an IV to get his fluids up, but if he won't eat, there's not much they can do. The shelter doesn't have enough funding for major operations like that."

Caleb thought of his investments, his savings, his life's earnings stashed away for emergencies. It'd be a rash decision to spend even a portion of it on this dog Valerie seemed so attached to. He doubted she'd even accept his offer if he tried.

"Is there anything I can do?"

That alone evoked a reaction he didn't expect. Valerie looked to him, a glimmer in her eyes like she was on the verge of tears. Was this really about the dog or something else? She seemed off when they left the coffeeshop, like something was on her mind, but there was no way he could ask. Not even now. Damn politeness. Damn social expectations. He wanted to jump from the first step to the tenth, but they had barely lifted their feet to climb this mountain. He couldn't push, but he wanted to. It felt right to.

"No," she finally said, her voice light and laced with that inner pain he so empathetically shared in. "I'll be all right. I left early, because there wasn't much else to do at the shelter with Brody gone."

"Did you have dinner?" Caleb asked as he pulled out his phone to check the time. "I know it's already after six, but – "

"I didn't have dinner," she interjected. "I... I don't know if I'm hungry, really."

Caleb knew that was a lie. He could hear her stomach growling from the driveway. "Well, I am. I was thinking of frying up some chicken."

A silent battle took place, and Valerie seemed to be teetering between taking back what she said and running away again.

"Can you keep Fido out of the way for a while?" he asked, gesturing to the ever-vigilant lab sitting in the foyer.

As if she finally realized Thor was still there, she nodded. "Yeah. Sure. I'll just put him in my room." She hooked her fingers under his collar and guided him away while Caleb kept a few yards of distance from them so as not to rile the dog.

He saw Thor scoop up the dog biscuit on his way to the hallway. Cheeky little bastard.

Caleb turned and went to the kitchen to start cooking. This might not have been much, but it was something. Better than not doing a damn thing to help her and looking like an ass. It was a simple gesture. One that couldn't be misconstrued as anything else but what it was. Just a meal.

That's what he told himself as he poured the oil into the deep cast iron skillet and turned on the eye. But when he took the chicken breasts from the fridge and she leaned in the doorway, Caleb wanted this to be more.

"So, you volunteer at a shelter?" he asked, hoping that making conversation would distract her from all those worries bottled up in her pretty head.

"Yeah. Just on the days I can leave the store early."

"How long have you been doing that?"

Valerie's lips pursed in thought. "About five years, I think."

Caleb pulled out a bowl and began taking down all the seasonings he would need for the batter. "You must enjoy it then."

"It's something to do."

That was a lie. Caleb could taste it in her words. It wasn't just something to do. If it meant nothing, she wouldn't feel so deeply for the animals she helped to care for.

"I bet the whole place would go nuts if I walked in there." It was more of an attempt to get her to smile than to degrade himself.

It didn't work. "Probably," she muttered as she crossed her arms and watched him mix the dry seasonings in one bowl and whip the eggs in the other.

"So, what's the story with you and the other witches running a coffeeshop? Or is there a story?"

She shrugged. "Not much of a story. It was Krystal's idea. She wanted to use the place as a way to help the community. We charm the coffee to help people out sometimes."

Caleb arched his brows and looked up, but she was too quick before he could ask anything further.

"It's a secret, so don't you dare tell anyone we do that."

He smirked. Telling secrets now. Maybe they were off to a better start than he thought. "I won't tell a soul." He hoped that no matter what she and the witches were up to in the coffeeshop, they were safe and kept a low profile. Humans were about as quick to believe in witches as they were in werewolves or vampires, but he knew enough about the witch's hierarchy system. If they stepped out of line, it was the pyre for all of them.

"And what about you?" Valerie asked, taking a few steps further into the kitchen, surprising and thrilling him at the same time. "You don't have a pack. What's the story with that? Or is there a story?"

Caleb let out a sigh as he sliced into the pink flesh of the chicken breast. "I've been in a pack all my life in one way or another. Maybe half a dozen different ones. It's not exactly safe to live outside of a pack. Not smart either. They're our support system in so many ways. It's not natural for someone like me to be alone. My... my inner wolf doesn't exactly like it that way."

Just when he thought this would be easy, he was voicing more honesty than he had ever been comfortable with.

"Then why move to Goldcrest Cove? You know we don't have any here."

He could feel his shoulder muscles tighten under the strain of divulging so much. "I know there aren't. I think that's why, despite everything, I'm liking it so far."

"But, you're living without a pack. Not smart or easy... Was your last pack that bad?" Valerie sat down at the table just across from his prepping station. So close he could reach out and dust her nose with a bit of flour if he wanted.

"Not bad, just... There were some things I just couldn't ignore any more about the way they were running things." Caleb continued to cut into the chicken, making tender-sized slices. That wasn't the entire truth, but she didn't need to know that. Not yet. She might not have fully understood the complexities of his disappearance. Only a werewolf as unique and complicated as he was would understand. Telling her the truth would only prove her friends partially right.

"What? You didn't want to eat Little Cindy next door?" she asked with a huff. Caleb shot her a look. Valerie lifted her hands in submission. "That was below the belt. My bad."

He ground his teeth. Though the insult wasn't deliberate, the mere idea that he, or any rational werewolf of his time would consider eating another human was sickening. "I've only ever met two other werewolves who fed on human flesh and they were psychopaths. Eating humans isn't even remotely recommended. It can make regular, tame werewolves like me into real murderers. The kind your friends don't like."

It was a gamble. This whole conversation was like walking on a bed of nails or through a field of landmines. But somehow, he couldn't stop himself. He wanted her to know, to understand, to trust.

"Is that where all the scary fairytales come from?"

He frowned. "Probably. Just like the evil witches in the storybooks. A few bad eggs ruined it for the lot of us."

Valerie cast her eyes to the mixing bowls. "Was it a bad egg that made you decide to leave your pack?"

He had taken for granted how observant she was. "Partially... But it was more than that." Caleb used his knife to sweep aside some raw chicken bits before taking another breast from the packaging. He needed to redirect this before it could get out of hand. "My wolf may be social, but I'm not. Never have been. I'm naturally a private person and tend to keep to myself. Big crowds, social gatherings, it's not something I enjoy as much as most werewolves."

"And your alpha didn't like that?" Valerie proposed.

Caleb shook his head as he continued to slide his knife through the meat. "Not one bit. Most of them tried to guilt me into coming along on their hunting trips or drag me to gatherings. I'd put on a show and fake it, but I would have rather been at home."

He looked up and caught the hint of a smile play on her lips. "So you're stepping out of your comfort zone to step back into your comfort zone?"

With a chuckle, Caleb shrugged. "In a way, I suppose I am... It can get confusing at times."

A dreamy, ethereal luster came over Valerie's eyes, and he could sense in that perfect moment that something took place inside her. What it was, he might never know, but his wolf did. She was happy. Just as she had been a few days ago when they collided in this kitchen.

"I get it. You want something, but at the same time, you don't want it. Your wolf wants a pack, but you don't want one."

That look was then mirrored in Caleb. For the first time, someone understood. His alpha didn't get it. His own wolf didn't get it. But she did. He could have kissed her right then and there for seeing past it all to grasp the root of his entire agonizing existence.

"It's a battle I fight all the time. Which to put first. Me or the wolf."

Valerie grinned and in that exact second, his hand slipped.

The sharp blade of the knife slid across his fingers. Blood became all he could smell, the pain sobering him from the dream. He dropped the knife and growled at the pain. His vision blurred for only a second before the colors began to shift in his perception. The golden eyes of the wolf had emerged in response to his injury.

He squeezed them shut, so Valerie wouldn't see and quickly turned away toward the sink.

"Whoa! What happened?"

She was out of her chair and behind him by the time the faucet was on and his cut fingers were under the running water. He could see the fleshy gashes and the bits of white bone underneath. Muscles and nerves had been severed, blood swirled with the draining water at the bottom of the sink.

So fucking clumsy, he chided himself. And in front of her.

"I just cut myself. It's fine."

Valerie was so near to him now. He could feel her heat against his side as she leaned over to see for herself. She hissed at the sight of it, but he wouldn't look her in the eye. Not while his eyes were still golden. With these eyes, he could see in near pitch-black darkness as if it were day. He could see for miles with a clear shot. But they never failed to terrify humans.

Then again, Valerie wasn't a human. She was a witch. She could handle his level of supernatural just as he believed he could handle hers. Still, he wouldn't lift his head. They had shared a moment, but he didn't want to share this. Not yet.

"That looks pretty bad," she said.

"It'll heal soon. I've survived worse."

He could feel her stare upon him, but only tilted his head further from her. Hands, thin and gentle reached out to examine. The feel of her skin on his sent such a jolt through his core that he wondered if he'd be able to keep himself on an even keel.

The thought of this woman taking down a man his size with just a touch was comical, though her intentions were anything but. He let her handle him, turning over to inspect the cuts from every angle until she was satisfied. If he had his way, their hands would have been joined for much longer than those few seconds while the cool water poured over both of their fingers. Hell, if he were able, he would have pinned her to the counter right there and taken what he had wanted since he first met her.

There was a pause before she left his side and began to rummage through a cabinet. When he glanced back to his wound, it seemed just as gnarled and bloody as it had been when he first cut it. These minor injuries should have healed by now. This was taking too long. Perhaps making it worse, he flexed his fingers to intensify his pain. He grunted and clenched his jaw, but still the edges of his skin and flesh didn't stitch back together.

Valerie set something heavy on the counter and he could smell the faint traces of antiseptic and latex. "You should wrap that up." She then began to pull out gauze, bandages, and packets of disinfectant. The gesture should have encouraged him.

"I told you, it'll heal. It just needs a little time."

Half a minute passed, the faucet water washing away the fresh bouts of blood that oozed from the cuts. And still, no healing.

"Not this much time," he grumbled.

A new scent blasted him from out of nowhere. Fear. Potent and overpowering. His wolf fed on it, but Caleb shook it off because he knew where it was coming from.

"It's not that bad, really," he told her calmly, hoping something of his dominance would help in reverse. Along with intimidating other werewolves, it could be used to give security and a sense of comfort, knowing that someone was in control.

Valerie backed away and he heard her whisper, "Oh shit," under her breath.

How he wished he could have looked to her, to cradle her face in his hands and make her believe that he was fine.

Staring at his cut, he saw the first stages of healing finally begin and he let out the breath he had been unconsciously holding. "It's fine now. Look."

But she wouldn't move from her place on the far side of the kitchen. Her heart continued to hammer in her chest, louder than the running water. Within the span of another moment, there was no more blood and the skin had completely sewn back together. He shut off the faucet and dried his hand on a dishtowel. His green eyes had returned, the wolf slinking back now that the danger was gone.

"See? Not even a scar." He held up his formerly marred hand to show her, but Valerie's stare was engrossed upon the floor in front of her. "You feeling okay?"

Valerie swallowed hard and nodded. "Yeah, I'm all right... Blood just makes me a little squeamish."

Why was she lying again? She had been able to stare at his fresh wound and even touched him before stepping into action to fix it. He knew plenty who became sick at the sight of blood and that wasn't squeamish at all. Something was wrong, but again, he knew not to press. He couldn't take things too fast.

"Maybe you should lie down. I'll finish up and let you know when it's ready."

Taking this as a dismissal, Valerie darted out of the kitchen and he listened while she rushed to her bedroom and shut the door hard. He cursed himself for whatever he did to make her this way. If he just hadn't cut his hand, she'd still be in the kitchen with him.

Three steps forward and five steps back. That's how it felt. This was supposed to be a game, not an awkward and out-of-sync dance. He thought he knew the rules by now, but apparently they didn't apply to her. She was unlike any woman he had ever met and it was as if he had to relearn everything. He didn't want to agonize over every little word, every gesture, every look of the eye, but he did.

As he cleaned up the blood-smeared chicken and rinsed off the cutting board, something from decades back came to Caleb. As far as he was considered, it had been a myth. Nothing more than a legend or a story werewolves told themselves to make them think that true love and lifelong partners were possible.

Some achieved that. They found a woman who could receive the gift – or curse, depending on who was asked – and they could have their happily ever after. Others settled for a "happy for now" arrangement and watched their partners grow old. Caleb, who had dated and been with women on and off over the last century and a half, didn't believe in the folklore.

It went along with the human notion of a soul mate. Two people who are destined to be together, no matter the distance or differences. It gave hope to those werewolves who thought that, because of their condition, they could never find love.

He knew plenty who bought into the lie, who thought they had found their mate, only to be disappointed when the end came. It'd come as a breakup, a death, a falling out of love, the list went on and on. But if it was true, if it was real, it would have never ended.

Caleb shook his head. Valerie couldn't be his destined mate. It was too ridiculous to think that he, a werewolf, could ever be mates with a witch. They may have had a connection, a sort of synchronization of frequencies, but that was all. It meant little in the grand scheme of eternity. He never bought into those concepts of fate or preordained collisions.

Valerie wasn't his mate, but he had to watch his heart, or he might have started to believe that she was.

Chapter 7

Valerie propped her head in her hand as she continued to flip through the chaotic, disorganized mess that was her family's grimoire. The ancient, delicate pages sometimes ripped under the force of her search, but she didn't care. She had to find an answer.

First it was the tea leaves, then Brody, and now Caleb seemed to be affected. When she thought deeper into it, she realized it wasn't just today. It was all through the weekend. Her phone battery draining so fast, the coffee going stale, and the seemingly inexplicable absence of nightmares. All of it pointed back to her. It had to. What else could it be? No other witch was experiencing these things. And if they were, they weren't telling her anything about it.

The pattern seemed random. There was no defining moment she could point to and blame for all of this. The only cohesion between it all was the fact that they were happening to her, and it had to do with energy. Something was sapping the life force out of everything.

There had to be a clue in her parent's spell book. Was she unconsciously pulling on all of this energy with her magic or was the cause something outside of herself? When she found nothing in the book or the loose-leaf pages that had been scattered on the floor, she turned to her digital files, the ones she had been compiling over the last few years.

The collection grew and grew with each generation, adding and merging with other grimoires as her ancestors married and inherited spells from other family lines. Her grimoire wasn't nearly as massive as Krystal's, but they at least had it stored and organized more efficiently. Valerie's was a hot, eclectic mess of magic, just like her.

But despite all that, she couldn't find a damn thing about involuntary energy transfers. Not one damn thing.

The knock at her door made her jump. Thor bolted from his resting place at her feet and began barking at Caleb through the wood.

"Come in, if you can," she called out wryly.

The door swung open as she swiveled in her office chair. Thor was right there to block him, tail erect and teeth gnashing at the man who stood harmless with a plate of fried chicken strips.

"Oh, for fuck's sake," Valerie grumbled as she went to Thor and pulled him back as she had done before. "Why can't you just behave?"

"He just feels threatened," Caleb said. "I don't blame him."

"Yeah, but he still needs to stop being such a turd." Valerie lightly bopped Thor on the nose. Not enough to hurt, but just enough to distract.

"I'm sure you know dogs can sometimes feed off a human's energies, right?"

That caught Valerie's attention. She hadn't thought about that. Could Thor's behavior and this magic issue be linked?

"So you think it's my fault he's so wacked out?"

Caleb seemed startled by the accusation. "No. Not your fault. He's like this even when you're not around. I'm saying he might react this way to strangers, because that's how he thinks he needs to react based on what he's picking off others. Not necessarily just you. In this case, it's all me. This is normal for my kind."

Then again, maybe not. Valerie let out a long breath and tried not to feel so damaged all of the sudden. Her magic was on the fritz, her dog was a nutcase, and everything felt out of control. That wasn't completely unusual, but somehow it felt that the pandemonium was managed before all this started. It swirled around her head in a congested jumble of disorder. Now, it was all crashing around her like a juggler who had fumbled with a bunch of spinning plates. Everywhere she stepped, there were shards ready to cut her and she couldn't find a broom.

"I brought you some food." Caleb handed her the plate at arm's length, so Thor wouldn't be triggered.

In spite of everything falling apart at her feet, Valerie found the strength to smile and took the plate. "Thanks."

"Are you sure you're okay?" Caleb asked as the silence grew too thick for either of them to tolerate. His gaze wandered toward her cluttered desk, and she could tell that a question sat on his tongue, but he said nothing.

"Yeah, I'm good. I've just got a lot on my mind."

He turned his attention back to her, those perfect emerald eyes making her world all dizzy and vivid. "If you ever need someone to talk to, you know where I live."

She dipped her chin. "Thanks, but I'm all right for now."

To tell him anything about her magic or the grimoire scattered across her desk would be too much. They weren't that close. Not really. Not even after that little confession of his about being a non-conventional werewolf.

In so many ways, she could relate. And if anyone could understand her mind, he could. There was nothing to truly suggest that, but it was just a feeling. A resounding trumpet call in her core that wouldn't let her push him aside anymore. Caleb might have been the one potentially good thing she had now. When all else was shattering, he elected to be her solid ground and a sounding board.

That's what he might have been, but Valerie didn't trust any of this anymore. Something had happened and until she could figure out what it was, she was back to square-one.

Caleb closed the door behind him, much to Thor's relief and Valerie stood there for a moment to gain her bearings. Then, she went back to her desk and set down her plate of chicken tenders. With Caleb's green eyes still fresh in her mind, she continued her search through the countless spells she had loaded into her personal database.

Within a few seconds, the screen dimmed and warned her that the power saving function had been activated. In a panic, she grabbed for the cord and plugged it in, but it was slow to recharge. The laptop was old. It was the same one she had used through high school and was due for a new battery anyway. That, in itself didn't seem odd. Still, she held her breath and hoped that was all it was.

She turned back to the grimoire and skimmed over the page one more time before pinching the fragile edge to turn it. When she did, it happened. A blackness like spilled ink spread over the parchment.

Valerie gasped and released the page, but the damage had been done. That corner became obscured, the penned words of her family heritage swallowed up by the magic that betrayed it. She threw her hands up and bolted from her chair to distance herself from the grimoire. She muttered tiny pathetic pleas and prayers that it would stop before it was too late.

Her heart pounded loud in her ears as she watched a quarter of the page age and wither. Then half. Then the whole. An entire spell was gone and it didn't slow until the adjacent page was just touched by the decay on its gutter margin.

Valerie stood, horrified by what she had done. Whoever had written that spell, whoever had constructed it themselves and tested it, might as well have just died in front of her. A piece of her ancestry was gone forever. All that was left was a brittle sheet of blackened parchment that looked like it would crumble at a touch, as if it had been burned so quickly that ashes hadn't had a chance to form yet.

Near the stack of grimoire pages was the plate of chicken fingers, puckered with green and white mold spots as if it had been sitting there for weeks instead of moments. Valerie looked all around for anything else she had inadvertently ruined, but there was nothing. Everything else was fine. Everything except for what she had touched with her hands.

Her nose tingled with impending tears as she tried to retrace her steps. Nothing had happened before Caleb came in. She had been so absorbed in looking for a reversal to this dangerous magic. She walked to the door, guided Thor away, took the plate, and that was it. They talked, but none of it was remotely close to resembling a spell.

Yet, there was that feeling. What Caleb made her feel.

She slapped her hand over her mouth to stifle her panic. Valerie knew what this was now. But it wasn't possible. She didn't want it to be. She shook her head against the thought. It had to be something else. But the evidence wouldn't lie.

Valerie was coming into her dark magic. And it was Caleb's fault.

Fear. Caleb despised that odor more than anything else, even his existence as a werewolf. It had been wafting from Valerie's room for the last few minutes and there was no way he could focus with it stinking up the house.

He sat in the dining room, his laptop open to his most recent chapter and a plate of chicken getting cold next to him. The harder he tried to think of the words, the more he became disconnected from the project entirely.

He rubbed at his eyes and let out a low growl of frustration. He wished he could have barged in there and demanded that she tell him what was wrong so he could fix it. His wolf needed answers, it needed to know she was all right. Still, he sat in place, applying every ounce of self-control in his arsenal.

That composure nearly failed him when Valerie's door opened and she rushed down the hall. Unable to keep himself rooted any longer, he stood and came to the living room to see her snatch her coat from the hook in the foyer.

"Going somewhere?" he asked, maintaining an even tone, though he wanted to charge forward and stop her flight. He would have grabbed her, whisked her off her feet, and planted her on the couch until every last bit of this anxiety could be extinguished.

He had never cared for anyone that much, and he had no reason to. Even now, he couldn't justify the feelings that neutralized most of his common sense. And after just a few days, he was done trying to figure it out.

Valerie spun around, her eyes wide as if she hadn't expected to see him there. "Yeah, I'm... I need to go see Krystal. I'll be back. Don't wait up or anything."

She headed out the door and Caleb felt his head tilt in confusion as he watched her disappear into the dark, cold night. Did this have to do with the altercation between her and the other witch from this morning? He sincerely hoped not. He didn't want to come between two good friends.

Caleb listened to her speed away in her Acura. The further and further she drove, the more he felt his spirit pull. It almost became physically painful to be separated from her. He squeezed his eyes shut and shook his head. He needed to relax, to get her off his mind somehow. She said not to wait up, but heaven and hell both knew that he would be sitting on that couch until dawn if it meant he'd be there when she walked back through the door.

Damn, what had gotten into him?

Valerie banged her fist on the front door of the Hayden Manor. That's what she liked to call it, anyway. It didn't have an official title, but the historical marker in the yard was enough to give it a reputation that was known by just about everyone in town. It was one of the few buildings in Goldcrest Cove to survive the ages of wars, storms, and every generation of witches that inhabited it.

The old architecture had been remodeled over the years, but the main structure and foundation remained much the same. It was upon this same door that she knocked countless times growing up. As a young girl looking to play for the afternoon, as a teen witch just coming into her magic, and now as a scared adult who needed answers.

Sierra, Krystal's older sister, answered first and Valerie freaked. Maybe she should have called first. Krystal might have been out on a date with Devin.

Sierra's dark brows rose in shock, but the space between them puckered with concern. "You look like shit."

Valerie gave her a look. They had known one another for just as long as she had known Krystal. Sierra was the one who always colored her hair, since she owned one of the best salons in town. She was the big sister to all of them, not just Krystal. There was the one time she didn't bust them for drinking beer for the first time in their junior year of high school. Then another when Valerie needed help with her math grades and Sierra tutored her, even when she had her own college homework to worry about.

It was for those favors that Valerie trusted her beyond words.

"I need to see Krystal," she said, doing a poor job of hiding her alarm. She was ushered into the warm foyer and the winter cold was shut out. It seemed that no matter the season, the house always stayed at a comfortable temperature. No doubt a former witch put a charm over the place to make it so.

Sierra crossed her arms. "She told me about the little tiff you two got into over the werewolf."

Valerie unbuttoned her coat and let out a deep breath. "I figured she would."

"You really don't know anything about werewolves, Val. If you did, you would have taken Krystal's side."

She couldn't stop herself and groaned, "Oh, not you too!"

Sierra was in no mood. "Honey, I've heard too many stories to think anything else. They're dangerous. Plain and simple."

Why did this have to be so hard? Why couldn't they just be open minded and accept that Caleb wasn't the same? Then, it dawned on her that they hadn't given him the chance. They hadn't talked to him. They hadn't seen him fixing dinner like a normal guy. All they saw was the wolf in him. All they saw was the label.

She had no words for Sierra. She had her own problems and fighting Caleb's battles for him was not on the agenda. Not tonight.

"Just promise me you'll be careful with him? I've got some wolfs bane in the garden if you want some?"

Valerie faked a smile. "No, thanks. I just came to talk to Krystal."

Only then did Sierra call for her younger sister, who was upstairs.

Light padding sounded down the polished mahogany staircase, but it wasn't her friend. The overweight Siamese cat named Artemis came to investigate the noise. He looked up to Valerie with that wise, no-nonsense stare, his tail erect and twitching.

"Still don't like me?" she asked the ornery cat. There were few outside of the Hayden family that the cat tolerated. Much like Thor, he was picky about his humans, except for Devin. Miraculously, he took to the non-magic cop like he was the best thing since the invention of canned tuna.

But Valerie, not so much.

The cat's eyes narrowed, as if in a glare, and then he sashayed into the kitchen. No doubt to look for a snack he didn't need.

A few seconds later, Krystal came down the steps, dressed in a pair of flannel pajamas. The coffeeshop had closed just an hour before, but Krystal had told them she would start making an effort not to chain herself to the back office every waking moment. They had Devin to thank for that. Meeting her Twin Flame had set into motion some incredible changes in Krystal. Not just with her dark, fire elemental magic, but her attitude. She wasn't so wound up all the time anymore. She let herself have fun and she finally learned when to leave well enough alone with the coffeeshop.

If only Valerie could say that her own Twin Flame encounter was just as beneficial. Even now, she didn't see anything good about her dark magic.

Krystal must have seen the same distress in Valerie's face and the offenses from earlier that day were forgotten. "Are you all right? What happened?"

Both of them would be looking for an excuse to blame her trouble on Caleb, but Valerie wouldn't give them the satisfaction. Still, there was no beating around the bush. It wasn't Valerie's style.

"I think I'm coming into my dark magic. I need to stop it. Can I look at your family's spell rolodex?"

Sure enough, her bluntness startled them both.

"You're going to need to rewind about twenty steps and tell me what's going on," Krystal demanded. "Did you meet your Twin Flame?"

Valerie shrugged and gestured like she didn't have a clue. "I don't know! He might have come through the coffeeshop or something. All I know is that all of the sudden, I'm draining the life out of things. And I'm not being dramatic either. Like, I'm literally sapping the fucking energy from stuff."

She went on to explain about her phone battery, the tealeaves, Brody at the shelter, and the grimoire page. There was no explaining the incident with Caleb and how his healing abilities had been delayed because of her. As far as either of them knew, he wasn't involved in any of this. If she could avoid admitting that part of the story, she would until her last breath. Telling her friends that she was attracted to a werewolf would be nothing compared to the shit storm that would hit when she told them he was her Twin Flame.

"And you're not doing it on purpose, right?" Sierra asked. "Not even a little?"

They were all still standing in the foyer between the kitchen and the living room where a fireplace crackled and hissed with a steady fire.

"Why would I want to do this kind of shit? I could hurt someone! I've already hurt Brody. He could be dead by now and I wouldn't even know how I did it."

All evening, she had tried to push out her anxiety about Brody. He didn't deserve any of this. All he did was love unconditionally the way dogs always did with those they trusted. And Valerie didn't want to think about how she had betrayed that trust. All because she couldn't bridle her feelings toward Caleb.

"Okay, okay." Krystal swept up her bangs, now infected by the same worry Valerie had been suffering for most of the day. "Let's go take a look at the rolodex and in the meantime, can you call mom?"

Valerie grabbed for Sierra's arm before she could reach for her phone. "No! Please! Don't call your mom! I don't want anyone else to know about this. I just want to find a way to fix it."

The two Hayden witches leveled on her. "You know that's exactly how I felt when I found out about my dark magic. I wanted to hide it, but mom said I had to harness it. Not bury it."

Valerie shook her head, her hair tossing with the frantic motion. "No, no, no. This needs to be buried. This isn't like burning a dinner or manipulating candle flames. I'm officially classifying myself as a danger to humanity here!"

Sierra took Valerie by the elbows and shook her. "You are not a danger to anyone as long as you remain calm. Krystal's dark magic has a trigger, just like yours will. Do you know what you're feeling right before it happens?"

She knew all too well what she felt. Giddy, light, damn near joyful. Something she never wanted to feel again if it meant she'd hurt someone.

"I get... I get happy." Valerie gave a pitiful, powerless shrug of her shoulders.

Sierra gave her the strangest look, but Krystal only nodded. "That sounds about right," she said. "But Sierra's right. I thought I was going to burn the house down if I wasn't careful. You're not a danger to anyone. We just need to find a way to channel this... Are you sure you don't want to at least ask my mom if she has any ideas?"

Valerie shook her head. "Nope. Not until we've tried everything imaginable. If I still drain the life out of batteries and shit, then we'll call her."

They could agree on that much and all three walked past the stairs toward the office where they kept their massive rolodex of spells. It was their version of the grimoire, the spells and recipes scrawled out on notecards they could easily flip through.

While Krystal and Valerie scrolled and leafed through the endless index, Sierra took to the bookshelves where histories and copies of the council records were kept. She dedicated herself to looking for any possible precedent for Valerie's new dark magic. If they could find someone else who had these same powers, the reasoning was that they could find out how they controlled it. It was in one volume where they found a case much like Krystal's, where a man could control the element of fire with hardly any effort at all after he met his Twin Flame. He was long dead, but his children had kept his grimoire safe. Photocopies of its pages were kept in a notebook in Krystal's room for her to study in her spare time.

Valerie prayed to every god and goddess she had some rapport with that they would find some answer that night. She wasn't sure she could leave Hayden Manor without at least understanding this dark magic more thoroughly.

About half an hour into their search, and suffering all sorts of questions about who her Twin Flame might have been, they were interrupted by Krystal's phone trilling. The song, "Wildfire" by Sarah Evans had Valerie wincing for a second before her friend answered it. Country wasn't her thing.

"Hey, babe," she said. "I'm a little busy right – "

She stopped, interrupted by Devin's deep voice on the other end of the line. Valerie couldn't tell what he was saying, but just by the tone, she knew it wasn't good. Krystal's expression pinched and her eyes darted from her friend to her sister and back again as she listened.

"And they're just missing?"

Valerie froze and crinkled the corner of the index card in her hand.

"Okay, um..." Krystal squared her shoulders and looked to the coffered ceiling paneled in dark oak. "We'll be there in a little bit, but... You know the rules, Devin." There were some more words and then goodbyes were given.

"Something tells me that wasn't a booty call," Sierra said as she abandoned her volume upon the bookstand to join them at the desk.

Valerie had known Krystal long enough to know that look in her eyes was a bad sign. Whatever Devin asked of her, she knew it wasn't good at all. This was something she couldn't understand or control, therefore she didn't like it. Nor did she like the fact that Devin had dragged her into it.

"There's... Well, he doesn't really understand it either, but you know the old cemetery where the founders are buried? Some are dug up."

Valerie went pale and she could feel a rush of cold sweep down her back, despite the warmth of the room. Sierra's jaw dropped and she was the only one capable of forming questions.

"Like, grave robbery? That's insane!"

Krystal pulled her long black hair over her shoulder and gripped it in her fist, something she did when she knew she was in over her head. "Devin said the caretaker made the call. No one's been in or out of the cemetery all evening."

"Why did he call you?" Sierra questioned.

Her gaze raked over both of them. "Because it doesn't look like the graves were dug up from the outside. He says it looks more like they've been dug up from the inside."

Chapter 8

Valerie hugged the jacket about her waist as they made their way from Sierra's jeep to the cemetery gates. Red and blue lights flashed against the brick wall and tree line beyond, splitting through the natural moonlight that would have streamed upon the pathways that weaved through the graves.

Devin and Aaron were the only cops in the cemetery, but the caretaker, Mr. Carmichael, remained to close up the place when the investigation was finished. By Valerie's estimation, he looked absolutely terrified. Probably less to do with the missing bodies and more to do with whether he would keep his job or not.

Krystal filled them in on the details during the drive. The caretaker had stumbled into one of the open graves that night while doing his final inspection before closing. It wasn't the typical rectangular cavity like someone had tried to take the entire coffin out of the ground. Instead, the hole was uneven, more circular with no corners. There were no piles of dirt beside the headstones as if someone had used a shovel.

The story Devin painted involved animals looking for an easy meal. As far as they knew, both Aaron and Mr. Carmichael bought it. But he knew better. Calling Krystal was a fair move on his part. If he suspected there was something more supernatural going on with the missing corpses, then getting the witches involved was the right thing to do.

Just as Krystal warned him, though, there were rules. Rules that they often broke for the sake of convenience, but they were walking on eggshells now. After helping him arrest the second-hand charmed murderer in October, Krystal made it clear that the witches couldn't have a hand in policing Goldcrest Cove again unless it directly threatened the magic-folk personally.

But the moment they came to the graves, they realized this would justify bending the rules a little. The missing people from the graves were family. The names on the tombstones were too familiar to ignore.

Even Valerie saw that one or two of her own family were disinterred and a lump rose in her throat. All the way there, she couldn't shake the unsettling thought that this was somehow her doing. Why wouldn't it be? She had visited this cemetery the day before when all of her dark magic began to emerge. It was in this spot where she saw Caleb in his wolf form and experienced the same sensations that once thrilled her. They frightened her now, because they meant nothing but death and decay. Story of her life.

Krystal and Sierra went to talk to Devin, who shined a flashlight upon the crime scene, so the two witches could inspect it for themselves and make what conjectures they could. Everyone's first thoughts were of zombies, but Sierra had told them there hadn't been a zombie issue in at least fifty years and those incidences were isolated to the deep south where voodoo hadn't died off in the wake of modern society. However, they wouldn't rule out anything.

Seeing the upturned graves for herself, Valerie began to doubt that this was her fault, but only minutely. Her dark magic destroyed and drained the life out of things. The corpses in this graveyard were already dead. What could she possibly glean from them? And there was a range on her abilities. The further she was from something, the less she affected it. That much she understood so far. There was only one grave from her family plot that was disturbed, but plenty more on the other side of the cemetery that she hadn't gone near.

Then again, she didn't know all the workings and loopholes of her dark magic. Maybe draining energy was just one facet. Valerie shuddered, not so much from the cold but from the not knowing what she had become.

"I knew you liked creepy shit, but I didn't think you'd want to come to a graveyard in the middle of the night."

Valerie sneered at Aaron who had come up to stand beside her near her aunt's empty grave. "You look pretty limber, Aaron. Why don't you bend over and suck your own dick?"

He chuckled and scoped around the inwardly sloping edges of the plot. "No need to be nasty. I'm trying to help too, ya know." Then, as if a switch had been flipped, Aaron was the picture of civility. "I'm sorry about what happened to Maggie. It looks like Krystal's grandmother was taken too."

Valerie glanced over her shoulder toward where her friends congregated. The Hayden family, Krystal's father's side and a few of her mother's side, who were not citizens of Goldcrest Cove until the early twentieth century, were laid to rest here.

"We haven't found any animal tracks, but Devin thinks they may be under all this fresh snow."

Again, she looked to the darkened earth and the snow clusters that reflected back the squad car lights from the parking lot. The snow wasn't all that new, but Aaron didn't need to know that.

"And it's a little dark, but so far we haven't found any bones or bits of clothes either."

"You're just the master of tact, aren't you?"

As stoic as Valerie tried to be in the face of all this, seeing her aunt's grave torn open got to her. She and her aunt weren't always the best of friends, but the woman took care of her after her parents died. For that, she owed the woman a lifetime of gratitude. Especially given that Aunt Maggie wasn't a witch. She hadn't inherited the gift of magic like her mother had, and so she had to tolerate cleaning up after another witch for the rest of her days. It wasn't easy, and her memory shouldn't have been desecrated in this way.

"I figured you would have wanted to know," Aaron replied, a note of irritation in his voice.

The stress and anxiety from the entire day bubbled up to vomit upon one of the few people she didn't care about hurting. "It's just a body. She's not there. It's not like she was murdered or her body stolen for some ritualistic shit."

Aaron's face turned stony in the cop lights. "Then why are you even here?"

She gestured toward her friends. "They asked me to come and I didn't have anything better to do."

A sly look came over him. "That's not what Devin told me."

Her eyes narrowed into angry slits. "You better tell me what the hell you're talking about or..." She couldn't voice her true threat. If she thought she could get away with it, she'd make sure his bowels were twisted up, so he wouldn't be able to shit right for weeks.

"He just said you've got a new roommate, that's all. I saw the guy earlier today and well..." Aaron waggled his brows in that suggestive way.

It was a thankful thing that few could see the pallor of one's face in the dark. Aaron would have seen Valerie's skin flush a deep red under the innuendo. She was completely aware of her thoughts as they slipped so fluidly and effortlessly into the gutter.

She remembered Caleb's ripped body speckled with water droplets. She remembered his piercing green gaze. The feel of his skin touching hers. The warmth and tenderness in his words and the way he seemed so attentive for no good reason. It didn't take long for the fantasies to manifest. The idea of his arms around her, pulling her in for a kiss that was both aggressive and sensual. She wondered what it would be like in bed with him, twisting under the sheets that would become damp from their lovemaking.

Aaron's flashlight began to flicker and finally went out. He cursed and banged it against his palm to make it come back to life. But it was no use. Valerie had drained those batteries completely dead with her imagining.

"I'm going to see if they need any help," she quickly said, rushing away from Aaron and leaving all her dirty thoughts behind her. He said he was going to look for more batteries in the squad car, which gave all four of them time to talk without fear of eavesdroppers.

"What do you think?" Devin asked the witches. "Anything?"

Sierra's eyes were focused upon her grandmother's grave. She, out of the two sisters, was the closest to the old woman. "If magic was used here, it's nothing good."

Krystal agreed. "Necromancy is a crime across the board."

"So no one in town is likely to have done this?" the cop asked, his expression hard and slightly intimidating. This was not Devin's usual demeanor. He was on duty, and as serious as sin.

"None that we know," Sierra replied.

A pause of silence hovered over the group before Devin finally asked, "Is it possible that something other than a witch could have done this?"

Valerie knew exactly where this was going and who their fingers would point at next.

Krystal was thinking the same. "It's possible."

"No way," Valerie blurted out. "No tracks, no blood. It had to be magic. And you said yourself there's no piles of dirt or signs that it was dug up from the outside. It has to be magic."

Nowhere in her outburst did she directly defend Caleb. She only stated the facts that they all knew. It was just a reminder, nothing more. But in her heart, she wanted to scream and curse them all for even thinking that a werewolf could have done this.

They all looked to her and at least Devin seemed ashamed for even suggesting it. The other witches, however, were still not convinced. Their prejudice ran too deep.

"We'll do some asking around and see if anyone's seen anything out of the ordinary," Sierra said. "If there's another witch or warlock around town practicing illegal magic, they can't hide for long."

"And as soon as there's enough light to see by," Devin added, "we'll get a team out here to search the woods for any of the bodies. Just in case."

Krystal was the one who had her gaze focused on Valerie. Maybe she was coming to wonder about all the fears Valerie secretly fretted over. Maybe she was thinking about the dark magic too. Still, without any documented precedent or pulling in someone older and wiser like Mrs. Hayden, they were lost in the dark. All they could do was hope that whatever happened at the cemetery had nothing to do with Valerie or Caleb. It was all just an unhappy coincidence that would sort itself out soon enough.

That's what Valerie tried to tell herself.

Caleb must have dozed off. The last thing he remembered was shutting his eyes after pausing the video game. The clock had read three in the morning, and still Valerie hadn't come home. Thor was harmlessly asleep in her room. All the while he fought off the urge to charge out the door every ten minutes to go hunt her down.

He told himself it wasn't necessary. She could take care of herself. She was a witch after all. Still, his wolf wanted her home. Wanted her in his arms and safe beyond a shadow of a doubt. Nothing could distract him from this driving force. Nothing could dull the pain of the aching heart in his chest that demanded it was close to hers. Fighting this inexplicable pull toward Valerie left him exhausted and confused more than anything.

Fatigue got the better of him, and the next thing he knew, he was awakened to the familiar rumble of her Acura engine. He cast aside the remote in his lap and rushed for the door, only to be stopped by Thor.

He'd had enough of the dog. In his half-wakeful state, he could feel his eyes turn their wolfish gold. His canines sharpened and elongated into fangs as he snarled back at the mutt. Claws extended from his fingernail beds, able to cut through the dog's flesh like butter if he wanted.

His wolf wanted to kill the dog, but Caleb wasn't so out of it not to see that would be foolish. He simply let his dominance discharge a silent show of power that could send the fiercest of beasts cowering for shelter. He'd get to the door even if he had to scare the shit out of Thor for the last time.

For a minute, the dog didn't back down and the coarse hairs on his shoulders bristled with the threat. Caleb only intensified his wolf's aura, making it impossible for the dog to feel or sense anything else but the monster within him. He was done trying to be Thor's equal and seized the rank of alpha immediately to obliterate the competition within the household. Anything to make this nonsense stop.

Only then did Thor finally back down. His tail tucked between his legs and he scampered out of the way with huffs and light whimpers.

Before Caleb reached for the doorknob, he reined in his wolf, forcing back the claws, fangs, and eyes that would terrify Valerie into believing what the other witches had been trying to tell her from the beginning. He was dangerous. A menace. A monster.

He stepped out onto the porch, dawn's light emerging from the east. He loved this time of the day when everything was still and cool. Even in winter. The hazy gray atmosphere was the first thing he saw upon waking, a reminder that all was well and the world continued to turn even if the night before had been pure hell.

Seeing Valerie gave him that same feeling. Now that she was home, safe, and in one piece, he felt he could breathe for the first time since she left. He couldn't wait for her to walk up the drive and came to her driver's side where she still sat, absorbed in some distracting thought.

He must have been too quiet, because she startled when he leaned one hand on the roof of her car.

"Goddess!" she exclaimed with a gasp. "You scared me."

He smiled, just glad to see her at all. "Sorry. You were out all night."

Dark lunettes hung under Valerie's eyes. Her hair was slightly messed as if she had been running her hands through it a few too many times. In the passenger seat was a folder of photocopied papers that he could only make out a few words in the outer margins.

Valerie closed her eyes and inhaled deeply before giving a nod. "Yeah, I just stayed the night at Krystal's..." She looked to him and must have seen the similar bags under his own eyes. "You didn't wait up for me, did you?"

He gave her a bashful grin. "I was... I was worried. I know you're perfectly capable of taking care of yourself, but you seemed pretty upset yesterday and..."

Just then, the engine on her Acura cut off. Her hands were in her lap, not even touching the key that was still lodged in the ignition. Valerie snapped awake and cussed aloud before testing the engine.

She turned the key, but there was little more than a clicking noise each time she tried it. Finally, she banged her hand on the steering wheel and covered her face.

"I take it this doesn't happen often?" Caleb asked, slightly amused by her mortification.

"No," she moaned.

"Pop the hood," he told her as he moved around to the front of the car. She did as he asked and he took a quick peek. Checking wires, the connections on the battery, and various hoses.

"Don't tell me you're a mechanic," Valerie teased as she climbed out of the car with her folder.

"I was back in the sixties in Arizona, but I've tinkered with them quite a bit from time to time. Just enough to keep up with all the new models." After inspecting everything he could think of, he closed the hood and met her gaze. If he wasn't mistaken, he believed he had finally impressed her. "My guess is that it's your battery or alternator. I'll know more once I test everything."

She snorted a laugh. "You have that kind of equipment?"

"Never leave anywhere without it," he answered, jerking his thumb toward his truck. "I keep it in the back seat with my toolbox."

Valerie shook her head in amazement. "You're full of surprises. And I thought I'd have to donate an arm and a leg to the car shop."

"That's just one reason I decided to learn about cars myself. Too many shops will gyp you in a heartbeat."

Her eyes raked up and down his body. "If someone gypped you, I think it'd be the last mistake they ever made."

His smile faltered for a second, but he chuckled off her joke. It wasn't far from the truth, though it was an exaggeration. "It might be... Are you working today?"

She nodded and pulled out her phone to check the time, but the screen wouldn't illuminate. "Damnit," she grumbled. "Do you know what time it is?"

Caleb fished out his phone from his jeans and wasn't too surprised to see that it had died as well. He failed to plug it up the night before while he waited for her. Then, he looked toward the horizon half-obscured by the trees. "I think it's just after six. The sun's not fully up yet."

"I need to get this thing charged and take a shower. I probably stink."

Caleb shook his head. "You smell just fine." He even shocked himself with that admission. "I mean, you don't stink anyway."

Valerie blinked and turned toward the walkway that led to the front door. "Well... Thanks, I guess. Coming from you that must mean something. Is your nose really as good as a dogs?"

Caleb followed after her. "Better than a dog's, unfortunately."

"That must get annoying," she remarked as she entered the foyer.

"It used to be. I've learned to tune a lot out."

"What else can you do?"

He went to listing his abilities as they made their way deeper into the house. "It's the whole gamut of things you'd expect. Smell, hearing, speed, strength."

"So, there's some truth to the movies in the end?"

Caleb gave her a lopsided grin. "Only some. I don't change on a full moon. I can change whenever I want. Totally voluntary."

Valerie moved to slip off her coat, but something compelled him to take it for her. His fingers hooked around the lapels and he slid it from her shoulders with ease. His knuckles brushed against her arms, and though there was a layer of cloth between them, the energy was still as potent as if she were naked before him. He could see the gooseflesh spread over her neck as she turned to look at him.

Her eyes were as wide as if he had just shifted right there in front of her. He stood there, gripping her coat with no excuse for his behavior, besides that it was an old fashioned habit. The scent of arousal tingled his nostrils and he had to force himself away from the temptation.

"Yeah, I kind of figured that part out when I saw you at the cemetery," she said. Her voice trembled, as if she had to catch her breath. "So, you never have to shift if you don't want to?"

Caleb slung her jacket on the hook and let his fingers drag down the wool fiber to savor in the warmth she had given it. "It may be voluntary, but it's not completely unnecessary. The wolf needs to run every once and a while." He locked eyes with her in the darkened foyer. "If I don't shift, the wolf becomes restless and irritable. He'll start scratching for a way out and completely take control if I don't let him."

Valerie's heartrate escalated, thrumming in his ears. "So, you really can become like a beast if you're not careful?"

"A ravenous, insatiable beast... Yes... It's always there, though."

"You do a good job of hiding it."

"It takes practice, but I have my moments when it becomes too much."

Valerie's gaze darted from his eyes to his lips and back again. "Have you ever lost control?"

He knew what she asked and he smirked. "Don't worry. You're in no danger from me."

He hadn't realized how close they were until he could feel her hot breath. His mouth watered for her kiss, the desire to taste and know how she felt against him nearly overpowering his restraint. His cock hardened and pressed against the front of his jeans just enough to snap him out of it.

One thing, and one thing only kept him from crossing the line. There was a sadness in those clear green eyes that he hadn't seen before. A deep-seated sorrow that she hid from the world, and maybe even herself. He wanted to understand it, if nothing else, so he could extinguish it permanently. A woman like her, strong and formidable, should never be seduced into misery.

Caleb broke away before he would do something he came to regret and fled toward the kitchen. "If I'm ever gone for the night, you'll know where I'll be."

He heard nothing from the living room or the foyer. Valerie hadn't moved or said anything. But he couldn't turn back. He couldn't look at her again until he was sure his heart was out of the danger zone. The thought of mates came back to mind and he wrinkled his nose in irritation. Mostly at himself for allowing such lies to enter for the second time in twenty-four hours.

"Do you want any coffee?" he called out to her, hoping that would wake her from whatever trance she had fallen into.

"Uh... Yeah, sure."

He wasn't totally convinced, but he did as she asked. He recognized the coffee grounds as the same ones he smelled inside the coffeeshop. Though the gold and purple logo on the black bag was enough for him to make the connection.

Valerie finally moved and he tracked her progress into the bathroom. More or less to distract himself, he pulled out the carton of eggs and package of bacon to fix breakfast. If he didn't keep his hands and mind occupied, he would have imagined too many things. Dangerous things. Like how she undressed, what her undergarments looked like, whether she washed her hair or her body first, if she liked to take a moment and bask beneath the hot water before bathing.

He could feel his wolf rise up again, golden eyes focused on the task at hand while his cock demanded other forbidden things.

"Keep it together," he kept telling himself. "Don't lose your head."

As if words were going to be enough to keep him at bay forever.

Chapter 9

Tuesdays weren't so busy. Valerie knew she could get away with dismissing herself after the morning rush to clean something in one of the back rooms. At least until she could get a grip.

She didn't trust herself with the coffee, the register, or any customer's credit card. Not while her heart and stomach were still fluttering over that incident with Caleb. Her head was still reeling as she showered and got ready for work. Her skin was hot to the touch, every nerve on fire. Just washing herself and running her hands through her own hair made her long for Caleb in a way she had never wanted any other man before.

By the time she was dressed, her wet hair pulled back into a painful ponytail, she was sure she had officially lost her mind. Just sitting beside Caleb in his truck was excruciating, but in a pleasant way. She wouldn't look at him. If she did, she was liable to kiss him and make the whole world rot. She imagined he was blissfully delicious, just like his natural scent that reminded her so much of that wild side she wanted to discover.

She kept telling herself that she was crazy for wanting a guy so badly, for yearning after something she couldn't understand. None of her feelings made sense. There was no single instance when she knew she needed Caleb. No exact moment she could point to and say it started there. It had just happened. It snuck up on her so suddenly and violently. Or maybe it had been there since the moment they locked eyes on one another and it took this total unhitching of her sanity to recognize it.

He had dropped her off a few blocks from the store, just to be sure that no one saw her riding with him. She didn't want anyone to have the excuse to blame Caleb for any of this, even though it really was his fault. Why did he have to come to Goldcrest Cove? Why did he have to knock her entire universe off kilter?

The little sleepover at Krystal's was hardly enjoyable. They managed to find six spells that were anywhere remotely related to energy transfers. Copies were made and sent home with her to study and practice that evening. Valerie wasn't sure how helpful they would be. They were more like temporary fixes. Spells to inhibit happiness, to make dull those feelings which were too intense. One spell helped to reverse the decay, which she would implement on her one ruined grimoire page.

Though the search had been relatively successful, it wasn't what Valerie wanted. It wasn't a cure, or a total reversal to banish the dark magic forever. If she could just forget that Caleb was her Twin Flame, rewind time and ensure they never met, then she would have rather done that instead.

When she came back from the storeroom where they kept the broom and dustpan, Devin and Aaron came through the front door. The equipment and keys on their belts jingled with every step, turning some heads in the coffeeshop. By now, everyone knew that Devin and Krystal were a couple. There was no use hiding it. They were too in love to bother being discreet. It made her wonder if she and Caleb could ever be like that.

Valerie knew what this would be about. Devin had said the night before that they would make a sweep of the woods around the pilfered cemetery to look for the missing bodies. She both did and didn't want to hear the news. If this had anything to do with her dark magic, she didn't want to be saddled with the guilt. If it didn't, she wanted to experience that relief and the unclenching of every tightened muscle when she learned that, for once, this disaster wasn't her fault.

Before she could make up her mind, Krystal was waving her over to join them. Aaron was carrying their drinks toward their usual corner table, leaving the cop and witches to talk real business.

"It's definitely magic," she heard Devin say as she trudged up to the counter. "We swept the woods and didn't find anything, but the minute we came back to the station, there was a flood of reports about other graves being exhumed across town. Even animals buried in backyards are gone."

That, Valerie wasn't expecting. A tremor of fear passed through each of the witches.

"So it's not an isolated case," Alexa remarked. She had been filled in earlier on everything she missed the night before, including Valerie's dark magic.

"Doesn't look like it." Devin leaned in closer to the counter. "And I don't think anyone at the station is taking it seriously, but there have been other reports. People are seeing their dead loved ones roaming around town."

"Sounds like zombie shit to me," Valerie sighed. This is what she didn't want to hear.

"And they're not freaking out?" Alexa asked, her voice a shrill whine of panic.

Devin shook his head. "I think it's people's unwillingness to believe in the supernatural that's keeping it from getting that far."

"Have you been able to get a hold of any of the... you know." After all her knowledge and training, Krystal still seemed unwilling to utter the word as freely as Valerie did.

"Not yet, but the chief's not putting anyone on the case either." Devin donned an uncomfortable look like his uniform was too tight. "The chief's been a little off his game lately, so it's not surprising."

Krystal gripped her dark ponytail over her shoulder. "Sierra called up Amber and Taylor yesterday, but they haven't seen any other witches in town."

Devin struggled with his next question, though he must have known it was on everyone's mind. "Is it... Is it possible that this is a similar case like what happened with Jacob Nathanson?"

Alexa was the first to glance at Valerie and then lower her gaze in shame. That name would haunt them for years. They caught the murderer and negated the second-hand charm, but no one was likely to forget how it all happened in the first place. Alexa certainly never could.

"We've been extremely careful about the charms since then," Krystal assured, defending herself and her friends. "And I can't think of any second-hand charm that would cause something like this. It's not like one person is going around to all these cemeteries and into the backyards of strangers. They couldn't possibly do that all night, and it wouldn't account for seeing dead people wandering around town. This is something bigger than a single charm."

That was a relief to Alexa, but not to Valerie. They were only narrowing this down further to come to the same awful conclusion she had already obsessed over for the last twelve hours. The emergence of her dark magic and this zombie incident couldn't be a coincidence. Just how she had done it, she wasn't sure.

"So what do you plan on doing?" Krystal asked her boyfriend.

Devin's lips drew into a grim line. "I was hoping you could tell me that."

All three witches looked to one another. Devin had turned to them as if they were the experts. If he knew how small they were in this gigantic pond in the magical realm, he wouldn't have even bothered asking.

Krystal knew leagues more than any of them. "We can go through our family grimoires for anything that'll negate the magic that brought the bodies back to life," Krystal said. "But some spells have their limitations."

"Like?"

Valerie frowned. "We may need a body or two. Some spells can only be cancelled out by the original caster. It all depends on who we're dealing with."

"Can you get your sister in on this?"

Krystal nodded. "Yes, but I'm going to refrain from calling in the cavalry until we've exhausted all other options."

Valerie knew exactly why. Bringing in her parents would open a can of worms they weren't willing to deal with yet. She made it clear to Krystal and her sister that she didn't want their parents anywhere near Goldcrest Cove until they understood more about what this dark magic was. If they could find a connection between these events, and if they were in over their heads, then they would make the call.

"What are your guys doing to help?" Alexa asked.

"Animal control is sweeping the woods, but they're wasting their time."

Alexa, feeling particularly sassy, remarked, "Better tell your roommate to stay out of the woods for a little while, Val."

Her face grew hot at the comment.

Krystal added, "If nothing else, so he'll be safe while we get this figured out. We don't need the town thinking there are wolves running around."

Valerie might have been mistaken, but she almost believed that was meant to be helpful and not snide or biting. "What am I supposed to tell him? That someone's going around resurrecting the dead?"

Devin, still new to the world of magic, let out a long sigh. Poor guy.

Krystal shook her head. "I don't want him knowing our business unless it's necessary. Tell him whatever you want, or keep him locked up in the house at night or something. Until we can figure out who's doing this and fix it, I don't want the werewolf meddling into things."

She said "meddling" as if Caleb were liable to come barging in and make things worse, though she couldn't imagine how. Part of her wondered if he might be of some help. While he tried to make small talk with her in the car, he mentioned that he wrote mystery novels. They could use a good sleuth right about now, and having one that was more aware of the supernatural than Devin might have been useful.

But she wouldn't offer it. If Krystal didn't want Caleb to know about the reanimated corpses, then Valerie wouldn't be the one to tell him. It might have been for the best. If the gang worked together, they might have figured out that Caleb was her Twin Flame. Then all hell would break loose, if it hadn't already.

It was just as Caleb suspected. Not only was her alternator shot, but her battery had been completely drained. He reasoned that the former must have quit before the latter. A hasty trip to the local car parts store was only the beginning of the project.

There was no garage for him to work in, so his hands became numbed by the cold metal as he worked loose her old alternator. He had been used to temperatures so high you could cook an egg on the sidewalk, but never this freezing. There was a reason he never ventured above the Mason-Dixon line.

But Caleb was glad to do it. Anything to lighten Valerie's load.

He had tried to lift the thick air in the cab of his truck with small talk about Goldcrest Cove, but she responded in short, clipped answers to cut him off rather quickly. There was a spark of interest in her eyes when he changed the radio station from country to rock, but that was all he was granted. Not even a friendly goodbye before she slammed the door and rushed up the slippery sidewalk to the coffeeshop.

For the last few hours, Caleb went over every word, every gesture, every look since yesterday to try and understand what was bothering Valerie. If living this long had taught him anything, trying to crack the code of the feminine brain was a futile effort. Time had not changed the fairer sex. They were just as complex as they were in the nineteenth century, if not more.

Whatever it was that troubled her, he hated to see her so unbalanced. She had been a spitfire when they first met. Feisty and in complete denial of the attraction between them. Maybe it was her own recognition of that attraction that was throwing her out of sorts. Caleb wondered if he knew her heart better than she did.

So deep in these musings as he tightened and untightened bolts on the Acura engine, he almost missed it. The breeze carried the scent to him just seconds before the crawling sensation down his spine sent him on alert.

Another werewolf was near. One that he knew. But that seemed impossible.

He waited, but heard little above the noise he made under the hood. "Do you think you're being clever?"

Unaccompanied by footsteps, a soft laugh confirmed it. "I still can't pull one over on you, can I?"

Caleb straightened and leaned around the popped hood to see Theo, his former alpha, leaning against the driver side door of the Acura. He wore a leather jacket similar to his own, as black as his hair that was pulled back at the nape of his neck. He had always kept it long through the centuries, he once told Caleb.

Hazel eyes twinkled with amusement as he looked to his former pack mate, the edges of his mouth curving in a deceptively friendly smile, encased in a thick goatee. Caleb knew that smile. It was the same one Theo gave when he was about to lay into a young werewolf for doing something stupid. Perhaps Caleb had been naïve to think that he would never see that smile again.

"You're a long way from Georgia. How'd you find me?" he asked, consciously keeping his heartrate steady and not letting a bit of fear leak out for Theo to feed on. The alpha would pounce upon it if given the chance.

"You think you're the first one to ever try disappearing?" Theo began. "You're sloppy. And you forget that I have connections."

Caleb huffed and turned back to the engine. "And I'm guessing you want me to ask you where I screwed up so you can boast about those connections." He grabbed for one of his adjustable wrenches. "But I won't."

Theo came closer and Caleb could feel the hairs on the back of his neck stand on end. The dominance the alpha naturally emitted was enough, but when he wanted to put a little force behind it, he was perfectly capable.

"And here I was, thinking we were going to be civil with one another."

"You lost the privilege of civility long ago."

"Don't be like that, Caleb."

"Like what?" he snapped. "Like a man who had to watch the people he trusted turn into murderers? Sorry if my lofty morals bother you."

Theo grabbed Caleb's shoulder and forced him to stand upright. "You know I didn't have a hand in what happened to that girl."

He hadn't thought about that girl's face in months. He didn't want to. Each time her memory came to flirt with his guilt, he pushed it away and dove deeper into his writing. That day was the worst of his life, next to the first night he turned into a wolf. The pain of the transformation couldn't compare with the pain of knowing he hadn't done anything to defend that innocent woman. She didn't deserve what they did to her, but it seemed like no one cared how he felt on the subject. They never did.

"You're the alpha," Caleb growled. "You could have overruled their decision."

Theo's eyes went hard. "That's not how the pack works and you know it. We're far more democratic. The votes don't lie."

Caleb jerked his shoulder out of his former alpha's grip and went back to tinkering with the engine. "Fuck the votes. And fuck you for letting them kill her."

"My hand did not spill her blood," Theo bolstered.

He cut a pair of golden, wolfish eyes toward his alpha. "Just because you wash your hands of the deed doesn't make you any less responsible for the crime... As am I..." His voice softened, but the rage continued to seethe beneath his skin. Before he could redirect his ire, he turned back to the car. "What do you want, Theo? Come to drag me back?"

Theo gave them – and their wolves – a moment to simmer down before answering. "Would it be so hard to believe that I came simply to check on you?"

"Given what you did to the last runaway from the pack, yes, it would." Caleb let out a curse as the wrench slipped and his knuckle rammed into the engine block. The bolt had become slick, and refused to turn easily.

"Kendrick ran away because he got into a fight with Ollie over a female and nearly killed him," Theo replied with a hint of annoyance. "He vanished under bad terms. You know all you had to do was ask."

Caleb managed to tighten the bolt on the new alternator and went to the second. "If I had asked permission to leave, would you have actually granted it?"

Theo sucked in a tight breath between his teeth. "Well, no... I probably wouldn't have."

"Then my reasons are justified."

"I wouldn't have let you go, because I would have rather worked through your grievances." Theo angled his head, so he could get a look at Caleb's pinched brows. "I gave allowances for you. I didn't force you to come on the hunts. I didn't make you attend every meeting. Do you know how much flack I caught for making you the only exception to the rule?"

Caleb glanced his way, but wouldn't buy into the lamented look. Theo was just trying to make it all fine, when it was anything but fine. "Can you bring someone back from the dead?"

Theo's nostrils flared. "No, Caleb. I can't."

"Then we're finished here," he replied. "I have no reason to go back to a pack that is so willing to take a life the way they did, and for unjust reasons."

"If I could go back in time and change what happened, you know that I would have tried all I could to spare her."

The wrench slipped again and Caleb had to take a deep breath. One more cracked knuckle and he was liable to tip the entire car over in his anger. "That's not good enough."

Theo let out a long sigh and allowed Caleb to finish working on the alternator before speaking again. "Then I suppose I'll have to leave you exiled in this miserable little town."

Caleb stood straight and held up one of his fingers, which was stained by oil and grease. "First of all, you have not exiled me. I exiled myself if anything." He held up a second. "And this town may be small, but it sure as hell isn't miserable. Besides the cold, I kind of like it here."

The alpha smirked. "You are aware that you're surrounded by witches, aren't you?"

Despite himself, Caleb chuckled. "Very aware." He stooped down to retrieve the fresh battery next to his toolbox. "I'm living with one."

Theo grimaced. "Do you hate us that much that you would rather live with a witch?"

Caleb caught himself smiling, and didn't bother to hide it. If his choices brought Theo pain, he'd rub it in. "She's not that bad. Out of the lot, there's really only two I get along with. Two is better than none, given how many are here." The pause made Caleb look up into his former alpha's contorted, disbelieving face. "It'll freeze like that if you're not careful."

"You do know what witches are capable of, don't you?"

Caleb nodded before returning to the task of replacing the battery. This was far less complicated than the alternator. "I do. We're under a white flag of truce at the moment, as long as I don't do anything to upset them. You being here might ruin that for me, you know."

"Mating with one of their own will upset them, if you hadn't figured that out."

A laugh came bursting from Caleb's mouth. "Whoever said I was mating with a witch?"

Theo leaned his forearms on the fender. "No one said a word. It was all over you when you said that you were living with one."

"You read too much into things," Caleb grumbled.

The alpha laughed. "I didn't have to read. It was a bright neon sign on your face. Whoever the witch is, you like her. Scents don't lie."

They certainly didn't, and Caleb must have become nose-blind to his own hormonal shifts. It had been a while since he'd had to regulate such things as lust or desire around another werewolf. A woman had never crossed his path that could tempt him like Valerie could.

A finger was jabbed in his face. "There it is again!"

Caleb swatted his hand away and just like that, they were laughing together again. As if the past hadn't happened, as if the pack hadn't executed that girl on that hot summer night. As if things hadn't blown up and they could be friends again.

"Just watch your back around these witches," Theo advised. "They can do a one-eighty on you at the drop of a hat. And they're tight too. Tighter than any pack I know. You cross one of them, you cross them all. And believe me, you don't want a coven of witches on your tail."

The errant thought had entered his mind that perhaps this attraction to Valerie could prove fatal. If he broke her heart, if he made one wrong move, she could end it all with just a flick of her fingers. And if she couldn't, the others could.

"You have experience with witches?" he asked as he tightened the last bolt in place to hold down the battery.

"Once in Scotland," Theo replied with a sigh. "That's where the hysteria started, and I wished to God that's where it had ended. Nothing challenges a witch more than persecution. If they had just been left alone, perhaps they wouldn't be as strong of a force as they are now."

Caleb wasn't entirely sure of that, but he had to trust Theo's word. He had been around far longer than any other werewolf he knew. To be sure, he had his flaws, but dishonesty wasn't one of them.

"They told me... They told me about werewolves who had been brought to trial before their council. Do you know anything about that?"

Taking up the rag to wipe off his hands, he turned to Theo who seemed uncomfortable with the question. "Yes and no... I know that it's a bit of a controversial thing. The alpha of the pack should exact judgement on their own kind. It's not the duty of the witches' council to police everything. I don't personally know anyone who has been executed by the council, which makes me question if they truly have. It could just be a carefully placed rumor to intimidate us into giving them a wide berth, which I completely believe. With all this feud business, they could be bluffing, just so we'd stop fighting for another century or two."

Caleb took his alpha's words to heart and nodded. "Well, it's working in reverse as well. I didn't exactly receive the warmest welcome."

Theo slipped his hands into his jean pockets. "I wouldn't expect you to. Witches have got to be some of the snootiest people I've ever met, ancient feud aside. Next to vampires, of course, but that's a different level of snooty altogether."

With a shrug of his brows, Caleb agreed with his old friend. For creatures with so many limitations, vampires talked a big game. At least a witch could back up her threats.

"I know I can't drag you back to Georgia kicking and screaming, as much as I would enjoy trying." Theo turned serious. "But if you stay in this town, and you get into some trouble, don't hesitate to call me. It's a long drive, but I'm willing to make that for you."

Caleb eyed the outstretched hand of friendship that Theo offered. He couldn't forget the sins of the past. The blood on their hands was still too fresh for him to ignore. He might have had a decent setup with Theo's pack, but upon principle, there was no way he could stay.

He could, however, make a choice in this moment. Taking Theo's hand and shaking it wasn't treason against his own ethics. It was an acknowledgement of a bond that should have transcended the drama that turned his pack upside down last summer. Shaking his hand would ensure that if anything should go wrong in Goldcrest Cove, he had an ally on the outside. It was insurance. Nothing more.

Caleb was confident that whatever this thing was with Valerie, it would not turn sour. If it was real, if it was meant to be and she was his true mate, then it wouldn't end in disaster as Theo predicted. It'd be worth it to peel back her layers and see what kind of treasure was hidden beneath.

Chapter 10

Valerie combed her fingers through her hair for the hundredth time that evening. Her nose wrinkled at the little dip of a wave in the silky strands on the back of her head, the evidence that she had worn it in a ponytail all day. She normally didn't, but she normally didn't shower in the morning either.

This entire day felt like a farce. She accomplished next to nothing at the coffeeshop and had spent the last couple of hours meticulously studying and practicing the spells she had copied from Krystal's family grimoire.

She should have been at the Hayden Manor with the rest of them. It had been agreed by closing time that all the witches of Goldcrest Cove would gather there with their grimoires and search for a solution to this zombie problem. Next to the murdering streak that Alexa had unwittingly caused, this was the only supernatural crisis to inflict the entire town. They needed to pull all their resources to send the bodies back to their graves.

And Valerie was stuck at her desk, trying to get a grapple on her dark magic that couldn't have shown up at a worse time.

She tried to tell herself that this training was necessary. But all she had managed to do was burn down half of her white, purple, and blue candles, and traumatize the apple she had been casting over for the last hour or so.

Two of the spells proved useless. Since it was happy, lustful thoughts of Caleb that triggered her magic, she tried the spell to make her mind go completely blank. All that did was waste half an hour as she stared at the wall in a dumb stupor. The other to neutralize all emotions left her feeling numb and depressed. That, Valerie knew for a fact, was not something she needed. She had spent too many years fighting that bone-crushing sadness to have to resort to it now.

The next she tried merely redirected the flow of energy. With her family grimoire safely stowed away where it couldn't be hurt, Valerie allowed her dark magic to bleed over the fresh apple on her desk. The shiny ripe skin turned black and shriveled until the fruit became rotten. Then, she made a conscious effort to return the energy. It took countless tries before the apple could be restored to its former freshness. It left Valerie even weaker than before, but it could be done.

That should have had her jumping over the moon, but after a few more rounds, all Valerie wanted to do was sleep for a thousand years. After the fourth restoration, she realized what it was. When she thought of Caleb, when she allowed herself to fantasize and imagine things, she wasn't exactly drawing upon the energy around her. There was no definite pull or draining. If there was, she would have been energized earlier this morning when she killed her car engine. That much power and electricity would have had her bouncing off the walls, but she felt no different. So whenever she'd reverse the flow, she was quite literally drawing upon her own energy to restore the fruit.

Valerie folded her arms over her desk and laid her head down with a groan. All she could think about was how unfair it all was. She had to go through this all alone. As usual.

Krystal had her mother and sister for support. Alexa was the baby of the group, the poor half-witch that deserved everyone's pity. Amber was too independent for her own good to accept instruction, and Taylor was a natural at magic so that she never needed anyone's help.

Valerie, she had no choice. She had no family to guide her. Never had. Her very human aunt didn't understand, and her parents died before they could play any significant role in her life. She didn't want to do this by herself. Hell, she didn't want to do it at all.

There was one spell she knew of. One spell that had taunted her plenty of times, but she never even dared to read it, for fear that it would seem too easy. A death spell. One to wipe it all clean. She didn't even know why it was in her family's grimoire. Someday, she'd have to copy it to her computer and finally see how simple it was to end it all. All she knew was that it would be quick and painless.

It was times like now when she couldn't see an easy way out that she thought of that death spell and wondered. But that's all she did. She wondered.

The light rapping upon her door wasn't enough to even startle her. She was just that tired. Valerie turned her head to see Caleb poke his way in. He'd been playing video games for the last few hours. They had barely spoken a word to each other since he picked her up from the coffeeshop.

Thor, who had been napping by the bed, lazily got to his feet and stretched, but he didn't bark. Didn't pitch a fit at all. It made her muse over what had happened while she was away. At least Thor seemed to trust the werewolf now.

"You all right?" Caleb asked.

Valerie lazily nodded against her arm. "Yeah, I've just... I've been working on my magic a bit."

His gaze traveled over the desk, starting at the apple and then circling around the candles. "I can tell. I've been feeling it all the way in the living room."

Her brows angled together. "You can feel the magic?"

"How do you think I knew what y'all were?"

Valerie hadn't thought about it. There was still so much she didn't understand about werewolves and what they could or couldn't do. She could sense the paranormal gene within him and other beings, but she never thought that he could feel it in return. It made her wonder if he felt her dark magic all those times it had slipped out on accident.

"It sure takes a lot out of you, doesn't it?"

Valerie nodded again and let out a long breath, the weariness settling in. "It's been a shitty day, too."

Caleb's mouth curved. "I can tell that too... Anything I can do?"

There was plenty he could do. He could lift her up and cradle her in his arms until all the bad things fell away. He could kiss her and test whether there was a breaking point to her dark magic. Maybe if she allowed herself to fully experience her triggers, then maybe she would understand its limits. In that, perhaps there was a solution.

On the other hand, getting too close to Caleb might level the whole house and make it look like two-hundred year old abandoned ruins. There was only one way to find out.

Valerie pushed herself up and stretched her arms over her head in an attempt to get her blood flowing again. "Mind if I watch you play a bit?"

Caleb seemed pleasantly surprised. "By all means."

Much to Thor's confusion, Valerie followed Caleb into the living room. The shooter game had been paused at a relatively safe spot. She knew this game well and had most of it memorized. She grabbed a throw blanket from the back of the couch and settled herself in the very corner of the sectional. Caleb took up the controller and resumed his play.

They were separated by at least three feet. A safe enough distance to play with. If his controller stopped working or if the fabric on the sofa cushions began to fade and unravel, then she'd know a line had been crossed somewhere.

Just being this close had her stomach in knots. She could feel her own pulse jumping in her neck. No matter how tightly she pulled the throw about her shoulders, she still didn't feel anymore protected from the danger of being so near to him.

It wasn't that he was a werewolf. She wasn't sure exactly when she had gotten over that little fact. It was more of the secret knowing of what they were. Two people destined to meet, fall in love, and ruin one another's lives.

The concept of the Twin Flame was one of the most fucked up creations in the universe. Two souls separated at the dawn of time, fated to come back together somehow. They were to challenge one another, to help each other grow and learn about themselves. That's what happened with Krystal and Devin.

It made Valerie sick to think about what it was that she and Caleb had to learn from one another.

The one obvious thing that stood out to her was that he was there to debunk all the myths about werewolves. But what was she supposed to do for him? She didn't know enough about him to even begin to guess.

"Shawn tells me you play some too?" Caleb asked.

It was then she realized how unfair she was to him. Over the last day or so, he had done nothing but try to get close and she pushed him away every time. Could she be blamed, though? She didn't want to hurt him. Didn't want to hurt anyone. Not again.

"That's an understatement," she replied as she brought her knees closer to her chest.

Caleb continued to jam the buttons and wiggle the toggle on the controller. "It's not every day you meet a true female gamer."

Valerie snorted. "You haven't been out enough."

He gave a breezy shrug. "That could be true."

She inhaled and suddenly felt fidgety, like she couldn't get her feet comfortable on the cushion. "I don't think I ever said thank you for fixing my car."

He smiled, but kept his eyes on the screen. "It was no trouble."

"I'll pay you back for the parts when I get paid."

Caleb laughed. "Seriously. Don't worry about it."

"Why?" she demanded. "I can afford it."

"I was doing you a favor."

A bit of Valerie's stubbornness chose now of all times to rear its ugly head. "Okay. So, if you won't take my money, then what do you want in return for the favor?"

Caleb looked at her and paused the game in the middle of a combat sequence. There was a potency in his stare that made her squirm. "Is it really that hard for you to just accept that one person can do a kind thing for someone else without expecting anything in return?"

"That's how the world works."

"Not my world," he affirmed. "You owe me nothing for the repairs. It's what..." His voice drifted for a second, as if he were trying to think of another word to replace the one he wanted to say. "It's what roommates do for each other, isn't it?"

Valerie gave a haughty half-shrug and the blanket tugged at her shoulder. "I've helped Shawn grade papers a few times and he buys me lunch on the weekends. That's the sort of thing I'm used to."

"Well, I'm not Shawn. I'm not like most of the men you know."

That was a fact if there ever was one. Caleb resumed his game and went straight into combat without missing a beat.

"Is it because I'm a girl?" she questioned. "I mean, you're almost two hundred years old, right? Are you just used to catering to ladies?"

One of Caleb's brows lifted. "I'd do the same for Shawn if his car needed fixing."

"So it has nothing to do with me being a helpless maiden or some shit like that?"

Valerie hadn't heard him laugh that hard before. "You? Helpless maiden? Hardly. I knew the moment I saw you in the coffeeshop that you could hold your own. You don't need a man to save you."

She didn't know how to feel about that. In one sense, it was the truth. Valerie had lived her life, dependent on no one but herself. Her aunt fed her and provided a place for her to stay, but all through school, she took care of herself. She learned how to wash her own clothes and cook her own dinners. The only exception might have been when she practiced her magic with Krystal and Alexa.

But within the same proud heartbeat, she felt called out somehow. Was self-reliance a flaw? Didn't guys want to feel masculine and in-charge? A strong woman would shatter that image and render a man useless.

"Some men are intimidated by girls like that," Valerie tested.

Caleb snorted. "Men have egos that are easily bruised."

"And you're not one of them?"

She watched his character's health bar on the screen go into the red. "As I said, I'm not like most of the men you know. I've lived long enough to learn."

Pushing her luck, Valerie pressed further. "Have you had to handle a lot of strong women in that long life of yours?"

Despite being close to death in the game, he smiled. "I'm proud to say that I have."

Valerie's heart went cold. "Oh?"

His eyes slid her way for only a second before returning to the game. Crimson blood splatters bordered the screen. The quickened, muffled heartbeat of the shooter became louder than the rapid gunfire.

"In fact, I prefer them."

Valerie let one of her bare feet slip out from the blanket, feeling her body grow hot. "And why is that?"

Caleb didn't reply right away. His thumbs slammed into the controller as he tried to navigate his way to safety in the game, but it was no use. His lips pursed when all the red faded to black and the death cut scene played. The menu came up, asking if he wanted to continue from his last save point or exit the game. He did neither and leaned back, setting the controller in his lap.

"The thing is," he began as he settled back like a philosopher ready to give a lecture, "a lot of people confuse having a strong personality with being a total bitch. A bitch is closed-minded, mean, hateful, and spiteful. A woman who is strong-willed has a mind of her own. She knows what she deserves and she's not afraid to ask for it. In some cases, demand it. She can hold her own and she has a confidence that can never be shaken. And if someone dares to cross her..." Caleb shook his head and hissed in a breath. "Heaven help the man, because she'll fuck him up in a hurry."

Just like that, Valerie knew he wasn't talking about her. Not anymore. Their definitions were vastly different. She was strong, because she didn't take shit from people. She did as she pleased, because that's how she had always lived. No one had the right to tell her what she could or couldn't do except herself. Perhaps that was why this dark magic frustrated her so much. She didn't want it, but she couldn't give it back.

But in return, she couldn't demand what she truly wanted. She let it pass by like some martyr. Never seizing her dream, never trying for something better. She stayed put, because she thought that's where she deserved to be. She wasn't all that brave, because she was terrified of losing what good she had in exchange for something she knew couldn't happen.

"That fits Krystal perfectly," Valerie said, brushing off whatever vague feelings of inadequacy she suffered from his words.

A puzzled look came over him. "I'm talking about you too."

She gave a mocking laugh. "You don't know me at all."

"It's still early," he said softly. "There's time for you to realize I see far more than what's on the surface."

She expected him to start listing off some long discourse of all the little things she did that made her look whole and secure. Right now, she could have used it. That reversal had her head spinning so much that there must have been a solid ten seconds before she could come up with something else to say.

"You didn't answer my question," she stammered. "Why do you like strong-willed women?"

Caleb's eyes twinkled like he had been waiting for her to ask. "They're a challenge. So many women today are ready to fling themselves at the first guy who shows them a bit of attention. It's the chase, but the word "chase" doesn't describe it well. It's more like..." His gaze wandered to the ceiling as he searched for the word. "It's like stalking. There's time to observe. Everything's slow and gradual. If you chase or pounce too soon, the game's over and there's no chance of getting what you want... It has to be easy. You take your time. You get to know her on her terms and her terms alone. Otherwise, it's forced. He has to earn her trust if he ever expects to have his prey."

Valerie knew Caleb wasn't using magic, but it sure as hell felt like she had just been charmed. The way his voice drawled, smooth and deep, made her toes curl without her conscious awareness.

"And once you have your prey, then what?" She was surprised at how gentle her own voice had become in response to his. She could see why he was an author. He had a way with words

"The real fun begins," he replied with a cunning grin. "A fool would try to tame her, but a wise man would refine her. Smooth the edges just enough. Polish away the darkness she tries to cloak herself in. He'll uncover a diamond in her soul. After he's done with her, she could never be scratched or cracked. Not by anyone. He has to leave her better than the way he found her."

Done with her? Valerie hadn't realized she was holding her breath. His green eyes held sway over her like nothing else she knew. She blinked and broke the spell herself before looking away. "You make it sound like she'd just be okay with someone barging into her life and making her into something she never was."

"She was always a diamond," Caleb said. "She just needed someone to make her realize it."

Valerie could feel his pull, his gravity entreating her to look up, but she wouldn't.

"And once she's caught," he continued, "she'll beg for the kind of refining he can offer."

"Not forced," Valerie whispered, more to herself than to him. She swallowed and began to think that this was a mistake.

She thought of what it would be like to be that woman. The one that he'd refine. Her imagination wandered to what kind of method he'd use. How he would run his hands along her curves to brush away that darkness. How he'd smooth down the edges of her with kisses in all the places that had never been touched by a man. The words that he'd whisper in her ear to calm that wildness in her soul. Calm it, but not break it. They would be wild and untamable together.

She inhaled a great breath to calm her racing blood, but it was no use. Flutters ripped through her body, her nerves singing and vibrating with such an energy that she felt as if she would bust. Caleb was under her skin now. Completely and irrevocably.

Just when she thought her own heart would burst from her ribcage, all went dark. The lights cut off, the television screen became black, and the only light to aid Valerie was the silvery glow sifting through the living room curtains.

"Shit!" she exclaimed, burying her face in her hands out of embarrassment. It was likely that Caleb could still see her.

"Where are the breakers?"

"They may not work," Valerie grumbled. It was likely nothing would work for a good while. Maybe a fuse had blown or the powerlines were practically turned to dust. She didn't know and dreaded to think of how much it would cost to fix.

"It's worth a shot. Where are they?"

Valerie blindly pointed in the direction of the bedrooms. "In the linen closet at the end of the hall."

The cushions shifted as he rose and almost noiselessly made his way toward the breakers. All Valerie could do was inwardly scold herself for allowing it to happen. She should have sensed it coming. The butterflies in her stomach, the tightness in her chest, the lightheaded euphoria. It all pointed to the disaster she was trying so hard to avoid.

A knock came at the door, making her flinch at the harsh sound. After listening to Caleb and the silence, she found it worse than any obnoxious alarm clock. It drew her further out of the dreamy state of fantasy that he had lulled her into.

Maybe it was one of the neighbors. If she cut out the power for the entire block, Valerie was ready to pull on all of her magic to fix this situation. Anything to just make it all go back to the way it was before she decided to sit with Caleb in the living room.

Sliding herself off the sectional, Valerie groped and toed her way in the dark, narrowly skirting around furniture and avoiding the walls so perfectly hidden by the night. The banging became more and more incessant.

"I'm coming!" she shouted to the impatient guest.

But when she opened the door, her mouth hung open. She hadn't seen the person standing on her porch in years. Not since the funeral. And even then, they didn't look anywhere near this young or alive.

Her Aunt Maggie glared at her, fists balled at her sides and wearing the blue dress they had buried her in. Valerie didn't expect a zombie to look so in-tact. The flesh on her bones wasn't rotting away, her hair looked as if it had been recently washed, and there was nothing to suggest that she had been dead at all. The only difference was her ashen, bloodless complexion.

"I know you had something to do with this." Aunt Maggie even sounded the same. The same withering, whiny voice that would scream at her from across the house whenever she was in trouble. "And you had better fix it, or so help me, I'll drag you to the cemetery and put you in my grave to replace me!"

Chapter 11

I t took a wealth of convincing to get Caleb in the driver's seat of Valerie's Acura. His two main arguments were that Valerie's strength wasn't up to the task of driving to Krystal's, and that Aunt Maggie didn't have a driver's license... because she was dead.

In all his decades of living, he had never seen or spoken with someone who had once been dead. Not in a séance and certainly not in the physical. He couldn't stop glancing in the rearview mirror to the ranting corpse, who seemed very much alive, but had no heartbeat and no pulse. It defied science, but then again, so did Caleb and Valerie.

The story of the empty graves and resurrected dead shouldn't have startled him as much as it did. Valerie filled him in on all the details before they left the house. That was before she knew that he'd be coming along. Her protests were weak and half-hearted, but he reasoned that the shock of seeing her aunt on her doorstep had a hand in that.

Now, Valerie had her eyes closed, head bent, and fingers pressed between her eyes.

"Headache?" he muttered to her.

She cut her eyes toward the backseat, and he understood perfectly. Maggie might have been her aunt, but they clearly didn't get along.

"And what about you?" Aunt Maggie chimed in from the backseat. "Are you a wizard or some shit like that?"

For a moment, Caleb wondered if Valerie inherited her sailor mouth from her aunt. "I'm a werewolf," he proclaimed, loud and proud. What was the harm? She'd go right back to the grave and the open, aghast look on her face was oddly satisfying.

"A werewolf? That's a first for me. I've only ever known about witches and wizards, thanks to my sister."

"Warlocks, auntie," Valerie corrected. "They're called warlocks, not wizards."

"Whatever! I'll call them magic men if I want to."

That's when she started in on another tirade about Valerie's father and how he always looked down on her for being the only non-magic member of his wife's family. "I can't help it if I was born without all your special powers. Lord knows I'd want them right now, just so I could go back to rest."

Valerie lifted her head and looked as if she had been struck by an important thought. "Did you... Did you see my parents?"

Parents? Caleb took his eyes off the road to stare at her expectant face. She had never mentioned losing her parents, though he shouldn't have been surprised. Here it was, so close to the holidays and there had been nothing said about visiting her family. He assumed they simply lived too far away or they weren't on speaking terms. He wouldn't have expected them to be dead.

"No, darling," Aunt Maggie replied. Her frazzled tone smoothed out to console her niece. "I didn't see anyone. The last thing I remember is the hospital, and then waking up in the coffin."

All this talk of death, graves, seeing dead loved ones, and coffins made Caleb more uncomfortable than he expected.

Valerie let out her breath, that expectant look now morphed by regret. "Take this left up here," she told him.

Caleb did as she asked, but all he wanted was to turn this car around and take her back to the house. This was all too much for her. Too much in one night. Her problems just seemed to be stacking and he realized now that there was little he could do to help. He had no magic, no way to make this all go away and help her feel better.

Telling her his master plan to win her affection might have been a mistake. It felt like one now, but when he saw that wild flash in her eyes, he thought they were on the cusp of something great that night. A releasing of all she had been holding back since the first day.

Maybe it was too soon. She still needed time to trust. She still didn't realize that Caleb only wanted the best for her and her wild spirit that was nearly smothered by the cares of the world. He'd do whatever he could to help, given his handicap.

They found the mansion and the line of cars parked along the curb in front of the lawn. All the lights were on and the multitude of voices coming from inside told him enough. The place was crawling with witches. The magic hit him like a damn wrecking ball the minute he stepped out of the car and into the street. The breath was knocked out of him, a spread of stars in his vision before he could blink it away.

Valerie felt none of it. And Aunt Maggie certainly didn't, as she continued to complain about anything under the moon. The spell, the witches, Krystal's family, and the inconvenience of having to sneak around at night.

"If someone saw you and recognized you," Valerie said, "it would cause a panic."

"I know that!" Maggie exclaimed. "Just because I've been dead for a few years doesn't make me stupid."

They were at the mouth of the drive before Valerie turned back to stop him, a hand extended out just inches from his chest. "It might be better if you stay out here."

He knew why. He could already see Krystal's sour face. They wouldn't let him inside the house, even if he promised to behave.

"I want to help," he insisted.

Valerie gave him a piteous look. "I know you do, but... there's just not a lot you can do."

He returned the look. "I'm sure there isn't, but I can at least try."

Her lips pulled, telling him that she thought it was a terrible idea. But then, she nodded and they walked up together. Aunt Maggie was the first to pound on the door, as she had done at their house.

Instead of Krystal or any of the witches he recognized, an elderly woman opened the door. Her snow-white hair fell in loose, gentle waves over her shoulders. She smiled and wrinkles formed at the corners of her clear blue eyes and wide mouth. Her features were dainty, delicate, skin pale and thin. One accidental scratch to her arm or cheek would tear her right open. And yet, there was a strength in her frame that convinced him she had to be related to Krystal in some way. It wasn't a muscle strength, but a firmness in tenacity and will that his wolf could sense. As if she had carried the burdens of the world and still managed to get dinner on the table.

"Miss Ruth!" Valerie gasped.

The old woman's smile widened. "Valerie! My, how you've grown!" Her gaze slid to her aunt. "And Maggie, dear, it's good to see you again!"

Everyone was speechless, even Aunt Maggie, whose mouth hung open. Caleb could only guess that this woman should have been dead too. And she must have died in the summer, judging by her lavender sundress.

When Ruth took notice of him, she neither seemed upset, nor perturbed by his presence. He could tell she was a witch, so she would certainly know that he was a werewolf. Or did death dull that sixth sense? "And who is this? You'll have to forgive me, but I haven't seen either of you in so long. Is this a husband or boyfriend?"

The idea that she would even suspect that was nearly hilarious. Valerie stammered before Krystal came to stand beside Ruth. Taking in the sight of her guests left her dumbfounded. And he wasn't sure if it was because of him or Aunt Maggie.

"You... You can't be here!" Krystal proclaimed.

"I know!" Maggie finally shrieked. "You girls need to send me back!"

Clearly, she didn't understand that the comment was meant for him.

Ruth propped her bony hands on her hips. "Did you lose all your manners? I haven't seen you for nearly fifteen years and neither of you have had the decency to say 'hello'. I know I taught you better than that, Valerie."

Valerie's head swiveled from Maggie to Ruth and to Krystal. Confronted on all sides, she must have not known who to deal with first. She threw up her hands and went forward to hug Ruth's thin neck.

"You hug her and not me?" Aunt Maggie bristled.

"Caleb, you need to leave," Krystal affirmed again, her glare as sharp and lethal as daggers.

Ruth embraced Valerie, but frowned to the younger witch. "I taught my granddaughter better manners than that too."

"He's a werewolf," Krystal muttered under her breath, still aware that the front door was wide open and the neighbors could hear if they wanted.

Valerie pulled back to let the nettled grandmother chide her kin. "That's no matter. It's cold out. Come inside – what was your name? Caleb, is it? Come inside. Werewolves drink tea, don't they? I have a pot brewing on the stove. I think you'll like this blend. It's one of my old recipes."

Now it was Caleb's turn to be unsure. It was Krystal's home, but the matriarch of her family was inviting him in with no conditions or reserves. Valerie shot him a look that told him not to squander this opportunity.

It was likely that Miss Ruth would be his defender that night. How could she, a woman who came from a generation grounded in tradition and protocol, openly offer her home to a werewolf? She would have known of the prejudices, and still she held back no measure of hospitality.

"Tea would be great," he said.

They all piled into the foyer and Caleb had to clear his sinuses of the overwhelming magic before venturing too far. Incense and herbs stung at his nose, and he wondered if some ritual were about to take place. All of the noise came from the living room to the right where a fireplace struck golden cascades of light upon the walls. The warmth gave the old home a cheery, welcoming air, despite the suffocating magic.

Caleb made the choice to say as little as possible and stay out of everyone's way until he saw an opportunity to interject. Still, he listened as he followed Ruth into the kitchen.

"Why did you bring him?" Krystal whispered harshly to Valerie.

"He wants to help. Let him," Valerie hissed in return.

"There's nothing he can do."

"That's what I told him, but give him a chance. He's not that bad of a guy, really."

Maggie interrupted them to ask Krystal, "Is your mother here? Would she know how to fix this?"

Right about then, they rounded into the living room and were greeted by the tribe of witches. By the smell of the space, they brought books as old as the house. Maybe older. They all said their hellos to Valerie and made their exclamations of surprise upon seeing Aunt Maggie. There was more chatter, but Grandma Ruth cut his concentration in two.

"Yes, I knew you were a werewolf when you came in," she said in a withered, gentle voice. "I apologize for Krystal's behavior. She really does know better."

Unsure if it was her hospitality or the edginess of being in a house of witches, Caleb's filter wasn't working. "No, she doesn't. None of them want to have anything to do with me ever since I came around."

Blue eyes assessed him before they turned to the pot of steeping tea. "Did you do something to upset them?"

"Nothing except move to Goldcrest Cove."

Caleb looked around the fully-equipped, spacious kitchen. Pots and pans hung from the rack above the island, potted herbs sat on the windowsill above the sink. Everything was clean and crisp, smelling of lavender and cleaning products. It looked like the set of one of those cooking shows on television.

"They're just scared, I guess," Ruth said with a sigh. "It's not often werewolves come around these parts. Especially if there are witches. You're very brave for staying here."

He wanted to tell her that bravery had nothing to do with it. It was all because of Valerie and his need to make a clean break from a bad situation. But he wouldn't trouble Ruth with that. She had enough to worry about, being dead and all.

"Have you met many werewolves?" he asked as she poured some of the tea into a cream-colored mug.

"Oh, yes. I visited a pack once in Virginia. Very friendly bunch. I made it clear I meant them no harm and all was well. That's all it takes. A nice, civil agreement on both sides. You don't get that too often these days."

He took the mug from her. "I'd have to agree with you on that."

She gave him a warm smile. "This will calm your nerves, but give you a little zip of energy. This late at night, we all could use it."

Careful not to burn his tongue, Caleb sipped on the bold brew. The taste was smooth with a hint of nutmeg that delighted both him and his wolf. "They should sell this at the coffeeshop."

Ruth seemed confused at first, but then nodded. "Oh, the coffeeshop. Krystal and Sierra were telling me all about it. I think they would serve it there, but I swore them both to secrecy. It's my recipe, you know."

Caleb took another sip and leaned against the counter, absently listening to the goings-on in the other room. Krystal could be counted on to tell them all that he was there. He caught onto Amber's excited voice, but the others were leery of him.

"So, which of my girls have you latched your pretty fangs into?"

Ruth's playful tone caught him off guard just as much as the question.

"I beg your pardon?"

Ruth gave a soft, husky laugh the way old women sometimes did when they talked about taboo things. "I raised them all, you know. In one way or another. I was there when Krystal and Sierra first discovered their magic. I babysat all of them while they practiced the craft in the backyard or in that same living room. I died with so many memories of them all giggling and screaming over little things like making a book levitate, making their first potion, or charming the cat into dancing."

Caleb relaxed. He could imagine Valerie, a little girl and full of spunk, sitting cross-legged on the floor and causing all sorts of mischief with her friends.

"They're all my little girls," Ruth continued. "So, which one is your Twin Flame?"

Confusion returned. "Twin Flame?"

"Oh, I'm sorry. I suppose True Mate would be a more familiar term. It's all the same, of course."

The tea must have been working, because Caleb didn't go on the defensive at the question. He glanced to the kitchen entryway that emptied into the foyer. They were all too engrossed over what he began to understand was their spell books. They wouldn't hear him. "I... I think it's Valerie."

He wasn't sure why he wanted to be so honest with this woman he just met. It must have had to do with the fact that whatever she learned tonight would go with her to the grave. With that many witches putting their heads together, the problem was bound to be solved soon enough. He didn't have to worry about the old woman snitching.

She nodded her head thoughtfully. "That fits. Valerie's a sweet girl. I'm sorry to see that her aunt left her. She must be all alone now."

Caleb remembered back to the conversation in the car about her parents. "She's got her friends. And she lives with another man. A human. He doesn't know about any of this."

Ruth straightened. "Living with a man? Is your Twin Flame married?"

He had lived so long in this modern world that he forgot how staunch the old customs were. "It's okay for men and women to live together now. We're all roommates."

That solicited a laugh. "A witch, human, and werewolf all living together. Marvelous!"

Emboldened by the tea, he asked, "Did... Did her parents die when she was little?"

Ruth looked down and nodded grimly. "Yes. In a car crash before she was two. She's lived with her aunt all her life. Maggie was the only family the dear thing had left in this world. When did she pass on?"

"Just a few years ago, from what I can tell."

The grandmother nodded as if satisfied. "Good. I'm glad she had someone for the important things. Maggie's not the best guardian in the world, but she was better than nothing. She let Valerie do just about anything she wanted, as long as she didn't bother her. I suppose I looked after her the most when she was little." Ruth turned plaintive. "Do be gentle with Valerie. She's had it rough, living with non-magic folk and all."

He could understand that. Neither of his parents were werewolves. No one understood him in those formative years as a teenager and young adult. He knew what it was to grieve for family, and how to move on from a blow like that. He still thought of them from time to time, but the sadness had worn away to nothing as the waves of life beat against it with each passing year. Valerie was an adult now, but her own pillars of loss hadn't been swallowed by the tide yet.

Miss Ruth let out a long sigh as she gazed toward the living room. "I hope, after all these years, she's forgiven herself."

Caleb grimaced. "Forgiven herself? For what?"

Old misty eyes turned to him. "For everything. For the death of her family, for being such an outcast, for just breathing." She blinked a few times to whisk away the coming tears. "I remember once, when she was four, coming up to me and asking if it was her fault that her parents had died. Something happened at school. I think some of her magic slipped out and she caused some trouble for the teacher.

But it made her wonder what else her magic had done. I had to explain to her that she was too young to have magic when her parents died, but that wasn't the end of it. There was a lot of crying, a lot of blaming, and a lot of heartache over the years. She seems all right now, but... I wonder if she's stopped thinking of herself as a... a bad omen, I suppose."

Caleb held his mug a little tighter. "I... I can't speak for her. I honestly don't know her all that well to know if she does or not."

Ruth gave him a loving pat on the arm. "That's all right, honey. This old soul can go back to the grave without knowing everything."

With a bit of shame for thinking it, he wondered if that could be his angle into earning her trust. It could bridge the gap between their worlds. They'd find a commonality in all the vast differences, and she would see that he could hold her bleeding heart steady in his strong hands. That almost felt like exploitation.

"But there are some things I *should* know. You said that you only 'think' it's Valerie. I saw the way you two were looking at each other."

Caleb only shrugged as he lowered his mug from his lips and gulped down the tea. "I don't know if she feels the same."

"Of course she feels the same!" Ruth said a little too loudly for his comfort. He didn't want any of the other witches to hear. "Twin Flames always know one another. It's never one-sided. How can you not know that she's the one?"

There was that term again. Twin Flames. He had never heard of it, but it made sense. That connectedness that seemed so obvious and instinctual. "We just met a few days ago."

"Twin Flames recognize one another instantly. Valerie knows her feelings and she won't be able to keep it a secret for long, I promise you. Not with her dark magic growing. It's still soon, so she might be a little scared, but it'll all come out. Just be patient."

Again, Ruth patted his arm with all the motherly tenderness he hadn't known in over a century.

"Dark magic?" he questioned.

A flicker of mischief passed over the old woman's face. "I'll let her explain that to you. It's a witch thing. I know it sounds foreboding, but it's nothing, really. She'll tell you about it in her own time."

Despite being a creature almost two hundred years old, Caleb wasn't a patient man in practice. He wanted Valerie and he wanted her now. But, just as he told her earlier, the thrill was in the game. Stalk, observe, and wait. That would make it all the sweeter when he finally had his fangs in her, as Ruth affectionately put it.

Valerie wanted nothing more than to bury herself alive in that very moment.

"So, it is a witch doing this?" Alexa clarified. They all – with the exception of Caleb who patiently waited in the kitchen – sat around the living room and listened with deep interest to Grandma Ruth.

Seeing the old woman after so many years was not only a shock, but a pleasant blessing. She, among so many others in her life, had been the most influential. She was the grandmother she never had. The only one. Both sets had died before she was born. Nothing but death ran in her family, she used to joke. But now, sitting on the floor near two literal zombies, it didn't seem funny at all.

"This is a very special sort of dark magic," Ruth explained. "There's only been a small handful of cases of it in the whole history of witches." She smiled to the girls she had helped to raise. "Luckily, it wasn't too rare, otherwise there wouldn't be a reversal for the magic."

Half of the girls jerked forward as if the old witch had the key to the universe. They had been combing through all their family grimoires looking for a solution to the spell. That search started long before Grandma Ruth showed up on their doorstep that evening. The only reason they hadn't knuckled down to business was because they wanted to take this opportunity to visit. It wasn't every day that someone came back from the dead.

Valerie should have felt the same about Aunt Maggie, but the feeling was hardly mutual. That old bat could turn to dust on the floor and she likely wouldn't shed a tear. The tightness in her throat was for a completely different reason.

"What's the reversal?" Amber asked hastily, her purple hair pulled back in a loose braid over one shoulder. She, along with Taylor, had come to the Hayden Mansion with their own grimoires to help in the search. Once more, they were all together to help their friends come to grips with dark magic.

"Oh, sweetheart, I don't remember it off the top of my head. Old age and all that, you know."

Some smiled, but cheerlessly, because it was so true.

"It's in my private grimoire," she said, then pushed herself to her feet. Krystal and Alexa, who were the closest, came to aid her.

"We already looked through our rolodex and it wasn't there," Sierra said.

Ruth's eyes twinkled and she shook a finger at her eldest granddaughter. "If you listened, I said my 'private grimoire'."

"You have one that you never gave mom and dad?" Krystal asked as she supported one of Ruth's elbows. They shuffled their way toward the hall and stairs, every witch pouring after her as if she were the Crone incarnate. Right now, she might as well be.

Valerie, too, fell in line, but let herself fall to the back of the flock as they climbed the stairs. As the others passed the kitchen, she glanced in and noticed Caleb was looking for her too.

His lips mouthed the words, "Are you okay?"

No, she wasn't. It was a lot. First her dark magic ruining a potentially romantic and insightful moment with Caleb, then her Aunt Maggie showing up, and now this might have just all been confirmed to be her fault from the start. No, she was far from okay.

But she nodded anyway and gave him a weak smile.

"I kept it in your mother's old bedroom," Ruth told them. "There's a handy little hiding spot under the floorboards."

Sierra and Krystal exchanged skeptical looks and it was the younger who decided to give the news. "They gutted her room a while back to make it into an office."

Grandma Ruth wasn't pleased to hear that at all. "What? After I made it into a wonderful meditation room?"

"Dad thought it would serve the family better to be an office when he wasn't with the council."

Mentioning that the room still held a magical purpose, even if it was an administrative one, settled Ruth's displeasure. "Well, did he pull up the floor?"

"No," Sierra replied.

"Then it'll be right as rain. We'll just have to move the furniture a bit for all of us to squeeze in, I suppose."

They reached the landing and Valerie couldn't help but take another look down to the foyer. Caleb was leaning in the kitchen archway, his thumbs hooked on his jean pockets and head tilted lazily as he gazed up at her. Valerie wasn't sure if she'd ever get used to that purposeful way he studied the world – and her. Every detail carefully noted and logged somewhere in that handsome head of his.

She steeled herself and turned away to follow the others into the office. It certainly was a tight fit. Bookcases lined the walls and a desk sat nearly in the middle, stacked with files and papers pertaining to things that none of them were supposed to know about. The council business was always a sensitive and secretive matter for Gordon Hayden, and he wouldn't have appreciated so many of them crowded into the room at once.

Grandma Ruth spun in circles, her white hair framing her face as she muttered to herself. "Now... Was it by the window... No... Well, perhaps. Moonlight comes through there quite nicely. It makes sense... But did I put it on the closet side or...?"

Without waiting for the old woman to make up her mind, every witch fell to the floor and began running their hands along the cracks and grooves. Nails tried to pry up the boards and fingertips tested knotholes. All but Alexa and Ruth were on their knees, bumping into one another.

Finally, Taylor let out a little yip of delight and then came the cracking of wood. Everyone looked to see her stumble backward on her rump and a piece of a floorboard between her hands. The tiny plume of dust hung in the air where she had yanked it up.

Like silly children, they crawled over to the hole and pushed aside the straw insulation. Krystal pulled out the aged grimoire bound in a leather that had been dyed a deep, rich shade of burgundy. A golden "J" was embossed on the front to stand for Ruth's maiden name.

Only then did everyone clamor to their feet and to the desk where they could open the grimoire and flip through the pages.

"Hold on, now!" Ruth cried. "That's my grimoire and I deserve to be the one to open it after so many years!"

Out of respect for the matriarch, they all scuttled aside and let the old woman pass. Her fingers, long and veiny, glided over the cover with such tender affection that Valerie felt hypnotized by the experience.

The cover and pages that hadn't been turned for well over a decade, crackled in protest to her handling. The illumination and delicate, precise calligraphy for every spell and potion was so gorgeous that soon, they were all entranced by the shiny new-to-them grimoire.

Like walking through a familiar house, Ruth found the spell easily. There was a sigil that needed to be drawn, while Ruth called for five black candles, five white candles, a bowl, sulphur, basil leaves, tamarisk, ginger, rue, peppercorn, pennyroyal, and rosemary oil.

"Really?" Amber questioned. "All of that?"

Grandma Ruth gave the most difficult witch a sassy look. "This is some old magic, honey. My grandmother taught this to me and she was taught by her grandmother, and so on. It's to reverse the effects of necromancy."

Valerie knew the term from her videogames. Reanimation of dead things to serve a purpose. Never had she imagined it would be an aspect of her dark magic – or someone else's dark magic.

Sierra and Taylor instantly fled downstairs to retrieve the items while they all rehearsed the Latin incantation that accompanied the reversal.

"Is it just for necromancy or... or all dark magic?" Valerie was scared to ask too directly, but somehow, Grandma Ruth looked as if she knew exactly what she was asking. Grandma Ruth knew everything, even if she had been dead for fifteen years.

"Sorry, dear. Just necromancy. And it'll be subtle enough that the caster won't even know it has been broken." That's when she turned to Krystal. "So, you need to call your parents and tell them what's happened. No more secrets or excuses. This is a powerful dark magic. They will have a list of all the witches and warlocks who have this gift and they all need to be accounted for. You know that necromancy is forbidden. The punishment used to be death, and it still is in some situations."

Valerie hoped that no one saw her face turn white. Death? She hadn't hurt anyone. Not really. And if she did, she didn't mean to. By now, she had reasoned that if her dark magic wasn't fueling her with all this new energy, then it must have been going somewhere. Why not into the completely lifeless bodies around Goldcrest Cove? It made sense to her, who knew so little.

All that mattered now, was that everything would be fixed. Then, she'd have to take preventative measures. Maybe if she turned herself into the council, they would know a solution. Or perhaps, if they couldn't find their culprit in this roster of necromancers, they would come to Goldcrest Cove and pick her up personally.

Either way, she was fucked.

Sierra and Taylor came back with everything. All the candles, the herbs, and oils. Grandma Ruth gave her directions and mixed everything into a bowl. The scent of the herbs made them all a little dizzy, and Valerie's thoughts drifted to Caleb downstairs. What would he be smelling? What would he feel? A spell this powerful would stretch across the entire town and he was already sensitive to the magic. Hopefully he wouldn't run out of the house and leave her stranded.

The circle was cast, the sigil drawn in white chalk on the floor. Grandma Ruth and Maggie – who was thoroughly weirded out by all the witchery going on – stood in the center, their ashen cheeks smeared with the herb concoction.

"This will send everyone's soul back to the ether and these forms we've taken will disappear. It's the herbs that will bind us to the others who have been awakened."

Aunt Maggie just nodded, stricken mute by the strangeness of it all. Valerie had always been careful never to practice her magic in the house when she was around. She wasn't sure how careful her mother had been when they were growing up, but Maggie was not pleased by any of it, regardless.

Final, tearful goodbyes were given to Grandma Ruth.

"Are you sure you don't want to call mom before... before you go?" Sierra asked, her voice thick with emotion.

Ruth sadly shook her head. "We've already given out final farewells. To have to give them again would be too much, even for my Catherine. Just say that you found the grimoire some time ago and put two and two together. You're both smart. They'll buy it." The old woman gave a playful wink and then backed onto the special sigil.

All six of the remaining witches distributed themselves in the circle and held hands. Magic concentrated within the circle, their mouths forming the complicated incantation that would send all the zombies back to their final resting places. It would be as if they were never taken.

The loose strands on the crown of her head rose. A tingling power passed through the connection they had made. The air became electrified, infused with their magic. One witch could accomplish much. Three could perform miracles. Double that, and there wasn't a force on earth who could stop them. That's how it felt to Valerie at least.

Three times they proclaimed the spell. That's all it took. Some had their eyes closed to focus on channeling their magic, but Valerie kept her eyes open. That allowed her to watch both Grandma Ruth and Aunt Maggie's forms begin to shimmer and flicker like a mirage.

Just before they disappeared completely into a pixelated distortion, Aunt Maggie gave her a smile and friendly wave. She had what she wanted. A way back to the afterlife or wherever it was she had gone to.

She returned the smile, and found she didn't have to fake it as hard. For the first time in years, she had a piece of her family back. It wasn't the family she wanted, though. For just a minute, she wished her parents had been resurrected instead. She had so many things to tell them, and she imagined that they would have words for her. They had been torn apart far too soon. She wanted to know what her mother's embrace felt like. What her father's voice sounded like. Just once, she wanted to look at them in the real, not just in a faded photograph.

The devilish thought came to mind that if she could just utilize her dark magic then perhaps she could bring them back from the dead. She'd do it quietly without anyone else knowing. Just for the chance to see her parents again, and then she'd give it up forever. Just for a few minutes, or maybe an hour. Just long enough to meet them.

But that was selfish. It would be pulling their spirits out of the universe, it'd be like reversing fate and death itself. There was a reason it was forbidden to practice necromancy. It was a perversion of the natural cycle.

But the tears on Valerie's cheeks didn't care about rules and laws. She wanted her family. She wanted to feel this togetherness again, to feel like she belonged to something. Krystal and the other witches were wonderful friends. They could never be replaced. But she still longed for the one thing that had been stolen from her, ripped from her life by the unfair reaper. That's what it was. Just damn unfair.

Chapter 12

They had been right. Caleb was useless at Krystal's house. If anything, he served as a necessary chauffer for Valerie. After that ritual to expel all the zombies from Goldcrest Cove, she looked dead on her feet. She insisted that she didn't need help getting to the car, but Caleb wouldn't let go of her arm. Valerie would have fallen into a puddle on the floor if he had.

It was a fortunate thing that Grandma Ruth had given him that tea just before the ritual. Something in it had made him immune to the effects of the magic that pulsated and radiated through the mansion. It merely glided over and around him, like he was a boulder in the middle of a swift-moving river. It barely touched his wolf, but it braced for the fallout that never came.

The effects of the tea calmed him, helped him to think rationally, even through the morning after. There was so much to consider. Dark magic, Twin Flames, zombies. It was a lot, and the internet could only help him so much.

A late-night search yielded nothing for the enigmatic dark magic they all spoke of, but there were countless resources about Twin Flames. It was just as Grandma Ruth said. The concept of the werewolf's True Mate and the witch's Twin Flame were one and the same.

A partner, typically romantic, who helped their counterpart in one way or another. To grow and learn, to expand spiritually and emotionally, to complement one another in this walk of life. They shared the same energy, the same essence, and it could never be brushed aside or ignored. It was everything the myths said about it, and everything he didn't want to believe. But it explained so much. Their instant connection, the pull of his spirit to hers, and why his wolf adored her more than anyone else he had ever met.

If Valerie was his True Mate, and he was her Twin Flame, then what did that mean? Where did they go from here? His usual tactics were pointless. The idea of the stalking game was to lure them in, but it seemed that they were bound in their souls already.

The only variable lay in the case where one Twin Flame denies the other. One was doomed to be the chaser, and the other bound to be the runner. Was that Valerie and Caleb? She was certainly behaving like a runner, skirting around their intimate conversations and pushing him away. Yet, he pursued her with no reservations. That game of cat and mouse could ruin them. Unless Valerie decided to give up and give in.

More interesting than anything else he read, was that Twin Flames were meant to heal one another. He could see that need plainly in Valerie, but he didn't need any healing. He had lived for over a century and a half. He had enough time to work out the kinks and the wounds of the past had scabbed over. What could Valerie possibly do for him?

Perhaps the most terrifying reality set in as he was pouring himself a cup of tea at six in the morning. Caleb was nearly immortal. He aged slowly. It had taken him this long just to appear in his early thirties. Witches aged like any normal human. If Valerie was his Twin Flame, she would grow old and die. They wouldn't be together forever. Could he bear that sort of loss?

Always the fatalist, he sighed and took a sip of his brew, processing through the grief he had yet to fully experience. He had lost family and friends over the decades, but never a lover. None that he was present for anyway. Could he hold Valerie's fragile hand as she slipped from this world? Would he be willing to live another three or four hundred years without her? And what of children? How would they turn out?

Caleb briskly shook his head. They hadn't even proclaimed their love for one another and he was already thinking of babies. Did that mean he loved her? That he was willing to spend the rest of his life – her life – with a witch? Settled in this little Massachusetts town without a pack? With half-breed toddlers running about?

The smile that softened the thoughtful pucker of his lips was his answer. If Valerie was willing, he would be too.

He tilted his head to listen for her again. She was still dead asleep, her breathing soft and steady, almost drowned out by Thor's occasional snoring in her bedroom. They didn't pull into the drive until close to one in the morning. After a fast shower, she had dragged herself to bed while Caleb stayed up all night with his little research project.

Glancing to the clock, it was time for her to get ready for work. He wanted to assume that Krystal and the others would forgive her for being late, or even taking the morning off. Then again, he didn't know how lenient they all were in that regard.

He set down his mug and went to making a batch of coffee for her. With a cup of the brew in one hand and a jumble of nerves knotted in his stomach, he went to her room. Thor didn't rise right as he cracked open the door. The dog, completely oblivious to him, must have been just as exhausted as his owner.

The room was dark, but he could pick his way through the cluttered mess on the floor toward her bed. He sat on the edge, knowing full well that this was all too forward. Not just for her, but for him. He never entered a lady's room without permission. But they were Twin Flames, weren't they? Did that shatter all etiquette?

The only part of Valerie he could see was the crown of her head, a tangle of dark hair against her pillow. The edge of the comforter was tightly tucked underneath her to block out the chill in the room. If she were a man, and if he had confidence in their friendship, he would have yanked the covers from her sleepy grasp and dragged her out of the bed.

Instead, he set the hot coffee on her nightstand, not twelve inches from her buried face. Valerie might not have been a werewolf, but she'd smell that pretty quickly. Patience paid off and he smiled when she shifted beneath the comforter.

A head emerged and green eyes squinted in the direction of the coffee. Without makeup, without perfectly styled hair, Valerie was even more beautiful. Natural, raw, and wild. Just as he liked her.

It took a moment before her groggy gaze landed on him. Valerie sucked in a breath and was back under the covers with a groan.

"It's past six," he softly told her. "What time do you need to be at work?"

Valerie grumbled out a, "six forty-five", but wouldn't come out again.

"It's best you get up then."

Before he realized what he was doing, his hand was on her leg. Just her calf, but it was enough to make her muscles seize beneath his palm, the blanket as their only barrier. She didn't move at first, and then jerked her leg away. He recoiled his hand, understanding his error.

"Sorry. Not a morning person?" Covering it up wouldn't change the fact that there was still a protocol in place. Twin Flames or not.

Valerie's hand slithered its way up and blindly reached for the coffee before she allowed the rest of her to resurface. "No, I'm not. Where's Thor?"

No doubt what she really wanted to know was why the dog hadn't chased him out already.

"Still sleeping," he whispered, gesturing toward the dresser were the dog continued to snore. "He's just as wore out as you."

That seemed to wake her up more than his sudden appearance in her room. She half turned over to look and after a few seconds of watching the dog breathe, she seemed to calm down.

He couldn't imagine her looking any more adorable than she did now. Her eyes half-shut, her lips relaxed and begging to be kissed. It'd be so easy for him to lean over, brace himself against her and have his way with her. He wanted to. He even inched forward just a tad before realizing he had fallen prey to the temptation and stopped himself.

His mind wandered to the future, of mornings when they would wake up beside one another. Of holding her all night long, her curves fitting against him as if they were made for one another. They hadn't yet. Hadn't even hugged. But he knew that's how it would feel. Somehow, instinctively, he knew that life with Valerie would be dazzling. The best years of his life would be spent by her side, and he couldn't point to one logical, rational reason why. Everything about her drove him crazy with longing. But she acted like she couldn't care less.

Valerie was wearing a plain black shirt with torn off sleeves, revealing her slender but strong arms that he hadn't had the privilege of seeing before.

As she sat up and took a long, deep swig of her coffee, he saw a bit of a tattoo peak out at him from the inside of her bicep.

"What's that?" he asked, his mouth running away with him.

Valerie smoothed back a bit of her hair and then opened up to let him get a good look. It was a simple design. Two circles touching with black dots in the center and inverted parenthesis touched the far outer walls of the circles, opposite from where they touched. He wished he could have reached out and stroked along that patch of skin and trace the bold black lines.

"It's a moon glyph," she replied, the coffee making her civil. "We all have one. The witches, I mean."

Caleb nodded. He had heard of moon glyphs, but it never interested him to learn more about them until now. "What does it mean?"

Valerie was half-way through another long draught of her coffee, and by the time she tipped the mug back down, it was as if he had never asked the question at all. "Do you mind leaving? I have to get dressed."

"Do you want any breakfast?"

She sullenly shook her head, eyes closed as she held the rim of her mug close to her lips, the steam rolling up from the brew. Valerie didn't just look tired or foggy, but downright ill. Though she was still stunning, her skin seemed to lack a certain brilliance. He wanted to convince himself that it was just because she was bushed after everything that happened, but he began to question her health instead.

"Are you sure you want to work today? You had a long night. What with the magic practicing and that ritual, you must be – "

"I'm fine," she snapped. "Please, just leave me alone."

And there, she spat her fire. But it wasn't the same sort of fire. It took on a harsher quality than he was used to. It was still a bit of sass and irritability, but there was a desperation in the order that made his wolf inwardly whimper. He wanted to fix it. Whatever it was. The way he wanted to fix it for that girl in Bainbridge who saw too much.

But Valerie didn't want it fixed. At least, that's what she made herself believe. So Caleb stood, the mattress creaking from the release of his weight.

"I'm making pancakes and bacon. If you want any, you're welcome to them before you head out."

He shut the door behind him and he thought he heard something of a sniffle from behind. Just why she made that noise, he didn't know. He waited for the saline scent of tears, but they never came, no matter how long he stood outside her door.

Had his gesture upset her that much? Or was this just another symptom of last night? He had half a mind to call up Krystal himself and tell her that Valerie was too sick to work. But once more, he pulled himself out of it. It was Valerie's life. That was her call to make, not his. They may have shared the same soul, but he didn't have to dominate her life. He wasn't her alpha. He had to learn that.

He wanted to fix every problem and shield her from the world that threatened to make her cry. He wanted to be her protector and her lover.

But he had to be patient. Damn patient.

She couldn't drink enough coffee. Her third mocha before noon was clutched between her hands, warming her palms as she tried to find her center.

Valerie couldn't think now. Not about the way Caleb's touch nearly sent her over the edge, or how she wanted nothing more than to grab him and pull him down into bed with her. She couldn't linger on the way he looked at her tattoo and how she wanted nothing more than to tell him everything about it, because he showed some vague interest. So few people ever saw it, and those who did would never ask. So she never got to tell them what the "life" moon glyph meant to her.

She didn't want him to care. Not about her tattoo, about her health, or anything. It activated her dark magic far too soon. By the time he left the room, that once perfectly red, unblemished apple ripened until it stank on top of her desk. She had no energy to restore it, so she threw the fruit away and denied anything from Caleb before she could get out the door.

All through the morning shift, she allowed herself to snap at Krystal and Alexa. She refused to work the register, spoke so little to anyone, and played off that she was just tired. That was partially true. Her eyes didn't want to stay open, her muscles and bones ached, and everything felt out of sorts. Being mean, forcing herself to hate and be cruel, was the only way to survive now. If she were happy, if she allowed herself to feel joy and peace like the world was all right, because she had Caleb, then they would have another zombie crisis on their hands.

Valerie felt as if she were torn between doing what was right for herself and doing what was right for the whole. This was the first time in her life that she could forget about her family, her childhood, and all the reasons she would be tempted to look at that death spell in her grimoire. Having Caleb, knowing that he was her Twin Flame, changed everything. As much as she didn't want to admit it.

Having him in the coffeeshop didn't help either. He had come in just an hour ago with his laptop and she let Alexa make his tea. She wouldn't even acknowledge his little wave when she turned in his direction. She played off like she didn't see him. That she was too busy to bother. But it broke her inside.

It was as if there were two little imps on each of her shoulders. One urged her to give into this happy feeling of being wanted and cared for, regardless of who it would hurt. The other told her to bottle it up, hide it, obliterate it if she had to. Anything to avoid another disaster, because her happiness didn't matter. It never did. Why should that change now?

These imps were playing tug of war with her heart and mind. All she wanted was for everything to just stop moving for a minute, so she could breathe.

"So, I called my parents," Krystal told them once the morning rush had ground to a near-stop. There were perhaps three other customers in the store – Caleb excluded from that number.

"What did they say?" Alexa asked, ever eager to see Krystal's parents again. The girl nearly worshiped any witch who knew more than she did.

"They said they would look through the register for anyone with necromancy dark magic and check on them." Krystal paused and looked straight at Valerie. "They said they wanted to make sure everything was all right, so they're coming."

"Fuck," Valerie hissed, unable to stop it from escaping her throat.

"Did any of those spells help?" Alexa questioned, her voice sounding so pitiful and sympathetic that Valerie couldn't even look at her.

"No, not really." She wasn't about to tell them how terribly they all failed. "I'm going to have to get creative or live in a cement box."

"No," Krystal crooned. "That's why I'm telling you that my parents are coming. Maybe we can talk to them and see if they know something. We didn't get much of a chance with my grandma last night, but now we have another grimoire to go through and – "

Valerie nearly slammed down her coffee. "Stop! Just stop! I don't want to talk about this anymore, okay? It's hard enough with everything else going on and... I just don't want to talk about it."

The two other witches were quiet for a moment. These sorts of outbursts weren't uncommon, but the glistening sheen over Valerie's eyes was unexpected. They had never seen her cry. Hell, Valerie couldn't remember the last time she allowed herself to ball her eyes out. This was as far as she'd allow the tears to come. No further.

"Is it about your Twin Flame?" Alexa asked. Out of all of them, she was the most romantic. Dreaming about knights in their shining armor atop a white horse. She asked for all the juicy details after a date, swooned over the slightest act of kindness, and ogled over every cute guy that walked in the coffeeshop.

But Valerie wouldn't cave. Not to her, who would latch onto the truth like a damn wolverine and never let go. If she knew Caleb was her Twin Flame, she'd never stop hearing that sweet, piping little voice.

"No, it's not."

Krystal saw through it and propped her hand on her hip. "You still haven't told us who it is."

"How should I know who it is?" Valerie shrugged. "He must have just been some random dude that walked in one day."

"When I met Devin, I felt that instant connection."

Valerie sneered. "Well, I'm not like you. I've never been all that gushy about guys before. You know that."

"But... Just... nothing? You don't feel a thing? No pull, nothing?" Alexa's sentimental mind just couldn't compute.

"Nope," Valerie announced. "Not a thing. Maybe I didn't see him. Maybe he just walked by the shop and didn't come in. It could be a number of things. We don't fully get all this Twin Flame shit anyway. You and Amber are the only ones who have. Maybe Amber never properly met her Twin Flame either. She never talks about him."

Both Alexa and Krystal seemed thoroughly disappointed. They just didn't understand that a happy ending was never in her fortune. No matter what her horoscope or tarot card readings said. Good things just didn't happen to her, and this dark magic nonsense was no exception. Nothing good could come of it.

"That's just so tragic," Alexa sighed.

"No, it's life. The fact that I crossed paths with my Twin Flame at all is damn inconvenient." Valerie took another sip of her coffee and wished there was something a little stronger in it.

"Promise you'll come over tonight?" Krystal asked, reaching out to take her arm. "My parents are bound to know something and I would rather have you ask them yourself. I'd feel weird telling them."

Part of her wanted to scream that she wanted as few witches to know as possible. She didn't want anyone, especially not the council, to realize how destructive she could be. That cement box might have been a joke, but who knew if it would become a reality.

Thankfully, she didn't have the chance to give her answer. A new customer walked in, and Krystal turned back to the register. Valerie, looking for any excuse not to deal with the crisis at hand, put down her mug and waited for the order.

"I'll be there," Alexa whispered. "If that would help you feel more comfortable."

Honestly, it wouldn't. "I appreciate that," was all she said.

Valerie didn't want to suffer forever. She didn't want to feel lost and desperate. She wished there really was a way to control her dark magic. Because, deep down, she wanted to enjoy this thing she might have had with Caleb.

But what if there was no help to be had? What if Krystal's parents saw her as a danger to society or a perverse witch who couldn't be trusted to live on her own? What if she opened up about all this dark magic and they imprisoned her? Or put her on that register of necromancers who had to be monitored at all times? What if, in her attempt to reach out for help, she was condemned for it?

It was like losing her parents all over again. Dealing with the grief and depression, but unable to turn to anyone for support. They would just label her and push her aside. She wouldn't survive that rejection. She couldn't.

Chapter 13

Caleb's hands stilled over the laptop keyboard. He hadn't been able to type one word. Not since Valerie and the other witches began talking. So many mysteries in what they said, and so many slashes that cut too deep.

She openly denied him. Denied they were Twin Flames. Grandma Ruth had said that Valerie would feel the same as he did. If that were true, she would feel this head-over-heels, too far gone, drifting in the clouds sort of ecstasy that he had felt. Until now that was. She had knocked all the air from him and he was plummeting back to earth.

It lined up with how she had behaved earlier that morning, but to be denied as if he never existed, as if they shared nothing, hurt far more than he expected. He thought she was different than the other witches.

The wolf came lose. In a harsh, unthinking decision that was so unlike him, Caleb resolved to do the same. If that's the way she wanted to play it, then he would too. He'd give her the cold-shoulder. He'd be polite and respectful, but the hunt was put on pause. Just until something changed in this stupid, frustrating game that he hadn't signed up for. He'd slink back into the shadows and wait. Wait for her to come to her senses.

Whatever this dark magic was, her friends knew about it and getting help involved older, wiser witches. He'd wait until all of that passed. Then she'd be ready for him again. And perhaps, by then, her friends wouldn't be so unforgiving of him, and she could finally admit their soul connection.

These distracting issues compelled him to close his laptop and sit back with his tea. He needed to clear his head before starting the next scene, otherwise he'd be writing in his own frustrations that didn't match the motives of the serial killer in his story. Not exactly.

He took a sip and watched the room, studying the diversity of the customers as he had a few times before. It was all casual enough, until the door opened. Something in the air instantly changed and his wolf growled at the intangible shift. Caleb watched the man that brought with him this uncomfortable feeling. It was nothing in the way he looked, but in his vibe and scent. And most intriguingly, the noises he failed to make as he walked to the counter to order a coffee to-go.

The coffeeshop wasn't crowded, but it wasn't empty either. Ever hyper-aware of his surroundings, he had pin-point focus on each person in the room. If someone left or someone came in, he'd notice the changes immediately. A new smell and another heartbeat. This man certainly put off an odor. It was so vile and rancid that Caleb wondered how long it had been since he showered. The subtle scent of the grave on Grandma Ruth and Aunt Maggie were nothing compared to this.

Another characteristic of the grave kept Caleb's attention. No heartbeat. Not even a faint, muffled one. He strained his ears, but there was nothing going on in that man's chest. He should have been dead. Instead, he looked very much alive. Standing straight, his skin slightly tanned by the sun, his black hair thick and curling around his ears, nothing seemed off. Maybe his brown, care-worn trench coat and leather gloves, but that wasn't so unusual due to the weather.

Krystal and the other witches weren't alarmed in the least. They treated him just as any other customer. Caleb narrowed his eyes upon the man, looking for anything else that would tell him who he was. His first thought was that this might have been another zombie that had risen from a cemetery. They might have purged the city of them last night, but what if this was a fresh one? The only off-thing is the man's skin tone and the way he wasn't dressed for a funeral, as the rest had been.

Not a hint of magic about him either. He didn't look at Caleb, didn't get a suspicious glint in his eye when he looked at the girls. He even properly paid for his coffee and slipped a dollar into the tip jar by the register.

The man turned with his cup and walked straight out the door. No mess, no confrontation. But that smell and the lack of a heartbeat didn't have him convinced. Caleb waited a while, sure that he'd be able to smell the man from across town. Then, he packed up his laptop and marched toward the counter.

"Look after this, will you?" he asked Krystal, who was the closest to him. He slipped the laptop underneath where they kept their purses.

"We don't watch – "

"I don't give a shit what you do or don't do for legal reasons," Caleb snarled, a bit of his dominance leaking. "I'm telling you to watch my bag. I'll be back for it."

Without another word, he turned, knowing full well that Valerie's stare was upon him, burning a hole through his shoulder blades as he left the coffeeshop. He didn't even look her way. It'd be too hard after all he just heard. He'd have to push her out of his mind for this one hunt.

The man was long gone from Johnson Avenue, but he could still follow his scent over the cold wind and snow. He turned to his right after he exited the store and followed the sidewalk down to Reichman Street. To the left was the historic, southern district of the city. To the right was the school, church, and park. The stench of death went that way.

Caleb came to the park and kept his distance. The playground was empty, too cold for any child to be out climbing on the jungle gym. He heard the pounding foot beats of a jogger toward the north end, and a couple walking their dog along the shoveled pathways. A few benches were caked with snow. Others, like the one that the dead man sat on, were cleared.

He was alone, sipping his coffee and staring across the patchy field of dead grass and snow. A thin veil of gray clouds masked the sun, giving Goldcrest Cove a dreary and somber feel. Caleb, knowing full well that he had not been detected, leaned against a tree just outside the park and watched the man over the iron fence that separated them. He was a good fifty yards or so away, but he could still hear him gulp down his coffee.

About fifteen minutes of nothing passed and Caleb was tempted to approach him when a police squad car pulled up along the curb near the park entrance. Out of the driver's seat came an older man – perhaps in his fifties - in an officer's uniform, his regalia noting him as someone important in the department. Maybe the chief, but he hadn't met the man before. He only knew that Devin didn't wear anything that adorned.

The cop looked around and then headed straight for his target.

Caleb turned so he wouldn't be spotted, shielding himself completely behind the tree, though he could still hear everything.

"So, was it them?" the cop asked.

The man who smelled of death, whose voice he marked at the coffeeshop, replied, "Yeah, it's them. All three of them."

"Shit." Gloved hands were briskly rubbed together to generate warmth. "That's going to be a problem."

"I think they had help," the other said. "A spell that powerful would take more than just three inexperienced witches. They're too young to know anything like that."

"Who would have helped them?"

"I don't know. All I know is that my work was undone."

"Do it again!" the cop insisted. "You're powerful enough. You can raise them all again and then some."

"It barely caused a stir last time," he snapped. "I can't just raise a whole cemetery and control them all. If you want true panic, I need to be able to manipulate a select few. It's too much to raise twenty or more at random and govern every last one. I'm not that powerful."

"Then what the hell are you good for?" the cop growled. "You've done it in the past and you can do it now. If you can't, you know I can just find someone else."

"No, no, no," the dead man replied frantically. "I'm just saying that I need to start smaller and work it up. That's all... The witches will be a problem, though. They must know I'm here and they'll call the council."

"Fuck the council. They can't touch you."

"No, but they can sure as hell make it difficult."

"Don't worry about them. I'll take care of that. You have a job to do and you'll do it." The cop lowered his voice and even Caleb shivered. "You still owe me. Cause a panic, and get me a soul. Kill the witches if you have to. In fact, if you do, I'll shorten our agreement by a few decades and you can go free to do your own business."

"We never agreed on killing other witches."

"Are you denying me?"

A long, pensive pause filled the park. The jogger continued on their route. The couple laughed.

"No. I'm not."

"Good. Then I suggest you get started. I don't want to be here any longer than you do."

The cop stood from the bench and walked away, his boots crunching against the ice and snow.

Caleb didn't need to hear any more. He pushed himself off the tree and began walking down Reichman Street again, though he wasn't exactly sure why. He wasn't sure what he just heard. And he wasn't even sure he knew who to tell. Would the girls know anything to fill in the glaring gaps of this conversation? Did they know something about their police chief that could explain any of it? What about them? Should he warn them? Their lives were in danger, but he had so few details to go on. He didn't even have any damn names. Once again, he felt useless.

He needed a minute to breathe and think. But how could he possibly think straight when he knew that Valerie's life was at stake?

Valerie had barely spoken a word since Caleb left. She had no strength to say anything beyond, "I'm going to go clean up the back." For an hour, she swept the floors, mopped them, and cleaned the toilets until they shined. And she took her time with it. Scraping up every piece of hardened gum under the sinks and polishing the fixtures until they glittered in the bathroom light. Anything to get her mind off Caleb and the way he just left the store. He didn't even look at her.

Again, those opposing imps yanked at her hair and ears. One wanted to feel offended, the other encouraged her to be thankful. Maybe he was falling out of love.

But that's not the way Twin Flames worked. They never simply stopped loving someone. They ran. Unexpectedly and without warning. All this time, she had thought she'd be the runner. Maybe it was Caleb.

It was all too tempting to feed on those bad thoughts, but they were like dynamite. They'd just explode and tear her apart later. She had to force herself not to care that he had unknowingly ripped her heart out and pounded it into the pavement. All because he didn't look at her when he left.

She cussed at herself as she scrubbed at the white porcelain with the toilet bowl brush. "Fucking Caleb. Fucking dark magic. Fucking Twin Flames."

So absorbed in this confused tantrum, she almost didn't hear the commotion up front. Valerie paused and listened, but couldn't make out the excited voices. She dropped the brush into the bucket of sudsy water and stepped out into the back hall. Now, the voices were clearer.

"We weren't expecting you until later," Krystal said, her tone noticeably strained as if she wasn't happy, but tried hard not to show it.

"Oh, honey. Necromancers aren't people to fool with. We packed our bags and got loaded up right away."

It was Catherine Hayden, Krystal's mother and one of the high witches on the council.

"I had a few meetings this afternoon, but this can be claimed as a business trip."

That deep, authoritative, masculine rumble of a voice belonged to her father, Gordon Hayden. He, too, was part of the council and quite possibly the most well-known warlock in this part of the country. Krystal and Sierra were practically royalty just for being their children.

The moment Valerie recognized these magic folk, she about-faced and made to go right back into the bathrooms until they were gone.

"Where's Valerie? I know she's working today."

She cringed at Catherine's question, knowing that her cover was officially blown. With a sigh, she closed the bathroom door again and went to meet her fate. Catherine's dark magic ability was to scry, seeing through time and space to know things that no one else knew. She shared that gift with Amber. So harmless. So easy. Why couldn't she have been gifted with scrying abilities, so she wouldn't be so terrified to face the Hayden family again?

Valerie shuffled out of the hall as Krystal was just explaining further details about the graves and bodies that were resurrected. More specifically, how Devin was working hard at the police station to keep the public panic to a minimum.

"I may not like that he knows about us," Gordon said. "But I do like how he's helping to take care of my little girl."

The man, who was well over six foot and built like a linebacker with a graying goatee, hugged Krystal about the shoulders. She looked like a pixie in the arms of a giant.

The smaller, more petite matriarch spotted Valerie and rushed forward to give her a hug of her own. "Oh, sweetheart! There you are!"

Not one for hugs, Valerie made exceptions for the Hayden family.

"I'm so sorry! If I had known earlier, we would have come last week."

A cold rush of fear shot through her and she went perfectly still. "What?"

Catherine pushed her back, her thin but strong hands taking a firm hold of the young witch's arms. Her warm, exaggerated smile fooled many into thinking she was innocent. But she knew just as much as Gordon, and wasn't afraid to get in between a threat and anyone she cared about. No matter how small that threat was.

"I know, honey," she said in a rather loud whisper. Everyone else at the counter was too absorbed in their own conversation about the necromancer registry to listen. "The minute I locked in on Goldcrest Cove, I found out. Why didn't you call?"

It was just as she suspected. Catherine knew about her dark magic. And it was likely that Gordon knew too. It would have been a long, silent, awkward three-hour drive from New York if he didn't. Did that mean they knew about Caleb too?

Valerie swallowed and tightened her jaw until her molars hurt. She had no answer. None that would satisfy Catherine. She knew better after spending all her teenage years trying to sneak around the woman and failing.

"It's all right," Catherine assured. "We're here to help. You don't have to do this alone."

That's what they always said. But something just never sounded right about that phrase. It was like when an adult told a child who had just received their first shots, "See, that wasn't so bad, was it?" Except, this was in reverse. They always said she wasn't alone, that she had help. But in the end, she never felt like she did. Not really.

Two things caught her notice. The first was that the coffeeshop was completely empty except for them. While lunchtime could be busy for some places on Johnson Avenue, it wasn't for Perfect Books and Brews on most days. The Haydens couldn't have come at a better time to discuss the necromancer problem, and she partially wondered if Catherine could foresee this lull in business.

She also wondered if the older witch knew that a werewolf was approaching their shop. She saw him walk across the front window, a hard and determined look on his face that startled her. Gordon noticed, and turned when the door swung open to admit Caleb.

All stood frozen where they were, mouths silent as all the witches and warlock stared at the werewolf, and the werewolf stared back. Mostly at the tallest man in the room. Valerie wished Caleb would have just looked her way, so he could see her muted pleas to behave. If he just did what Gordon said, there wouldn't be any trouble. But she could already see the storm clouds in both of their eyes. It was as if two alphas were about to clash.

"And who the hell are you?" Gordon asked, taking two lumbering steps forward to confront him.

Caleb straightened and his chest rose a little with pride. "Caleb Lancaster."

"What are you doing here?"

The air inside the shop thickened and nearly choked Valerie. She knew that Gordon could be sensible. He knew the laws better than any magic folk alive. He wouldn't use magic so openly in his daughter's coffeeshop. At least, she hoped he wouldn't.

Caleb's gaze wavered for just a minute and finally landed on her. She gave the slightest, but perceptible shake of her head to tell him not to tangle with the warlock.

"I left my laptop in here earlier," he said calmly. "I came to get it back."

Gordon looked to his daughter. Krystal picked up on the cue and went to grab the bag from under the counter where Caleb had left it. She was about to walk forward and give it to him when Gordon intercepted and did the task himself.

It was like something out of an old Western where two cowboys bowed up to one another. Valerie half expected Gordon to say something like, "This town ain't big enough for a werewolf." Luckily, he wasn't so corny. Instead, he was damn terrifying.

He held out the laptop to Caleb. The werewolf reached out and grabbed the strap, but the warlock wouldn't release right away. Without a sound, without so much as blinking, Valerie could feel the shift in the magical energies.

Caleb must have felt it stronger than any of them, or he was the target. When his face pinched as if he were in some immense pain, she understood.

"Don't you ever get near any of my daughters or their friends again." Gordon's voice was so low, so guttural that Valerie almost didn't hear him. "Do you understand me?"

Caleb stiffened, but his whole body began to tremble as if every muscle had contracted at the exact same moment. He squeezed his eyes shut against the pain, but he wouldn't concede. And he said he wasn't an alpha.

"Stop it!"

Valerie glanced around to see who had spoken, only to realize the frightened screech came from her own lips. And she would have charged forward to get between the men if Catherine still didn't have a hold on her.

It was just enough to break Gordon's sway over Caleb. The pain subsided, the magic recoiled back into the warlock, and everyone could breathe again. Gordon released the laptop to Caleb, and the weight of it caught him off guard, because he nearly dropped it.

The werewolf quickly regained his strength and he only nodded.

Krystal and Valerie had both talked a big game when they first met Caleb, but neither of them had hurt him. Not really. Gordon was the first to demonstrate what a magic user could do if they knew the right things.

She hated it. Every bit of it. She had been hesitant of him at first, even scared. But she knew him now. Caleb wouldn't hurt her or any of her friends. He wanted to help, but Gordon didn't know that. He only saw the race, the label, the stigma.

Unlike the last time he left the coffeeshop, Caleb looked at Valerie. Anger burned in his eyes, but it wasn't reserved for her. Though it would throw her under the spotlight, he gave her a nod. Much like the one he had given when no one else wanted to serve him. Once more, she became his advocate.

And for once, Valerie didn't care if she got in trouble or suffered for her loyalty to a werewolf. It was in that moment that she knew she was lost. Lost to this whole Twin Flame shit.

One pure and powerful feeling formed in her heart, filling her chest like a dense, thick foam that stopped all air from reaching her lungs. She shuddered and tried to breathe, but it was no use. The one thing she swore she would never do had happened right there in the coffeeshop. She fell in love.

Chapter 14

H e should have known how badly that would go. With every intention to tell the girls about all he heard at the park, he had gone in with a hopeful attitude. That warlock asshole was the wildcard. That, he hadn't been expecting.

Upon Valerie's subtle hint, he played nice, but the arrogance of the man reminded him of some of the more ruthless alphas he had tangled with in the past, and the wolf in him wouldn't bow to his magic. Valerie was the only reason he backed down from a potentially bad situation.

It was for her sake, and less to do with Krystal or any of the other magic folk, that he sat at Devin's desk inside the police station. Many of the cops and staff were out to lunch, but Devin had a mountain of paperwork in one corner of his desk and a homemade sandwich in the other. He wasn't going anywhere, and that was to Caleb's benefit. He needed someone who would listen.

It was a long shot, given that his girlfriend had some strong opinions about werewolves, but his bet was placed on the fact that Devin didn't grow up in the magical community. He didn't even know werewolves existed before Krystal told him recently. His regard for Caleb's race might have been somewhat malleable at this point and he would take full advantage of it.

Devin returned from the breakroom and offered the extra canned soda to his guest, mostly out of formality. Caleb took it, but didn't pop the top right away as the cop did.

"So, Mr. Hayden didn't like you very much, did he?" Devin ribbed.

"That's putting it mildly," Caleb grumbled. His head still ached with the near aneurism the man had stricken him with. "I'm sure he would have killed me on the spot if the girls weren't watching."

"I wouldn't doubt it." Devin took a swig of his soda and set it on the table before dragging his sandwich to sit in front of him. "The way Krystal talks about werewolves, you'd think there was an all-out war going on or something."

Caleb let out a long breath, but wouldn't make any comment to that. It was better he remained ignorant. "I was going to tell them about something involving your police chief, but I didn't exactly get the chance."

Devin's hands stilled over the napkin wrapping and looked up from beneath his dark brows. "Chief Nickels? What's he got to do with anything?"

"Possibly everything, but I don't know how to piece it all together. I was hoping that you'd be able to help." He then proceeded to give a play-by-play of everything that was said on the park bench between Chief Nickels and their mystery corpse.

The entire time, Devin stared, ignoring his sandwich and drink as he was completely engrossed in Caleb's story. When he was finished, Devin settled back in his chair and his gaze went vacant.

"That doesn't sound like the chief at all," he said. "If he was anything supernatural, Krystal would know it and tell me. And I can't see him knowing anything about the supernatural either, let alone working with one. It just doesn't make any sense."

Caleb shrugged and set his drink down on the edge of the desk. "I'm only telling you what I saw and heard."

Devin scratched at the back of his neck. "The chief's been acting a little off lately, I'll admit that."

"How so?"

"He's not in the office as much. Doesn't talk. He usually eats a few donuts from McRae's, but lately he hasn't been getting any. He's not as focused on his duties. He even pushed aside this whole zombie apocalypse shit, thinking it wasn't anything important."

"Probably because he's in on it," Caleb added.

The cop shook his head. "It just doesn't seem right."

"I'm more concerned about the girls than the chief. If this man really intends to hurt them, I can't allow it."

Devin smirked. "Believe me, they can take care of themselves. And now that Krystal's parents are in town, they're the safest they'll ever be."

Caleb's nostrils flared. "That's not good enough for me."

"Well, what the hell are you going to do about it then? So far, you've been wasting time talking to me."

Caleb leaned forward. "I need you to talk to Krystal and the others. Tell them about what I saw and make sure they know what's going on. I can't get to them. Not after what her father did to me."

Thoroughly amused, Devin tilted his head. "Oh, is the big bad wolf scared of a little magic now?"

He would have snarled at the man if he didn't need to be on his good side so badly. "It's called self-preservation and maintaining the status quo. But that's not going to stop me from getting to the bottom of this."

Now he sounded like a detective in some cheesy, cheap-budget mystery film.

"Will you tell them for me?"

Devin held up his hands. "What do you want me to say?"

"Don't tell them that I had anything to do with it. Tell them you saw the chief."

Devin gave a wry smile. "I can't hear over the distance of a football field."

"Come up with what bullshit you want to tell them. Just don't mention me or they'll automatically assume it's untrue."

"And how can I know that you're telling the truth now?"

His mouth opened, but the words stuck. He cared for the witches. Their attitudes and all. Maybe he cared just because of Valerie, or there was something about the girls that reminded him of a werewolf pack. They were loyal and worked together for a common good. That in itself was admirable, even if he didn't have feelings for one of them.

Then, something came to mind. Devin was the Twin Flame to Krystal. He heard them talking about it earlier that morning. He would understand the power and intensity of what it meant to be bound by their hearts and souls. If he confessed this one tiny truth, maybe it would be enough for Devin to take him seriously.

"Valerie is... she's my Twin Flame. You know what that is, right? So you know that I'd do anything to make sure that she's safe and protected. Even if it's not by my hand. I wouldn't make something up like this just to lead them on. I care, dammit. Whether or not I want to, I do. I can't walk away from this."

Devin studied Caleb's face, searching for those tells again that would give him permission to disbelieve. And once again, he'd find none.

He finally nodded. "You have my sympathies, then. I know what it's like. I can't walk away either." The cop leaned his elbows upon his desk. "What's the next move? I can try and get someone to tail the chief for a bit. Maybe see if he's going places he normally doesn't go or if he's meeting with people."

Caleb nodded. "You do that. I'm going back to the park to see if I can get a lead on the other guy. His scent shouldn't be that hard to track. Not like it's going to get lost amongst the living, anyway."

Devin grimaced. "It's just so strange that this guy is dead too."

"I think he's the necromancer," Caleb boldly stated. "If the chief's got some sort of deal with him to raise the dead, he must be. He even admitted it, saying all of his work was undone because of what the girls did."

The cop nodded in agreement, but still seemed unsettled by the whole thing. "And here I thought witches were the worst of my problems."

"Trust me, I've been around for almost two centuries and I'm still learning new things."

Blue eyes widened. "Two centuries?"

Caleb winced. "Yep, you still have a lot to learn."

"Well, do you know anything about necromancers?"

"Not a thing," Caleb replied. "But I'm going to get a crash course before the end of the day. Guaranteed."

"Where do you keep the strong stuff?" Valerie whispered to Sierra once they were alone in the kitchen.

The kettle hadn't stopped whistling since they all arrived to the Hayden Mansion, but she needed something with more punch. Especially after the day she had.

Sierra looked to her, then glanced toward the archway that led to the hall. Krystal was a stickler for any kind of liquor in the house. She wouldn't have appreciated Sierra hiding bottles all over creation, but she did anyway.

"I had to hide my last stash," she whispered in return before quickly hurrying toward a part of the kitchen that was rarely used. In a cupboard, behind a false wall in the back, lay her bottles of whiskey and vodka. Just what she needed for an evening like this.

Her parents were visiting with Alexa, Amber, and Taylor in the living room. They all made time for the Haydens whenever they came to Goldcrest Cove, no matter the circumstances. Amber was bored by the council talk, but Alexa and Taylor drank it all up. Instead, the purple-haired innkeeper stuck by Mrs. Hayden and talked about business and the other goings on in the town.

They came together, for the second night in a row, to discuss the necromancer problem. The problem she had caused.

Discreetly, two tumblers were taken down and two splashes of the amber drink were poured for them while the mini quiches were still baking in the oven. Krystal never failed to make a little something for them during these family meetings.

Valerie threw back her shot and let herself dissolve in the burning liquid that left her throat feeling scorched. She squeezed her eyes shut as they teared up, but she refused to cough.

"Are you really that worked up about this?" Sierra asked.

Valerie carefully set her glass down and took the bottle from Sierra's hand to slosh out another round. "More than you know."

When she brought the glass to her mouth, Sierra reached out and took her wrist to stop her. "My parents are here now. They'll take care of it. You should be drinking to celebrate that all this will be behind us by tomorrow."

The concerned look Valerie received was enough to keep her from taking that second shot of whiskey. She put it down and exhaled. "That's... That's not all I'm worried about."

"Then what is it?"

Valerie, for the thousandth time that day, felt like a pitiful mess. She had never wanted to love a guy. She never thought she would be capable of it. To feel this deeply, to want something so badly that her very being felt like it would come unraveled if she didn't get it. Caleb, without saying much or doing anything, had stolen her sanity.

It had taken her that long to figure it out, and her whole life to understand what love was. It was staying by someone at their worst. Even when she was a bitch. It was stepping out to do something small, but meaningful. Like bringing her coffee in the morning. It was offering up their time and attention when it was taken for granted. Like how he cooked and fixed her car.

At every turn, Caleb was demonstrating his love and she couldn't be bothered to make a stronger defense for him when the rest of the witches abused him. She refused his company and apart from the tiny instances before she realized the connection to her dark magic, had been nothing but rude to him. She didn't deserve him, but she still wanted him. And Valerie felt selfish for it.

Before Sierra could stop her, she took the shot and slammed it down on the counter.

"It's my Twin Flame," she said shakily, willing herself to stay together just this once. "I know who it is, and it's driving me crazy because I can't... I can't be with him. This whole dark magic bullshit is messing everything up. I have a chance at having something real and genuine, and it's all fucked up because of me."

A gentle hand rested on her shoulder, but if Sierra expected her to start bawling, she wouldn't. She had enough sense not to do that in their house with so many people in the next room.

Valerie's grip was on the neck of the whiskey bottle, but Sierra intercepted before another glass could be poured. This time, she set it far out of reach.

"There are a lot of reasons to drink," Sierra said. "Drink to a hard day, to a good day, to a birth, or to a death. But don't ever drink over a boy."

She was always dishing out wisdom. Being a hairdresser was much like being a bartender. She had to be a good listener and give sound advice. Valerie saw the sense in what she said and slumped against the counter, her elbows propped up and face in her hands, looking just about as pathetic as she felt.

"Is he... Is he already married or something?" Sierra questioned, fishing for who it could be. Valerie would have to drink a lot more for her to confess the name of her Twin Flame.

"No. He's very much single."

"Then what's the problem?"

Valerie looked up at her friend. "My dark magic basically sucks the life out of everything when I'm happy. When I'm thinking about him in a good way. In a... a nasty way." Sierra smirked like a Cheshire cat at that. "So how can I be with him, if all I'm ever going to do is hurt him?"

The older witch nodded. "I see your problem... Does he know about you?"

"He knows who I am... He doesn't know everything though." It wasn't exactly a lie, but it was only half-true. Caleb knew she was a witch, but not about all the little things in between. All the things she wanted to tell him, to spill out of her soul, so someone could see her scars and understand her pain.

Sierra seemed to pause in thought and then gestured toward the archway where a peal of laughter came floating through. "Let's get my mom to help. She knows a lot and if she could help with Krystal's dark magic, I'm sure she can help with yours, even if it is a little... different."

Different. That seemed to sum up her entire existence. Different.

Krystal came through the archway and snatched up the pair of oven mitts from the kitchen island before she noticed the scene in the back corner. "Is that where you've been keeping it?" she nearly screeched.

Sierra rolled her eyes. "Now I have to hide it again."

"No! Pour it all out or give it to Amber or something. We don't have any use for it."

The elder sister stuck out her tongue at the younger. "You know you can use this for cooking sometimes."

Krystal waved her off and turned, her black ponytail whipping about her shoulders. Taking the quiches from the oven, she set the pan on the potholders before taking another look at Valerie. "Are you okay?"

Sierra was quick to her rescue. "Just worked up about all this zombie and dark magic stuff. Needed something to loosen her up."

Just two shots and she was already pretty loose. The whiskey had warmed her stomach, but it did little to silence her fears about Caleb and whatever twisted future they had together. Catherine might have been able to help with her dark magic, but how long would it be until she was able to be with Caleb the way she wanted? Could the witch work miracles?

The door knocker came alive, and despite the alcohol in her system, Valerie jumped. Her skin tingled to think that perhaps it was Caleb come to check on her or stand up to Gordon.

Krystal grinned to them and rushed toward the door without an explanation. Then again, that smile was all the explanation they needed. Devin's voice rumbled from the foyer and more footsteps pattered into the hallway. As far as she knew, the two men in Krystal's life hadn't met yet.

This, Valerie had to see. She and Sierra went to the archway and watched the meeting unfold. Both proud men evaluated one another in silence before Gordon offered out a handshake. It was far more civil than what he gave Caleb and Valerie couldn't help but feel a bit offended over it.

"It's good to finally meet you," Mr. Hayden said with a smile that could almost pass for pleasant. There was still a bit of hesitance there, as if he wondered if the match would last. Mixed magic couples often didn't. Alexa's family was a great example of that. Being Twin Flames, however, would help.

"It's great to put a face with the name," Devin replied. "Krystal's said nothing but good things."

"She better. I am her father, after all."

The two continued to shake hands and Valerie wondered if this was some sort of strength contest after a while.

Catherine touched her husband's arm to redirect his attention. "Don't break his hand, honey. He needs that in his line of work."

They finally released and Valerie stole a glance toward Krystal. She didn't seem the least bit nervous about the meeting, but she rarely showed that sort of weakness. There was far more permanency in their relationship than most. They were Twin Flames, after all, and her father wasn't likely to get in the way of that.

"Yes, you're a police officer, right?"

"Yes, sir."

"I assume you're here to help us, then?"

For some reason, Devin's gaze flickered momentarily toward Valerie and a chill rushed down her spine. "I have, but I've also brought news."

At this, every witch in the house was at the archways and listening in from a safe vantage point.

"Our chief, James Nickels, has been acting odd lately. So my partner and I decided to put some surveillance on him, especially when he was really eager to brush this whole missing bodies case under the rug."

Gordon's brows furrowed as he listened intently.

"We planted a hidden microphone on him and managed to catch a conversation earlier today and I think we can use it to fill in a few missing pieces."

Valerie knew damned well that their little police station didn't have the budget for a microphone that small. Instantly, she thought of Caleb and wondered if any of this had to do with him.

"Do you have the tape?" Gordon asked.

Devin pursed his lips. "No, we don't. Right after we listened to it, our server got hacked and it was wiped from the hard drive. There was no way I could retrieve it." He reached for his back pocket. "But we wrote down the script before it was deleted."

He read off the dialogue that went back and forth between Chief Nickels and the mystery man. With each line, Valerie felt as if she'd turn into a puddle on the floor. It wasn't her. None of this necromancy magic was because of her.

Not trusting her legs to support her, she retreated into the kitchen and perched herself upon a stool while she continued to listen. They talked about a deal, about magic, and a threat upon the witches that undid it all. Whoever this guy was, he was to blame. Not her. It was such an overwhelming relief that she had to stop herself from laughing out loud.

Her hand covered her mouth, her eyes brimming. *It wasn't her fault.* That's all she could think of. Not that there was still a necromancer on the loose who had evil intentions, nor that that their lives were potentially in danger. Nothing but the relief that she was blameless. Finally blameless.

"That's it?" Gordon asked.

"Yes, sir. Nickels walked away after that. We've got a man trying to track down the one he was talking to."

"The council called earlier today to confirm that everyone with this ability is accounted for. Whoever this is that made a deal with your chief hasn't been recognized by the council."

Amber's voice joined in. "Would it be someone new to this magic?"

"Likely not," Catherine answered. "To be able to resurrect that many bodies, they would know a lot about the craft. He also said that he can control several bodies at once, which is something very few necromancers can do without practice."

"But they would have had to slide under your radar, right?" Sierra questioned from the kitchen archway.

"It appears they have," Gordon said. "Or, they could be under the jurisdiction of the European council. It'll take a little while to get a hold of them and have them check their own registries."

"If that's the case, they're in America without our approval." Catherine didn't sound the least bit happy about that.

"Who is going after this man?" Gordon demanded. "He has to know what he's up against. Don't tell me you sent one of your own."

For the first time that evening, Devin fumbled for an answer. "He's... He's aware of the situation with the bodies and he's capable. I can assure you that."

That's when she knew for certain. It had to be Caleb. Devin wasn't so stupid that he'd send another cop after a magic user, and it was likely that Caleb insisted on going after the necromancer if he was the one to hear the conversation in the first place. But how long ago? Was he all right? Did he need backup?

The strength she had lost just a few minutes before returned and she was ready to run across town in the snow to make sure that Caleb was all right. But she couldn't. Not with the Haydens still there and everyone ready to help her with her dark magic. She'd have to stay, and so would the fluttering moths in her stomach. At least until she had Caleb in front of her again, whole and unharmed. If this necromancer was as strong as Krystal's parents believed him to be, a werewolf was no match for him.

Chapter 15

Finding the necromancer's hideout wasn't hard at all. Tailing the man himself was another matter. It had taken Caleb just a couple of hours to locate the place. A foreclosed home near the edge of Goldcrest Cove, the yard overrun with weeds and signs stating "No Trespassing" were posted everywhere. His scent was all over the place, but it was stale. At least half a day old.

It provided him a starting point. All across town, he tracked the walking corpse. Some houses were visited, and he lingered at the harbor for a spell. His final stop, to Caleb's dismay, was the Hayden Mansion. The curb, once more, was lined with cars. One of which was new to his reckoning, it had to belong to Krystal's parents. They were all inside, chatting away late into the evening, totally unaware that they had come close to their enemy.

Oddly enough, the necromancer didn't stay long. He must have known powerful witches were about the place and had enough sense not to try anything. Not tonight.

The scent grew stronger as the light continued to fade. Now all that was left was the waning moon and stars above to light his way to a cemetery just on the east side of town. One of the ones that hadn't been touched in the recent upheaval. These graves were all intact and hadn't been disturbed. Yet.

Caleb kept his distance, skirting around the cemetery and slinking into the dense woods to cut around the backside. Crouching, he navigated his way between bushes and trees, his feet barely making a sound against the forest floor. His eyes had gone golden now to help him see through the darkness, and they never deviated from the necromancer.

His mind ran through the scenario. Should he shift? Should he stay human? Could he manage to get close enough to the necromancer to attack, or should he play the diplomat and try to talk his way out of it?

Caleb watched and assessed, studying the man's movements as he weaved through the headstones. His head swiveled, as if he were looking for a certain name, picking his way through the dead for someone specific.

He was being smart now. More exact, just as he promised Chief Nickels. But why? Why did he want to cause a panic? What was the point in that? Was it something personal? Devin said he didn't think the chief knew about the supernatural, but how long had he been working with the necromancer? So many holes and not enough information to fill them.

Caleb paused when the necromancer stopped suddenly in front of a row of five headstones. They seemed old, the marble darkened by years of neglect. Even with his sharp eyes, Caleb couldn't make out the names or dates carved into the faces.

All was quiet. Not even a breath of wind. So quiet he could hear his own heartbeat, pounding away at a steady, calm rhythm.

A twig snapped, and Caleb forgot himself. He spun to look, only for a second before he realized he had let too much of the wolf control his reflexes. When he turned back to the cemetery, the necromancer was gone. Absolutely vanished.

Caleb took a step, and then he felt it. Within the span of just a few seconds, magic pulsated from his right. Then came the impact. As if the aftershock of an explosion had knocked straight into him, Caleb flew through the air and collided with a pine.

The wood splintered upon collision and he fell to the ground. His spine and ribs had effectively been broken. His breastbone, too, had been split from the force of the attack. If he only had one of these injuries, he might have been able to pick himself up and charge at his assailant. As it was, he could barely lift his head from the frozen earth he had landed on. He needed more than a couple of minutes for the bones to mend.

The necromancer marched toward him, his footsteps loud and clumsy in the brush. The magic hit him again, blasting him to his feet and sending him rolling. He roared at his attacker as he scrambled to right himself and gain traction on the ice and snow.

Once his back was healed, he felt he could at least make a decent counter. Fangs and claws unsheathed as Caleb let a partial shift take over. His muscles swelled, tightening against his clothes as he imbued his body with the strength of the wolf. He'd need it.

The necromancer's gloves were off, his palms glowing blue with power. His face was twisted in a scowl, and this guy knew who he was up against.

Caleb didn't show the least bit of hesitance or fear when he came running, ready to rip out whatever dead heart lay dormant in that chest. The warlock drew back a hand and sent another shockwave to debilitate him.

Using his enhanced speed, Caleb dodged it. He would have been little more than a blur as he darted from the ground to a nearby elm, scaling its branches until he was above the necromancer. He leapt, thinking he would use the element of surprise.

It didn't work.

The necromancer turned as if anticipating his move and jabbed with his magic. It knocked Caleb in midair and he went tumbling backward. As soon as his feet hit the ground, he was moving again. Venturing close and then moving away, he searched for a blind spot. A weakness. Anything to give him the edge he needed.

Each and every time, he narrowly escaped a massive blast from the necromancer. It was as if he had some sort of foresight, or could see him perfectly in the pitch black darkness of the forest. Caleb might not have known much about witches and warlocks, but this sort of power seemed excessive. Either he was more than he seemed, or there was something terribly wrong about this.

He charged one last time, coming up straight from behind. All weapons were bared, quiet as the wind upon his approach. Still, the necromancer turned and caught Caleb by the throat. The necromancer lifted him with one cold, icy hand as if he were a doll.

The same pain that Mr. Hayden had inflicted upon him radiated through Caleb's veins. He roared in agony, his strength failing him as he feebly scratched and reached for the necromancer.

It was as if lava were encasing his bones, searing him from the inside out. The necromancer's eyes went black as a moonless night as he poured out his magic to kill Caleb.

All he could think of was Valerie and what this man would do to her if given the chance. She might have had an edge on the necromancer, being a witch herself, but if she were to lose, if she were to fail in stopping him, she'd suffer this torture too. Caleb rebelled against it and against the darkness that closed in around his vision.

He fought harder, flailed his weakened limbs more wildly to free himself, but it was of little use. The warlock had him.

Just as he thought the end was near, the magic receded. The hand upon his throat no longer felt the same. The grip loosened, the fingers shrunk and turned boney. His palm no longer blazed with the magic that was close to destroying Caleb.

Then, it was as if a switch had been flipped. The necromancer dropped Caleb into the snow. His body, heated by the magic, melted the ice around him to create steam. Though weak and his blood still burning, he wouldn't take his eyes off his opponent.

The necromancer, just as perplexed and even more furious by this strange turn of events, had pulled up his trench coat sleeve. Though his vision was spotty and hazy, Caleb could see what had happened. His arm had become withered, as if a thousand years of decay had caught up with him. The skin had turned black and charred, his blood completely gone, leaving only a gaunt skeleton of a form.

He hastily pushed up his sleeve to inspect further until he came to the first patch of unharmed flesh. In faint blue ink, Caleb saw a tribal tattoo. Its form hadn't been marred by the decay.

The necromancer let out a relieved sigh and looked to his opponent. "You're lucky it's not time yet."

That was all he said before he turned and strode away as if nothing had happened. His confidence in Caleb's enfeebled state was proven valid. He could barely move and just one breath took tremendous effort. But he was alive. Alive to fight again on another night.

As he lay still in the snow, letting his body heal and recover from the immense damage, he thought about what had happened. Did Caleb do that to the warlock's arm, or was it something else? Did the necromancer, since he too was dead, have a limited reserve of magic? Was that reserve depleted? Why else would he stop? And what did he mean by "it's not time yet"? Time for what?

Once more, he was without answers and nothing could be connected. Not yet.

"So, I'm not sucking the life out of things?" Valerie asked, nearly choking on the burning sage.

The last half hour had been spent clearing out one of the spare rooms upstairs, leaving it bare except for the myriad of sage bundles, incense burners, and a carton of crystals and stones. With Valerie, was Catherine, Taylor, and Amber. The others, the less experienced witches who were still too young to understand what needed to be done, were downstairs.

"No, honey," Catherine Hayden assured sweetly. "Not at all." The older witch took up the stones and passed them out to the others.

Valerie sat quietly in the middle of the circle they had drawn in chalk on the floor, a circle that was meant to help release all of the negative energy. The three witches evenly spaced out the various crystals. She recognized a few, only from her light personal research and the endless lectures from Alexa on the subject. The amethyst, black tourmaline, and selenite she recognized for sure.

"It's just a very rare form of magic," Taylor said in her mousy, quiet voice. "At least, I've only heard of one or two cases of it in this region."

She was the resident expert in all things related to energy and harnessing it naturally from the earth and nature. The nursery caretaker spent many hours with Alexa in her greenhouse, going over all the meanings associated with herbs and stones. Valerie had been invited on a few occasions, but refused. Now, she wished she had gone. That knowledge would have come in handy now.

"You see," Catherine began as she placed the incense burners just outside the ring of crystals, "Whenever the positive, enriching energy within you starts to bubble up, it's pushing out all the negative energy. It's like rising water pushing up air through a cylinder. Our spirits normally compensate for the change, but your dark magic is releasing that negative energy too quickly and too violently. So it begins to infect the things around you."

"And that's why the apples rot and the power goes out?" Valerie said.

Amber gave a nod. "Exactly. Your yang is evicting your yin, which throws you out of balance. There should always be an equal amount."

"So, my happy is pushing out my sad and it's making everything else sad."

"Sad and dead," Amber emphasized.

"Not so coarse, dear," Catherine chided. "But, in a nutshell, that's what it is."

Valerie took in a breath, but wasn't sure whether to be relieved or worried. At least that explained why she never seemed to be able to absorb the energy of the things she was killing, and why pouring all the energy back drained her so much. It wasn't a give-and-take system, but a completely fucked up pressure release valve.

The mechanism of it made sense, but just because she understood it, didn't make it any easier to cope. It was like when she first found out about what her body had to go through every month just to be fertile. Or when her chest began to grow and she had to wear bras. Learning about the inner workings of her dark magic seemed like going through a rite of passage. Or maybe a trial by fire.

"And we fix this... how?"

"There's no fixing it," Taylor explained. "Only coping with the side effects."

Valerie waited, but no one chimed in. "And we do this..."

"You have to learn to release the negative energy more carefully and safely," Catherine said as she placed the last of the burning incense sticks. The room was beginning to smell like a flower shop, a potpourri bowl, and a million broken bottles of perfume had exploded. Her head was dizzy from the potency of it.

"And to do that, we're going to wipe your slate clean," Taylor announced proudly with one of her award-winning smiles. For a timid, quiet little thing, she had a huge heart that Valerie could appreciate.

"Is that why you got everything out?" Valerie asked as she looked around at the barren walls and empty corners of the room.

"Yep," Amber replied. "Wouldn't want you disintegrating away the furniture."

"If you can't be nice, I'll send for Sierra instead." Catherine's hands were on her hips, shooting daggers with her eyes at Amber, who couldn't seem to curb her tongue tonight. Valerie didn't mind, but then again, Amber and Valerie had a lot in common.

"Don't upset the balance of the room!" Taylor warned, finding her courage in the task that was practically made for her specialty.

That snapped them all into place. Valerie waited patiently for the setup to finish and then turned imploring eyes to Catherine. "What do I have to do?"

She thought to protest, to tell them all that she would rather go take it out on the necromancer herself than sit there and endure the ritual. But then that would admit to them all that she was scared, which she was, but she didn't want them to know that.

"We're going to set up a barrier around you and let you just work out all that negativity you've been bottling up."

"Sounds a lot like an exorcism," Valerie muttered.

Amber shrugged. "It kind of is, but it's not permanent."

Valerie's eyes widened just a bit. "Not permanent?"

Catherine knelt beside her on the other side of the circle. "You won't have to do this all the time, but you will have to maintain the balance on a regular basis. We'll give you tools to make it easier."

If she didn't think it would stoke the matriarch's ire, she would have groaned aloud. Instead, she looked to the ceiling, wishing this was over already, so she could go home and wait for Caleb.

She hadn't heard from him, meaning that his search for the necromancer might have been unsuccessful. If that was the case, she wondered how many of the witches downstairs would care. How many would go looking for him too? How many would try to help if he was in danger? Was Devin even up to it? He was influenced by Krystal, after all. Maybe he sent Caleb after the warlock just to put him in harm's way.

The unsettling feeling in the pit of her stomach wouldn't go away. Not when she felt so betrayed by her friends. But they weren't exactly betraying her. Just Caleb. But by proxy, it was an offense upon her as well. That's how it felt, anyway. One more confirmation that they were Twin Flames.

She shook her head at how absolutely fucked up this whole thing was.

"What's wrong?" Taylor asked. The empath likely picked up on her down-swing.

"Just unburying all that negativity, so it'll come out easier."

She meant it as a snide joke, but Catherine didn't seem to get it.

"Very good. That's the spirit. You'll feel much better after all of this. I promise. And I'll show you some easy rituals you can do in the morning before work to get you off on the right start."

Valerie cut her eyes at Amber, who never failed to pick up on her sarcasm. The innkeeper witch smirked and positioned herself in relation to Taylor around the circle. They'd need to form a triangle to create the barrier that would keep the room and everyone else in the house safe from her bad juju.

"One question," Valerie started in before they had a chance to begin. "Will I... Will I have to be put on a registry like the necromancer? I mean, this is really similar to their magic, right? And it's not like this is a good sort of magic."

Catherine gave her one of those sympathetic smiles. "No, we won't. Not as long as you make an effort to keep this all under control."

Valerie, like a child eager to prove that she was very sorry for something she had done, nodded quickly to the condition.

The triangle was formed and all of the sudden, Valerie felt as if she were being put on a sacrificial altar.

"So, just relax for a minute while we get this up, and then we'll walk you through the purge."

Now Valerie's hands began to shake in her lap. "Let's call it a detox or something less ominous than a 'purge'."

Amber smiled. "Not an exorcism?"

"Not that either."

Catherine slid them both a look before beginning in on the brief, but powerful incantation.

Within a few seconds, an invisible veil fell around Valerie. She felt the shift in the air as it dropped around her. Sounds from the outside became muffled and it seemed as if everything contained within the barrier was hermetically sealed. All the while, she could see her friends as plain as day.

It was a good thing that Valerie wasn't claustrophobic.

Catherine came to sit in front of her, less than four feet away. The woman nearly had to shout at her through the barrier. "You need to trigger your dark magic. Put yourself into a meditative state and focus on it."

She wasn't usually the one to suffer from nervous jitters. She had made a point of being so put together, especially around others. But right now, she was the center of attention. The star of the show and they all expected fireworks like what Krystal managed to do at her first training ritual. Valerie didn't want them to see what she could do. What kind of damage she could inflict. Even if it was all contained.

She shook her head. "I don't know what the triggers are."

Catherine lowered her brows. "No lying. You know exactly what triggers it. We're not judging here and we can't see inside your head. You have nothing to fear from us."

Valerie felt heat spread across her shoulders and prickle down her back. Catherine had to know. Or at least have a good idea. Why else would she say, "we're not judging"? She knew about her Twin Flame, and she didn't seem to care. No doubt she understood their connection, and who had brought out the dark magic in her now.

Her lips tightened as she laced her fingers together upon her crossed ankles. With her eyes closed, it didn't take her long to enter that calm, meditative state. It had been a long time since she had let her mind run completely blank. Not since the last time she came home from a funeral.

Then, once she knew everything was still, Valerie let her mind and heart wander. It left the Hayden Mansion and ventured to the recent past. It revisited the moments she and Caleb shared. At the coffeeshop, at her home, in his car, at the cemetery. She brought up his green eyes in her vision and found them not powerful enough to stoke the dark magic. Not until she remembered the gold of the wolf.

Tingles exploded through her core and down her thighs at the memory of his naked, glistening body standing in the bathroom. That was the first morning after they met. Was it then that she fell in love? Or was it when they shared a moment in the kitchen? Or on the couch when he played his game?

She recalled his touch and her blood sang with each of his caresses, both real and fictional. Daydreams crept their way in to distort the truth, but she didn't care. In her mind's eye, their bodies intertwined in ways that hadn't really happened. Not yet. Maybe not ever, but she wouldn't let herself dwell on that.

The idea was to fill her up with such powerful energies that the negative was eradicated from her soul. A clean slate. That's what they all needed.

She could feel his hot breath on her neck and the way his mouth would have felt if it slid across her collarbone. Valerie tried not to let her ecstasy show, but it was too late. Her jaw, once clamped tight and aching with the effort to hold it all together, loosened and her lips parted. Her head tilted and the tension started to build more and more as she thought of what it was like to be naked in his arms, to feel their bodies pressed together in the throes of hot, animalistic sex.

But she dispelled that from her mind at once. Caleb would never be rough with her. He'd be a gentle lover, dragging it out slowly and deliberately to drive her mad. She hardly knew the man, and yet she felt she knew exactly what his lovemaking would entail.

All the things she thought she could never have, all the dreams and the plans for a future spun like twisters in her head. A home of her own. A family. Happiness. True and priceless happiness. All within reach. She allowed herself to believe it. To believe in love and fate and everything she thought would never be hers. In her fantasies, Caleb wanted an orphan. He wanted the damaged one. He wanted her and only her.

The floor tilted out from underneath her. From the tips of her toes to the crown of her head, Valerie became light. Her aura burst and it burned like a beacon. Was this what it was like to surrender? To give herself wholly over to the joy that her ancestors had whispered about? Was this hope? She believed it. At this point, she'd believe anything, because it all seemed possible. There was no necromancer, no dark magic, or anything that could shatter this perfect image of the life she now thought she deserved.

Valerie opened her eyes, confident that she had done it.

The smoke from the burning sage swirled around her in a fog of cleansing power. The aromas of the incense filled her senses. The crystals so carefully arranged around her began to vibrate and hum with their healing energies. Catherine and the others were still in the room, safe and well as they watched her in fascination.

The only thing to suggest that something was amiss, was the peeling wallpaper. The barrier had done its job for the most part and quarantined her dark magic.

Catherine gave her a candid smile. She was proud. And for once, Valerie was proud of herself too. If she had to do this every day, it might have been worth it. Nothing in the world could compare to this bliss. Nothing except maybe one thing. But Caleb was the only one who could give that to her.

Chapter 16

Caleb hadn't expected Valerie to be home. He had rather hoped that she would have stayed with Krystal. It might have been safer there. At least all the witches would be together, in case the necromancer changed his mind.

Once he had recovered from the short-lived battle, Caleb checked the cemetery for missing bodies. He had been prepared to call Devin the minute he saw something amiss, but there was nothing. Not one plot had been disturbed. The necromancer had fled, and covered his tracks. There was no lingering scent in the snow to follow. No tracks. Nothing. It was as if the necromancer had never been there.

Which made it seem all for nothing. What had Caleb accomplished? Putting off the inevitable? It was clear that he injured the necromancer somehow in the fight, but he was a warlock. There had to be ways for him to heal himself. And once that happened, he'd come back just as strong as before.

As he trudged up to the house, he began to wonder if Devin had pulled through for him. It was too late in the evening to call him now with more details, but did he at least relay what he had previously found to the Haydens? He hadn't heard a word out of the cop, and he wasn't going to count on Valerie being a chatterbox. As it was, she would probably still give him a wide berth.

A few new smells greeted him when he stepped onto the porch. Something was burning, but he couldn't place it. When he opened the door, the aroma hit him hard and he had to clear his throat before attempting to take another full breath.

Half of the lights in the house were on, and by the hurried rush of footsteps, he knew that Valerie wasn't asleep as she should have been.

She soon appeared, clad in her typical pajamas. Her demeanor was anything but typical. She stood at the end of the front hall, her posture straight, stare fixed upon him with a kind of eagerness he had never seen out of her. She was full of energy. His wolf could tell that much, but there was no accounting for it. Not this late.

"You should be in bed," he remarked, well aware of how tired and dogged he must have sounded.

"I... I couldn't go to sleep knowing you were out there looking for the warlock."

That surprised him and a bit of vigor returned as he hung up his jacket on the hook with the rest. "Devin told you?"

She shook her head and straightened even more, looking something like a meerkat on alert. "I figured it out for myself. He didn't give you away, if that's what you were wondering."

Caleb nodded. "Good. I didn't want Krystal's parents to go on a rampage."

Valerie smiled, a wide, pleasant sight, especially after all he had been through. "They didn't. But they were helpful. They've got a list of all the necromancers who've been at least documented by the council and everyone's accounted for. None are missing or anywhere close to Goldcrest Cove."

Knowing this would startle her, Caleb asked, "Did they check for the dead ones?"

Her eyes went wide. "Dead ones? Why should they – "

"This warlock doesn't have a heartbeat. That's one thing I couldn't have Devin tell you, because he probably couldn't come up with a good way to explain how he would know that. And he stinks like he's been dead for years."

Valerie's mouth tried to form words, but nothing came out for some time. "Well... That changes things. And the part about Chief Nickels being in on this?"

"That's true. I saw him with my own eyes talking with the man."

"Could you give a description to Krystal's dad? Maybe he can – "

"No," Caleb replied with an exacting tone. "I'm not talking to that man or getting anywhere near them until this is all over."

He passed by her to go to the kitchen, her eyes following him before her feet could.

"Is this about what he did today?"

"It's about maintaining a status quo," he said as he pulled out a water bottle from the fridge. He barely had time to take care of himself all day. He turned to her and cracked open the cap. "If he wants to think I'm some bad guy, then let him think that. I'm done trying to convince any of your friends of my innocence."

That silenced her just long enough so he could take stock of this new place they were in.

He wasn't sure what brought on this bout of brutal honesty. Maybe it was the culmination of everything that had happened that day, or the fact that his body was still sore after being inundated with so much magic. Or perhaps it was because he was talking to Valerie. The one other person on this earth who could possibly understand him.

He took a swig of water, never taking his eyes off of her across the kitchen. Valerie certainly looked to be teeming with things to say or to ask. Her fingers twitched at her sides. Her heartbeat and breaths were elevated. Was it nerves or excitement? Not even his wolf was sure, but they could both agree that something was different.

She wanted to talk. Wanted details. Almost acted like she gave a damn about him. She said she couldn't go to sleep knowing that he was in danger. What had changed since that morning?

Whatever it was, Caleb would take advantage of it. If she was willing to step back in the ring, he would too.

"So, did you find him?" she finally asked.

Caleb nodded. "I did, but it didn't end well."

"Are you okay?" Valerie took a single bounding step forward, as if ready to strip him bare and check for non-existent wounds herself. He would have gladly let her as long as he could return the favor.

"I'm fine now."

"Now? So you weren't earlier?"

Caleb smirked and leaned his shoulder into the fridge. "Sharp one... We got into a fight. It was careless of me, really. I got too close tailing him near a cemetery and he must have known I was there. He might have killed me if..."

He paused and watched the change in her. Valerie closed her eyes and her hand gripped something he hadn't noticed before. It was a pendant necklace, the single purple stone braided with cord.

On her, it seemed so out of place that he had been surprised he didn't notice it before. Its style was better suited for Krystal, who wore long skirts and blouses that make her look every part the earthy witch that she was. He preferred the black leather and studded jewelry he had found on the bathroom vanity.

The atmosphere transformed, but only for a few seconds. A heaviness had settled in the aromatic air and then lifted just as quickly. No visible change, nothing to suggest that magic had been used, but he had a feeling it had been.

"You all right?"

Valerie opened her eyes, a hint of trepidation poisoning their beautiful depths. "Yeah, I'm good... But... Did you kill the warlock or...?"

Caleb blinked and forced himself back into their discussion, though he was ready to pull her further off track. "No, I didn't. I didn't get a chance. I should have known better, that with his arranged attacks I didn't have a chance. No magic, after all. I'm only good in close-quarters combat." Caleb found himself unconsciously turning the water bottle cap in his hand. "But something did happen. I'm not sure what to make of it."

He then told her about the warlock's hand and how it had shriveled up and rendered him useless. It had been the only thing to save him from death.

"I've never heard of it, but if this guy is dead like you say he is... all bets are off." Valerie pulled out her phone from her flannel pajama pants pocket. "I need to tell Krystal or Mr. Hayden. I don't know how I'll explain it, but – "

Caleb was on her in a minute, seizing her hand that held the phone before she could dial. "No, I said I didn't want to involve them."

He could feel it now. That energy, that vivacity. The very air around her was altered. It had once been burdened with griefs and sorrows that she wouldn't dare show or speak of. She kept a field around her at all times, keeping the world at a distance. Valerie had been a bird trapped in a cage under her own request.

That cage had been broken. She had freed herself and he missed it. Valerie had done it without him. And she permitted him closer for the first time. Caleb glanced to her lips, so full and inviting. It would have been easy to kiss her now, as it had been before in the foyer. Only now, she didn't turn from him. Didn't retreat or shy away. Everything in her stance, her aura, and her scent told him that she was ready to finally let their souls connect again since they had been split at the formation of existence itself.

Valerie had been willing, but Caleb held back. When her own gaze fell onto his mouth, her breaths ragged and sweet upon his skin, he edged back and released her hand. The game had resumed and it was too early to take his prize.

Dazed, she watched him turn and retrieve his water bottle from the table.

"I'm going to see if I can find him tomorrow," Caleb told her. "Or maybe tail Chief Nickels and see if he can tell me anything about this deal he's made with the warlock."

Valerie's hands were shaking as she replaced the phone in her pocket. The urge to comfort her, or to pounce too soon, had to be pushed back. His wolf hated him for it, but Caleb knew better. Now was not the time.

"I'll, uh... I'll look in my family's grimoire for anything about that arm decaying stuff. It's a long shot, but maybe it'll hint at something."

"Not tonight," he pled. "Get some rest and do it in the morning."

She smirked and a bit of the courageous girl resurfaced. "It's already morning."

Glancing to the clock, she was right. One o'clock again. "We're forming a bad habit," he remarked as he took another drink. "I'm going to make myself something to eat and then go to bed. I suggest you get a head start."

He set the bottle down before taking refuge in the fridge. He'd need to cool off after what had almost happened. Her fire could spread far too easily. And if he had any hope in winning this game, he'd need to keep his distance. No matter how hard it was to resist her. Especially like this. He had thought she was beautiful before, but this refreshed, revived version of Valerie appealed to him even more. He always knew she was a firecracker, and her fuse had finally been lit. Whatever dazzling display she had in store for him would be well worth the suspense. It still killed him to trace the light tread of her shuffling feet down the hall and to her room. If only he could have gone with her.

He looked like shit when he first walked in. It was all Valerie could do not to slip into hysterics. His shirt was torn and bloodied, his hair disheveled, jeans stained and wet from the snow. She noticed the way his face sagged with fatigue, how his eyes lacked that usual intensity that excited her.

And she noticed when it all came back. When the life returned to his expression the more they talked. She clung to that hope when Caleb had told her about the necromancer almost killing him. She couldn't allow herself to dwell on the negative when she was so close to figuring out all the quirks of her dark magic. The amethyst necklace Catherine had given her served as a suitable grounding agent, but she needed something stronger to keep out the negative energy. Once it was inside of her, she knew that it would escape eventually. Then she'd hurt someone. Namely Caleb.

Lying in bed with Thor fast asleep under her desk, Valerie listened to his movements in the kitchen. He had said he was going to make a quick snack, but it sounded more like a feast. Pots were being taken out. Water boiled on the stove. She thought she heard the cutting board too. Either he was much hungrier than he made out to be, or he was prolonging going to bed.

She wished she could have done the same. Anything to stay in the same room with him. Anything to have him close, to feel his breath on her face and the warmth of his skin.

Checking the clock, it had been an hour since he sent her away. In just a few more, she'd have to get up and get ready for work, but she wasn't the least bit tired. Love kept her awake. Longing made her eyes stay open. Desire kept her ears straining to hear his movements.

Her heart told her she couldn't stay in her bedroom anymore. Too much had happened that day for her to remain under her covers alone. Her Twin Flame was in the next room and she was done pretending. Done fighting.

Quietly, so as not to wake Thor, Valerie slipped from her bed and into the hallway. The savory aromas of garlic and basil told her whatever he had cooked was bound to be good. Most of the noise coming from the kitchen had gone quiet some time ago, replaced by the clatter of a single fork upon a plate.

Valerie knew all too well that she could never sneak up on a werewolf, but something stopped her from stepping into the light that slanted through the archway. Her legs were shaking, her heart painfully thrumming against her ribcage the longer she thought about what she'd say or what she'd do.

She knew exactly how she wanted this to end. Naked, in bed, sweating, and with Caleb. But how? He hadn't exactly been cold, but he hadn't been the tenderhearted man she had come to love. Some of that had to be in response to her. He couldn't have fallen out of love and she wouldn't allow herself to believe that he was the runner. They would stand their ground and face this now. Both of them.

Caleb was seated at the dining table, his dirty shirt slung over one of the seats, leaving him bare-chested and enticing. His fingers spun a fork loaded with spaghetti, almost obsessively, but he wouldn't take a bite. She stood there, watching him watch his food.

Look at me, damn it, she thought to herself.

"Couldn't sleep?" he asked.

She was so new to this. She needed to say something clever and sexy. Something to get his attention and make it utterly clear about what she wanted. Valerie had always been a blunt and honest person, but asking for a man to want her, to take her, was something she never had to do. Admitting her feelings and giving herself over to them was new territory too. What words could possibly be the right ones?

In response to her silence, Caleb finally tilted his head up and looked upon her with those green eyes that made her world fragment. Before, she tried to contain the blast, to hold the pieces of herself together. Those days were done and there were no words.

She rushed forward and before she could talk herself out of it, her hands were on his face, and their lips connected. Soft, warm, with a hint of garlic from his meal. At first, she felt his shock in the form of rigidness, and then he gave in.

He was out of his chair with his hands on her faster than she could realize. They glided over her curves as his solid body pressed into her own. He had her against the wall as their kiss deepened. They devoured one another like hungry, lustful beasts that had never known any taste sweeter than what they sampled in the kitchen. Tongues played as hands roamed. Hers traveled along the contours of his hard muscles, his upon the feminine hills and valleys of her form. Her nose was filled with the tangy scent of his sweat and the aroma of the forest that clung to his skin.

All the while, Valerie hadn't a single thought outside of Caleb. Her soul begged to be touched and he obeyed without her ever uttering a thing. She moaned and gasped whenever he got it right. And she adored how he would tremble and hold her tighter when she let her nails trace long lines down his back and shoulders.

His kisses ventured along her jaw and down her neck, nipping and licking like a pup that had been gifted a bone. With each teasing bite, electricity shot through her core and limbs, nearly rendering her limp. Caleb must have sensed her weakness. His hands cupped her ass and pulled her clean off the ground. Her legs wrapped around his waist for stability and she could feel his hard shaft pressing through his jeans, eager to meet her. By the hot dampness in her pajama pants, she knew something else was ready for attention in the same way.

"I should have done this days ago," she gasped, surprised she could find her voice at all.

The movements of his mouth on her skin made her shiver. "The minute I laid eyes on you in the coffeeshop, I should have taken you into the back."

"I don't think I would have stopped you."

Valerie never knew what it was like to be held like this. To be secure and safe, needed and desired. All that tension, all the doubts and guessing were obliterated. Caleb was her Twin Flame and the heat between them rose to such heights, she was sure they would melt all the snow in Massachusetts.

Tiny gasps escaped her lips as her head tilted back against the wall. Her fingertips pressed into his meaty, powerful shoulders. Higher she was lifted, until his mouth was upon her chest. Only her shirt separated her skin from his teeth. She couldn't stand it. She let go of him just long enough to tug it off. Cold air hit her and the bare wall against her back chilled, but he made up for it. Her amethyst necklace was spun around, so the jagged edges of the stone wouldn't hurt her.

His mouth seized the soft flesh of her breast the moment she was free of her shirt. Valerie let out a cry and arched her back. This was unlike anything she had ever felt. She had sex before in high school with inexperienced boys who just wanted the deed to be done and over with. They had no skill, no finesse. Caleb wasn't anything like those boys. He had lived long enough that he knew how to pleasure a woman, how to draw her to the brink with just a touch. Just a kiss. Just a few caresses and she was putty in his strong, capable hands.

To feel their bodies together, grinding as he continued to pleasure her, was like no magic she had ever known.

So when Caleb's mouth released her and she was lowered once more to face him, she groaned at the unfairness.

"Trust me," he whispered. "I'm not going to stop now. Not after all this damned waiting."

Her eyes cracked open to see why he had gone so still and the breath caught in her throat. Staring back at her wasn't a man, but a wolf. His gaze, once green like the lush forest, had turned golden like the rising full moon. Its hungry depths were iridescent in the dark, burning through her. To her own amazement, she wasn't frightened. How could she be? The wolf was part of him, just as magic was part of her. If Caleb could look past it, so could she.

And yet, there was a nervous look about him, as if he feared what she would think or say. He should have known that after playing this stupid game, she wasn't going to throw in the towel. Her hands gripped the back of his neck and pulled him in for more kisses. Claiming, hot, unyielding. Her nails drove in like spikes, demanding that they stay locked like this for eternity.

Caleb had other plans, and unfortunately he was stronger than her.

He pulled her from the wall and moved just a few feet over, so he could set her on the counter. His hands were free to bury themselves in her hair and she loved the feeling. Better yet, she wasn't afraid to let him know. Her legs hooked around his and pulled them together again. Their hips moved to imitate what their spirits needed so passionately. Their souls had been apart for long enough.

Caleb, to her horny frustration, leaned back from her kisses. His gaze, sultry and fierce, drank in her half-naked body. Something in that should have made her blush. She should have felt vulnerable, exposed. But it felt right. All of it. Only because it was with him.

"You know what's funny?" he asked breathlessly with a shake of his head. "I can write a bestselling novel, but I can't find a single word to describe you."

Desperate to catch her breath, Valerie muttered. "That bad?"

His lips spread in a devilish smile, exposing the fangs she had discovered with her tongue earlier. "No. That good."

Then, with a slowness that infuriated her, his mouth descended upon her shoulder, blazing a new trail with kisses and nips down her chest to find her nipples. The breath she had tried to catch escaped her in a rush and Valerie spiraled out of control.

The kitchen began to spin, and she was given to a world of new and indescribable feelings that all rushed between her legs like lit fuses burning their way to the dynamite. Unconsciously, she found herself rocking and grinding more urgently in an indulgent rhythm against what little of Caleb she could reach in this position. Greedy and selfish, she wanted all of him and she couldn't wait.

Her hands rushed to the front of his jeans and fumbled with the button and zipper. But he caught her first. He seized her wrists, just as he had done earlier that evening when they were sensible, and pinned them to the upper cabinets, so he could continue his work on her taut, aching nipples.

"Slow down," he growled.

She shook her head, making her all the more dizzy. "No... Please..." Now she just sounded petty.

His smile widened. "I like it when you beg, but I know what I'm doing."

His tongue flicked and spun in intoxicating patterns until she was sure she'd come right there in the kitchen before he ever had a chance to go further. Valerie whined and whimpered, unwilling for this to be over so soon.

Just when she thought she couldn't hold it any longer, Caleb released her breasts and met her lusty gaze. "Can you behave?"

Her courage and fire returned, she grinned. "Never."

Caleb was no less pleased by her answer. He let go of her wrists and seized her ass again to slide her from the counter. Her hands were freed, but she couldn't reach all the important places she needed to conquer before this was over.

He carried her across the house and to his room, her world bathed in black before entering a silvery blue haven. The night was clear and the last of the moon's rays splashed across his bed. The room was permeated with his scent, despite it only being his for a few days.

Valerie was dropped to the mattress before Caleb was straddled on top of her. Again, she groped for his jeans, but he captured her again, just long enough to torment her with more kisses, more caresses in places that ached and tingled.

Soon, her pajama pants were on the floor, along with her panties. Completely naked, she lay there and waited. She looked up to see Caleb's face immersed in shadows, but she could see what he was doing. Admiring her again, his leer raking up and down from the vixen-like stare to the way her legs parted to invite him in. The gold of his eyes sparkled and its affects spread like stardust in her veins.

"I know the word," he finally said as he pulled at the flaps of his jeans to shed them. "Perfect."

Valerie stopped her tortured writhing. *Perfect.* He thought she was perfect. Her eyes stung and she swallowed back the lump that rose in her throat. He was just saying it, because they were having sex. He didn't mean it. It was his dick talking. That's what she wanted to believe.

And still, there was something in the way his hands lingered over her ribcage and waist, how he grazed in all the right places and lit her up as they went. Maybe he wasn't lying. Maybe it wasn't just a trick of lust. Maybe he meant it.

Lost in this startling revelation, she hardly noticed the sound of his jeans hitting the floor with his underwear. But she noticed instantly when his nails outlined the inside of her thighs and drew across her wet and pulsing folds.

A cry escaped her and her legs spread to give him room. Obediently, her hands stayed tangled in the sheets while he toyed with her. She would have forced him to take that final plunge if he hadn't subdued her. So strong and forceful. He was in complete control and she loved it.

"Oh, Goddess! Don't stop!"

A seductive growl added to the overall pleasure of the moment. "Not until I hear you howl with me."

A smile crawled across her lips at the thought of it. Both of them, wild and untamable. Their souls really were the same. Across time, distance, and race, they were so much the same.

One tiny touch to the nub above her folds made stars dance in her vision. He did it again and again until she couldn't see straight. The pressure in her belly grew until she thought she'd burst, but Valerie gloried in it. In all of it. The sinful, molten rapture of it.

Then, in a rush of skin and muscle, Caleb was atop of her, his hands cupping her breasts and mouth lapping at her nipples. Her legs were over his hips, and she could feel the tip of his silky cock at her front door. She lifted herself, guiding him, urging him.

One sound was all it took to break his restraint. A growl. A deep, insistent growl that rumbled from her clenched teeth.

Caleb filled her, slipping into the core of her desire so easily, like they were perfectly designed for one another. In truth, they had been. She didn't have long to wait, but he had. Almost two centuries of it. She couldn't imagine what kind of other worldly revelations this did for him, but she knew how it felt for her.

Every lock, every door, every chain that had kept her down, had been eradicated. Her soul and spirit soared with his, spinning and whirling in a fitful tornado. Their frequencies aligned, their heartbeats skipped in unison. The harder he pounded into her, the further down the rabbit hole she fell with him, never to be seen again on this side of the looking glass.

They all told her how Twin Flames were destined to be together in the end. They all told her how the relationship was supposed to help her grow and learn on some spiritual level. But none of them had told her about this existential hurricane of bliss. This joining of beings that defied the laws of the universe themselves.

Valerie wanted it to last, to hold onto it forever and a day. But it wasn't over. Caleb, with his face buried in that lovely place where neck and shoulder met, growled just as she had, his sharp canines only adding to the innumerable sensations her body had never known before.

The orgasm, long and blissful, rocked her body and sent her into wild shrieks she had never heard from her own mouth before. Light exploded behind her eyes as she craned her head back to let it ravage her body.

Complete and utter surrender. That's what it was. Surrender to Caleb, to the future, to her past, and to everything she thought was real and immutable. This proved her wrong. So utterly wrong. Because feeling him come, feeling his cock throb with her, became her definition of real. Caleb was real. What they had was real. What she felt was real. And she knew that she never wanted to be without it. Never.

Chapter 17

Dawn had come all too soon for Caleb. Those hours spent in his bed, tangled in all that Valerie had to give him, were short, but sweet. They lay beside one another, exhausted and damp from sweat. Their lovemaking seemed to have no end. They came again and again, insatiable beyond words. They didn't need to tell one another that they were ready to go again after the first or the second, or even the third. Their spirits spoke to one another on a whole other level that he couldn't begin to understand.

Savage and raw with just enough tenderness to make it last. She had been as hard as diamonds, but moldable in his embrace. He too, found himself in the duplicity of give and take time after time. Wanting to submit himself to her undeniable will, but to enforce his own dominance. In the end, they were equal in the act and nothing could have been more harmonious. Nature's design couldn't rival what they'd created in that bedroom.

He recalled how she had taken him in all the ways a man could be taken, and vice-versa. Her hands, slender and skillful, had slid along his cock so masterfully he thought there was nothing better. She proved him wrong when her mouth and tongue were added into the mix. But he thought the best of it was when she demanded control, how she wouldn't take no for an answer and climbed on top to ride him just before daybreak. The sun caught her eyes at the exact moment they began to blur with ecstasy. It was the same look she gave again and again, but each time was like the first.

Valerie finally succumbed to sleep and he watched with engrossed fascination. The steady rise and fall of her chest as lungs expanded with each slow breath. How her dark lashes twitched every now and again as she dreamed. Her hair, a black and burgundy muss, filled him with pride. Because he was the one to muss it up. He was the one that made her quiver and beg. He was the one she wanted.

He thought it almost comical the way she charged into the kitchen and instigated the whole thing, when she might have been the one holding back the most since the beginning. His stalking game either worked too well, or hadn't done a damn thing. It was all her. Her decision to bust down the walls that divided them. Her decision to bound across the lines of civility and breach through the veil that separated them.

Caleb couldn't be sad or disappointed over the way things had turned out in the end. The goal had been reached, and no matter how they reached it, this felt right. They only had known one another for a few days, but this is where they were meant to be.

His fingertip drew a line from her shoulder, down her side and to her hip, where his hand flattened and stroked along the curve of her thigh. Without much prompting at all, her knee lifted so he could have a better hold.

A smile tilted the corners of her lips, and even in her sleep, she let out a tiny moan of pleasure at his touch. He felt his eyes turn golden, his one and only regret out of their lovemaking. His wolf wanted her too, and the passion of their sex enticed him forward like a moth to her flame. Thank God he didn't scare her. That was the last thing he ever wanted to do.

Valerie stirred and her gaze found his. She had seen nothing but these golden eyes for hours. If he thought he had any control over it, he would have implemented some.

"Really?" she said with a groggy smile. "How many times would this make it?" Caleb smirked. "Does it matter?"

Her hands were on him before anything could be decided. He let out a long breath as his stiff cock was taken in her capable hands. His eyes rolled into the back of his head and he began to wonder if the rest of the day would be a mirror of the night before.

In kind, his hand found the familiar path up to her femininity and discovered her just as wet and ready as his nose indicated. The smell of her arousal was enough to drive him to the edge of madness. Her taste, that much more. Like nectar straight from the gods. And that's what he began to see her as. A goddess in all but immortal divinity. And he was the mortal who didn't deserve her, but took her all the same, because she demanded it. He would be a willing worshipper for the rest of his life, drunk on her essence.

He slid inside, her warmth curling around his finger. Valerie gasped and her hand tightened over his shaft in response to make him echo her. Up and down she rubbed with the same speed as he pleasured her, their hands becoming the tools and poor substitutes for the real thing. But it was the foreplay of it, the imagination and understanding of what was to come that thrilled them both.

Eager lips found his and they slid into the kiss. They didn't stay there for long. Valerie pushed him onto his back and she kissed her way down his chest, flicking her tongue over his nipples as she went. He ground his teeth to subdue the growl, but it came out anyway.

Down she went, lingering over his hips and abs, following their lines as she had done countless times before in the last few hours. He watched every second of her descent. A tiny pearl of moisture upon his tip caught her eye and she ravenously enveloped her mouth over it. He wove his hand into her hair, urging each lick and suckle as she savored and tasted his cock.

"Does your wolf like this too?"

He chuckled at the thought of it. "Every part of me likes this, because you're the one doing it."

Caleb groaned at each skillful stroke, at each brushing of her teeth along his sensitive shaft. Yes, she was a goddess that could rip his heart out and dash it to the floor for all he cared. As long as she loved him like this.

When he felt close to the brink, he tugged upon her hair and brought her up again with the intent to turn her over. A silent battle of wills took place. She wanted to ride him again, but he wouldn't allow it. He wanted to take her this time. It was only fair after she had done all the work.

Using his strength against her, Caleb whisked around until she was on her hands and knees upon the bed, and her hips in his hands. Carefully positioning her, he slid his cock inside. Heat met with heat and she gave out a long, blissful cry.

He thrust, admiring the way her back and shoulders moved with each measure. With one hand, he reached around and caught her nipple between his fingers. Her cries grew louder, more urgent, more pleading for release that he was willing to prolong until the end of time. Because she was his, and he was hers.

She came just seconds before he did and he relished in the raging pulse that encased his cock so luxuriously. They collapsed on the bed once more when it was all over, panting and ripples of light flowing between them as they began to spiral down from the high.

Now it was his turn to be overcome by drowsiness. Caleb's eyes closed and just as he felt on the edge of sleep, he heard her phone vibrate in her bedroom. Valerie, of course, wouldn't hear it.

"Your phone's going off," he mumbled.

Valerie scooted closer, her bewitching hands upon his chest as her head nestled against his shoulder. "Let it go off."

"It might be Krystal. You're probably late for work."

"Fuck work," she said cheerfully as she kissed his collarbone.

He found that amusing, though he should have expected such an answer. "You need to give them some reason why you're not coming in then."

"Why? It's none of their business."

Caleb took her hand and laced their fingers together before she could start another wildfire. "You don't want them sending a search party. What would you tell them if they came barging in here and they saw us together?"

Valerie let out a long breath and let herself take a break from driving him to distraction. "I don't have to give them an explanation for anything."

He paused, picking his next words carefully so as not to rile her. He remembered what she had neglected to tell them the day before in the coffeeshop. Was she still ashamed of him? "You could tell them your Twin Flame is a werewolf and I'm sure they'd accept it."

She sat up immediately, her amethyst necklace dangling from her neck. Her green eyes flashed with surprise. "You... You know about Twin Flames?"

Oddly gratified by her startled look, he ran his thumb along her cheek. "Grandma Ruth mentioned it. I found out the rest."

A miniscule hint of fear came and went, like the blinking of an eye. Valerie licked her lips thoughtfully and then settled back onto the mattress, propped up on her elbow. "What else did she mention?"

Caleb wouldn't allow her to be discouraged. Not after all they had just been through. "She told me to be gentle with you. That you've been through a lot with your parents and your aunt. As a witch and a woman, you haven't had it easy... That you blamed yourself for a lot of what you had to go through as a child... You had to grow up too fast and I know what that's like."

They may have still been in the same bed, but Caleb felt instantly shoved away. A barrier dropped, the one he thought had been torn down when she first kissed him. In a desperate attempt to keep her there, he held her hand tighter.

"I don't want any sympathy." Her melodic voice turned hard and nettled. "I never have. That's why I don't talk about it. Grandma Ruth had no right to say any of that."

He leveled his own stony glare with hers. "I'm glad she did, whether she had a right to or not. Because I don't pity you. I understand you. I've had to watch my parents die as well. I've watched every one of my family pass away, all my friends, my acquaintances. It used to be impossible for me to open a newspaper without seeing an obituary for someone I knew. I understand how hard it is to feel... to feel alone. To feel helpless..."

Caleb knew he couldn't keep any secrets from her. Not after all he just confessed. She had to understand the whole truth of why he was in Goldcrest Cove. "Remember that bad egg I mentioned? The one I was running from in my old pack... That was me. There was an incident."

Valerie froze, and he knew where her mind must have gone. He held her tighter.

"There was a girl in Bainbridge. She was getting mugged and I happened to be there, but not... not as myself. I had gone for a run that night and the wolf saved her. The newspapers all said it was a dog, but she was smarter than anyone expected. She showed up at a pack meeting. She found out everything and was threatening to tell somebody." Caleb swallowed, remembering her terror-stricken face. "My alpha put it to a vote. Whether to let her go, kill her, or turn her so that our secret would be hers. No one wanted to let her go for obvious reasons, but the majority elected to turn her... It didn't go well. She fought the change and the wolf wouldn't take her... She died."

Valerie lowered her gaze, but wouldn't say anything.

"I try to convince myself, on most days, that it wasn't my fault. I had been her defender once, so I should have been it a second time. I could have done something to save her, but I didn't. I had been too reckless and got too involved. I should have been the one they punished. Not her. I couldn't abide by what they did, so I left." He kissed the back of her hand. "And I'm glad I did, because I met you. And I've had time to grieve and forgive myself, as I know you can too."

The veil began to waver again, but it wouldn't buckle just yet. In her eyes were the signs of deference.

"Maybe that's why we're Twin Flames," he continued. "Maybe I'm supposed to help you understand that it's okay to be lonely and grieve. It's okay to walk through the valley of the shadow of death, but you can't sit there for your whole life like you deserve to be miserable, because they're gone. I spent too long in that valley to ever think that was a place we deserve to be. You are worthy of happiness and love, no matter what happens to you or what you've done."

Valerie seemed on the brink of some devastating emotion, but she wouldn't take that final step. He tried not to read into it, tried not to think it was because she didn't fully trust him. These things took time. If he had learned anything after living for so long, it was that. Trust, love, and healing all took time. Even for him, and especially for someone like Valerie.

"If you think I'm going to get all weepy, you'll be disappointed."

Once more, he smiled to her and wasn't sure if he'd ever love her more than he did in that moment. She hadn't pushed him away, hadn't recoiled from him for his confession. This was going well so far. "I would only be disappointed if you think for a second that I was going to run away just because of a little baggage."

"It looks like you've got some baggage of your own, too." Valerie took a steeling breath, though he could see her eyes mist a bit. "So, you know. We're Twin Flames. I can't see it changing much, though."

Caleb's brow furrowed. "It changes everything."

She shook her head. "I don't think it will. You're still a werewolf and it's going to take a lot more than this bit of news for them to change their opinions overnight. If anything, it's going to make a bigger stink."

"Then we'll deal with the stink together... Right?" Caleb leaned up and kissed her, slow and sensual. Probably the most sensual kiss of the whole morning. Before, they were driven by a wanton need for one another. This kiss communicated everything that his heart wanted to say, but his mind couldn't.

When they disconnected, Valerie looked as if she had just taken a shot of morphine. Bleary-eyed and pliable, she simply nodded and then fell into him. His arms encased her, softening her fall from heaven.

He'd hold her as long as she wanted, as long as it took to let her know that her world was all right. Until she felt safe. He never had someone there for him, but he could be there for her.

She thought he would ruin it all with that after-school-special speech. He might have tainted his image in anyone else's eyes with his story about what happened in Bainbridge. To her own amazement, it didn't. If anything, it made it all the better. They had only one secret now, and it made breaking the news about Twin Flames that much easier. Krystal had to explain her dark magic quite a few times before Devin finally got used to the idea, but Caleb was ahead of her in every respect it seemed.

Valerie couldn't regret that, or anything else they had done. Even once she was back in her clothes, she blushed and grinned like one of those love-struck airheads in the movies. Not in a million years did she ever think that would be her. Never had she thought she could walk on air and feel totally and completely adored.

The amethyst necklace had done its job and absorbed every last bit of negative energy she had to expel over the last several hours. Of course, there was little to expel at all while she stayed horny and with Caleb. All the same, she excused herself to cleanse the crystal while Caleb fixed a pot of coffee for her and some tea for himself.

Poor Thor, who had to patiently wait out all the loud, hot sex, was eager to be let out into the yard for some fresh air. Valerie, still on a high despite the moment of seriousness, met Caleb in the living room. Clad in only his jeans again, chest bare and smelling like an erotic dream, he handed over her coffee mug with one of those charming smiles she could never get enough of. This had to be an illusion. How could she ever get anything this good?

"I texted Krystal and told her I was drained from all the... the stuff that happened yesterday. She seemed to buy it." She nearly gave herself away again. Caleb might have known about Twin Flames, but the dark magic might have been a little too much for now.

They sat beside one another on the sectional and she curled her legs up on the cushion, contented to lean into him. One arm wrapped around her shoulders as if they had been doing this for ages, for a lifetime. Valerie still couldn't get over how perfect it all seemed. If she could only stay like this forever.

"Good. You'll have the day to rest while I make another go for this necromancer."

Caleb took a sip of his hot tea as if he hadn't just sent Valerie into a panic attack.

"Bullshit! You're not going after him!" She sat up straight and nearly spilled her coffee. "He almost killed you! Leave it to Krystal's parents!"

The werewolf wasn't impressed with her argument and set both of their mugs on the coffee table before a mess could be made. "I'm not going to fight him this time," he replied with all the calm she couldn't muster. "I'm going to try and talk to him. I can't really threaten him to tell me the truth, but I can at least make a case to move on away from Goldcrest Cove or something."

Valerie grabbed for the waistband of his jeans. "It's too dangerous and I'm not going to let you leave this house if that's what you plan on doing. Not without me."

A flicker of something wild and angry passed over Caleb's expression. "If it's dangerous, I'm certainly not taking you."

"Yes, you are! I have a better chance in combat with the guy if it comes to that."

Caleb took hold of her hand that was fastened to him. "You weren't there last night when I fought him. No offense, but he's way out of your league. I'm not going to put you in harm's way. You'll stay here and that's final."

She gave him a simpering, but challenging smile. "I'm a witch. What are you going to do about it?"

He opened his mouth to give his answer, but must have thought better and closed it. A muscle in his jaw tightened as he tried to think. He came out with nothing and gave a huff. "I'm not going to sit around here all day and do nothing when innocent people are somehow at risk."

"You don't have to sit around. I'll just go with you. Besides, you said so yourself that you weren't sure where he ran off to."

"I know where his house is," he insisted. "I can pick up the trail there."

"Suppose he knows you were tailing him and he covered his scent once he went back? Suppose he changed his hiding spot? He could have totally disappeared off the map for all you know."

Caleb wasn't pleased with that dose of reality, but she was quick to chase it with something better.

"I think we should go see Amber," she said confidently.

That might as well have been like a curveball coming right out of left field. "Amber? What the hell can she do?"

Caleb never thought he'd be back on the porch at Rose House. But after what Valerie explained, he deemed it necessary. If Amber could give them any hint about the necromancer, it was worth it.

Before he raised his fist to knock, Valerie took two steps away from him, though she had been on his arm up the porch steps. He tried not to feel offended. It was only a formality until they could openly confess their attachment. Hopefully that would be sooner rather than later. After all this necromancy business was over with.

The door swung open before his knuckles had a chance to make contact with the wood. Amber's smiling face greeted them. "It's about time you two got out of bed and showed up! I wondered if you two had taken another roll in the sheets with how late you were."

They exchanged alarmed looks. The innkeeper turned and walked inside, assuming they would follow, but they both stood, aghast and confused.

"Did you...?" Caleb whispered, gesturing to Amber's back.

Valerie shook her head. "I didn't say anything to anyone."

"You didn't have to," Amber answered back from the sitting room. "I saw it coming weeks ago!"

So, Valerie wasn't exaggerating. The witch really could scry. They stepped inside and now that the guise was pointless, their hands intertwined as they followed Amber.

The purple-haired innkeeper turned and clapped her hands in a gleeful spectacle that annoyed Caleb more than it should have.

"Oh, I can't tell you how excited I was when that premonition hit me!" she cried. "You two are just perfect for each other. I know you can't really see it now. But I do. Or, saw. I saw it… Whatever." She waved her hands and motioned toward the Victorian sofa. "Just take a seat and we can get started. I've still got to get dinner in the oven for tonight."

"Who else knows?" Valerie asked meekly as they sat down together.

Amber settled herself on the coffee table in front of them, the wood creaking under her weight, but holding steady. "No one… Well, Mrs. Hayden might, but she might have been more worried about the whole necromancy thing."

"She knew about my dark magic."

There was that word again. Caleb looked to her, searching her expression for that usual timidity whenever the term "dark magic" was brought up in a conversation. But there was nothing. No fear, no hesitance or sudden rush of anxiety. She was, however, thoroughly piqued by Amber's deceptiveness. That must have explained the innkeeper's uncanny friendliness when he arrived.

"If she knew anything about Caleb being your Twin Flame, she didn't tell me. That's all I know." Amber brought her hands together and excitedly rubbed her palms. "Okay, so you saw the warlock, right? Did he touch you?"

Caleb scoffed, still mystified how she could know so much. "I'll say he did. Tried to choke me."

Valerie's hand tightened around his and he gave a reassuring squeeze in return.

"Perfect," Amber said with a little too much enthusiasm. "If he touched you, it makes my job a ton easier. Give me your hands." All three joined hands to form a triangle. "I don't normally try these things with fewer witches, but I've been getting better."

"Valerie says this is your... special skill?" Caleb still didn't like the concept of being so close to magic when it was performed. If this could have been done without him, it would have been all the better.

"My dark magic, yeah. Now, hush for a minute, so I can get a clear signal."

Caleb grimaced. She talked as if it were something like a magical GPS tracker. In a sense, maybe it was.

Amber closed her eyes and he could already feel the flood of magic travel through limbs, circulating like an electric current. Not painful or terribly uncomfortable, but definitely odd.

He half expected her to go into some trance or watch her head whip around like in The Exorcist. Instead, she seemed to drop into a calm meditative state. Occasionally, her face would pinch or her lips would twitch into a tiny smile as if she saw something favorable.

A long moment passed with nothing to show for it. Then, Amber's eyes opened wide with absolute terror. "Holy fuck!" she screamed.

"What?" Valerie and Caleb asked in unison, all scooting to the edge of their seats.

Amber immediately let go of their hands and stood, but upon shaky legs. Her complexion turned pallid as she absently walked about the sitting room, wringing her hands and muttering incoherently like a mad woman. Above it all was the stench of fear.

Valerie went to her friend and took her by the arms. "What did you see? Did you find him?"

The frightened witch jerked as if she had just been woken up from a vivid walking dream. She looked from Valerie to Caleb and then pressed her palm to her forehead. "Yeah... Yeah, I found him. This is way above my paygrade, guys."

Caleb was on his feet now and went to her, charged with purpose. "Wherever he is, I'll go and take care of it."

Amber let out a short scream and seized his jacket sleeve. "No! Don't! Don't get anywhere near this guy. If not for yourself, then for Val's sake, okay?"

"Is it really that bad?" Valerie questioned skeptically. "The man's dead."

"It's not about the warlock. It's about... about who he's working with."

"Chief Nickels," Caleb said. "We already knew that."

"It's not Chief Nickels," Amber insisted. "Not completely, I mean... It can't be all his doing."

Valerie shook the witch. "Start making sense! Who is he working for? Do you have a name?"

She shook her head and that paleness returned. "No. Not a name. Just a feeling and it's not a good one. I couldn't see a face either. It's... I don't know what it is, but this is way beyond all of us. It's not just necromancy shit. There's this whole other scheme and... I really don't even want to look any further into it."

Caleb looked to Valerie before saying, "What are we supposed to do? I can't tell Krystal's father that I've had anything to do with this."

"Well, you're gonna fuckin' have to, because there's no getting around it." Amber strode away toward the hall. "I need a drink. You want one?"

They both declined and Amber left them alone in the sitting room.

"Maybe I can lie and put myself in your place," Valerie offered distractedly. "I'll say that I'm the one that went after the necromancer and Amber scryed off of me."

"No. I won't have his wrath come down on you."

She gave him a wary look. "But you're not going to let it go, are you?"

"Not if it's really that bad."

Valerie stomped her foot. "Damnit, Caleb! You don't have to run off and be some big hero just to prove you're on our side. Are you doing this because you want to impress everyone else? Because if you are –"

He wouldn't listen to another word. Caleb took her face in his hands and kissed her hard on the mouth. Once her bones had turned to mush, he let her go. "I'm doing this to protect you. I have from the start. Everything I've tried to do was to make sure you're safe above all else. Hell, if I thought I could convince you to leave town with me, I would. But your life and friends are here, so I can't ask that of you. If you stay, I stay. And if I'm staying, this bastard's gonna have to leave."

Whether it was the kiss or the gallant speech, it worked. Valerie softened and she nodded. "All right... But I think we need to tell Mr. Hayden anyway. We'll make him listen to what you have to say... *I'll* make him listen."

It was a step. A small one, but a step toward finally coming out about their relationship. If Amber knew and didn't object, that was a start as well. Having one more witch on their side might not turn the tide completely, but it would set the hurdles on a lower rung.

"Let's have him come to the house and we'll talk there," Caleb suggested. "It'd be better if he comes into my territory than me trying to trespass onto his."

Chapter 18

Nothing in the world could beat the feeling of her hand tucked securely into his. Except sex. But this was much easier to do when Caleb was in the driver's seat, his eyes on the road that would lead them home from Rose House.

While her curiosity burned to know exactly what Amber saw, her mind had sunk to darker places. With country music on the radio, reality set in. Valerie hardly knew Caleb. That didn't seem to matter as much before, but now, somewhere in the back of her mind, it did. It was like those women running off with someone they just met at the bar or getting married after knowing one another for a week. Twin Flames might have been the exception, though she couldn't shake that feeling like they were going a hundred miles per hour down a dirt road with sharp twists and turns ahead and no brakes.

Valerie thought of the future, of all their differences. They might not have been running now, but would one of them venture off course after a while? What if she couldn't stand the way he brushed his teeth, or he lost patience with her when she was being neurotic?

Even further, she wondered what this would mean for their lives in Goldcrest Cove. Would their relationship blacklist them from other witches and werewolves? What if Caleb got the itch to be part of a pack again and wanted to move?

But one desperately important detail had escaped her up until now, and she couldn't keep quiet about it, not even when his thumb stroked over the back of her hand so tenderly it made her want to melt in her seat.

"So, how is this going to work?" she asked.

"What do you mean?"

Valerie shifted, as if straightening her legs would make this any less awkward to talk about. "Well, you're practically immortal, right? You've been around for a while and... I only know of one way a witch can live forever, but it's forbidden and – "

"Don't think," he commanded gently as he brought her hand to his lips and kissed it. "We don't need to worry about all that right now."

She forced herself not to go soft, just because he knew being sweet would pacify her as it had before. "But I'm going to worry about it. It's kind of a big deal. I don't want to be the withered old hag while you're still looking like a hottie."

He cocked a brow at her. "You think I'm a hottie?"

A bit of a blush rose to her cheeks, of all times, after the morning they just had. "I hate to break it to you, but everyone does. Even Alexa."

Caleb chuckled and she reveled in the sound of it. "Good thing I only have eyes for you then, huh?"

He glanced her way with that smoldering, sexy twinkle in his eyes and she wondered how much time they would have alone before Mr. Hayden and the rest of them showed up to the house.

"Let's just worry about this necromancer and then we can get to all those annoying details. Deal?"

This time, she was supple to his request and only nodded. Just at the exact moment, the truck engine began to sputter. Her eyes went wide and she dropped Caleb's hand. Dwelling on all those bad thoughts must have invited in more negative energy than she realized.

He cursed aloud and pulled the truck over to the side of the road. "I forgot to fill up. I've got a jerrycan in the back. Won't take me long to get her up and running again."

Valerie let out a breath and slumped. "Oh, good. It's not me."

Caleb looked to her in puzzlement. "Why would it be you?"

And there, she trapped herself. Valerie refused to look at him and kept her eyes on the snowy shoulder of the road. They were still a good ways off from the rest of the town with a small stretch of woods on either side. A perfect place for a conversation like this, but a terrible one to be caught without gas.

"Is there something you need to tell me?"

Valerie stammered, hating how she had been caught. How could she possibly explain dark magic? Twin Flames would have been bad enough, but having to instruct Caleb on the complexities of magic seemed too much. She had hoped that this sort of discussion would be planned and thought out more thoroughly.

"I... I really don't know how to put it into words right now."

Sympathetic to her distress, Caleb said, "That's fine. Let me get this taken care of and you can think on it." He kissed the back of her hand again. "And don't think I'll forget. Because I really want to know." He kissed her wrist, then her forearm, making his way tenderly up to her elbow. "I want to know everything I can about you, as long as you're willing to tell me."

Even through her coat sleeve, his kisses drove heat through her like spikes. Who needed a heater when she had a sexy werewolf to woo her?

Caleb flashed her a smile and then hopped out of the truck. Valerie took a breath to calm herself. If she wasn't careful about her energy, they'd never make it home and they'd be stranded. She was in no mood to go tramping through the snow.

There came the metallic scrape of the can on the bed of the truck and she thought she heard the dull pop of the tank lid. But then silence. No sloshing or chugging of the gasoline. After a few seconds, she peeked into the chipped side mirror.

Caleb was standing there, jerrycan in hand while he peered out into the woods next to the truck. He didn't move, but every line of his powerful, masculine body told her that something wasn't right.

She turned in her seat and opened the door, only to be barked at.

"Get back in the truck," he ordered. He had never spoken to her so severely. At first, it scared her into doing just like he asked.

That didn't stop her from rolling down the window with the crank lever on the door. "What's wrong?"

Caleb set the jerrycan back where he had gotten it, all while never taking his eyes off some unseen target amongst the trees. "Just stay in the truck. Lock the doors until I get back."

Without another word, he marched down the shoulder and into the forest. Valerie let out a huff of disbelief. To her eyes, she saw nothing out of the ordinary. Just the same woods she had grown up with and passed by countless times. But to a werewolf, maybe there was more. Something obviously had him peeved. Whatever it was, it was bad enough that he felt he could start giving her orders.

She did as she was told, but kept her stare centered upon the forest, watching for any sign of his return. If he wasn't back in five minutes, she told herself that she'd go after him and suffer the consequences later. He might have been more dominant, but there was one thing he would come to understand. Valerie wasn't an omega, or some pack underling. She was more stubborn than that.

He didn't know whether to curse or thank providence for picking up the warlock's scent. It was faint, almost imperceptible above the pines and frost. But it was there on the wind and he followed it. Leaving Valerie in the truck might not have been the smartest thing he could have done, but he didn't want to risk losing this opportunity.

Caleb would do as he said he would. Just talk. He'd meet the man under a white flag, just to get answers, if he was a willing donor.

A quarter of a mile deep into the wilderness, he came to a dead end. The scent cut off abruptly, giving no lead in any direction, not even up. Never had a trail gone cold like this. Caleb looked around to the pines and elms, keeping all his senses open to the trap he didn't expect.

"I suppose I should thank you."

Caleb spun to face the warlock leaning against the trunk of an elm. He instantly showed his hands in a sign of capitulation. "Thank me for what?"

"Bringing one of the witches right to me," he said, his eyes flashing with sinister intent. "The question now is whether I should hold her hostage to lure the rest of them out, or kill her to send a message."

The wolf in him raged, but Caleb kept up his submissive guise. "There's no need for any of that."

"You've all been muddling in my affairs too much for it to be anything else but necessary."

Caleb narrowed his eyes upon the warlock, trying to place him in time. He didn't talk like anyone born in the last century. He would know.

"They're trying to protect their town," he defended. "Nothing more."

"And you? What's your role in this? You can't be working alongside them."

Caleb nodded and took a testing step forward. "I am. They're my friends."

The warlock gave a laugh. "Friends? You're a fool to think they'd want anything more from you than a bodyguard. You're perfect for it. In fact...."

The warlock extended his gloved hand toward Caleb. The fingers arched as his wrist rotated in a slow, but stiff manner. "I think I'll take advantage of you for a moment, if you don't mind." He huffed. "Well, as if you really have a choice in the matter."

Magic shot from the necromancer's palm and Caleb turned to escape it, but it was no use. Its tendrils wrapped around his body and seeped through his clothes, then into his skin. He let out a shout as it laced its way through his blood and nerves, infecting his system until he couldn't move another inch.

The magic was as painful as he thought it would be. Hot, burning, liquefying into his bones and taking over everything. Just before it reached his brain, he felt the shift. He could do nothing to stop it, nothing to ease his agony as he usually could during the transformation.

Bones snapped and cracked out of joint. Skin gave way to black fur. His clothes ripped and pulled against him as his form changed. But he didn't completely shift. Not as he usually did into a wolf. What he became was something else. Something unnatural and beastly.

That's all he understood before darkness swelled in his vision and dreaded unconsciousness took hold. He didn't know what the warlock had planned, but all he could think of was Valerie sitting defenseless in his truck.

His fifteen minutes weren't up, but Valerie couldn't stay put. A dark, foreboding feeling gripped her stomach and refused to let go until she followed after him. Maybe it was just something silly, like a wolfish instinct to take a trip into the woods. It was more likely that Caleb sensed something coming and wanted to meet it on his terms instead of waiting for it.

Whatever it was, Valerie had to know for certain, so her heart would stop rioting.

The snow chilled her ankles as she stepped slowly and carefully into the trees. Thankfully, the underbrush wasn't as overgrown as it would be in the spring or summer. That made the way clear for her to follow his footprints. After a while, she attempted to match her stride with his, stepping where he had stepped, so there would only be one pair of prints instead of two.

She called out his name, but there was no reply. Nothing but the crisp crunching of her shoes against packed snow. A cold wind slammed into her face and she stopped, heeding its warning. Valerie searched the maze of trees for anything that remotely looked like Caleb. But she saw nothing for yards in any direction. This was definitely the way he went.

Her eyes followed his trail up ahead and found it had stopped near an opening in the forest. The snow was disturbed and flattened, like he had fallen down or there had been some scuffle there. The intention in going after him had been to alleviate some fear that he was in trouble, but this only proved her gut right. Something was wrong.

Now, she felt like one of those stupid girls in a horror movie who went walking alone in the dark with a killer on the loose. She turned one more time to look for him, even peering up into the trees with their twisted, bare branches. Nothing. Not a single trace.

She let out a long breath, letting it mist in front of her mouth. Then, the hairs on the back of her neck began to prickle. She thought it was just the cold and her nerves. That idea was shattered when she felt that sort of sixth sense that something was drawing closer. Like a force was descending upon her, stalking, lurking.

Her own set of instincts kicked in and she used her magic to throw up a shield as she turned to face it. Valerie let out a cry as something dark slammed into her defenses, hard enough to throw her backwards and break her walls completely.

She fell into the snow and watched as the creature ducked and rolled away in the opposite direction. At least her shield had helped her before it broke. Powder flew up as the creature regained its footing and charged for another attack.

If the snarls and gnashing fangs weren't enough to tell her what it was, the muzzle, fur, and pointed ears did the trick. This was what she expected werewolves to look like. Monstrous, massive beasts from the Hollywood movies that only CGI could create. Part man, but mostly wolf, and bigger than either. Golden eyes rimmed in a hellish black glared above the wrinkled jowls as it growled at her.

In her heart, she knew it was Caleb, but at the same time it couldn't be. He would never go after her like this.

"Caleb, stop!" she cried as he dashed closer, kicking up a slush of snow with his paws as he ran. He didn't stop. Didn't even seem to hear her.

Valerie struggled to her feet and could feel her heart break as she used her magic to throw him back again. A pulse, much like the one she had used the night she found him in her kitchen, was enough to send him crashing against a tree. The wood splintered and she heard the crack as the trunk split in two with the force of the impact.

Caleb only shook his head and rose to his feet again, ready for more.

"You know me! Snap out of it!"

Again, it was like he had gone deaf. Or maybe his wolfen form couldn't comprehend human speech. Valerie pulled on all of her magic to defend herself. The forcefield she erected would be enough to keep him out, and the pulses could weaken him after a time. That was the idea, anyway. But how long could a werewolf endure this? He could heal and his stamina was insane. It was likely she couldn't outlast him, but she could hold until he came out of whatever it was that made him go crazy.

Rage, rather than fear, fueled her magic. Someone had to be behind this. She could almost sense the enchantment over Caleb. Just who, she couldn't say. Maybe the necromancer, or maybe – she thought to her regret – it was Mr. Hayden. She wouldn't put it past the warlock to try and make a point to his family. If he wanted them to be afraid of werewolves, this sort of stunt wasn't completely inconceivable.

Whoever it was, Valerie knew it was up to her to break it. Between her repulses, Valerie continued to try and talk him down while extracting what magic she could. It was difficult, and required Latin words she couldn't remember completely. Undoing someone else's charm wasn't something she knew well. But she had to try.

"The words that bind thee," she muttered, "I release. The magic that compels thee, I free. The... The power that... oh shit, what was it..."

Still, Caleb kept coming with all the force of a damned tornado, pounding into her shield, clawing for her and snapping his sharp teeth just a couple of feet from her nose. Valerie shoved him back and she began to lose her resilience. She could see the filmy, rainbow barrier of her shield begin to flicker and fail as Caleb stood for another round, no less tired and no further convinced that she wasn't his enemy.

Valerie let it all drop just for a second, so she could regain some energy, but she'd never had to do this on her own before. She could charm coffee and perform rituals with other witches, but battling an enchanted werewolf was new ground for her. Stubbornness and pride wanted her to win, so she could tell them all that Caleb was never a threat. Love kept her from dealing the fatal blow that would end it. Despair made her drop to her knees and wish that their Twin Flames were enough to make him understand the truth.

It was a fucked up way to die, but Valerie would have preferred dying at the hands of her Twin Flame than anyone else's. Caleb would eventually wake up and find her mangled, half-eaten body and probably hate himself for eternity, but what else could she do? She couldn't hurt him. Not really. And if her words weren't enough, then what more was there?

There was courage. The kind of courage that Caleb believed she had. The kind that kept her from looking for that one spell in her family's grimoire. The courage to keep fighting and keep living. She stood, doing what all witches advised against. She pulled on the very last of her reserves, the last bout of magic that would leave her totally defenseless if she used it.

Caleb crouched low, his furry mane bristling around his head. He knew the magic was nearly gone. He knew if he made one more lunge, he'd have her. So he leapt, closing the space between them. Valerie threw up one last repulse, but she braced, knowing it might not have been enough.

The missile of magic didn't hit its target. She heard a collision, as if two trucks had plowed straight into one another in a fit of roars and growls. Valerie looked up and blinked. Wrestling not too far from her was not one, but two werewolves. She could tell which one was Caleb by his dark fur, but the other boasted a coat of brown, tan, and black. It reminded her of a German Shepherd, but this was no dog. It was definitely a werewolf, who matched Caleb in size and strength.

Too stunned to move, she collapsed in the snow and watched them roll and tear one another apart. She remembered when there had been a massive dog fight at the shelter a year or so back. Two dogs, who seemed to get along, suddenly jumped on one another and it took three male volunteers to separate them. This reminded her of that, but the consequences were far more obvious and brutal than that little scrap in comparison.

Blood stained the white snow where they struggled. Fangs and claws ripped into one another without mercy. Yelps and beastly noises such as she had never heard before echoed across the forest. They moved too quick for her to even track.

Who was this second werewolf? Where did he come from? Did he know Caleb? Was it his fault he had gone rogue all of the sudden?

But the werewolves were the least of her worries. So engrossed in the battle, unsure whether to cheer on her lover or not, she didn't hear someone approach until it was too late. An arm snatched her up. She screamed, but a leather glove slapped over her mouth to quiet her. The odor of something rotten made her gag.

"This will be easier if you don't struggle," the man muttered in her ear as he dragged her away. Her feet beat and kicked, but he was far too strong. "Just be a good witch and do as I say."

Fat fucking chance of that.

Valerie, drained from the fight with Caleb, found just enough magic left in her to blast this guy into next Tuesday. She let it burst from her body as if she were the atomic bomb that had just detonated. The warlock was flung into the air. The moment she was free, Valerie ran. She didn't even know where she was running to and the expending of her magical reserves had her dizzy and reeling.

She thought of Caleb and the other werewolf, and didn't know who had won – if anyone had won. Theories raced through her mind about the werewolf, the warlock that tried to grab her, and why he wanted her alive. Theories that she couldn't keep straight or make sense of. All she knew was she had to keep running and get to some semblance of safety before anyone realized where she had gone.

She needed more time to build up her magic before she could go back and have any chance of coming out the victor.

She stumbled in the snow several times before getting just enough footing to run a good stretch. Too caught up in her escape, she didn't hear the commotion going on behind her. Shouts, roars, and the zing of magic made it sound like a full-on battle. Who the combatants were, she couldn't tell.

Heart pounding wildly in her chest, she kept going until she collided into something solid, but giving. Valerie screamed at the vague color of black, thinking she had just ran into Caleb. But Mrs. Hayden's perfume calmed her immediately.

"It's all right, honey!" she said, gathering the frightened witch into her arms. "They're taking care of it. You're all right."

That meant Gordon had to be close by. Valerie craned her head around to where she had run from, and realized just how short of a distance she had managed in what felt like an eternity of running. A mass confusion of colorful magic blurred the scene and she couldn't even see Caleb or the other werewolf anymore.

"Don't hurt him!" she screamed to Gordon, thinking that he'd blame Caleb for the whole thing.

She tugged away from Catherine, but the older witch held onto her firmly to keep her away from the battle.

"He won't hurt Caleb," she assured carefully. "He's just after Emmett."

"Emmett?" Valerie wondered if that was the other werewolf. If that were the case, she still didn't want Gordon doing something stupid. It was the werewolf who saved her life.

"The necromancer. I called Amber and she told me."

Likely, Catherine sensed all this trouble before it ever started and knew exactly what Valerie and Caleb were up to. But she wouldn't let herself worry about that now. Not until she found Caleb, in wolf or in human form, somewhere in the fray.

Bursts of brilliant neon shades shimmered and exploded through the forest as the two warlocks continued to do battle. If that was how powerful Emmett, the necromancer, had been, she wouldn't have stood a chance. Her, nor Caleb.

The moment she caught sight of the two werewolves loping away from the two warring warlocks, Valerie's lungs released their breath in one huffing gust that left the rest of her like jelly. Only Catherine's motherly arms kept her upright.

Her mouth formed his name, but her throat couldn't make the sound. But souls needed no voice. She saw Caleb's dark form turn and look to her. All malice and fury were gone from his wolfish face. All that remained was regret, and she saw it in the way his ears folded back and tail tucked low between his legs.

The enchantment was broken. Her old Caleb was back, and she reached for him with a shaky hand of amnesty. He was hesitant at first, taking a few paces and then backing away, too scared to approach her after all that he had tried to do. She couldn't imagine what had been going through his head, but it didn't matter. None of it did. She still needed him, still loved him.

Caleb glanced to the lighter-colored werewolf, as if for permission. Just one nudge was enough and Caleb made his way toward them. Catherine didn't warn him away as Valerie had expected. She permitted the werewolf in all his glory to come forward.

Now, up close and not fighting for her life, Valerie could fully appreciate how beautiful he was. Though his fur was matted in places by half-frozen blood, Caleb was a wonder. Absolutely magnificent.

Still, he came to her like a child bent on a scolding, or a pup who would be whacked with a newspaper for doing something bad. Valerie would never punish him or hate him for what happened. Catherine transferred the young witch from her arms into his, and she basked in the warmth of his fur.

Strong arms wrapped around her and she buried her face in his pelt, loving how, even as a wolf, he smelled just like her Caleb. She held fast as if they'd be torn apart the minute Gordon was finished with the warlock.

Tears that hadn't been shed in all the other heart wrenching moments before now, came spilling over her cheeks. Relief and love brought them out and they dried against his chest. There wasn't a warmer, more welcoming place on earth than in his embrace.

Chapter 19

Theo may have been content to smoke a cigarette in the middle of the trapping circle, but Caleb paced. The magic still glittered in his veins and crawled across his skin. The last of its potency was thoroughly beaten out of him by his former alpha.

The bastard had stayed in Goldcrest Cove after they had their talk in the driveway. Caleb wasn't sure whether to hate the werewolf for it, or be glad that he had stuck around town. If it hadn't been for him, the necromancer might have had his way and Valerie would be dead.

He still couldn't believe, after all he had tried to do to her, she forgave him. Hell, she wanted to hold him and be there when he shifted back into a man under Gordon's watchful eye. She had seen far more of his beastly nature than he would have ever wanted her to see, and still she accepted him. This Twin Flame connection was stronger than he ever imagined.

"You're going to make me dizzy," Theo complained with the cigarette dangling from his pinched lips. "Quit your pacing for a few minutes, will ya?"

Caleb looked toward the Hayden Mansion again, listening to the pitiful interrogation taking place inside. "How can I when she's in there and I'm out here?"

Theo cracked a slick smile. "She's perfectly safe. That asshole of a warlock is making sure of that."

He certainly was. The minute he had the necromancer weakened and trapped in a binding circle of his own, Gordon Hayden had turned his attention to the two werewolves. They were under arrest by the order of the High Magical Council, under his authority, until they could be properly questioned. Their involvement with the necromancer was a prime focus of his, and Caleb was sure he wouldn't get a fair trial. Not after he had almost killed Valerie. Theo might have gotten off as the hero in the whole scheme, and he'd be sent home.

"You really like her, don't you?" Theo questioned as he took a deep drag. At least he had something to calm him. Caleb could never stomach the nicotine.

His feet wouldn't stop moving as he answered without missing a beat, without one bit of hesitation. "I love her. More than I've ever loved anything and I almost killed her."

Theo, the one who always had an arsenal of sarcasm, was bullied into silence by Caleb's condemning tone. After a short pause, he realized in all the hysteria he had forgotten something just as important as Valerie's wellbeing. His gratitude.

"I didn't get to say it before, but… thank you for being there."

That cunning smirk returned and he nodded. "About time you said it. And you're welcome. I had a feeling something was happening, so I decided to keep a sharp eye for a few days. Looks like it paid off."

It did, and Caleb was in Theo's debt for a thousand years for helping to save the woman he loved. If only they could have just as long together.

Their conversation from the truck came back to haunt him as he waited. There were obstacles in the way of their happiness. Too many to count. Gordon was the biggest. His wife seemed more open to negotiation, but if the patriarch had his way, Caleb would be thrown out or imprisoned. Then he'd never see Valerie again.

"It doesn't sound like it's going well in there," Theo commented as he blew his last puff of smoke into the afternoon air above them.

Gordon was losing his temper, and the necromancer, Emmett, danced around the questions masterfully. "I found out plenty if he'd just swallow his pride and ask me."

"But you're a werewolf," Theo teased. "Heaven forbid a warlock ever ask a werewolf for anything helpful."

"I'm surprised he even let us have these pants," Caleb mentioned. Though they still didn't have shirts to fight off the winter chill, he could be thankful for the warlock's consideration to modesty. Caleb's clothes had been lost in the impromptu shift, while Theo's were left behind in the woods and no opportunity was given to retrieve them.

"I think he did it, so you wouldn't shock the witches."

He raised a brow at his former alpha. "Yeah, seeing a dick as small as yours might make them pity you."

Theo flung his cigarette butt into the snow outside the trapping circle. "Mine would make them faint. Yours would make them cringe."

They laughed and Caleb shoved his alpha, which sent him banging into the invisible wall that magic had created. There was no leaving until Gordon was done with them.

That moment might have come sooner than he thought when the back door opened to the kitchen and the warlock marched out, wrapping a scarf around his neck to keep warm. It was more than he was willing to give to the werewolves.

Theo and Caleb both straightened and willed themselves not to shiver in front of the man who was far from happy with the way things were progressing.

Theo could always be counted on. "Won't the son of a bitch talk?"

Gordon glared and he wondered if the warlock would lash out with his magic upon the alpha. "No, he's not. So you're going to tell me everything you know and now."

A hearty laugh rumbled from Theo. "Bullshit! Why should we tell you anything? This isn't our affair. That's your problem in there. Not mine."

Caleb, however, wasn't so obstinate. If he could play on the warlock's sensibilities, it'd put him in better standing when it came time to make his case for Valerie. "He was going to use me to attack Valerie and the rest of you."

Gordon was visibly shocked by his openness, but took advantage of it. "Why?"

"He didn't tell me. But he didn't want you or the witches to get in the way of his plans with Chief Nickels."

Studying eyes narrowed upon him. "How do you know about Chief Nickels?"

"I was the one eavesdropping on their conversation in the park. I told Devin to relay the information to you, so you'd at least get the heads up. I knew something was off about Emmett when he came into the coffeeshop yesterday."

Gordon took a step closer to the circle, well within arm's reach if the magic didn't bar them from one another. "Were you the one tracking him last night?"

Caleb nodded. "I found him near a cemetery. I stopped him from doing another... whatever it is that he does. We got into a fight, but he stopped when..." He hardly knew how to describe it or how to even make sense of what he saw, but Gordon was impatient.

"Say it! Why did he stop?"

"He let me go when his hand started to rot. He rolled up his sleeve and I saw it. It was like all the decay from being dead was catching up with him. He stopped and said, 'You're lucky it's not time yet.' Or some shit like that."

Gordon nodded and he could see the warlock putting the pieces together. "He is dead. Completely dead. Emmett was born in the seventeen-hundreds. He was the first necromancer in America before the witch council sentenced him to death for his crimes against humanity. But he won't tell us who raised him or why."

Caleb, in kind, came as close to the edge of the circle as the magic would permit. "Did Amber tell you about what she saw? Maybe it has something to do with that."

He looked as if ready to disprove the idea, but Gordon turned pensive before walking away.

"Hey! Can we at least come inside?"

Gordon ignored Theo's plea and reentered the house without a word. Caleb let out a sigh that turned frosty coming out of his lips as his former alpha muttered curses upon the warlock.

"So much for getting on his good side," he grumbled.

"I don't think he has a good side," Theo added. "He better let us go soon. I'm down to my last cigarette."

Caleb's eyes lifted toward one of the windows that overlooked the backyard where they were trapped. It was just at the right moment, because he was privileged to see Valerie gazing from one of the second story rooms. She gave a tiny smile and wave, but her heart wasn't in it. She knew, just as well as the werewolves did, that this was unfair.

His lips tightened and he nodded to at least show that he was well, despite being a little hungry and his toes frozen senseless upon the frozen ground. These were just small prices to pay for being close to her.

Valerie stepped to the side of the window, so Caleb wouldn't see her clutching the amethyst pendant in her hand.

The room they had used last night to cleanse her of all that negative energy had been repurposed to contain Emmett, the necromancer. He sat in the center of the room inside an impenetrable trapping circle forged by Gordon and Catherine. There was no way to break it, except by their command. Nothing was permitted in and nothing could be taken out. Emmett might as well have been in a steel box.

Despite this imprisonment, he said nothing. He'd barely lifted his eyes from a knothole in the floor on the opposite side of the room. Catherine was skimming through her mother's old grimoire to find a truth charm or a spell to help them see inside the warlock's twisted mind. She did that while Valerie and the other witches were entrusted with Emmett. For the first time in her memory, the coffeeshop was closed in the middle of the day, because there was no one there to man it.

"I don't get why you were with him," Alexa muttered to Valerie as she peeked out the window to the two werewolves down below. "If you hadn't been there – "

"Then he might have hurt someone else," Valerie interrupted. She'd make no excuses or apologies for her behavior. Not to them.

Alexa blinked at her snapping tone. "I was going to say, then he wouldn't have hurt you."

"I don't care about that," Valerie mumbled as she glanced back to the necromancer. Her stomach turned to think of how close she had come to getting killed. Or worse. And it was all because of that bastard.

"You should have," Krystal joined with just as much fire. "Don't you see that he used Caleb against you?"

Valerie shot daggers with her eyes at her friend. "He would have used Caleb against all of you. Not just me."

"But you were conveniently closer."

"Just shut the fuck up, okay?" Valerie groaned. "It's over and done and no one got hurt."

"But seriously," Alexa pleaded. "Why were you driving around with him?"

Valerie pressed her fingers between her brows to fight off the headache.

She didn't want to have this conversation with them. Not now. It wasn't the right time and she was liable to bite someone's head off if they so much as made one smart remark about Caleb being a werewolf.

Up until now, they believed that she wanted nothing to do with Caleb. She'd done a fair job of hiding this from the world, but now it had been dragged into the sunlight. She felt like a harlot who had been caught in the act. None of them would understand. How could they when they let their ignorance blind them? Not even their friendship, which she thought could survive just about anything, could open their eyes to make them see that it wasn't the end of the world for her to love a werewolf.

"They're Twin Flames."

The voice they hadn't heard for hours finally spoke up and startled them all. They looked to the necromancer, whose dark eyes were riveted upon Valerie with a cold, knowing stare. Ice spiked in her blood. How did he know?

"You're lying," Krystal scoffed.

"What reason would I have to lie? They are nothing to me."

Krystal stepped daringly close to the necromancer, but they all knew well that he was powerless. "To create trouble. That's what you've been doing since you got here."

Emmett's voice was calm and level to the point it was eerie. "It's not my problem if you let something as natural as a Twin Flame attachment birth dissention within your little coven."

Valerie nervously rubbed on the amethyst, willing her intention for it to absorb all this negative energy before it ruined her later.

"Isn't it, like, nearly impossible for them to be Twin Flames anyway?" Alexa suggested. "They're completely different races."

Krystal looked to her friend in mild disbelief. "Devin's a human and he's my Twin Flame."

"Yeah, but it's not the same thing. He just doesn't have magic. Caleb's something else entirely."

"It doesn't matter if it's possible or not, because it's not true." Krystal gestured to Emmett. "He's just lying to make us fight or something."

"It's not like he can get out, though. What good would it do to get us mad at each other?"

Krystal's face screwed up in disgust. "You can't believe anything he says, Alexa. Besides, it's too ridiculous in the first place. Tell her, Val. Caleb isn't your Twin Flame. He couldn't be."

But she wouldn't look at them. None of them. In some respects, she was ashamed that she hadn't come out with it already. Maybe things wouldn't have gotten this bad and Gordon would have let Caleb and his friend into the house where it was warm. Maybe they would have accepted his help before Emmett had a chance to cause more mischief.

She couldn't dwell on what might have been if she'd had the courage to speak up in the first place. All she could do now was release this burden and tell them the truth. The whole, unpopular, controversial truth.

"Caleb is my Twin Flame."

Her voice was surprisingly even, not shaky or choked with emotion. She might as well just have stated what color of shoes she had been wearing, as opposed to confessing something that was sure to cause an uproar in the Hayden Mansion.

Krystal and Alexa were too stunned to speak for a solid minute. The eldest was the first to break the silence.

"How long have you been keeping this from us?"

"Since I put two and two together about my dark magic. I didn't think it was him, but it just makes sense with how I feel. How I've felt since I first saw him in the coffeeshop."

"How you feel?" Krystal cried. "He's a werewolf, for Goddess' sake! How can you feel anything for him?"

At this, Valerie spun with violent abandon. "You don't know him like I do! You haven't even tried! You have no right to judge me for what I feel for him! We didn't judge you when you were getting involved with Devin. We all thought it was a bad idea, but he was your Twin Flame and we accepted it! Why can't you just accept this?"

Krystal's mouth hung open.

"This whole time, you've known he was your Twin Flame and you let us bully him like that?" Alexa asked, clearly the more sensible one of the two.

"What was I supposed to say? 'Don't say those mean things, I love him'? Do you know how hard it is to tell you guys anything when you're on a roll sometimes? Besides, would you have been any less shocked if I had told you days ago?"

Krystal was frozen in her incredulity, and it seemed that Alexa had only latched onto one part of her self-righteous speech.

"You love him?"

"No shit, I love him!" Valerie blurted out. "He's my Twin Flame. Of course I do!"

It didn't occur to her until that moment that Caleb was a werewolf, and though he wasn't in this room or in the house, he could easily hear from the backyard. She gulped back the fear, thankful for this burst of bravery as she faced her most trusted friends and ruined every bit of esteem they might have had for her.

"Now, doesn't that feel better?"

And Valerie had just enough bravery to march up to the necromancer and scream, "Shut your fucking mouth!"

"Valerie!" Catherine gasped from the doorway. "There's no need for that!"

In the presence of the motherly witch, she withdrew and crossed her arms. She hadn't realized how undone she felt until she tried to reel it all back in.

Catherine was carrying the leather-bound grimoire in her hands as she entered the room. Half expecting to be sold out by her friends, Valerie retreated to a corner and sulked over her lonely future. Neither Krystal nor Alexa gave her away, but listened to Catherine's report.

"I found a truth charm, but it needs these ingredients for a tea. Can you go get these, honey?"

Krystal gingerly took her grandmother's book and nodded before leaving to do as she was told. Gordon passed her on the way in. No looks were given, no words exchanged. They were all dutifully employed with their part in the scheme and Valerie was all but forgotten. She could be glad for that. Then she could slip away without ever being noticed. She was sure they wouldn't care anymore. Not now that her humiliation was complete.

"Who is it?" Gordon demanded of the necromancer. "Who are you working for?"

As before, Emmett didn't open his mouth. He only stared at Valerie as if she were somehow part of all of this, as if she were the one who should have been answering these questions.

"Who is it?" Gordon repeated. "Namtar? Ahriman? Erlik? Vanth? Name him!"

"Demons?" Catherine asked.

This might have been the only thing to grab the necromancer's attention all evening. His head slowly turned to fix Gordon with a glare. "Wouldn't you like to know?"

Valerie grabbed for the amethyst stone again and knew that it was beginning to fill with all her dark energies, but there was no place to expel it. No safe place to dump it. Not here.

"Name him! What demon raised you? Certainly not a powerful one if your body is continuing to rot away."

The witches looked to one another and then to the undead in the circle. He was unfazed by the accusation.

"So the mutt did give me away." A rueful smile played on his mouth. "How predictable. It's incredible that the beast trusts any of you."

Alexa glanced to Valerie, but wouldn't explain it to the elders in the room. They didn't seem to care.

"Tell me the demon's name and we can help to release you of his power."

"What makes you think I want to be released?"

Gordon's patience was slipping and they could all feel it. "In any other situation, you'd be brought to the council and executed for your perversion of nature, as you were three hundred years ago. But you're already dead and I can't imagine you feel nothing because of it. Why did he raise you? You should have better sense to know that whatever it is he's promised you is a lie, so why be loyal to him?"

"Whoever suggested I was loyal to him?"

Catherine was quick to return with, "You're doing this for yourself then? That's not what we've been told."

"Maybe they lied to you," Emmet offered with a raised brow.

Gordon's gaze shifted toward the window that overlooked the backyard. Valerie knew what was going through his mind. If he knew the whole truth, as she expected, then he would know that it was Caleb who had listened in on Emmett and Chief Nickels' conversation.

It then clicked for Valerie. "There's a demon in Chief Nickels?"

"Holy shit," was muttered by Krystal who had come back in with the prepared truth tea for Emmett. "A real demonic possession? Is Devin – "

"Devin should be fine," Gordon declared. "Demons are only ever after one thing and as long as Devin hasn't gotten in his way, he's safe."

That gave Krystal some comfort and she passed over the mug of tea to her mother, along with the book. The transfer was a little clumsy, but not a drop was spilled.

"What makes you think that any of you are safe? For all you know, those two werewolves could be working for me. They could be feeding you lies just to throw you off track."

Gordon grumbled and took the tea from his wife. "I've had enough of this. You'll take this and we'll get the real story."

Using magic as an extension of his own limbs, Gordon forced open Emmett's mouth. As if the tea were put into a zero-gravity atmosphere, it floated in a steady stream from the cup and straight onto the necromancer's tongue. He fought it at first and tried to bat the serum away, but Catherine used her own magic to restrain him further.

The strangled sounds of the warlock resisting the tea sickened Valerie, but she watched on with expectation, just as eager as the others to know the truth. But not every eye was on Emmett. One pair, the one that belonged to Krystal, was fixed on her in such a resentful way that Valerie almost couldn't stand it.

Had she no sympathy? No compassion? Couldn't she see that Valerie was just as torn up about it as the rest of them? She had to keep this secret for all the reasons they had validated.

Drastic plans began to take shape. Hours ago, the idea of leaving Goldcrest Cove had nearly broken her heart. Now, it seemed the only solution. Caleb would be glad to leave after all of this, she was sure. Maybe they could go back with whoever this other werewolf was that waited with him in the yard. They'd leave and go someplace where neither of them could be judged for what they shared. Some place where she could study her magic in private and he wouldn't have to be under the surveillance of a pack. They could be alone, but together. At least they would be at peace.

Emmett's coughing and sputtering forced her to set aside her escape plans for a minute. The shift was instant and almost palatable. The heaviness in the room sank through the cracks in the flooring and totally dissipated as if the morning fog were giving way to a clear afternoon.

"Thank the gods!" Emmett managed to cry between his coughs. "It took you long enough to figure it out." He shrugged. "Though, I can't say I was particularly ready for this moment, but I suppose that's what I deserve."

Though the warlock now displayed an uncharacteristic liveliness, they were determined not to be fooled. Gordon handed the mug back to his wife and stepped up to finish what he had started.

"Tell me who the demon is."

Emmett nodded and something about him was disarming. "Gladly. His name is Jolem. At least, that's the name he's given me, but he's gone by others over the millennia."

"Did you make a deal with him?"

"I did. Part of that deal bound my tongue, so I couldn't tell you anything. I know I've caused a great heap of trouble for you, but let me explain my reasons."

Emmett opened his mouth to begin the tale, but Gordon harshly cut him off before he could begin. "I don't care about your reasons. Why are you in Goldcrest Cove?"

Off put by the warlock's rudeness, Emmett looked annoyed, but didn't fight the truth tea. "Jolem is addicted to fear and chaos. I'm not the only one who has fallen into his services, but he finds amusement in harvesting fear in different forms and by different methods. I'm just a footnote in his history."

Catherine stood beside her husband, equally regal and serious as she joined the interrogation. "So he's been using you to create fear in Goldcrest Cove for his... addiction."

"I recognize the name," Gordon told his wife. "Jolem gains power from the fear and agony of others. Raising the dead would cause a panic in the town and the demon would have a buffet."

Emmett rose to his feet within the circle, alarming the younger witches for only a second.

"Precisely," he said with a snap of confidence. "And thanks to that potion, I can finally tell you everything. You can imagine my relief when I found out I was right about this town. I knew some of the magic folk who founded Goldcrest Cove and I suspected some of their descendants would be here."

Gordon narrowed his eyes in suspicion. "You knew they were here and you allowed Jolem to bring you?"

Emmett grinned. "In fact, I suggested it. Of course, I made it seem as if it were his idea in the first place. Start small and work his way up to mass hysteria. I knew if I tried anything with necromancy, especially as sloppy as I did, any witch would find out about it and be on my trail in no time."

The three witches who watched on were aghast at the reality of it.

"You used us?" Krystal asked. One look from her father deterred her from speaking out of turn again.

"In a sense, I suppose I did, but you have to know it was for good. I wanted you to find me and Jolem, and I put my trust in the right families." His kind smile was enough for Valerie. She didn't like him, but she no longer hated him. With all that truth tea in his system, he couldn't be faking any of this. They had been pawns in a grand scheme that none of them knew about.

"What's Chief Nickels' involvement?" Gordon asked, straightening the trial back on its original, direct course.

Emmett, once more, was happy to give all the information he needed. "Jolem always chooses a body to possess that he can use as a source of information and power. The chief knew all the families in town, where the oldest cemeteries were, and he could push aside any report that came in regarding my spells. He would claim them as unimportant and they would go uninvestigated. His idea was to create a lack of confidence in the police, so more townspeople would panic. And then you three stepped in before it could get out of hand, which stole away Jolem's satisfaction."

Once more, he sent his appreciation to the younger witches. Now they were the heroes?

"Where is he now?"

"At this time of day, most likely with his wife," Emmett replied cheerfully. "One thing that Jolem has tried to do, at least in part, is allow the man to live as he normally does while still utilizing him for our deal."

"And the werewolves?" Gordon demanded. "What are you using them for?"

Emmett snorted. "Nothing at all. I assumed there would be none in Goldcrest Cove. Not with so many witches here, I didn't think a werewolf would come within a hundred miles of this place. Imagine my surprise to find two. The first, I knew had some connection with the little dark one there." He waved toward Valerie. "The second arrived quite without my knowledge."

Catherine passed a sympathetic look to Valerie, but Gordon might as well have had blinders on.

"Why did you use them?"

"I pride myself on improvisation. I might not have had use for him before, but I never squander my prospects. I needed to get captured if I had any hope of bringing this to an end. I knew where the witches would be, and therefore where the werewolf was likely to spot me. It all started when I went to the coffeeshop. I went with the excuse to spy on the girls, but intended to catch the attention of the werewolf to begin the chase. Unfortunately, unless I directly threatened one of your own, I couldn't be found. Part of my own free will was stolen from me in the contract. I was under some obligation to make it seem as if I was still working for Jolem while also planning his demise."

Valerie, too overcome with relief, added her own voice into the mix. "So you put an enchantment over Caleb and made him attack me."

Gordon's temper wasn't reserved only for his daughter and he gave a harsh shake of his hand to tell her to stay out of it all.

Emmett respected her enough to say, "Only to weaken you, and then I'd take you hostage. It worked, of course. And here we are." He opened his arms as if to show them all how well his plan had succeeded.

But, now what?

"I assume you have the next fifty steps mapped out?" Gordon remarked snidely.

"Not entirely," Emmett admitted. "The rest is up to you and your family. I can destroy Jolem from here, but he needs to be free of Chief Nickels. If I try to destroy the demon now while he still possesses a body, he will kill the host and I have enough reverence for life not to let that happen."

Gordon was not convinced. "Demons can't be destroyed easily. You're sure you know how?"

The necromancer grinned. "Of course, I do! I didn't at first, but after some extracurricular research, I know exactly how to kill him, so he can't feed off the suffering of others again."

"And we just need to cast him out of Chief Nickels?" Catherine clarified.

Emmett slung his hands into his trench coat pockets. "It won't be easy, but I believe you'll find something in that grimoire that will do it. Demonic magic has been lost to the ancients, I've discovered. Some older texts may have the proper incantations. I made sure to raise Ruth, because I knew a witch of her caliber would know things. And if she didn't know them, she could give you the necessary resources." He jerked his chin to her grimoire.

That's all they needed. Gordon looked to Krystal. "Call Devin and tell him we're forming a plan. He needs to be on standby to help."

She nodded as she pulled out her phone and rushed out of the room.

"How long does the tea last?" Gordon asked his wife.

"At least ten hours," she replied as she began to flip through the pages for the exorcist spell they needed.

Valerie's head was still spinning from all this information. It was like the final pieces coming together to reveal this masterpiece of a plot. All of it to take down one demon. They all played a part, and Emmett was the orchestrator to conduct the symphony. Only the last pages of this grand finale were left blank. How exactly could he kill a demon if the knowledge was lost?

The necromancer shuffled forward to confront Gordon. "I'm curious how you found out I was working with a demon."

The warlock gave the prisoner a hard look. "You may have used the werewolf for your own plan, but he was still loyal to us. He told me about your flesh decaying after using too much magic. If you had raised yourself of your own power, you wouldn't be limited like that."

Emmett smiled and nodded. "Very good. I wondered if he had caught onto that when we first met. My apologies for almost killing him, miss." This time, he gave his attention to Valerie. "I didn't realize his usefulness until afterward when I found out you were his Twin Flame."

Gordon, couldn't have turned around fast enough to pin Valerie with his flashing eyes. "You're what?" he shouted.

Valerie jumped and backed into the corner, willing herself to be smaller and wishing she knew a spell to disappear completely.

Catherine came to her rescue and stepped between her and Gordon before he had a chance to unleash his fury upon the little witch. "Let's handle one crisis at a time, darling," she soothed. "We'll take care of Jolem and then we'll discuss this further."

Valerie lowered her gaze to the floor, unwilling to meet the burning glare of the closest thing to a father figure she ever had. Being the center of so much hostility made her want to fire back with just as much as she received, but she didn't have the strength to fight anymore. Not about Caleb or her place in Goldcrest Cove. As far as she was concerned, she was over it all.

Alexa came to her side and touched her arm, as if that would make it all better somehow. Valerie didn't shy away from one of her few defenders, but she felt if there was ever a time to run away, it was now. Even the muscles in her legs tensed for the race to leave Hayden Mansion behind.

"And you're absolutely sure you can destroy Jolem if we set it all up for you?" Catherine asked of Emmett, her husband still fuming from this bit of unpleasant news regarding Valerie.

The necromancer paused, perhaps more for effect, because there wasn't an ounce of doubt in him. "I am most positive, ma'am. It's not in the timing I would have liked, but everything is bound to come to an end, and this is mine... So yes, I am sure."

Chapter 20

He could feel her sadness. Almost taste it. It had finally happened. Her friends and adopted family had turned against her. If Caleb could have saved her the anguish of losing their favor, he would have. He knew what it was like to be the outcast, the one that went against the grain.

Caleb growled and cursed at the trapping circle that kept him bound in the yard while Valerie's world fell apart in that upstairs room. He needed to hold her, to tell her that it would all be okay. Though it would be a small consolation, he'd show her that even when the world cast her off, he was there to catch her.

But even as he yearned to be by her side, he listened to the necromancer's story. So, they were all on the same side after all. That afforded some solace, but his fate remained in the balance. Direct from the horse's mouth, he was innocent of anything devious. But would Gordon still allow a werewolf to live in his hometown? He didn't have much hope for it.

"Looks like we'll be let loose soon," Theo said after they had drawn out the last of the truth from Emmett.

"It appears so," Caleb sighed. "If we're allowed back to my house without a guard detail, I should have a spare shirt for you."

Theo, out of cigarettes, was reduced to pacing along with him. No wolf liked to be caged as they were. "That's big of you. As soon as this is all over, I'm gone and I suggest you come with me."

Caleb's lips were ready to pull into a growl, but he resisted. "I'm not going anywhere without Valerie, if I can help it. Now that I found her, I'm not giving her up just because some warlock doesn't like me."

"You know, you won't be able to keep her forever."

His nostrils flared. He didn't want to think about those things right then. "I'll make it work. I'm not going to leave her that easily."

Theo huffed. "A werewolf witch. That'll be the first. If you turn her, that is."

Caleb shook his head. "I'd never do that to her, but we'll figure out some way."

Testing the trapping circle, Theo absently kicked snow outside the magical lines that had been drawn. "If you won't turn her, then you'll have to find some other way to lengthen her life."

"Or shorten mine."

That earned him a scathing look from his former alpha. "I never thought you to be suicidal."

He took a breath and urged his wolf into a calm again. "Not suicidal, but I've lived long enough. Life without her... it might as well be pointless."

Theo rolled his eyes. "No woman is worth that much."

"She is," Caleb ground out. "You clearly haven't found your True Mate."

"Nope, and I hope I never do if it'll turn me into a suicidal romantic like you."

Contrary to everything, all the bitterness, the anxiety, the rage, Caleb had the ability to smile at his old friend. "You don't know what you're missing."

The back door opened and Gordon appeared, this time without a coat or scarf to keep him warm. He didn't need it. He only took a single step outside to give some dismissing wave. The field that kept them bound to one stretch of yard immediately dropped. The smothering magic had been released and the werewolves were free.

"Both of you come inside," he ordered before turning his back, trusting they would do as they were told.

Caleb, still hoping for some amnesty that came with capitulation, hurried toward the open door into the house. Theo didn't move. When he turned to the alpha, his dark eyes were focused on the fence that bordered the property and the freedom just beyond.

"Don't even think about it," Caleb warned. "You don't want him chasing you down."

Theo grimaced. "He doesn't need anything from me."

"You don't know that. Besides, I want you to meet Valerie."

A wicked grin darkened his features. "You sure you want me to have a chance at stealing her away?"

"Quit fucking around and get in here before I have to drag you."

Theo didn't seem that motivated, but he followed Caleb into the pristine kitchen to be intercepted by Gordon and Catherine.

"Where's – "

"Valerie is upstairs," Gordon interrupted. "She's none of your concern right now. I'm sure you heard Emmett. You two are free to go and I want you both out of Goldcrest Cove by dawn."

Caleb's wolf roared in protest and he struggled to keep his rage bottled as it seethed in his veins. The hateful words scorched his tongue, but he knew they would do him no good.

"Not sunset?" Theo quipped, eliciting a special scowl from the warlock.

"It would be if I thought we couldn't use your help."

Though he was tempted to hate the man even more, he made a show of listening.

Gordon continued, "Emmett says that we need to cast the demon out of Chief Nickels, so he can destroy it. The demon is like a fear junkie and that's the only way we're going to get him alone. Devin's going to work with us to make a trap for him and we need you two."

"I'm not doing a damn thing for any of you." Theo looked to Catherine and gave a respectful nod. "Pardon my language, ma'am. This isn't my problem."

"If you don't help us," Gordon said, "I can easily arrest you both for trespassing into our jurisdiction without permission."

Caleb blinked at this news. "There's a law against our kind living in the same place?"

"That's not the point," Theo grumbled. "He's blackmailing us into doing his dirty work. You're no better than that dead warlock sitting upstairs."

"I'm giving you a choice to help us and prove that your kind aren't as selfish as we've been led to believe."

Catherine touched her husband's arm, that universal sign between a married couple that she had just as much right to speak as he did. "What he means is that we aren't part of your... pack, but we can at least be friendly. We don't see eye-to-eye, and we don't understand one another as we should, but we have a common goal." The old witch looked right at Caleb with as much tenderness as he could expect of a mother. "Do this for Valerie, if you're unwilling to do it for yourself. If... If it's true that you two are Twin Flames, I know she means a great deal to you. This town and everyone in it means a great deal to her, too. Help us for her sake."

Caleb didn't have to think about that for long. Everything he had done was for her, if not for the town too. Catherine was right. She was his world and her safety and wellbeing were his top priority. Whether that meant he would go to prison or be executed for breaking some law he didn't even know about.

"How do we know you won't double cross us when it's all over?" Theo asked. Caleb could have punched him through the damned wall.

Gordon stiffened. "You don't know. I think that's why they call it 'trust'."

Theo snorted and Caleb slammed his fist into the alpha's chest. He heard the bone crack beneath his knuckles, but he'd recover soon enough.

"We'll help you. Just tell us what we need to do."

The alpha was far from appreciative, but with his breastbone snapped in two, he wasn't likely to voice it. Catherine appeared mildly startled by the show of aggression and took a step back against the kitchen island. An aura of gratitude could be felt from Gordon as he explained their plan.

"Devin's going to call Chief Nickels about a disturbance just on the edge of town. He's going to tell him that there's a crowd and he needs backup to get it under control. He'll make it sound like it's something the demon can benefit from. We would normally make a trapping circle around the chief, so we can cast out the demon, but they take a kind of magic that we haven't practiced before. We'll need help detaining the chief while we take care of the demon."

"And you want us to detain him?" Caleb asked.

Gordon, tossing aside what was left of his pride, replied, "That's what I'd like."

"When?"

"We're calling in Enforcers from Boston. They'll be here in a couple of hours, but we'll wait until nightfall."

He saw no problem with it. The idea of a demon might have frightened some, but Caleb was insensible to it. He feared the warlock upstairs more. If a demon had to employ the services of a dead necromancer, it showed just how powerless he truly was.

"What do you want us to do until then?"

The warlock gave a shooing gesture toward the front of the house. "Go home. Devin has your number. He'll call when we're ready for you. Pack your things and be ready to go when it's all over."

A vice clamped tight over his heart. *Leaving.* He just got here and he would be leaving again. "Can... Can I speak with Valerie?"

Caleb felt as if he were the subordinate again, taking orders and asking permission like a criminal who had lost all their rights, or a servant who had little value beyond what he could contribute. His wolf continued to balk and fume, just as

Theo's did. He didn't like it any more than the alpha did, but at least Caleb had enough sense to stay civil while it still profited him.

"No," Gordon replied pointblank. "She and the other women are guarding Emmett to ensure he holds up his end of the bargain and I don't want her to become distracted."

"It's just for a minute," Caleb begged, though he wouldn't stoop so low as to grovel at the feet of the warlock.

Gordon's face turned red. "I don't care if you two are Twin Flames or not. I won't tolerate you under my family's roof. You two will leave and wait for word. If you leave town or you don't come when you get the call, I will send my Enforcers and they won't fail to catch you."

Theo's chest recovered just enough for him to wheeze out. "They can try."

A low, threatening growl from Caleb might not have done much, but it was enough to make Theo behave again.

"We'll go... Don't think me ungrateful, but... allow me to say one thing." Caleb waited for some reprimand, but it didn't come. "I love Valerie and I know she loves me. Don't be surprised if she goes with me in the morning."

It might have been arrogant and assuming, but he felt as if he knew Valerie's heart well enough. She might have been tied to this town in her heart. She might be turning her back on her own family. But Twin Flames only came around once in a lifetime, and she understood that just as well as he did. She wouldn't waste it now that she found it. That's what he was betting on.

By the looks of the pair, however, they didn't seem to think so. And they had known Valerie for longer. Caleb could only hope that he wasn't missing something, something that would make him look like a fool to the whole coven.

He loves me.

Valerie had said it over and over again in her head. They were Twin Flames. It was a given. But he had never said it. Not once in their lovemaking or at any point afterwards. But the full and complete knowing of it was like a bolt of lightning, starting from her head and passing through to her feet in a rush of energy she was sure she'd never experience again.

He loved her and he had to leave.

Listening on the stairs had been a silly and girlish thing to do, but when she saw that Gordon had invited Caleb and his friend in, she couldn't help it.

If she had been the strong woman that she was before all this shit happened, she would have marched down and given Gordon a piece of her mind. She would have threatened to leave too if he was going to force Caleb out. But then, her werewolf had made that promise for her. And he had been right. The notion of leaving had filled her mind even before she knew for sure that Caleb would be going too.

For once in her life, the stars were lining up in her favor. Sort of.

Waiting for the Enforcers to arrive had given her time to think it all over. Leaving was the only solution. Her friends didn't like her anymore, and she had no family to keep her here. She had enough work experience in the coffeeshop to get her another job somewhere. Attachment to the coven had never been a big deal, though she felt she did owe them a lifetime of gratitude for training her when they could have turned her away. She knew what she would pack, what she would pack it all in, and that she could take Thor with her.

And still, something deep in her gut told her that leaving Goldcrest Cove was a mistake. She wanted to pass it off as a fear of change, of the unknown. It wouldn't be unknown, because Caleb would be there and they would take care of each other. There was something about making this decision so quickly and decidedly that wouldn't settle. Just that morning, she was swooning and moaning beneath the sheets with him. Now, they were independently considering running away together.

Maybe it was all too fast. Part of her wanted to think it through, but what was there to think about? She loved him, and he loved her. Wasn't that all they needed?

"I'd say we all play cards, but I'm guessing it'd be a bother."

Valerie's mind was miles away when Emmett spoke. Krystal and Alexa had left just a few moments ago to properly close up the shop for the day. They had left it in a mess when they got the call from Catherine, and it would be another half hour or so before Amber or Taylor could come as the backup.

Gordon and Catherine were in the other room in a conference call with members of the council to talk about Emmett's fate. He would be returned to his previous dead state, of course, but there were other details to discuss that went over her head. Neither did she care.

That left Valerie in the room alone with the undead necromancer.

She turned and for the first time, realized how dark the room was. The sun was close to setting and soon, it'd be dark enough to set their plan in motion. Much of Emmett was draped in darkness.

"Nope. No card games," she said as she crossed the room to turn on the overhead light.

"I apologize if my outburst earlier had ruined things for you, but I felt it needed to be said."

Valerie gave him a strained smile, mostly because she felt he deserved some kindness. Just why, she wasn't sure. He had nearly terrorized Goldcrest Cove, threatened her, almost killed Caleb, and caused a heap of trouble for countless people. But that was all under the demon's influence. Like the werewolves, didn't he deserve to be heard?

She sat cross-legged on the floor in front of him, the impermeable shield of the trapping circle ensuring her safety. "It would have come out eventually, I guess... I just wish they would have taken it better than they did."

Emmett nodded in understanding. "People can be ignorant. Three hundred years hasn't changed their hearts and I'm sure three hundred more won't do it either."

Compassion wasn't something she felt that often for complete strangers. "You seem like a decent guy," she said, picking through exactly what she wanted to say. "Why would you make a deal with a demon like Jolem when you knew people would get hurt? It doesn't make sense."

The curve of his mouth took a grim turn as the truth tea worked its magic. "I did it for love. Plain and simple."

Valerie wanted to laugh, but she found that love was no laughing matter anymore. "You're going to have to tell me a little more than that."

The warlock shifted to sit a little closer. "It's good to see that someone's willing to hear me out. And as a reward, I'll tell you something I haven't told them." He thumbed toward the adjoining wall to the room with Gordon and Catherine.

"My wife was like you," he began. "That is, her dark magic was like yours."

Valerie went pale and waved her hands for him to stop. "How did you know that?"

Emmett gave her a kind look. "My dear, I may be dead, but I can see the dark magic in you. Also, I've seen the way you hold that amethyst and how it's clogged with your negative energy. You're learning to cope with your dark magic, which is more than my wife tried to do. The gods bless her, but she feared it. Every day, she fought against it by refusing to find happiness in the world. She wouldn't let herself enjoy our marriage. She wouldn't laugh, wouldn't smile. She festered in the energies she contained and would never cleanse herself as she needed to. It killed her in the end. She died just four years after we wed."

Valerie could see that even after three hundred years, the man's heart broke for his wife. His throat worked through the emotions that were still so fresh, but he continued.

"My dark magic is the opposite of yours, and my wife's. I find joy and happiness natural. I always have. It takes a real effort to make myself angry and hateful. Part of Jolem's contract instilled me with these dark feelings to make it easier to do what needed to be done. You see, while you expel death, I radiate life."

"So, when you let yourself feel bad, the good comes out and overflows."

He nodded. "The complete opposite of you. It's how I can bring the dead back to life. I learned to master it with small things. Rabbits, birds, dogs, and the like. I raised my first human when the midwife of our town couldn't save the life of a stillborn. I did it again when a child fell and broke their neck while playing in the woods behind our cottage. They were miracles, as far as anyone else could see. My wife and I were Twin Flames as well, and I thought that a miracle in itself. I knew, if she would just let herself feel joy, I could take away the pain and death that destroyed her. But she never would, because she thought it would hurt me. So she kept it in."

"And it killed her." Valerie's voice was little more than a whisper, but in the deathly silence of the room, he heard her perfectly clear.

"It did... And I had to raise her. It was what caught the attention of the council. It was a budding little thing then. Not as prominent and far-reaching as it is now. But they found out about me and they found me guilty of perverting the natural order. Death was part of life. Suffering a part of joy. They thought that changing fate or altering it in some way was wrong and they executed me for it."

She squeezed her eyes shut. "That doesn't seem right at all."

"No," he insisted. "It was right. While it did no harm to anyone, and it might have been a selfless thing to do, it was wrong. I see that now, and unfortunately my reputation as the first necromancer amongst the colonies had a greater impact than I would have ever expected."

Emmett straightened. "Jolem gave me life and promised me that if I did as he said, he'd take me to where they reinterred my wife. You see, I did manage to raise her, but the council reversed the magic. I never found out where they laid her remains, but Jolem said that he did. He said if I did his bidding, if I used my magic to inspire fear so he could gain more power, he'd take me to her and I could raise her again. We'd have the life we were meant to have as husband and wife... as Twin Flames."

Valerie thought it sounded like something out of a terribly-plotted romance novel. "You know Jolem probably doesn't know where she is."

He laughed. "Oh, I know it. But I thought, if I could just do as he wanted, I'd have enough time to find her grave and do it myself. But I've been back to my old village. It's gone now, and so is the cemetery. I needed time to find her."

"But you said yourself that raising the dead was a perversion."

"It is," he said with a nod. "But... I only wanted to do it so I could apologize to her. Apologize for all those years I spent nagging her to be better, to try harder. All those years I spent letting her destroy herself when I could have done more to help." Emmett leaned closer. "I need her forgiveness. But now... I suppose I'll never get the chance."

Emmett took a few seconds to compose himself before leaving the subject of his wife for possibly the last time. "But I did something better."

Valerie watched as he took off his trench coat with some effort because of the enclosed space he was in, and then rolled up his long sleeve shirt. A few inches below his elbow, began an intricate pattern of tattooed lines and symbols. None of which she recognized.

"This is what will kill Jolem. About six months ago, when I realized that my magic did have its limits upon this body, I began to search through archives and records for something that would break my ties with the demon and destroy him."

Valerie came closer to inspect the tattoo, visually tracing the lines as it wound up his bicep and disappeared beneath the rest of his shirt. "But what is it?"

His face lit up with excitement. "It's a sigil. It's only activated if it's destroyed. If I chose to use too much magic, my body will decay. If its progress consumes the tattoo, it will be Jolem's demise."

Valerie's mouth hung open. "This is how you're going to kill him once he's cast out of Chief Nickels?"

Emmett nodded. "Yes. I had intended to wait until I found my wife, but... I fear the worst. That her body may never be recovered. Now is as good a time as any."

The gears in Valerie's brain began to turn. It all made sense now, except for one thing. "But this circle keeps you from using magic. How are you going to destroy the tattoo if you can't make your body decay?"

There had never been a more heartfelt, sorrowful smile in the existence of the universe than the one that Emmett gave Valerie in that moment. "That's where I need your help."

Chapter 21

"I don't like this," Theo grumbled to Caleb as they both warily eyed the Enforcers. Four warlocks who didn't look like much at first. Upon further inspection, they carried themselves like policemen in civilian clothing. Average, but his wolf knew that they would be formidable in a fight.

"You've said that several times already."

They answered Devin's call, all to Theo's griping and complaining about the whole affair. It had been a chore just to keep him from skipping town. When they arrived at the designated spot, there were three squad cars with their flashing red and blue lights along Jackson Creek Road. Yet, the only officer on the scene was Devin. Gordon had enlisted help hijacking the others from the station to keep up the ruse.

Devin had done a fair job of making it look like a crime scene. Yellow police tape stretched across the line of trees they now took shelter behind. Only Devin stood out near the road to receive the Chief when he arrived.

They'd been briefed about the plan half a dozen times. The chief would be taken through the trees as close as possible to the trapping circle. Once he passed the point of no return, Caleb and Theo were to grab him and keep him still while the warlocks did their work. Just as Emmett said, there was a spell in Grandma Ruth's book designed to cast out the demon. As soon as it was released, Devin would give the word to the witches back at Hayden Mansion and Emmett would take it from there.

Knowing the plan backwards and forwards did little to put the werewolves at ease. Caleb blamed the presence of the powerful and trained warlocks. He continued to tell himself that this was for Valerie. As soon as he was done here, he'd go to her and make his proposal.

The last few hours had given him time to make up his mind. He'd ask her to leave Goldcrest Cove with him. He'd declare every secret feeling he harbored in his heart and lay it all bare before her like a man who had nothing to lose. In the end, it'd be everything. There was still time for her to change her mind. Her friends could be with her now, persuading her to do the sensible thing and let the werewolf leave town without her.

Caleb knew he had one card working in his favor. They were Twin Flames. Destiny made them inseparable. They might have not known one another for too long, but he felt he had a stronger connection with Valerie than anyone on this planet. That had to count for something.

"I'm out of here the minute it's done," Theo said, shifting his gaze to the dancing police lights.

"I'm sorry you had to get pulled into this."

The alpha huffed. "I've been pulled into worse. Believe me."

"Ever dealt with demons?"

He shook his head. "Not once."

Caleb cracked a smile as he slung his thumbs through his belt loops. "You'll have something new to tell the boys when you get back to Georgia."

Theo's head swiveled. "You're not coming back to the pack?"

"I told you I wouldn't and I'm standing by that."

With a roll of his eyes, he turned back to the squad cars, the flashes of red and blue illuminating the regret in his face. "Suit yourself. You're making a mistake being alone. You know that, right?"

"I won't be alone. I'll have Valerie."

"Don't count your chickens before they're hatched. She might not be as willing to leave her own kind as you are."

"I know her. You don't. Let me make that call."

Theo grabbed Caleb's shoulder and gave him a friendly shake. "My friend, I'm going to give you a good piece of advice. It doesn't matter what race they are. Women are fickle creatures who are apt to change their mind at the drop of a hat. Nothing is set in stone with a woman. Not ever."

Caleb thought how Valerie had fought her feelings so hard in the beginning, how she had acted like she hated him. The transformation was extreme and pleasantly so, but Theo might have had a point. She had changed her opinion of him so quickly. But he couldn't allow himself to think that she would prove him wrong. Not in this.

"Thank you for your advice," he said coolly. "But we'll just wait and see."

The sound of a new engine met their ears and they moved to get a better look down the road. A fresh set of squad car lights rounded the bend.

"There he is," Caleb said before snatching at Theo's sleeve. "Let's back up, so he doesn't see us too soon."

They both retreated deeper into the thicket to join Gordon and the Enforcers, who were no less wary of the werewolves as they were of the demon they'd have to exorcise. Caleb ignored them. If they all did their part, then this would be over and they could go their separate ways.

Caleb listened as the chief pulled up and was met by Devin.

"You said there was a crowd," Nickels griped. "What happened?"

"We were able to get them under control and send them back into town."

Caleb heard a heavy, disappointed sigh. "Fine. Where's the body?"

"Just behind here. We think the killer dragged the victim into the trees."

"Is someone coming from Boston to do an inspection?"

"Yeah, I called them as soon as we confirmed it was a murder."

Caleb was impressed by Devin's coolness under pressure. No wonder Gordon and the rest of the witches believed his lies about the eavesdropped conversation. Not a single hitch or bit of hesitance in his story whatsoever.

The two officers strode toward the fake crime scene, discussing the phony details Devin had invented to make the illusion complete. Devin lagged behind and once Chief Nickels passed the mark, he gave the signal to the werewolves.

With their inhuman speed, they raced forward in a blur. Caleb took Chief Nickels on the left, and Theo took him on the right. Before the older cop could see their faces, they whisked him deep into the forest where the Enforcers were ready for them.

Though Gordon said the demon couldn't be caught in a trapping circle, one had been drawn in the center of a clearing. All three were bound inside and Caleb could feel the pull of the magic.

"Get your hands off me!" Chief Nickels shouted, pulling and tugging in vain against the supernatural strength of the werewolves.

Gordon and the other Enforcers took their places in the circle.

"I call forth Jolem," the council warlock declared in a voice fit for an alpha.

Chief Nickels went completely still, but neither Caleb nor Theo loosened their hold. They had been warned of the craftiness of demons. Their guards would not be so easily let down.

Their captive then began to laugh at Gordon who stood with the grimoire open in his hands.

"Emmett betrayed me, didn't he?" the demon asked, a voice just a note deeper than Chief Nickels'. "I should have figured as much."

Gordon didn't feel the steadily mounting tide of tension and power emanating from Nickels' body, but Caleb and Theo did. They exchanged cagy looks as Gordon ignored the villain's beginning monologue and dove right into the spell.

"You think a few words are going to stop me?" the demon cackled. "I'll just find another body. I'll get what I want and none of you stupid warlocks are going to get in my way."

Gradually, the demon inundated the human's body with its own strength. Caleb and Theo, who didn't have to put so much effort into holding him steady at first, found themselves jerked and jostled like a pair of unruly toddlers.

Magic swelled around the circle, arcing and fizzing between the warlocks who followed in the Latin chant. They saw everything. The glowing red eyes of the possessed man, the way the werewolves struggled to keep him still, and how a mysterious wind whirled around them in an eddy of power.

Gordon was the only one who seemed concerned, but he never stuttered, never allowed himself a moment to doubt for the werewolves' safety in all of this.

A mist, the blackest that Caleb had ever seen, began to seep from Chief Nickels. Out of every pore and orifice in his body, it leaked into the air above them, gathering into a cloud of evil.

It was all enough to make Caleb squirm and want to run. But he couldn't. Not when they were so close. Not when Devin was already dialing the phone to let the girls know that it was time.

Valerie knew what she had to do. She just wished to all the gods and goddesses that she didn't have to. If what Emmett said was true – which it was beyond a shadow of a doubt – that sigil tattoo ran across most of his body. Including the important parts. If she did what she was asked, what was required, it would be murder. To destroy a demon, a soul would have to be forfeited. And Emmett decided long ago that it would be his.

But was it murder? The man was technically dead and operating under the power of the demon and his own magical reserves. He said when Jolem was banished for good, Emmett would deteriorate to dust anyway. She'd just be helping him along. It was like some witch's version of euthanasia, which Valerie had her own opinions about to begin with. Still, her amethyst necklace was silently stowed away in the downstairs bathroom. She wouldn't need it for this.

For hours, while the other witches kept guard over the necromancer, she battled within herself about the plan. Emmett had told them that he had his plan set in motion, but he wouldn't tell anything further, which made Catherine suspicious that the tea was wearing off too soon.

Like a caged animal, she paced in her corner of the room, torn and undecided. But what was there to decide? This was the only way to kill Jolem. If they didn't, Emmett warned that he would just inhabit another body and the timing would be all off. Tonight was the night. It had to be. There was no room for uncertainty or reluctance. But that was all Valerie could feel flaming in her gut.

Catherine's phone rang and Valerie went cold, knowing full well what it meant.

Every witch, including Amber and Taylor, came forward. The whole crew was present. All seven were dedicated to helping Emmett eradicate the demon's spirit. Only Valerie was needed. Like the warlock said, she was the only one who could do it because of her dark magic.

The room was so quiet that they could hear Devin's rushed voice on the other end of the line.

"They're doing it! The werewolves are having trouble keeping him still. Whatever he has to do, he better do it quick!"

Catherine looked to Emmett and altered his prison just enough so he could use magic within its boundaries. "Start your ritual. If you need more magic, we'll assist."

Emmett rose to his feet, that confidence pouring from him as if the thought of Valerie's insecurity had never entered his mind. It might have been an easy thing for him to want to throw away his own life, but it wasn't so easy for her. How could it? She wasn't used to death and she wasn't about to start getting used to it now.

The warlock shucked off his jackets and then peeled away his shirt to reveal the amazingly complex, but utterly beautiful sigil tattoo etched across his entire torso. A ripple of emotion spread across the room. Uneasiness, a bit of fear, and awe. Even Valerie was struck by the intricacy of it.

His calm, kind gaze fell upon her and he gave his nod to tell her that he was ready.

With shaking steps, she came closer to the circle.

"What are you doing?" Catherine demanded.

The tea hadn't worn off so much that Emmett couldn't answer. "I need Valerie's dark magic for this. I've already discussed it with her."

Krystal ran to her friend and took her arm. "Whatever he wants you to do, you don't have to."

Valerie turned to the one person she thought she could trust, the one person she thought would always have her back and support her. Today, and this whole week, proved her wrong. Her spirit was sick from it all, and one last disapproving action wasn't going to make a difference. They weren't friends anymore.

"No, I have to. I'm going to make this right."

She yanked her arm free and hurried again to stand in front of Emmett. No other witch stopped her, though they couldn't possibly imagine what it was she was about to do.

The warlock turned over his palms in front of him to receive the negative energy and Valerie stretched out her own to pass it on.

"You know what you have to do."

Emmett's voice was so calm, so smooth that it almost made her more compliant to the whole thing.

"And you're ready?" she questioned, more or less to delay this gruesome business.

He nodded. "I am... If you can find a way, any way at all... Tell my wife what I said earlier. I failed to do it myself, but I have a feeling you're just resourceful enough to do it."

Her throat was too thick to answer him and she nodded in return. She couldn't refuse a dead man's last wish.

Without any other word or order between them, Valerie let herself slip away. Her thoughts, one by one, were consumed by Caleb. Just the previous night, she had been able to fantasize and make up things about the werewolf to inspire all the gushy, romantic, happy feelings to expel all her negative energy. Now, she didn't have to use her imagination.

Her heart reviewed their sex, the way his hands had caressed her curves. How his kisses set her soul on fire. How his love made her feel alive and special for the first time in her life. Everyone left. Everyone died. Everyone turned their back on her, but not Caleb. He loved her.

Valerie glimpsed to Emmett's exposed fingertips and saw it was working.

"Val! Stop! What are you doing?" They all screamed and made to intercept or pull her away, but she was too aware of them. She threw up a shield to keep them all out. She couldn't stop. Not now. Even if she wanted to.

Channeling all of her negative energy, the decay spread through his fingers to his hands, down his wrists and up his arms. Skin darkened, shrinking around his bones. The blood in his veins dried and turned to ash. Muscles and tendons snapped and shriveled. All the while, Emmett could feel it. He winced and grunted at the pain of dying for the second time.

The decay crept close to the tattoo. When it touched the first sweeping line of the sigil, it glowed a bright and luminescent blue. As his flesh beneath the tattoo continued to rot away, more blue wove its way around his arms and up his shoulders, painting his body as the sigil began to do its work.

So much pain and destruction, all for a few happy thoughts. Valerie felt ashamed and rotten herself. But she couldn't let go. She'd be killing Emmett, but it also killed the demon and would save countless others through the centuries to come. All things worked for good in the end, but Valerie couldn't bear to look into the warlock's twisted face as he suffered this torture.

Caleb and Theo gripped hard upon the chief's arms as he thrashed and pulled with more vigor than they would have ever expected from a man or a demon. Gordon and the other warlocks continued to chant and let their magic swirl in crushing currents inside the trapping circle.

Still, they held on, knowing that if they let go, the demon had the potential to escape. Even if his wolf writhed and begged and pleaded for a reprieve, Caleb wouldn't give up.

The demon, black smoke billowing around him like a cracked and broken smokestack, paused for just a moment. His expression, once triumphant in the face of his exorcism, morphed into confusion, and then finally gave way to fear.

Amongst the ebony smoke, tiny sparks of blue popped and hissed. It was just a few at first, but then more boiled up to surround the particles of the formless demon and disintegrate him. This wasn't the same purple and greenish magic that flowed amongst the warlocks as they stripped the spirit from its host. This was Emmett's work.

"No... No! It's impossible!"

Driven by this new foretelling of annihilation, the demon fought harder against his captors. Theo and Caleb were tossed off within just a moment of this frantic battle. Theo crashed against the inside of the trapping circle and sank to the ground. Caleb was sent rolling and he could feel a bit of blood dribble from his nose.

Weak, and sure that a rib had been broken, he leapt up and dashed for the chief again before he could step out of the circle. Caleb tackled him about the waist, diving straight into the black mist himself. He could feel the magic of the banishing spell as it crackled around his ears.

He heard Devin, still on the phone with Catherine.

"They can't hold him for much longer! Hurry up!"

Valerie felt the trickle of blood roll down her upper lip as she pushed harder and harder against the negative, forcing it out of her with such force it was giving her a headache. And the decay still had half of his body to consume.

"They can't hold the demon for much longer," Catherine told them.

An idea must have occurred to Emmett, and thankfully the parts of his body used for speech hadn't been aged away yet. "Drop the circle!" he demanded brokenly.

Valerie understood and added, "I need to get closer. Nothing between us."

There was only a moment's hesitation in the old witch before she did as he asked. The trapping circle was obliterated and like magnets, Valerie and Emmett reached for each other.

His skin felt slimy and paper-thin. His bone splintered beneath her grip like dried leaves. She held onto his forearms, just below where the tattoos started, and the decay quickened, heaving across his core for one final push.

When they touched, a pulse of light coursed through Valerie. Emmett was exchanging his own energy for hers. It was a transfusion of magic, of light and darkness, of death and life. They became each other's yin and yang, sun and moon, black and white. A complete and total reversal.

The magic and splendor of it nearly blinded her and she couldn't see much through the inexpressible tears that blurred her vision.

Soon, the sigil was completely irradiated, its blue and silvery light the most vivid thing in the room. Valerie blinked away the moisture from her eyes so, she could see the last smile Emmett would ever give in this world.

He never found his wife. He never completed his mission. But she heard his words in her head as clear as if he were speaking them. He thanked her and all the other witches for freeing him from the demon. Now, they would both be put to rest. The essence of their spirits would scatter into the universe.

The lines of the sigil became inflamed and fattened, the blue hue displaced by a pure, white light as hot and blinding as the sun. It devoured him and she looked away when it became too much for her eyes. A sizzling noise like an autumn wind in the trees filled the room.

All at once, Valerie wasn't holding onto a solid form anymore. Emmett's skin and flesh pulverized into dust that drifted to the floor inside the trapping circle. There was nothing left and she looked to the clumps of remains in her shaking palms.

The room fell dark again and Valerie stood in the center, the other witches staring at Ground Zero. They'd likely never see this ritual again as long as they lived.

Her whole body sputtered with the flood of energy that Emmett had given her as his last parting gift. He had sacrificed everything for them, and she helped. Grief for a man she didn't know made her limbs weak.

She fell to the floor, but her knees didn't hit the hardwood. Hands and arms gently lowered her. Her friends, the witches she had grown up with, caught her in time. Despite being filled from head to toe in so much light, Valerie began to weep. She had never cried so hard. Not even at a funeral.

Words of encouragement were given from every witch in the room, congratulating her on doing what none of them would have had the strength of heart to do. If only they had known that Valerie wasn't as strong as she had made them believe. This broke her more than she had anticipated. All she wanted now was Caleb. He had as much of a part to play as she did. It was the thought of him that aided her in the ritual. The thought of his love and the future they had together.

It was like a million firecrackers exploding around him, but Caleb hung on, pinning the chief to the ground with nothing but his own bodyweight. Theo had come to his senses and joined him in the dogpile.

The chief flailed and raved, screaming out his own curses in a language none of them knew. All the while, Gordon and the other warlocks extracted the last of the demon. The black smoke coiled and spat within the circle as the blue and silver magic of Emmett's spell did its work. It ate up the darkness, replacing it with bursts of light.

The warlocks fell silent and watched the spectacle. Caleb and Theo felt the chief's body go limp beneath them as the last of the howling rage died away. They turned to the sky and stared as the evil, shapeless spirit was engulfed by the magic.

When there was nothing left to take, nothing left to destroy, the light sparkled like every constellation in the sky had gathered just to thank them for this service to humanity. Then, like a collapsing star, it burst and evaporated before their eyes. The only light that remained came from the squad cars that flashed from the street.

Neither man, warlock, nor werewolf said a thing at first. All were too weary and dazed by the incredible ritual to jump for joy or scream their victory cries.

Chief Nickels was safe – perhaps a little bruised – but unconscious. Devin gave the final report to the witches over the phone and hung up before coming into the clearing. The Enforcers turned to one another and gave quiet congratulations on a job well done.

Theo and Caleb recovered from their battle wounds in enough time to stand and face the council warlock as he approached.

Gordon closed the grimoire, his gaze tracking between the two werewolves. Without a word, he held out his hand to Caleb. Pride balked at the idea of shaking hands with the man who had blackmailed him into this trouble. Camaraderie and the need to be the better person, told him to take the damn peace offering.

And so he did, and he shook it firm to make a good impression.

Gordon then extended the same olive branch to Theo, who had more ego to wrestle with than any of them. And still, he shook the warlock's hand. Not as a friend, but as one who had shared combat with him. That was enough.

And just like that, it was done and over. Devin enlisted the help of another Enforcer to take Chief Nickels back to the car with the assurance that he would remember nothing by morning. They knew how to replace memories and wipe the minds of anything magical. It was what they were good at.

If only Caleb could forget all this nasty business, and the threat that still loomed over him. He had less than twelve hours to get his stuff together and leave Goldcrest Cove. He wouldn't count on Gordon's generosity to change his mind.

Valerie would come home after they dealt with Emmett, and Caleb would make his proposal before dawn. He knew the words, he knew his heart, and though it'd be a long road ahead of them, they'd be together. That was all that mattered now. That hope of a future, of a love stronger than any magic, was all he had left.

Chapter 22

A nd that was it. Valerie signed her name at the bottom of the letter. One last parting word to her friends before she vanished. It was a short letter, saying how sorry she was for disappointing all of them with something that was far beyond her control.

Her Twin Flame was in the living room, hauling up the last bit of his luggage to take to his truck in the drive. She'd leave her car here and tell Shawn to sell it or use it for himself later. The teacher was still out of the state, but Caleb would call and settle things. She hated that she'd be leaving him to deal with the rent all by himself, but Caleb said he'd be leaving a parting gift that would help Shawn get through the next six months without them.

Valerie didn't pack much. Just her favorite clothes and her family's grimoire. Her laptop was easy enough to carry and they could get dog supplies for Thor wherever they would settle. She assumed that Caleb had a plan, or at least a vague destination in mind.

But that didn't seem to matter. So long as he agreed to take her with him. When he asked her the night before to run away together, it made the whole arrangement so much easier. There were no tears, no fuss, no farewells or empty promises. They'd go on as they had and roll with the punches as they came. She wouldn't have wanted it any other way.

She folded up the letter and wished she had some fancy envelope to put it in, so it wouldn't get damaged. She wasn't even sure it'd slip under the door of the coffeeshop, but she couldn't think of any other place to put it. The girls would see it when they came to open up first thing in the morning.

Valerie expected to feel something like remorse, or maybe a last minute change of heart. But in the end, it felt right. Goldcrest Cove didn't feel like home anymore. Caleb was home and the only place she felt accepted.

There was, however, one hitch in the plan. He didn't know everything. Last night reminded her of that. Caleb was still clueless about her dark magic and the flipping in her stomach had more to do with that than leaving the only place she had ever known.

With a deep breath, she stood from her desk and took one last look around her room. It'd be someone else's soon. They could have her sheets, her posters, her records, and her furniture. Then her gaze fell upon her alarm clock. She hadn't packed that. It belonged to her parents, its vintage flip-numbers keeping the time since before she was born.

Valerie strode across the room and snatched it up. She could start life with Caleb outside of Goldcrest Cove, but not without this clock. Besides the grimoire and a few other keepsakes, it was one of the last things she had of her parents.

She carried it, along with the goodbye letter, into the living room. Thor sat near the kitchen, his tail thumping against the tile, tranquil but curious. There was just enough room in the back of the truck cab for him. And if there wasn't, Valerie would have let him sit in her lap. There was no way she'd leave her dog behind.

This house held so many memories. Some good, and some not. Watching Shawn play videogames on the television, Krystal cooking in the kitchen after Aunt Maggie's funeral, the back porch where she and Alexa had practiced some magic together one late night. And of course, every corner, every shadow, had been touched by Caleb in some way. But there would be a lifetime of new memories to cherish.

Valerie snorted at herself for being so sentimental. The house and her room had never mattered before. Why should it now?

Caleb came from the foyer for the last time and put his hands on his hips. "Is that going too?" he asked, motioning to the alarm clock.

She nodded. "I'll put it in myself."

"Do you want some coffee before we go?"

Just as Gordon asked, they'd be leaving before dawn. She hadn't gotten much sleep over the last few days, and it seemed that coffee was the only thing keeping her standing.

"I want to sleep some in the truck, but... there's something we need to talk about first."

The tremor of anxiety in her voice brought on a look of worry in Caleb's handsome face. "What's wrong? Not getting cold feet, are you?"

She gave him a tired smile. "No. Not cold feet... I just need to explain something that I really haven't had much of a chance to talk about before."

He blinked and took slow, cautious steps toward her. "Is this about what you brought up in the truck yesterday?"

Valerie nodded. "You might want to sit down for this."

Side by side on the sectional, and with all the care of a woman on trial, Valerie told him about her dark magic. With her heart in her throat, she told him about how meeting him had brought it on and how it had helped to vanquish Jolem the night before. She gave him the facts, the pros and cons, the rituals and practices that she'd have to do for the rest of her life.

Caleb listened, his intense stare almost distracting. She looked forward to a lifetime of those gorgeous green eyes, as long as he would have her with all her flaws and high maintenance.

When she was finished and gave the worst of the news, that it was happiness that could cause so much damage, Caleb took the alarm clock and letter from her, so he could hold her hands.

"I want to make one thing perfectly clear," he began evenly. "I don't care if you have the power to kill me with a kiss. I don't care if you make the whole house rot away after we make love. I don't care if you burn the entire forest away with your laughter. Because I love you, and that means I'm in this for the long haul. I don't know how we're going to make everything work, but I know one thing I can and will do." He kissed the back of her hand, sending skitters through her arm. "I want to make you so happy and full of life that there won't be a bit of darkness left in you to remove at all. I want to be the reason you never have to wear that amethyst or choke me with sage smoke. I may have brought on this dark magic, but I want to be the reason you never have to worry about it again."

Valerie's mouth twitched and pulled into a smile as she felt a fresh bout of tears coming on. They were tears of joy, of relief. She shook her head. "I've done enough crying, Caleb. Don't make me cry now."

Caleb cupped her cheek in his hand, eyes full of warmth and love that she never thought she deserved. "Only if those are happy tears. I'll make you cry them every day."

She sniffled and covered his hand with her own, still in disbelief that all of this could happen within the course of just a week. In that time, she had met her Twin Flame, killed a demon, and was moving away from the place she had been born and raised. Never had she thought it would come to this, but she regretted nothing. Because they had each other.

Caleb leaned over the steering wheel to watch Valerie do the bravest thing he could imagine. He'd had to do it too many times, and he left a piece of himself in every town he passed through. There were still remnants of him in the pack he abandoned. Leaving took more guts and heart than anything else he could imagine. Even murder was easy, if the feelings were right. Walking away took more.

She stood at the front door to Perfect Books and Brews, the letter in her hand, frozen in this final act. The truck continued to run, but he had turned off the music out of respect. A few long moments passed by as she made her goodbyes to the shop she had made with friends she might never see again.

Part of him lamented this course of action. If he had never come to Goldcrest Cove, he could have saved her the trouble. But then he remembered that things wouldn't have fallen into place as perfectly as they had. Everyone was where they needed to be at the right time and under the right circumstances. And technically, not one person had been truly harmed or killed in the process. Emmett was already dead and the demon didn't count as a person in anyone's book.

They had averted a potential crisis, and that much he couldn't begrudge. He just wanted this heartache to end for Valerie, so they could go on and be happy together.

Finally, Valerie slipped the piece of paper just above the door jam where it slipped through with a little wiggling. He heard the tap as it hit the floor and her deep inhale as she turned and made her way to the truck.

"Are you ready?" he asked again when she shut the door.

Valerie, probably in an effort to distract herself, reached behind and petted Thor's head as he laid down across the back seats. The poor dog must have thought they were on their way to the vet or some other nasty place, rather than on an adventure.

"Yeah, I think so."

"I booked a hotel in Virginia for the night. We'll stop there. It's about ten or eleven hours, but It's up in the mountains. I thought you'd like that."

Valerie looked to him, her eyes misty as she smiled and nodded. "I think I would like that."

Caleb put the car in drive and pulled out onto an empty Johnson Avenue. It was still too early, even for tourists. He doubted anyone might have been awake at this hour. He turned down Reichman Street, the one road that would take them straight out of town. They passed the shops she had known all her life, the church, the schools she had gone to, the park she must have taken walks in. Every place held a memory.

As she sniffled, Caleb took her hand and held it tight.

"It's just the cold," she said.

"Uh huh. Keep telling yourself that." Caleb straightened and gripped the leather of the wheel a little tighter. "We can always come back to visit. Preferably when it's warmer."

She nodded. "Spring is really pretty up here. Summer can get a little crazy with the marina and all the tourists, but it'd be nice. If you think we can sneak back in without anyone knowing."

"Oh, they'll know. We just have to let everyone simmer down first before making any plans."

Silence continued before Valerie made an effort to put it all behind her and turned on the radio. She skimmed through the stations, looking for anything that wasn't playing Christmas tunes.

"You know what's funny?" she asked with a huff. "Tomorrow's Yule."

"Okay?"

"It's just something we always celebrated." Valerie rolled her eyes. "If you believe in that sort of thing, it's when the God is reborn of the Goddess. It's a time for new things and change... It's just kind of ironic that all of this is happening right around this time."

Caleb didn't buy into all that spiritual stuff, but if she did, he would listen and respect it. She would do the same for him. "What would you do to celebrate?"

Valerie settled in the passenger seat as some classic rock floated through the dash speakers. "We'd have a little party at the Hayden Mansion. Krystal's parents would come, and Alexa's mom, even though she's not a witch. We'd eat snacks all night – no big dinner or anything. Catherine would go around the room and we'd give something like a New Year's Resolution, but for Yule instead. We'd do a little ritual to send out our intentions for the new year, like what we want to accomplish, what we want to have manifested. Just witchy stuff. Afterward we'd play cards or other games."

"We can do something like that tomorrow in the mountains if you'd want. I won't mind."

She gave him a sweet, sympathetic smile. "It's all right. We can make new traditions. Besides, I already know my Yule Resolution."

Caleb slowed down at the last light before officially leaving Goldcrest Cove. "And what's that?"

"To start all over with you."

He wouldn't tease her for that. He kissed her knuckles as he had done earlier that morning and thanked the universe that they had finally crossed paths. He had never felt more complete, more at home.

He made the turn onto the highway that led to the interstate when he caught sight of the two squad cars blocking the road. Caleb let go of her hand and slowed just as Devin, Krystal, and another officer stepped out of the vehicles.

"Oh, fuck..." Valerie muttered, sinking low in her seat out of embarrassment.

They were alone on the highway, and it was a good thing, because Caleb was ready to unleash all that anger he had been bottling up since the beginning. He had no more patience to spare.

He pulled the truck over and ordered Valerie to stay put while he handled it. His strides strong and purposeful, he plowed ahead to meet them before they could get too close to his truck and upset Valerie.

"You told me to leave, and so I'm leaving. What else do you fucking want from me?" All that hostility was targeted at Krystal. He was smart enough to know that none of this was Devin's fault. But it was his job to defend his woman.

"Please, just calm down," Krystal said, ignoring that Devin had wedged himself between her and the werewolf. "We know what you're trying to do, but we can't allow it."

Caleb waved his hand toward the truck. "I'm not kidnapping her! She wants to go with me. I told your father that yesterday."

She raised her hands as if to pat down his fiery temper while Devin reached for his gun more as a warning. "I know what you said and I know what he told you, but we can't let you leave like this."

Caleb stiffened in shock. "So, he's going to arrest me? After I kept up my end of the bargain, he's got the fucking nerve to – "

"No one is getting arrested," Devin interjected. "If you'd just calm down, we'll explain."

He didn't care if the other officer knew anything or not. Caleb wasn't holding back. "I have just as much right to live here or leave as any of you do. I was willing to go and play ball even though I thought it was a bunch of bullshit."

The truck door opened and slammed behind him. Valerie wasn't ready for this. He didn't want them to leave on bad terms with her friends. Not like this.

"Val, get back in the truck," he ordered her.

He might as well have been trying to tell a cat what to do as she stalked up the road to join him. "Just let us leave, Krystal. It's not like you want us here anyway."

The other witch's brows knitted together as if she had actually been hurt. "Don't want you here? We'd always want you here."

Valerie, too far gone to be convinced otherwise, shook her head and she shared in Caleb's ire. "If you don't want Caleb here, then I'm not wanted either. Where he goes, I go. You should understand that better than anyone else in Goldcrest Cove. I know you think it's disgusting, but I love him and now that I found him, I'm not going to let you or anyone else tear us apart."

Caleb couldn't have been prouder of his Twin Flame, though he wished it wouldn't end this ugly. Before, it would have been a clean cut. They'd leave, there would be no fuss or argument. Just leaving quietly. Now, it'd be so much more complicated and two friends were about to know just how nasty the other could be.

Krystal drew up to her full height. "You're right. I do understand what it's like. And I'm... not so much disgusted as I am hurt that you didn't just tell me from the beginning."

"How could I?" Valerie screeched. "You were going on and on about him and it's like we were living in the dark ages. Judging each other and being all bitchy. It's not right and telling you anything was just going to make it worse."

"I could have helped. I could have stopped talking like that, at least for your sake. I could have tried to have an open mind." Krystal's voice took a pleading turn and all the men could do was watch.

"You would have just tried to convince me to leave him, like you are now."

Krystal stepped forward, exasperated. "We're not trying to separate you! My parents talked it over and they want him to stay!"

Caleb didn't trust it. "And he's not going to arrest me?"

The witch shook her head and lowered her voice, so the cop waiting by the running vehicles was less likely to hear her. "No, he won't. Yes, you needed permission, but the council is the one to give the permission, and... after last night, he wants to give you another chance. I told him about how you've been good for Valerie, how you've wanted to do nothing else but help with everything, and my mom added her own two cents. She knows you two can't live without each other, and we all knew that if you left, Val would leave too. My dad thinks it may be good to have a... a guy like you around in case things go bad again. He thinks he can trust you and he wants you to stay." She gave a huff of a laugh. "He even said he'd help you guys with the rent just to ensure that you don't leave."

All anger sank straight out through his pantlegs. "Do you swear by all that?"

Krystal gave him a resentful look. "Why would I lie? I may want Valerie to stay, but do you think I'm that eager to have you for a neighbor?"

While he could have been offended at the insult, Valerie cut him off.

"What makes you think we even want to stay after everything? Like you said, you don't want him as a neighbor, and I don't want to have to deal with your condescending bullshit all the time. We don't just want your permission to stay, we want your acceptance too."

The witches glared at one another before Krystal bowed her head. "I know I've been mean about the whole thing lately, and… it's going to take time for me to get used to the idea, but you have my word as your oldest friend that I do accept this. Goldcrest Cove wouldn't be the same without you. Who else is going to keep Alexa grounded and Aaron from getting too cocky?"

She thumbed toward the other officer, who simply folded his arms and cocked a brow. Valerie wrinkled her nose at the guy and Caleb knew there would be some explaining about that relationship later. But right then, a choice had to be made.

"It's up to you," Caleb said to Valerie. "If you want to stay, I'm staying with you. If you still want to leave, we have a place to go. Whatever you decide, you have my support."

The others seemed nervous about the ultimatum. They looked to the loaded-down truck and to Valerie, breaths held and hearts bursting with hope that she'd make the decision they favored. They had to know that it all came down to her. Caleb, though he didn't like the idea, would put up with the witches if they could put up with him.

The ball was in Valerie's court. Her fate was in her own hands now.

She ran her fingers through her hair, frustration written in the lines that creased her pretty face. To them, this must have seemed like an easy choice. Pick family. Pick tradition. Pick stability. Over the years, those things had given her what she needed, but not what she wanted. He thought he understood her mind more than any of them, but even if she chose to stay, it wouldn't change anything for him. Just as she said, where he goes, she would go. Never again would they spend a day apart as long as he had anything to say about it.

Several moments passed, all three vehicles running on idle that cold winter morning. Valerie lifted her chin and looked her friend square in the eyes. "You've been like a sister to me. Do you know how much it hurts to know that you don't approve?"

Krystal's lips tightened into a thin line before she replied, "I think I do. Just about as much as it hurts me to know that you think I'd give up on our friendship just because of who you love."

The sadness between them ballooned and Caleb knew it would pop soon. Devin couldn't have seen the tears coming, but the werewolf could smell them. Nearly taste them in his own mouth as they fell down the cheeks of the witches.

"I thought it would be better to leave after everyone reacted to the news the way they did."

Krystal shook her head. "We were just shocked. It was like a bombshell, Val. We never suspected it would happen. But don't think I disapprove or something, because I don't... You can't choose who you love. And if we can all get used to Devin, we can get used to Caleb."

The two men passed each other amused looks, unsure how to take that comment.

"But I don't want you to just get used to him," Valerie said. "I want you to accept him like you accept me. You don't have to love him, but just... accept him."

The witch and werewolf looked to one another and he did his best to keep the wolf out of his eyes as she studied him for what seemed like an interminable time. "You know I can try. He hasn't done anything to make me think bad of him. Except steal you away."

Valerie shook her head. "He could never steal me away. I'd go willingly, just like you'd follow Devin anywhere he went. You get that, right?"

Krystal's face fell. "So, you're leaving?"

After another moment of deliberation, Valerie bit her lip. "No. We're not leaving. Not as long as we're still wanted here."

That face that had fallen into dismay lit up again. "You're always wanted! Both of you!"

A few seconds later, the dam broke. Valerie and Krystal closed the distance between them, colliding in an embrace that Caleb honored by stepping away.

It wasn't quite what he had expected. He didn't think they would ever change their minds. Ignorance, apparently, had its limits. For Valerie's sake, he was glad for that. Only time would tell if they could truly be civil and get along. And as long as they held to their promise this time, there wouldn't be another clandestine escape. Even if there was, he'd be with her every step of the way.

Devin came around, leaving the two witches to their reunion as he came to Caleb's side. "I was there when Gordon gave his decision. He means every word."

Caleb slipped his chilled hands into his jacket pockets. "Let's hope for Valerie's sake that he does. If he tries to cross me, it'll be bad news for him."

Devin leveled a look. "I would defend Krystal's family from you, if it came to that."

Caleb smirked. "You won't have to worry about me. Valerie will be more than enough for Gordon to deal with. You know how headstrong she is."

By the look the cop gave, he expected he knew exactly how much of a handful Valerie could be. And Caleb was looking forward to a lifetime spent learning everything he could about the witch that stole his heart.

About the author

Sheritta Bitikofer is an author of paranormal and historical fiction. She lives for the deep, engaging stories that enthrall readers from cover to cover. As a wife and mother of eclectic tastes, she can be found roaming Civil War battlefields, haunting her local coffeeshop, or relaxing with a plate of chili cheese fries.

Follow her for upcoming novel releases

www.sherittabitikofer.com

Also by Sheritta Bitikofer

The Native

The Irishman

The Scholars

The Convicts

The Soldier

The Outlaw

The Deviants

The Unsinkable

Keeper of Light

Bulletproof

The Nexus

<u>Bewitching Brews</u>

Bewitching Fire

Bewitching Darkness

Bewitching Hearts

<u>Wolves in the Open</u>

Highland Howls

Silver Screen

Mourning Moon

<u>The Decimus Trilogy</u>

The Beast of Verona

Amber Ashes

Saving the Beast

<u>Redemption Duet</u>

The Rose

The Lion

<u>Standalones</u>

Escape

Clouds

Passions

By The Book

www.ingramcontent.com/pod-product-compliance
Lightning Source LLC
Chambersburg PA
CBHW031307280626
47169CB00017B/490